NO. 23 BURLINGTON SQUARE

JENNI KEER

Boldwood

First published in Great Britain in 2023 by Boldwood Books Ltd.

Copyright © Jenni Keer, 2023

Cover Design by Alice Moore Design

Cover Illustration: Alamy, Shutterstock and iStock

A CIP catalogue record for this book is available from the British Library.

Paperback ISBN 978-1-78513-961-1

Large Print ISBN 978-1-78513-957-4

Hardback ISBN 978-1-78513-956-7

Ebook ISBN 978-1-78513-954-3

Kindle ISBN 978-1-78513-955-0

Audio CD ISBN 978-1-78513-962-8

MP3 CD ISBN 978-1-78513-959-8

Digital audio download ISBN 978-1-78513-953-6

Boldwood Books Ltd
23 Bowerdean Street
London SW6 3TN
www.boldwoodbooks.com

To my four darling boys, who are all now men.
You make me proud every single day.

PROLOGUE

1

AUGUST 1927

Number 23 Burlington Square, Kensington. It had taken Mercy a while to find as she wasn't familiar with this part of London, and one grand Georgian terrace looked much like another. The green panelled door stood at the top of five wide stone steps, and she rapped loudly on the brass knocker, gripping her crocodile skin handbag tight. The style of the bag was dated, purchased many years ago by her mother, but it had great sentimental value to Mercy. She didn't have many nice things and no one had brought her gifts for so many years – but then all the people who had truly loved her were dead now.

The front door swung inwards and a rosy-faced woman stood in the doorway, almost as wide as she was tall, with a house apron tied around her substantial middle. It looked home-made, one of the horseshoe pockets at the front sitting lower than the other, and the fabric possibly recycled from an old summer dress – tiny blue forget-me-nots with bright yellow centres in clusters across the fabric.

'Mrs Mayweather?'

She nodded and hovered on the step.

'Agnes Humphries, but please call me Agnes. Come in, dear girl. I've just baked a fruit loaf. Do you like cake? You look like you could do with a bit of fattening up. There's hardly any meat on your bones.' She tutted. 'What is it with girls nowadays? I'm certain the young men want good, childbearing hips and a bosom to match, not the scraggy bags of bones that wander about in those shapeless frocks that seem so fashionable.'

Mercy, fully aware she was a bit on the thin side, did not like having it pointed out, but nonetheless stepped into the thin, dark hallway – narrow only because of the proliferation of furniture. There was a mirrored hall stand to her left, hung with an assortment of coats and scarves, and a black silk top hat stood on the highest shelf.

'Do you have a gentleman caller?' Mercy asked, immediately on her guard.

Her prospective landlady followed her gaze.

'That, my dear, has been there thirty-eight years. I had hoped its owner would return to reclaim it, but it's probably time to accept that he never will.'

She sighed as the pair proceeded down the hallway, squeezing past a bow-fronted sideboard, piled with clutter and clothes brushes, a tall bookcase stacked haphazardly with books, and a high-backed wooden chair, half-hidden under abandoned articles of clothing. This was clearly a woman who held on to all sorts of things, not just top hats.

'I must warn you that I have already interviewed a couple of prospective lodgers as I take the matter of who lives under my roof very seriously,' Agnes said over her shoulder. 'We're like a family here at number 23.'

Mercy followed her past the bottom of the staircase and into the front parlour, where an attempt had been made to tidy up – although brass microscopes, further piles of books, and china ornaments covered every available surface. The Victorian fashion for filling your house with a multitude of possessions to display your wealth may have waned, but this house felt like a time capsule of all things last century.

A bright yellow taxidermy canary perched on top of a glazed cabinet behind the door studied Mercy as she passed. Agnes absent-mindedly stroked its soft yellow head.

'Sunny. He had such a beautiful song. We had him nine years and I was so upset when he passed that Papa had him stuffed. He was my mother's, you understand, and we lost her when I was a young girl. The gentleman I interviewed this morning knew the Latin name and such an awful lot about birds. I was most impressed.'

Agnes directed her to a seat, and Mercy hoped her lack of ornithological knowledge would not put her at a disadvantage. She gripped her crocodile bag tightly, as she sat forward on the lumpy sofa, too upright to be comfortable and too nervous to smile.

'We're all still in shock at the sudden death of Mr Blandford,' the older woman said. 'Particularly old Mr Gorski, who rather enjoyed their afternoon teas and games of cribbage.'

'Did he pass away in the house?'

'He did but I can assure you that the room has had a thorough clean. Gilbert, the young man who rents the attics, helped me burn the bedding. But it was just a cut that turned septic. Nothing contagious. We all miss him terribly but the Lord saw fit to take him and we should not question His wondrous plan.'

Did God actually have a plan? wondered Mercy. Her life thus far had been far from wondrous. If there had been some lesson in all the cruelty, then she dearly hoped He would reveal it soon. Perhaps coming here was His plan, and that she could still make a positive difference to someone's life. But then, that's what she'd been foolishly led to believe before.

'Tea?' Agnes nodded towards a large square wooden tray on the table before them, already prepared in anticipation of Mercy's arrival. The dainty pale pink cups and saucers were scattered with tiny flowers, like tossed confetti, but the sugar bowl and one of the saucers did not match, Mercy noticed.

'Please.'

The older woman continued to talk as she poured, and a mangy black cat with a missing ear wandered into the room. It rubbed itself against Agnes's legs and gave a deep rumbly purr, before jumping onto the sofa, sniffing the air between itself and the unknown visitor, and finally curling up next to Mercy.

'So...' Agnes slapped her thighs and placed the cup with the matching saucer in front of her guest. 'We have young Gilbert up in the attics. Very obliging chap, if somewhat of a loner. Still, he makes no noise and pays his rent on time. Fiddles about with one of those box cameras and photographic glass plates, and has a penchant for dark corners. Bit like a vampire with a complexion to match.'

Her potential landlady really didn't hold back with her pronouncements, Mercy noticed, but there was no edge to her comments. She was merely stating facts, even if most people would choose, out of politeness, to keep such facts to themselves.

'The second floor comprises the rooms you have come to view. It's a lot of stairs, so I'm pleased that you have young legs. Mr Gorski is on the first floor. He's crippled with arthritis, but was a world-famous pianist in his day. Those fingers of his won't cooperate any longer, and it's heartbreaking to see. Used to console himself with his gramophone – close his eyes and move his hands in the air like he was conducting the orchestra, but I haven't heard it played in recent weeks and that worries me. Mr Blandford would sit with him from time to time, listening to his records. "No idea what I'm listening to, Ag," he'd say, "but it keeps old Mr G happy and I like to spread a little happiness." He was kind like that.'

Agnes settled back into her chair, and Mercy nodded but was far too nervous to take everything in. 'The ground floor rooms are mine, and the Smith family have the basement. Nice enough but the children can be noisy. Luckily, Mr Gorski is too far up to hear them, and they have their own entrance at the front.' She paused, perhaps realising she'd not given Mercy a chance to speak yet. 'But enough about our little household, tell me a bit about yourself.'

She stared at the young woman expectantly, before dipping her hand into one of the apron pockets to pull out a small notebook and opening it up. She slid a shiny black pencil out between the spine and the pages, licking the end in readiness. 'Your letter said you have a steady job and can offer good references,' Agnes prompted.

Mercy adjusted her position, crossing her thin ankles and then uncrossing them, giving herself time to think. When you had things to hide, it took all your concentration not to trip yourself up with careless words so she resolved to stick as closely to the truth as she could. It would be easier that way.

'Um, yes,' she said. 'I work at Pemberton's, on the glove counter.' Everyone knew of the big department store in the city, rivalled only by Selfridges. 'I have a reference from them but I've only been there a very short while, and one from Mrs Donnington, the schoolmaster's wife who has known me all my life.' She produced two cream envelopes. The contents of both were true. She was a clean and tidy individual, but Mrs Donnington had supplied a false address, that of a sister in Shropshire, after Mercy had begged her to make it impossible for anyone to trace her back to the tiny Suffolk village and the life she'd fled from.

'And where are you currently staying?'

'Oh, I erm, well, I'm at my aunt's. She's been very kind but I need rooms of my own.' Mercy didn't have an aunt. Not one that was still living, at any rate. Her current lodgings were temporary and in a not altogether pleasant part of the city.

'So very modern.' Agnes sighed. 'Young ladies able to rent rooms and hold down jobs – although shop work was not considered entirely respectable in my day. But then women largely stayed at home or worked in service until they got married – unless you were of the class where you didn't have to work, and could spend your days embroidering handkerchiefs until a wealthy suitor banged down your father's door and begged for your hand.'

There was a melancholy look about the older woman's eyes and Mercy wondered if she'd had romantic disappointments in her past. *Miss* Humphries, the advertisement had said, and she wore no wedding ring, but had she loved and lost? Mercy felt a wave of empathy because she had loved and lost too. She twisted the thin gold band around her finger, acknowledging to herself that war was a cruel and terrible thing, separating sweethearts – sometimes for ever.

'My sister married well but I don't see her very often,' Agnes continued. 'She's the only close family I have left... Well, her and my niece. Lovely girl but rather a flighty piece. Hangs on the coat tails of those Bright Young Things. Running around corset-less and dancing to jazz, with a shingle haircut and a tendency to say things just to shock, but a kind girl, nonetheless.'

Agnes looked lost in thought and Mercy assumed she was contemplating her wayward niece. 'And they do say blood is thicker than water...' She rested her chin briefly on her plump knuckles in contemplation. 'Tell me a little about your family, Mrs Mayweather?'

'Please, call me Mercy.' Her surname and married status made her uncomfortable, even though it offered her a protection of sorts. A single woman in London would be so much more vulnerable. 'My father died not long before I married, and my mother was taken by the influenza epidemic. My husband...' She swallowed hard. 'I... I lost him in the war, so I'm quite alone.'

'Oh, you poor darling girl. But so many young women are in the same boat. Hundreds of thousands slaughtered on foreign shores, and yet you don't look old enough to have been widowed for nearly a decade.' Agnes's bottom lip wobbled, and Mercy thought how emotional this woman must be to feel so moved on her behalf – a complete stranger.

'I married young.' Almost too young, but without a father, Roland had offered the security she craved, and her mother had been relieved to hand the farm over to more capable hands. 'Such pretty cups.' Mercy held hers aloft, keen to change the subject.

Agnes blushed. 'They were my mother's. Daphne, my sister, thinks I'm silly to hold on to all these keepsakes and souvenirs. She says it's mawkish, but I can't bear to part with the memories.'

'There's nothing wrong with a touch of nostalgia. Sometimes the past was simply a nicer place.' Mercy gave a weak smile. 'And such lovely books. I've often dreamed of having the time to read, to lose myself between the pages of a novel, travel to far off lands, and go on wondrous adventures.'

'Indeed. I have sailed a dozen oceans and visited hundreds of cities all from the comfort of this very room. Not so much through novels, mind, more often travel journals.' Agnes frowned. 'But surely there is always a spare half an hour in the day to curl up with a book?'

Mercy shook her head. 'My mother-in-law was very... demanding.'

The curious look she received from Agnes made Mercy wonder if perhaps she had said too much, but the older lady glanced down to her notebook and returned to the matter in hand.

'To business then. Absolutely no gentleman callers, and the front door is locked at ten every night. There is a privy out the back

and running water up to a shared bathroom on the first floor. Mr
Gorski has priority but tends to use it mid-morning and I assume
you'll be gone before then. I can provide breakfast and supper, but
it's extra, as is laundry, and I'm not keen to take on more as I
struggle as it is. My legs aren't as young as they used to be. I could
really do with another pair of hands...'

'Just lodgings, thank you.' Mercy could barely afford the rent,
never mind extras, but it was important to be in a respectable
neighbourhood. One of the places she'd viewed the day before had
been quite unhygienic and she didn't like the lecherous looks she'd
got from the landlady's husband. An idea occurred to her. 'I'd be
more than willing to take on some of your workload, if you'd
consider me for the rooms. After all, I'd be quite literally on the
doorstep.'

'Now there's a thought. I could knock a few shillings off the rent
maybe... Oh, dearie me, it's so hard choosing a new lodger. All three
of you have your merits. This house and the people within it are
like family, so I must choose wisely. However, you haven't seen the
rooms yet. You might not be enamoured of the two sets of stairs,
and I'm afraid there is a touch of damp along the back wall...'

But Mercy knew in her heart she wanted to live there more than
anything. It was obvious to her that Agnes was a good woman with
a kind heart, that Burlington Square was a delight, in all its summer
glory, and most importantly, that the house was a hundred miles
away from Suffolk and everything she was running from.

2

As Agnes closed the door to the timid young lady she sighed. Why did Mr Blandford have to die so unexpectedly? The household had been a perfect blend of residents. Young Gilbert in the attics might be odd and unsociable, but he always paid his rent on time and did any little jobs she asked without complaint. Perhaps he could be persuaded to leave his silly photographs and trays of nasty chemicals for an afternoon and listen to Mr Gorski's ramblings? Much like herself, and anyone over fifty, she conceded, the old man had a propensity to look backwards – to talk about the good times and rue the bad, whereas the young looked forward and anticipated brighter days ahead. It's what made the household work – the optimism of youth and the wisdom of the old. Even Jemima, down in the basements, whose life was an endless stream of dirty napkins, meal preparations and cleaning, was forever engaging the other residents in lively discussion – spurred on by her husband's firm belief that a social revolution was on its way.

It broke Agnes's heart that number 23 was no longer a family home. Her father had been a respectable man of business, with a portfolio of investments and a moderate income, but ill health had plagued his final years, and his sharp mind had dulled. Persuaded to put money into unwise commercial ventures, their finances had dwindled to almost nothing. After his death, she was bequeathed the house but very little income, and was forced to make economies in order to remain. Partly her need for money, and partly her genuine altruism, the post-war housing shortage gave her the idea to rent out the rooms. She couldn't bear to leave a lifetime of memories and move somewhere smaller, and so compromised by sharing it.

Initially, she only rented out the basement, as it was fairly self-contained, but was eventually forced to give each of the first, second and third storeys their own door, and rent them out too. And everything had been just dandy until poor Mr Blandford had unexpectedly succumbed to sepsis. Off to the Mad Hatter one night, for a drink and merry chatter with some friends. Dead by nightfall of the next. All the more shocking for the speed in which it took the dear man.

And now that she'd interviewed the three most promising applicants, Agnes Humphries had to make a decision.

She wandered into the front room and desperately wished she had the wisdom of King Solomon, although sometimes she wondered if she had any wisdom at all. Gilbert was forever berating her for being too trusting, especially when peddlers turned up on the doorstep offering things for sale that she didn't think she needed, but was made to believe she did... And yet deciding who to give the rooms to felt just as momentous as Solomon deciding the fate of a child. If only she could cut the metaphorical baby in two... well, three.

Clara, her niece, *was* family and that had to mean something.

'Aunt Ag, how could you not tell me you had rooms going?' she'd said, as she'd theatrically kissed her aunt's cheek and collapsed into one of the high-backed armchairs. Her long legs seemed to stretch out forever, and Agnes tried not to tut at her shocking hemline. 'Mummy is keen on me coming here, and Daddy is being so terribly unreasonable. It's awfully tiresome living out of a suitcase but I simply *must* be in the city. Rural life bores me and London has it all; the culture, the night life, the freedoms. Oh, and the cocktails. Daddy wouldn't know a highball if it bounced in front of him.'

The truth was, as Agnes found out when she received a letter from her sister the following day, that Clara had been thrown out of the family home and was currently staying goodness-knows-where, and sleeping on the chaise longue of goodness-knows-who. Daphne, however, had been frustratingly vague on detail. She'd merely hinted at a bedroom scandal, and informed Agnes that her husband, after years of tolerating the increasingly unacceptable behaviour of his wayward daughter, had finally snapped.

But Agnes, even though she loved Clara with every fibre of her being, knew that her niece was trouble. She suspected Mr Gorski would be horrified should the young woman start entertaining gentlemen in the rooms above, never mind displaying her calves and strutting about like one of those movie stars (which Clara did have a tendency to do). By allowing her private rooms of her own, would she be encouraging this pleasure-seeking lifestyle? Agnes wasn't convinced she was the balm to that strong-willed niece of hers, whatever her sister believed. It seemed like a brutal choice between family and the stability of her household.

And then there was Stephen Thompson. Old enough to be beyond the exuberances of youth, he'd answered the advert the very morning it had appeared in the newspaper, and turned up at the doorstep every inch the gentleman, with his white shirt, striped necktie, and matching jacket and waistcoat. (Agnes noticed the shirt cuffs were a little worn and the shoes needed a good buff – but this must be the lack of a woman in his life.) He had a respectable job in

a bank, and would undoubtedly be the least trouble. Even the way
he wore his hat told her that he would be a boon to the neighbourhood.

'As you are no doubt aware, moral integrity is placed above all
with banking staff,' he'd stressed. 'We pay a surety in the form of a
bond when we are employed, and an impeccable character is paramount in an institution that cannot afford to court scandal or
dishonesty.'

Everyone knew that bank work was higher paid than other clerical positions, and all prospective employees were, by necessity,
thoroughly vetted. Even Daphne could not fail to approve of such a
man, and she disapproved of most things.

His polite enquiries about the other members of the household
were also an encouraging sign. He'd been fascinated by Mr Gorski,
and stressed to Agnes that he was an ardent, if uneducated, admirer
of classical music, despite never taking up an instrument himself. It
was, he proclaimed, surely in his blood. Perhaps, pondered Agnes,
he would make a suitable replacement for Mr Blandford and volun-
teer to spend some of his leisure time with the old man – even take
over the Sunday afternoon tea ritual. She regretted not asking him
if he played cribbage.

But – and wasn't there always a but – the women had stirred
something in her, albeit for different reasons. She loved the
refreshing vibrancy of Clara, for all her faults. Her niece was living
a life she wished she'd had the courage to lead herself. And she felt
bewilderingly protective towards Mercy – that nervous scrap of a
woman she'd seen last. Ultimately, she was convinced the young
widow was running from something. That poor woman was alone
in the world and if Agnes didn't help her, who would? Her heart
went out to them both, but her feelings towards Mr Thompson
were strangely indifferent. The bank clerk might be the sensible
option, but did he really fit at Burlington Square?

Agnes spent a restless night, changing her mind on several occasions. Which of the applicants would it be? She knew only too well that this simple decision could potentially alter the fates of everyone involved. Three very different choices. Three very different paths the lives of all at the house could take. She chewed it over with her cat, Inky, as she made breakfast the following morning, before finally deciding on her new lodger.

She waddled down to the front room, opened the drop of her tiny walnut bureau and took out a sheet of cream paper to begin the necessary correspondence...

PART I

CLARA GOODWIN

3

FRIDAY, 5TH AUGUST 1927

Agnes dipped the nib of her pen into her father's pewter inkwell and began to write.

c/o Lily Harcourt
  Darling Clara
    The rooms are yours as soon as you want them, for how could I possibly refuse my favourite niece? Thomas Humphries' blood runs through your veins, as surely as it runs through mine, and that forever ties us. I have always believed that family is one of the most important things in this world, so the thought of having you in the house once more brings me joy. Burlington Square holds such fond memories and I hope that we can make more of our own...

Agnes paused as she heard Gilbert padding down the stairs, doubtless with a black leather folding camera in his hand, off to take photographs of goodness knows what. (She'd never quite worked out what he did for a living. Surely taking family portraits couldn't be very lucrative, but he never seemed short of money.)

Mindful of her other lodgers, she remained anxious that Clara's behaviour might upset the apple cart if unchecked. Later, she would write to that timid young widow and mention Mrs Johnson's boarding house two streets away. It would have been useful to have her help with the housework, but surely Clara could run a few trays up the stairs – after all, that girl did nothing else with her days. That's what Daphne was really asking of her – to mind her niece and perhaps teach her some responsibility.

'Gilbert,' she called, 'could you pop this in the postbox for me, please?'

He appeared at her door and nodded.

'I won't keep you a moment.' She dipped the pen again, and finished the letter.

> ... *I'm sure I don't have to remind you of the house rules, but will do so regardless: no gentleman callers and the front door is locked at ten o'clock every evening.*
>
> *I look forward to your arrival.*
>
> *Aunt Agnes x*

– who was absolutely certain she *did* have to remind Clara of the house rules, and desperately hoped she hadn't made the wrong decision.

4

It had been one hell of a party the evening before. An Egyptian-themed gathering and more champagne than was good for her, Clara's pounding head reminded her that with every high, there followed a crashing low. Tut-mania was rife, and Clara's evening had been a blur of ostrich feathers and bandages, scarab jewellery and hieroglyph-covered fabrics.

Jack had kissed her again, as she'd known he would. He'd been making thick kohl-lined eyes at her all night, and Neville had been making similar eyes at him from the slit in the thin strips of linen he had artistically wrapped around his head from the moment he'd stepped out from a wooden sarcophagus. Apparently, the two schenti-clad and alarmingly muscular young men he had hired to heave the aforementioned coffin into the venue were *absolutely* not his type, but he'd still ended up going home with one of them.

Her father was always irritated when he knew Clara was in the company of Neville Brigden. He'd long had his suspicions regarding the young man's proclivities, and these had later been confirmed, somewhat unprofessionally, by the Goodwin family solicitor, who was in the employ of both families. His services had been urgently required on a couple of occasions when their only son had found himself tangled up in some embarrassing brushes with the law and the family hoped to avoid a scandal along the lines of Lord Arthur Somerset, Oscar Wilde, and their ilk. Reginald Goodwin consequently forbade his daughter to hang around with 'that sort', but Clara paid him no heed. She liked Neville. He kept his hands to himself and talked to her of serious things – actually interested in her replies. Jack was only interested in one thing, and her devil-may-care behaviour made him hope he might get it.

She lugged her case to the top step and knocked. There was a lurching feeling in her stomach as last night's largely liquid supper, peppered with a handful of salted peanuts, threatened to resurface. A cigarette would settle her insides, she decided, flipping open a small silver case from her purse and placing one between her lips.

Thank God for Aunt Ag. And for Mummy. However disgusted her mother was by the whole sordid affair, she still looked out for her daughter. Just as well because Clara was getting desperate. Daddy had banished her in a temper, paranoid that whispers of her disgrace would get out – the *real* version, not what her father had told his chums at the club. But several weeks later, and her friend, Lily, was growing tired of finding a worse-for-wear Clara draped across her upholstered furniture of a morning. And all this because Philip was some phenomenally distant relation of Queen Mary, so it was imperative that the press didn't get a whiff of what she'd been up to, semi-naked, in a guest bedroom of the Goodwin family home.

'Clara, sweetheart!'

'Aunt Ag, darling lady.' She whipped the cigarette out and held it between her manicured fingers, air-kissing either side of the older lady's plump cheeks, and then stepped into the hallway, leaving two pale cream pigskin suitcases and matching hatbox behind her on the top step.

'Don't smoke in the house, darling. It lingers in the fabrics.' Her aunt's sing-song voice drifted into the front room behind her as she tumbled across the battered sofa. God, this threadbare thing had been around since before she could remember. It was lumpy and hideous, and Clara recalled curling up on it as a small child and finding the damn thing uncomfortable even then.

'Have you eaten?' The older woman appeared in the doorway and deposited the cases inside the door with a pant. 'I could rustle you up some eggs. You look so painfully thin. Like that dreadful wizened Tutankhamun when they unwrapped him.'

Charming, thought Clara, remembering her aunt's inability to filter the things that popped into her head before they reached her mouth. Perhaps she should have covered her naked body in brown boot polish and turned up as a mummified corpse to the party – that would have been a scene-stealer to upstage even Neville's dramatic spectacle.

She shook her head, unable to face solid food just yet.

'Daphne said you fancied a change of scene?' Aunt Ag began tentatively. 'And I'm so looking forward to having you here. I often think back to when the house was a family home.'

'You were so lucky to be cherished by such wonderful parents. I don't think I am loved in the same way.' Clara sighed. 'Merely tolerated.'

All at once, everything was too much for the young woman. She stubbed her cigarette out in a small scallop-shaped dish that sat on a side table, and burst into tears.

'Oh, sweetheart. I don't believe that's true for a moment.' Her aunt waddled over to her niece and perched on the wide arm of the sofa, pulling the distraught girl to her bosom. 'Nothing and no one are worth your precious tears,' she said, cradling Clara's head. 'Besides you'll ruin that... distinctive makeup of yours, and we don't want that.'

They sat together for several minutes, Clara releasing the emotions that had been building for weeks, as her aunt silently absorbed them like a colourful sponge. Finally, the young woman pulled back and looked into her aunt's concerned eyes.

'How do you do it?' she asked. 'Live alone, with no one to share your troubles with, to kiss away tears when everything gets too much, to tell you that you are special and loved?'

Clara was now convinced that becoming an elderly spinster was her fate too, although she was determined to be one of those feisty old ladies who spoke their mind, wore unsuitable clothes for her age and drank like a drowning fish. It was either that or a loveless marriage, and she was certain the former was the preferable option.

'Sometimes you don't have a choice.'

It was common knowledge that Aunt Ag had never married, although Mummy said there had been at least one serious suitor, back in the day. It appeared that by the time Clara's grandfather had passed on, his oldest daughter was beyond marriageable age. And, she acknowledged, her aunt had never been quite the beauty her own mother had. But for all her indelicate frankness, she was a good listener, and possibly the least selfish person Clara knew. She'd get nothing but honesty here, something that her parents had never afforded her, but could she bring herself to reciprocate and be honest with her aunt? That was the real question.

'What's this silly nonsense about, eh? I always saw you as so strong, Clara.' Her aunt rubbed a plump thumb across her niece's wet cheeks.

'But I'm not. I'm very, very much lost, alone and frightfully scared.'

'What can a girl like you possibly have to vex her at such a young age?'

Clara considered for the briefest of moments that she would share her troubles, but the gold lettering on the spine of a large brown leather King James Bible on the top of a bookcase caught her eye, reminding her of Aunt Ag's steadfast faith. She wouldn't understand, and certainly wouldn't hold back at telling her niece how God would judge her and find her wanting. Clara simply couldn't bear to hear it.

Regretting that she had given her aunt cause to worry, she determined that, much as she had always done, she would deal with this alone.

5

The repeated *beep-beep* of a motor car horn woke Clara up early the next morning.

She'd slept much of the previous day and, yet again, partied into the night. After a much-needed afternoon siesta, she'd inadvertently offended her aunt by leaving the tray of carefully prepared supper untouched, declined her offer of a cup of tea (a French 75 would have gone down nicely but Agnes wasn't really the cocktail-making sort), and announced that she was off to the Pink Slipper with Neville (where she definitely would get a French 75 and the opportunity to dance her troubles away).

Her aunt had been disappointed that she should want to go off gallivanting on her very first evening, but had wished her a lovely time as she waved the motor car off. She had perhaps later regretted that sentiment when Clara banged loudly on the front door at 2 a.m., having forgotten her key *and* the curfew, and then sung 'Bye Bye Blackbird' loudly up the stairs, swaying from side to side and clutching at the banister for support.

The horn beeped again, and Clara pulled the quilt above her head. The room smelled of man – cheap aftershave and lingering

Brilliantine – and the dated décor assaulted her eyes. Oh, how she missed the obliging, on-hand staff and comforts of home, the room service of a good hotel, or even the simple femininity of Lily's sofa. She didn't want to be at Burlington Square but current options regarding places to lay her dainty, sleek, black-shingled head were limited. Aunt Ag was at least in the right part of London, and certainly nearer to the night life than Hertfordshire.

There was a sharp rap at her door.

'Someone is out the front, asking for you.' A disembodied male voice floated towards her.

'Urgh...'

Beep-beep.

The rapping got louder and more impatient.

'All right. Hold your horses.'

Clara rolled off the bed, smoothed down her dishevelled hair, and pulled her pink satin robe tighter around her body. She walked into the main living area, groaning when she saw a half-drunk bottle of champagne by her abandoned shoes, and plodded across the faded blue and gold oriental rug.

On the other side of her door stood a young man with serious eyes set in shadowed sockets. His dark brows were pinched together and he had a pasty complexion, as though he and sunshine were only passing acquaintances. Gilbert, she assumed.

'Deal with the entitled show-off downstairs in the red Morris Oxford,' he ordered. 'He's woken everyone up.'

'Well, hello darling, and a very good morning to you, too,' she said sarcastically as she floated past him and towards the staircase. A red Morris Oxford meant Jack, and she really wasn't in the mood, especially as he'd been the reason she'd left the party early.

'I'm watching you, Miss Goodwin. Don't take advantage of Agnes just because she's a kind soul and related to you.'

Yes, Gilbert. His words made her feel uncomfortable because

her father had shouted similar accusations at her when he'd given her the 'change your ways or leave my house' speech: she was spoilt, she was ungrateful, and she was using people.

'Says the man who locks himself up in the attic and doesn't tell anyone what he's up to.'

Despite sporadic visits to her aunt over recent years, she'd barely glimpsed the lodger who lived on the top floor. Aunt Ag said he was a photographer of sorts, but he was unnervingly vague regarding his subject matter.

Clara descended the two flights of stairs and was greeted by her aunt.

'Oh, darling.' She frowned. 'In your negligée?' The older lady proceeded to unlock the front door, and the sudden glaring rectangle of sunshine aggravated Clara's fragile head.

'Clara, darling!' Jack's voice came from the silhouette in the door frame and gave her squinting eyes some respite from the blinding light. 'You look utterly dazzling. What a chap wouldn't give to wake up to such a heavenly sight every morning. Why did you flutter off so early, my little nightingale?' He stepped into the hallway and looked adoringly up at her. 'The party didn't get going until three. Mitzy announced she'd stump up a bottle of fizz to the first person to come back with the most outrageous hat, so we leapt in the old jalopy and hared around Piccadilly, until Neville won by showing up with a policeman's helmet. Totally shriek-worthy. And then, when I deposited Lily at her abode in time for kippers and coffee, she asked me to drop the rest of your things off on the way back to my little flat.'

Jack's 'little flat' had four bedrooms, but it was all relative when your parents owned half of Somerset.

Clara glared at him and he cast his eyes downwards. 'She had everything boxed and ready to go. I could hardly refuse,' he finished.

'You mean to say that you haven't been to bed yet?' Agnes asked Jack, still hovering in the hallway and wide-eyed.

'All in good time, dear lady. All in good time. I'll shut the old peepers in a bit, never fear, as I'll need my energy for tonight – Mitzy wants to try the new club on Carnaby Street. I say, Clara, couldn't shout me a cup of noodle juice before I head off, old thing?' he asked. 'Got the very devil of a head.'

'No men in the rooms,' Agnes reminded Clara, who was suddenly grateful for this rule, if nothing else.

'You'll survive, Jackie. You always do. Just dump my stuff and someone can bring it up later.'

She turned to head back upstairs just as Gilbert came trotting down, a Kodak folding camera in his hands. Stepping aside to let him pass, and still cross that he'd been on her back for something she'd had no control over, she couldn't resist a passing jibe.

'Off to see your friends? In daylight, no less. You'll need a spade.'

Her aunt tutted. 'That's not kind, dear. Just because he has no friends and looks like a corpse.'

Jack reappeared with the first armful of Clara's rather colourful belongings and placed them inside the door. As if the hallway couldn't get any busier, another figure appeared. A middle-aged man in a smart, if dated, suit joined the merry throng. He took off his bowler hat and Clara noticed shocks of silver running from his temples.

'Oh, Mr Thompson,' her aunt exclaimed. 'Did you not get my letter?'

'What? Yes, yes, but I was just passing and thought I'd drop by to say that I'm still interested in the rooms if it doesn't work out with the new lodger. Your letter implied you felt obligated, if somewhat reluctant, to offer the rooms to a troublesome relative, and I thought if that situation proved to be temporary, you might be of a mind to reconsider me.'

Clara paused her ascent and threw her aunt an inquiring glance. Agnes's cheeks flushed a hot pink.

'Clara Goodwin.' She bounced over to him from the bottom step and stretched out her manicured hand. The alarming cherry red of her Cutex liquid polish was another modern fashion Daddy found unpalatable. 'The troublesome relative.'

The man took Clara's proffered hand, although was clearly unsure what to do with it, and cleared his throat. 'Ah, yes. Yes, of course. Delighted to make your acquaintance.'

'I'm not sure I used those exact words, but family is important,' Agnes hastily explained. 'Our Clara is simply a bit headstrong, as all the young women seem to be nowadays, and I was terribly sorry to turn you down, Mr Thompson. You would have been a most welcome addition to the house...'

Her aunt wittered on, clearly not blessed with the knowledge that the more you apologise, the guiltier you sound. But Clara wasn't bothered by her aunt's description of her. She knew she was a handful and almost revelled in it. That was the problem with boredom; it could push you too far the other way.

Mr Thompson nodded politely as Clara studied the stranger's face in more detail.

'...And you seemed such a charming fellow, despite only being a clerk when many your age are bank managers...' Agnes was yet again engaging her mouth before her brain.

'I know you, don't I?' Clara finally said, in the pause.

'I doubt that very much,' Mr Thompson replied, scrunching up his brow and looking faintly alarmed.

'I do. You live on Daddy's estate, or rather you did when I was younger.'

'Reginald Goodwin's daughter?' His brow crinkled into a perplexed frown. 'Goodness gracious, the last time I set eyes on you, you were about twelve. And *you* are the niece of Miss Humphries?'

A look passed across his face that she couldn't quite understand, but it puzzled her. It was as if he'd been told the horse he had wagered his life savings on had fallen at the first fence. His shoulders drooped in a resigned slump, as he pulled a pocket watch from his waistcoat and half-glanced at it.

'Oh, do look at the time. Excuse me, I must dash.' And he spun for the door, almost bumping into Jack, who'd returned with a second bundle of clothing, Clara's fox-fur coat balanced across the top obscuring his vision.

Clara shrugged and put the curious man out of her mind. The less she thought about home right now, the better.

6

A week later and Mitzy had wangled some invites to a party up in Belgravia, with rumours that one of the Mitford sisters might pop by. It was yet another themed occasion, and Clara suspected the sublime had now descended into the ridiculous. Everyone was expected to attend in a costume that had some link to childhood, and Neville had threatened to arrive on a wheel-mounted rocking horse in a baby napkin. Clara tied the most enormous yellow bow around her head and used safety pins to raise the hem of a dated pre-war dress Lily had loaned her to a scandalous height. She just needed some childhood toys to complete the look.

How could anyone live with so much clutter? Clara asked herself as she rummaged through a tall chest of drawers in one of the ground floor rooms her aunt had filled with several lifetimes of possessions. Aunt Ag never threw anything out and was bound to have something suitable. Jack had offered to swing by and collect her at ten, but she was running dreadfully late. (Not once had it occurred to her that she was leaving to go out at the very hour her aunt had expressly asked her to be in.) It had taken longer than she'd anticipated to pin up the stupid dress and he was due any minute. Her endeavours were finally rewarded when she opened the tall Victorian wardrobe, the pair to the one in Agnes's own bedroom, and a small collection of dolls and playthings stared down at her from the top shelf.

She grabbed an ancient china doll in a bottle-green dress, and a spinning top she remembered from visits when she was little. Tutting at her aunt's open velvet jewellery box on the side – honestly, anyone could walk in and steal the treasures within – she returned to the narrow hallway. Maybe *that* was how Gilbert funded himself. Would Aunt Ag even notice if anything went missing? There was a cheery *rat-a-tat-tat* on the front door and she opened it to Jack, who had rustled up something approximating the school uniform of a small boy – a stripy blazer and matching short trousers. He was a handsome man, she recognised, with his high cheekbones, pencil-thin moustache and lazy smile. She felt a wave of something wash over her as she looked into his eager face. It wasn't love, but he was a sweet man, for all his unwanted adoration.

'Let's go, darling,' Clara purred, which sounded wrong from the lips of a woman dressed as a seven-year-old. 'This house is drier than a sun-baked desert and I know a little something fizzy will perk me up no end.'

Agnes floated into view at the end of the dark hallway, her grey curls tucked away in a hair net, and a pale dressing gown reaching to the floor. Jack caught sight of her from the corner of his eye and jumped.

'Good God. I thought the old bird was a ghost,' he muttered. 'Wandering around at this hour. Gave me quite a fright.'

'It is my house,' Agnes pointed out, as she advanced towards them. 'And what are you doing with Lady Winifred, Clara? Give her back this instant.'

'It's just a doll, Aunt.' She rolled her eyes. 'I'll bring her back tomorrow.'

'Absolutely not. She isn't to leave this house under any circumstances and I'm far from enamoured that you've rummaged through my possessions without permission. Much of what I own has enormous sentimental value. I made it crystal clear that my lodgers should be in by ten. I need to lock up of an evening and know that both my property and your virtue are secure.'

'Then I shall see you in the morning. It's highly likely we shall be dancing until dawn. These things often don't get going until the early hours.'

Noting Agnes's shocked expression, Jack made attempts to reassure the older lady.

'Don't worry, Miss H, I'll keep the strangers at bay. I shan't leave her side all night.'

'It's not the strangers I'm worried about.' She gave the young man a pointed look before swinging back to her niece. 'And you can't stay out all night. That's not the behaviour of a well-brought-up young lady. It's the behaviour of a harlot.'

Clara rolled her eyes, slid Lady Winifred onto a small hall table by the door, and slipped out into the night.

7

THE CHINA DOLL

Agnes's favourite doll had a pale complexion. In fact, she was so pale, her skin was paper white. Her glossy face of finest German porcelain and eyes of the brightest blue were framed by the shiny helmet of ceramic hair that sadly could not be brushed, but would forever look immaculate.

The doll had been given to Agnes on her sixth birthday and she spent many an afternoon pouring imaginary tea into dainty cups with her oh-so-sophisticated friend, *Lady* Winifred, discussing which cake to eat first, or passing comment on the behaviour of the staff. (Poor Ann never could lay a fire properly and Polly's pastry was always overworked.) By the time Agnes turned eleven, Lady Winifred had become a valued confidante. Did she know why her mother was so exhausted all the time? What should one expect if a baby brother or sister came along? And when a baby sister did come along and it was apparent her mother was dangerously ill, she talked to her friend long after her candle was out, asking for advice and looking to her for strength. Those sapphire eyes held so much wisdom and understanding. For Winifred was a grown woman, with her narrow waist, wide hips and long, graceful limbs of stuffed cloth. She had lived a full and exciting life, been on adventures and had surely experienced all manner of difficult life circumstances. And Agnes was just a girl.

When Agnes's mother died, Winifred was put on the top of the wardrobe, her tiny leather-booted feet dangling over the edge at awkward angles, and propped up by a hatbox so that she could oversee the young girl from afar. Suddenly the time for dolls had passed, because Agnes Humphries was too busy for frivolous entertainment and, at the tender age of twelve, was forced to grow up exceptionally fast. She became the mother her five-day-old sister would never know, and henceforth she had neither the time, nor the inclination, to play with dolls.

The only play acting she indulged in for the next twenty years involved her desperate attempts to be an adequate replacement mother to Daphne.

8

Clara stumbled downstairs the following afternoon, swathed in her voluminous silk dressing gown, in search of tea and sympathy. There was a small gas stove in her rooms, but she really wasn't the domesticated sort. Besides, if her aunt was catering for Gilbert and Mr Gorski, surely there would be enough for one extra. And Aunt Ag obviously enjoyed caring for people, despite never marrying or having children of her own. Such a shame because she would have excelled at both states of affairs. Some people were absolutely top-drawer at things like that.

A steaming mug was slid towards her across the pine table, but it appeared she was only going to get the tea. The sympathy was noticeably absent, even though the last thing Clara needed, as she nursed a headache from hell, was to be chastised for having fun.

'Your whole day is backwards, young lady,' her aunt said, avoiding eye contact. 'You remain in bed until the afternoon, at which point you rise and treat everyone you come across as staff. There is no offer of help, or consideration for the feelings of others, and I don't see you trying to become a useful part of this household.'

Delicious baking aromas circulated the room, even though Clara knew that it would be a while before her stomach was sufficiently recovered to receive anything solid.

'But my head is absolutely pounding.'

'Well, what do you expect, my girl? I enjoy a tipple as much as the next person, but it seems foolish to me to have so much that you suffer for it afterwards.' There was a pause, and her aunt's kinder side won out. 'I'll rustle you up some raw eggs with a splash of Worcestershire sauce. Mr Blandford swore by it.'

'I'd rather have a Bloody Mary.'

'Clara! Language.'

'That's what it's called,' she whined.

Her aunt retrieved a bottle from the tall cupboard on the back wall, and two eggs from a basket on the windowsill. It took seconds to whip them together.

'Drink your tea, try to swallow those eggs, and then nip upstairs for some clothes. By the time you return, I'll have laid a tray of afternoon tea and cake to take up to Mr Gorski.'

Without waiting for a response, her aunt slid a glass containing the revolting-looking hangover cure towards her, and then turned her attention to the rather more appetising fruit loaf baking in the oven.

* * *

'Come in, come in,' a quivery male voice commanded, and Clara opened the door to find an old man seated in a leather upholstered wing chair across the room from her. He had two fluffy white tufts above his ears, which blended with the bushy beard beneath, and a dearth of hair on the top of his head. His nose was large but straight, and either side he had tiny crystal-blue dots for eyes. It was an intelligent face, she acknowledged, quickly convinced those bright buttons saw right through her. There was something about the way they darted about that made her suspect his brain worked so much faster than the worn-out body it occupied.

Clara knew Mr Gorski lodged on the first floor but hadn't yet paid him much attention. She wasn't very good with fragile, old people. They required time and patience – the first of which she had more to spare than she would have liked, and the second she did not possess at all. Her aunt, however, had been kind enough to take her in and was clearly beginning to struggle with her mobility, and so Clara took a deep breath, walked towards the old man and placed the tray on the small table that was directly in front of him.

'Alexander Gorski,' he said, holding out a twisted hand. The palm had folded in on itself and his fingers fanned out at an odd angle, like the broken wing of a bird. Arthritis, Aunt Ag had said. She peered at the proffered appendage. How terribly awkward.

'Please, take a seat and keep this old man company? You must be Clara?' His accent belied his foreign origins as he rolled the R in her name.

As she slipped into an adjacent chair she realised she was staring, which was terribly impolite, and so quickly became charming Clara, seductive Clara, fake Clara. It helped to conceal the real Clara – vulnerable and afraid.

'An absolute pleasure to make your acquaintance,' she purred. 'And I am, indeed, the wayward niece I'm certain my aunt has already had cause to complain about.'

The old man briefly raised both eyebrows but didn't comment.

'My parents saw you give a concert many years ago in Vienna when they toured Europe.'

They'd mentioned hearing Alexander Gorski play Beethoven before the war (exceptionally well, according to her discerning father) when the old man had moved into Burlington Square –

Mummy consoled by her sister's need to take in further lodgers because she was at least attracting 'the right sort of people'.

'Ah, when my hands worked properly and God gave my life purpose. There really is something quite spiritual about music, don't you think?'

'Sensual rather than spiritual. I feel it is something one should move to, rather than listen to sat stiffly in a chair, although I suspect my choice of music differs greatly from yours. It's jazz that speaks to me the most: the squeaks of the trumpet, the rumble of the double bass, and how the vibrations of it pulse through my body. It gives me such a buzz, particularly when I'm dancing. Rather like sex,' she added daringly.

'My dear girl, if you're trying to shock me,' he said, leaning forward to assess the cake, 'I fear it will take more than that. I may be old but I understand sensuality, all too well. The gentle caress of a woman's breath across your skin, the sweet smells that linger in the air after two people have shared their bodies, the uncontrollable heat that rises within when you are near to someone you long to touch but cannot do so at that moment... And, yes, music can indeed be sensual.' He closed his eyes for a moment, lost in thought. 'Debussy's *'L'après-midi d'un faune'*... I was there at the 1912 ballet première, you know?' He chuckled as he opened his eyes and looked directly at her. 'The gentleman next to me booed, but the sculptor, Rodin – you have heard of him? He stood up and cheered. The finale was most erotic.'

Clara, to her consternation, blushed. Something she was rarely prone to do, and the old man reached out his hand and gently patted her knee. 'I can play and win any game you choose, my dear, because I have been around longer than you and seen it all before. Ah, every generation thinks it is the first to discover carnal pleasures and that is not so. Your modern dancing may be liberating, your skirts may be emancipating, but I beg of you, be careful. Men do not have to live with the consequences, and that often leads to unfettered recklessness.' He paused and reached for the sturdy mug of tea on the tray, and stared at it as though it might have the answer to whatever was clearly preying on his mind. 'Because it is often the women who suffer the most.'

He shakily brought the mug to his mouth, the bright blue dots losing their sparkle for a moment.

'Don't worry about me, darling man,' she assured him. 'I'm living a life of unparalleled privilege and enjoying every moment. A carousel of parties and dances, good times and dear friends.' And she gave an enigmatic smile as if to prove her words.

'And yet your aunt told me you have been thrown from the home by an irate father, so I can only assume that things are not as rosy as you paint them. Particularly as, according to the charming Miss Humphries, you lead a hedonistic life that benefits no one – least of all yourself.' Honestly, her aunt couldn't keep a secret if it was locked in an underground vault and someone else had the key. 'And so I wonder to myself if you are lost,' he finished.

'Sorry?'

'That's when we start misbehaving, isn't it? When we become a warped version of ourselves to hide the pain or the disappointments.'

'I have no idea what you're talking about.' She waved a dismissive hand. 'Times have moved on since the war, that's all. Daddy simply doesn't understand. Isn't it why so many young men sacrificed themselves in lands far away? So that we would be free from oppression and judgement?'

'They died for a world that would see no more fighting. And this, I believe, they have achieved. But they also died so that we could live together in harmony, for society to be more equal, for everyone to flourish. Forgive me if this sounds brutal but they did not die to allow spoiled individuals to strut about, unable to see the harsh realities of the world around them.'

'You think me spoilt?'

'I don't think you care much for your aunt or the people in this house – arriving home in the early hours, banging and shouting. Expecting her to run around after you.'

'So, she *has* been telling tales?'

'She simply says what is on her mind, without censoring herself to take account of people's feelings. And I rather like that about her. If you ever want an honest opinion on something, then your aunt is the person to ask.' He paused, sizing her up. 'If you are brave enough to hear what she has to say, that is.'

Clara stared at the outspoken man in disbelief. There was no need for him to attack her, merely because his own life had proved a disappointment.

'The pity of it all is that you strike me as a butterfly – flitting about the world from flower to flower, catching the eye but serving no purpose. When in reality you could be a bee – produce something useful, gather the nectar and give us all honey. Music was my honey. A lifetime's work to enrich the lives of others. It became my focus to distract me from the pain of those things I could not have.'

Making a move to stand, for she really didn't want to be judged further by this unnervingly astute old man, she contemplated his words. Perhaps she did need a distraction, some cause or passion she could devote herself to, because she was fairly certain that most of the things she ultimately desired in life, she would never be able to have.

9

Despite her conversation with Mr Gorski, Clara failed to temper her behaviour, and after another week of drunken antics she was caught trying to smuggle Neville up to her rooms (whether her aunt realised he was no threat to her niece's virtue or not was moot). Aunt Ag summoned her to the kitchens to have words, and those words proved brutally to the point.

'I realise times have changed, even if I have failed to change with them. If you want to play fast and loose with young men, that is your choice, but it's not fair of you to do so under my roof. I support anyone's right to make their own decisions in life, but I don't believe your choices are even making you happy.' Perhaps she'd been speaking to Mr Gorski. Clara could just imagine the pair of them tutting over the younger generation and shaking their heads. 'Talk to me, Clara? Tell me what's behind this giddy behaviour.'

Clara shook her head, afraid to start speaking lest everything should come flooding out. She was torn between wanting to confide in her darling aunt, and petrified of incurring her judgement.

'You told me you feel lost and alone, and yet I always see you surrounded by friends. To be alone in a crowd is a very sad thing indeed. If you're going to break the rules, do it because *not* conforming makes you happy, rather than because you simply don't know what else to do.'

'I am trying,' Clara pointed out. 'I've been taking the dinner trays up to Mr Gorski.' The old man's perceptiveness unnerved her however, and she hadn't lingered after that first visit. She didn't need reminding of her inadequacies.

'But you're in and out in a flash. It wouldn't hurt you to give him some time. He's been so lonely since we lost Mr Blandford. Besides, you are making me more work than you're saving me. Yesterday morning I found a nail polish stain on the bedside rug in your rooms when I changed the bedding. You've helped yourself to my medicinal brandy, taken food from the kitchen outside of the meal-times I have established, and then left me the crockery to rinse afterwards. I don't have staff to clear these messes up, Clara. You'll never find a husband if you don't present yourself better.'

'Finding a husband has never been a priority,' Clara said, inspecting her glossy nails, the result of the unfortunate spillage, and contemplating a further colour change. What was her aunt getting her drawers in such a flap about?

'Don't become an old maid like me. It isn't a life I would recommend. We are the superfluous women, trained only to be wives and mothers, and when that doesn't happen we're left without fortune, often alone for the greater part of our lives and, in my case, forced to take in lodgers to make ends meet. They do say if you don't marry, all that is left is to teach, go on the stage or walk the streets...' She counted the possibilities out on her fingers. 'And you may find these are your only options if your father decides to cut you off once and for all.'

'Going on the stage rather appeals.' Clara gave a wicked grin, and tilted her chin to the ceilings as though the eyes of the audience were on her that very instant. Her aunt was right however, and Clara was still inordinately frustrated that she'd been born a woman. It was so restrictive.

'Don't be so flippant. Without the protection of, and income from, your father, what will become of you?' Agnes stirred the contents of the aluminium saucepan, before deftly lifting the kettle from the hob with her stripey knitted pot holder just as it began to whistle.

'I've always taken care of myself. I don't need a man to protect me – father or husband. Don't lament your spinsterhood. No one tells you what to wear, what to think, or even how to vote.' It vaguely annoyed Clara that women her age still didn't have a say in the running of the country, but she simply did not have the drive to do anything about it. Ironic, as Daddy was a politician.

Agnes shook her head as she turned off the gas hob and scraped some scrambled eggs onto a waiting piece of thin buttered toast.

'We're so very different, Clara, and I am thankful because it takes all sorts to make a world, but the spinster life is solitary. As you so astutely pointed out, I have no one to help me make decisions, no company in the evenings and no one beside me in bed at night.'

'Really, Aunt,' said Clara, looking coy. 'Satiating the desires of the flesh is no reason to marry.'

Agnes's cheeks coloured up to match the row of recently pickled beetroot jars on the table.

'You vex me at every turn, young lady. I love you, and make allowances for your behaviour, but even Gilbert berates me for being a soft touch. I am beginning to suspect that there are far more deserving lodgers out there, who would respect this house and the people within it. I shall ask you to leave if your conduct doesn't improve... Look at me, Clara. I mean it.'

Clara was momentarily thrown. She had, as Gilbert suspected, thought her aunt a pushover. Someone who would tolerate her behaviour without confronting it. Apparently not. Added to which, he was apparently chiming in with his unwelcome two penn'orth. Yes, Clara knew she had a selfish side, but she did care about others – dear old Aunt Ag more than most. The thought that this kindly old lady was considering throwing her out was sobering.

'So, you think more of some doddery old Polish man's opinion, and that of the freak in the attics, than you do about your own niece?' Even as she said the words, she recognised she was being unfair, but lashing out was all she knew.

'You're dreadfully unkind about young Gilbert. I don't want you picking on that lad.' Clara pouted. 'He's socially awkward but kind at heart. He brought little Ellen Smith her first pair of shoes – smart red ones they were – because I'd mentioned how things were tight for the family. He may be odd, with his vegetarianism and inability to hold a decent conversation, but I feel inexplicably protective towards him, for all his scurrying and secrecy.'

'Exactly,' Clara said. 'He has something to hide. Mark my words, all is not as it seems. You have no idea what he's doing with that camera of his. Ask yourself why he's out so much at night? I wouldn't be surprised if he's taking photographs of scantily clad ladies and selling them to disreputable magazines.' She twitched her eyebrows suggestively.

'Clara! You can't go around saying things which are simply untrue.' Her aunt looked faintly alarmed at the thought, though. It was clearly not an option she'd considered. 'Besides, in my experience, those who draw attention to themselves and pretend to be something that they are not, also have secrets.' She gave her niece a penetrating look, and the young woman shuffled uncomfortably in her seat.

Agnes poured the scalding hot water into the small teapot on the breakfast tray and covered it with a knitted cosy. She added a sturdy mug and a teaspoon and stood back to admire her handiwork.

'You need someone to love, Clara, because love makes you put others first. When you have a child of your own, or a husband whom you adore, you will make sacrifices and be glad to do so, because the wants and needs of that person come first. Indeed, I do not resent my father for the sacrifices I made on his behalf.'

Clara's relationship with her parents had always been tricky, but she did love them, and it made her sad that she was on bad terms with her father. She would never be as close to him as her aunt had been with her own father, but maybe he'd had enough time to get over his unreasonable outburst. Perhaps, she decided, it was time to see how the land lay.

Agnes's front room was an eclectic mix of furniture, all crammed into the small space since she'd been forced to contain herself and many of her possessions to the ground floor. Consequently, the room had no clear identity, and the large desk in the window looked out of place. It had belonged to Clara's grandfather – not that she remembered him because he'd died before she was born.

She walked over to it and picked up the receiver of the stick phone that Mummy had absolutely insisted on paying for – as though she was the big sister, and Agnes was the baby. Was it having a husband that had allowed her mother to reverse the roles over the years? she pondered.

Clara asked the operator to connect her, and waited for the click as the telephone in Hertfordshire was picked up.

'Oh darling, I don't think it's wise to ring here. At least, not for the moment. Daddy is still furious about your behaviour and needs more time.'

Neither were prepared to discuss the incident, most especially because they were on a party line and you could never be quite certain that the operator wasn't listening in. But even after Clara had been caught in flagrante delicto, and they had faced each other in the confines of the guest bedroom, her mother couldn't bring herself to use any factual language to describe the perceived sexual wickedness of her daughter. It was as if by refusing to acknowledge what had taken place, all the unpleasantness would go away. So terribly British and so terribly wrong.

'We both know Daddy's in London for parliamentary business today.'

There was a pause. Neither were quite sure how to proceed.

'Agnes wrote to say you'd settled in. I was so pleased. When I bumped into Lady Rigby a couple of weeks ago, she hinted that you'd been sleeping on a girlfriend's sofa – Jack must have said something – but I really don't think that's the thing, darling. It makes you look poor and desperate.'

Clara ran her glossy thumbnail across her bottom lip, enjoying the way it glided seamlessly back and forth.

'I'm both though, Mummy, aren't I? Daddy has temporarily stopped the flow of pennies and my money won't last forever. Hotels are so terribly expensive.'

'He's worried that everything will get out. He dines with these people, darling. He sees Philip's father at the club when he's in town. It could affect his position. Look what the honours scandal did for Lloyd George.'

'My... indiscretion is hardly of that magnitude.'

Her mother sniffed.

'Well, as it appears that Philip's engagement is still on, perhaps all is well. Alice's mother was seen out purchasing a new hat, and there was an announcement in The Times. They've brought the wedding forward to next month, which makes me wonder if

Alice's parents have got wind of something and hurried it all along.'

Clara inhaled so quickly at that unexpected piece of news that she made herself cough. So nothing had changed and she must accept that she'd simply been a pre-marital fling. Of course the wedding would go ahead, she realised; it had never been a love match, after all. Alice's family money came from textiles and they needed the patronage of Philip's family and their exemplary heritage. Word was the Surrey estate was deep in debt.

'Let Daddy see that your silly nonsense is done with. Persuade him that you were an unwilling participant and get a ring on your finger. He simply wants to see you settled.'

Yes, and off his hands. If she could be tucked away in some rural country house, preferably nursing a baby, then she wouldn't cause him any more embarrassment, she mused.

'Honestly, at this point I don't even care if he's got money. A good family name and a bit of land will be enough. Jack has always seemed keen, and he's got all three. You don't have to love the man. Goodness, Clara, most of us find ways around it.'

But Clara would dig her elegant Spanish heels in over this. Aunt Ag had reminded her that being happy was more important than conforming. For a young woman who had spent a lifetime not fitting in and feeling miserable, she was damned if she was going to settle for a marriage that led to more of the same. She wanted to hold on to the possibility of her fairy tale ending, like those in the books her aunt had read to her when she was little. Books that had offered an escape when, snuggled up on the shabby pale blue sofa at Burlington Square, she allowed herself to believe that anything was possible.

'Marriage isn't for everyone. Maybe I want to pursue a career? Be someone in my own right, not just some man's wife.'

'Oh, darling, you don't have the temperament for work, and I'm certain whatever you tried would be eminently unsuitable, and just embarrass Daddy further.'

It was those final words that made her realise returning home would not be a good idea at the moment – if ever. Somewhere deep inside, Clara knew that all Aunt Ag wanted was for those she loved to be happy, whereas her parents wanted her to conform so that *they* could be happy. They would always see her as a disappointment and, for all the lack of fine dining, attentive staff and an ever-bulging purse, she would rather remain accepted for who she was at Burlington Square – even with her aunt's frustrating restrictions and rules – than viewed as a disappointment at home in Hertfordshire.

10

Delightful curls of smoke twisted and ribboned in the hot summer air, spiralling and dissipating towards the heavens from the end of Clara's cigarette. Things were pretty grim, she conceded, as she admired her patent leather T-bar shoes, twisting her feet first one way and then the other. She was perched on her aunt's front steps, with her long legs stretching down to the pavement below, and revelling in the warmth of the late August sun. Remaining at Burlington Square was not ideal, but she'd simply have to make the best of it.

There were a multitude of people dashing about the square and she wondered where they could possibly be going, until she realised that most of these scurrying figures were probably off to work. It was so easy to forget that the shopgirl and the factory worker were real people, who were at the beck and call of others for the duration of their day, when she'd never had to scurry to a place of work in her life.

At least these people had a purpose; they had perfume to sell, or furniture to assemble. What purpose did she serve? Why should she heave herself from her bed every day and face the world, be sociable and entertain her friends, if doing so didn't make her happy? Perhaps it was time to put a stop to the endless hedonism. Aunt Ag was right: a large dose of philanthropy might even make her feel better about herself.

She took another drag of her cigarette and noticed how glorious the gardens in the square looked. They were a slice of tranquillity in a heaving and often unpleasant city; a small but well-kept shared green space, giving residents the merest taste of escapism from the oppressively tall buildings, throngs of rushing people and grime of city life.

So engrossed was she in the scene before her, that she didn't notice she had company.

'You're very pretty.' A squeaky childlike voice shattered the silence. 'I thought perhaps you were a lady with your lovely dress and shiny hair, but Grandma says smoking isn't ladylike, so I'm not sure what you are.'

Clara turned to her right and was confronted by two inquisitive faces on the pavement below. They were surely sisters, as they were so similar in appearance. A woman, not much older than herself but considerably shorter, clutching the arm of a tall, angular-faced man, came up behind them. She had a further child balanced on her free hip. How could someone so young practically have a litter of the damn things, Clara thought, with another quite clearly on the way? The swell of her stomach underneath the dangling legs of the youngest girl was the giveaway. Eurgh... to be nothing more than a baby factory, she really couldn't think of anything worse. That was all Jack wanted, really, someone to produce a few Rigby juniors to keep the family name going. Well, that and a good time until he got bored of her and found amusement elsewhere. She recalled him ramming his tongue down her throat as though he were excavating a mine, his hands tugging roughly at her hair as he tried to elicit a response from her. It was all about him and what he wanted. He had no idea what she wanted, what made her feel good, how or where she wanted to be touched.

'Excuse the little 'uns,' said the man. He un-looped his arm from his wife, as Clara studied the couple in the sunshine. The woman wore a hard expression, her suspicious eyes focussed intently on Clara, but she gave nothing of herself away. With a smile and a more relaxed air, she could have been rather attractive, and her fresh-faced husband, with his chiselled jawline, would turn any lady's head.

'You must be Miss Humphries' niece?' he said. 'I caught sight of you a couple of weeks ago.'

Ah, now she remembered him. He'd been nonchalantly leaning on the railings as she arrived to visit her aunt, giving her the most libidinous look and making some remark about her legs. He was a rather good-looking chap and he knew it, with his easy air of confidence and cheeky wink. There had been no indication that he was married.

'I'm Nicholas and this is my wife, Jemima.' He didn't introduce his daughters, she noticed, but it was just as well. She had no interest in children and wouldn't remember their names anyway.

His wife said nothing but continued to study Clara intensely. The soul-piercing eyes of this young woman made her feel uncomfortable and a shiver rippled up her arms despite the heat. It was as if she could see through Clara's glossy veneer and bravado, and knew her for the fraud she was. Perhaps she was also assessing her as competition. Clara knew that when she entered a room, most women stepped back into the shadows, and Jemima was already somewhat in the shade with her dowdy cotton dress and dated hairstyle.

'Clara Goodwin.' She reached out an elegant hand but neither of them took it. 'I've been forced to move in with my aunt through circumstance but expect the situation to be temporary. Mr Blandford's former rooms are somewhat small and lacking in refinement. Aunt Ag, bless her, has deplorable taste in furnishings, but needs must.'

'He was a nice man,' said the tallest of the girls. Clara looked startled for a moment. She'd almost forgotten they were there – lurking below her like ants on the pavement. 'He had a head like a giant egg and couldn't do all the buttons on his waistcoat up, they were all pulling to pop open, but he sang a lot and said terribly funny things.'

Nicholas, standing behind his daughter, mimed taking a drink and rolled his eyes. Ah, so Mr Blandford was a dipso. Had Aunt Ag mentioned that? She couldn't remember.

'Strong drink is the work of the devil. Grandma told me. And I knew he would die because she said it leads to an early grave.' And she crossed her tiny arms with great conviction.

'Matilda!' It was the first word Jemima had spoken. 'Don't be talking about Mr Blandford like that. The poor man was the victim of an unfortunate accident.'

'I liked him,' Nicholas said. 'Generous with his time *and* his money. Always happy to help a neighbour out in times of trouble. Friends should be there for each other, don't you think, Miss Goodwin?' He gave her a curious smile. 'On hand to help with each other's needs?'

'Absolutely,' she purred.

'We need to get these three fed, Nick,' Jemima reminded her husband, scowling at Clara, before walking to the gate.

'Lovely to meet you, and I'm sure we'll be seeing you around,' he said, guiding the remainder of his family towards the steep steps that led to the basement. As they began to descend, Clara took what she hoped was a seductive drag of her cigarette and blew smoke out lazily from between her cupid's bow lips, turning her head slightly away as though she had no interest in these people at all.

Funny how life could turn on the toss of a sixpence, thought Clara, because there really was a sight for her weary and disillusioned peepers. Barely five minutes ago she'd been despairing at her situation and feeling thoroughly alone; now, her body thrilled with the pops and fizzes of a new attraction. And then she sighed, realising that, although you can't control who you fall for, she did have the rather unfortunate habit of falling for those who were already attached.

'You know where to find me... us... if you need anything. Anything at all,' Nicholas said, the last to disappear below street level.

She nodded because it was a tempting thought. Her body felt alive again – a response Jack continually failed to elicit. Perhaps she would ingratiate herself with the young family and see where it led. Suddenly living at Burlington Square didn't seem quite so beastly, after all.

* * *

After finishing her cigarette, Clara hopped down from the steps and walked over to the Burlington Square Gardens. By realigning her sleep pattern with the rest of the human race, she was now able to appreciate the joy of this green space during daylight hours. Despite the less than wholesome smells that sometimes drifted from the Thames, and the lack of a sweeping skyline, she already felt better for taking herself outside and reconnecting with nature.

She slipped through the gate and walked along the gravel path. There was a young woman sitting on the central bench, who shuffled along as she noticed Clara approach.

'There's plenty of room,' she said, so Clara reluctantly sat at the far end.

The woman looked up at her, nervously down to her knees, and then back up to her glamorous companion. Clara, used to the adoration of others, made the decision to be kind.

'What a glorious morning.'

'It is, but I shouldn't be here really. My lodgings are further out but I came for an interview here a few weeks ago and fell in love with this neighbourhood.'

'A job interview?' Clara was intrigued, despite herself.

'No, I work at Pemberton's. I was here for rooms at number 23.'

'Not the glove lady?' Clara couldn't help grinning as she made the connection.

'Yes. Mercy.' The woman tentatively stuck out her hand, clearly confused as to how this glamorous lady knew about her, and Clara shook it.

'You might not be so friendly when you realise I'm the reason Aunt Ag didn't give them to you.'

'Ah, the niece. She kindly wrote to me after the interview and I understand completely. Besides, Mrs Johnson's boarding house is an improvement on my last place so I'm not complaining.'

'You left quite an impression on her. Several times she's rued her choice. I'm rather afraid I can be somewhat of a handful.'

There was a pause as the two women smiled at each other.

'Beautiful bag,' Clara said, spying the crocodile skin handbag by Mercy's feet.

'It's not terribly fashionable, but my mother bought it for me and I can't bear to part with it.'

Clara recognised another sentimental soul and realised Mercy would have got on splendidly with her aunt. In fact, she would bet her last cigarette this woman was the helpful sort, who would abide by the curfew and not stumble in at five o'clock in the morning, waking everyone else up.

'I haven't shopped at Pemberton's for an absolute age. Splendid store. I'm not sure I could stand on my pins all day long, serving fussy and ungrateful people like myself. But how deliciously exciting.'

'I've always worked. I grew up on a farm and was milking cows before I could even read. Farming's not just a job; it's a way of life.'

'What brought you to the city, then?' Clara felt uncomfortable. It was becoming increasingly obvious that this young lady needed the rooms far more than she did.

'I wanted to prove to myself that I have a value.' She shrugged. 'The hours are shorter at the store – you're never really off-duty on a working farm – and the people here are so much nicer. My mother-in-law was very bitter about what happened to her son and blamed me. I needed to start again. Work out who I am.'

Clara remembered Aunt Ag mentioning how jumpy the widow was. She could see for herself that the woman was perched on the edge of the seat, not relaxed enough to lean back, and her wide eyes darted around when she heard voices.

'I wish I had a purpose other than the unwritten destiny of all women to become wives and mothers,' Clara said. She knew she would make a simply terrible job of both, not possessing one single maternal bone, and the inevitability of bearing a child through marriage petrified her. She did not want to go through the pain of childbirth, or endure the dependence of another. 'But I simply don't know what I could do. Shop work is rather beneath me.' She immediately realised her error. 'No offence.'

'None taken.' Mercy smiled. 'You doubtless have a better education than me, and can aspire to occupations out of my reach; clerical work, teaching and such.'

'I was far too restless for book-learning.' She crossed her elegant legs and sighed. 'If style and sparkling conversation were on the curriculum, I would have passed with distinction. I have no skills other than looking beautiful, surrounding myself with beautiful things, and floating around dance venues drinking cocktails. I excel at all those things.' She smiled to herself. 'If only someone would pay me to have a good time, I could be so fabulously wealthy. Perhaps I'd better settle for a loveless marriage with good financial prospects after all.'

Mercy gasped, and reached out to grip Clara's arm. 'No,' she said, as the nervousness that had hitherto danced across her face was replaced by a look of pure horror. 'Don't *ever* do that. Marriage is absolutely not to be entered into for any reason other than love.'

11

After her conversation with Mercy, Clara tried to offset her guilt at taking the rooms from a more deserving applicant by pulling her weight and spending more time with her aunt. Her determination to apply the brakes to her self-indulgent lifestyle, combined with her dwindling finances, resulted in a less frenetic social life for a few days. Aunt Ag was delighted to have the company of her niece in the evenings, and Clara was content to be loved simply for who she was. Curled up with her aunt on the sofa, talking about old times and listening to the older woman's no-nonsense philosophy, she felt the most content she'd been in a long time.

But her friends missed her, and Neville was most displeased that she'd abandoned them for the 'call of cocoa and the companionship of a dreary old dear'. She was eventually persuaded by an unusually persistent Jack to join them one late August evening at the Sixty-Three.

She pulled out her rather crumpled peach silk evening dress from the teetering pile of clothes across a stick-back chair. Her bedroom resembled a church hall jumble sale, as she still hadn't unpacked properly. It was at times like this she missed having staff, although there was something to be said for not having the beady little eyes of some maid judging you from the corner of every room. She slipped the dress over her head and it slid down her body, as she assessed her reflection in the mirrored door of the ugly Victorian wardrobe that stood in the corner. As she swished from side to side, the bow motif of rhinestones across the left shoulder caught the light, and the hemline skimmed the top of her knees in a manner her paternal grandmother had proclaimed utterly scandalous. But then Grandmama was a wealthy dowager with little to do all day except lament her lost youth and criticise anyone who had the gall to enjoy theirs.

Clara knew she was attractive. Jack continually declared it, and even the eyes of the married Nicholas told her so. She knew it was terribly naughty of her to flirt with her neighbour, but she revelled in stirring up a little jealousy between the couple. Meeting the young family had reminded her how thrilling the chase of an unsuspecting quarry was.

As she skipped down the two flights of stairs, she encountered a sullen-faced Gilbert coming through the front door, camera in hand. Initially, he paid her no attention, but as she fluttered past, he stopped directly in front of her, blocking her exit.

'Can I take your photo? Here. Now.' His eyes narrowed, and Clara tried not to mind his total lack of social skills. A 'hullo' would have been good manners.

'What? No. I'm going out.'

'I'll give you five pounds.'

Normally, she would have sneered at the young man and carried on her way, but five pounds would be awfully handy, although she was curious as to why he wanted a picture of her. Either he was yet another ardent admirer, or he wanted her image for unwholesome purposes.

'I'm not taking my clothes off so that you can sell sordid photographs of me to some *artistic* magazine.'

Gilbert's pale face flashed the only other shade in its limited repertoire, turning an embarrassed pink.

'It's the dress I'm interested in. It won't take a moment and no one will even know it's you. I don't care about your face.'

'Then I hardly see the point, darling.'

'Right.' He looked disappointed. 'I should have known you don't need money.'

Not wanting to admit her financial situation, Clara reconsidered the proposition.

'And there will be no funny stuff?'

Gilbert shook his head. 'You're *really* not my type.'

'Ditto.' They stared at each other for a moment. 'If you're quick then,' she acquiesced. There was, as yet, no motor car horn to announce the arrival of her lift. 'And pay me promptly.'

'I just need to grab something.' Gilbert disappeared into Aunt Ag's front room and returned with a cut-glass champagne coupe from the tray of assorted glassware on her sideboard. As a landlady, she left this room accessible to all her lodgers, offering a communal space they could freely enter. She'd confided in her niece that a cheery hello from a returning Mr Blandford had often been the highlight of her day, and that even Gilbert occasionally popped down for a cup of tea – albeit with minimal conversation.

'Hold this.' Gilbert thrust the glass at her and she raised an eyebrow. 'Oh, and wear this.' He scooped up her apricot felt cloche hat that she'd carelessly flung on the hall stand earlier.

He fiddled about with his camera and instructed her to stand on the half-landing, with the coupe aloft and her face tilted away.

'I'm far too high up, darling,' she complained.

'It's perfect.' He moved the camera to his waist and looked

through the tiny window. 'Hold still,' he instructed, and pressed the shutter.

There was a timely beep from the street and Clara relaxed her pose, tripping back down to the hallway, her hand outstretched and both eyebrows raised expectantly.

It took Gilbert a moment to realise what she was demanding, and he rummaged in his pockets to find a small roll of bank notes, before counting five into her waiting hand.

'Almost a pleasure doing business with you,' she said.

And, as she drifted into the chilly London night, she realised, despite his protestations to the contrary, the poor misguided soul must have it bad to happily part with such a sum just to have a permanent keepsake of her.

* * *

An hour later, after a thrilling ride through central London in Jack's motor car with the top down, Clara, Neville, Mitzy and Jack arrived at the Sixty-Three.

Sometimes, when Neville had his way, they went to the Pink Slipper – a divine spectacle to behold, with golden walls, pink stucco Grecian columns, and enormous flamingo-coloured light shades. It attracted a more avant-garde clientele, and it wasn't just the ladies who wore make-up. Jack, however, preferred the Sixty-Three – not least because Neville tended to be better behaved at this more respectable venue.

It was the second club the notorious Mrs Bayswater had opened – the previous one having been closed down for selling intoxicating liquor in breach of licensing laws. This new venture, at 63 Gerrard Street in Soho, offered copious amounts of alcohol, plenty of dancing and stunning monochrome decor. Rather cleverly, Clara thought, Mrs Bayswater also served breakfasts to keep her clientele until the early hours. Neville was often keen to end the evening, albeit technically at the start of the day, with kippers, coffee and a slice of bread and butter.

Oftentimes, the patrons enjoyed themselves too much and fights broke out – the wearing of evening-dress no guarantee of the calibre of the customer. West End gangsters mingled with theatrical types, English nobility and even minor European royalty. Rudolph Valentino (Lord rest his soul), Prince Christopher of Greece and Evelyn Waugh had all been spotted at the club on occasion.

They secured a table and Neville whisked Mitzy off for a spin about the floor before the poor darling had even sat down, leaving Clara alone with an unusually pensive Jack. She couldn't put her finger on why, but he was restless, his eyes unable to meet hers and his body language different somehow. He hadn't even acknowledged the American millionaire chap he'd recently become acquainted with – which was most unlike him as Jack liked to be seen with popular people. Perhaps that was why she'd always jogged along with him so well. Neither minded being the centre of attention, and she suspected it had been the start of his infatuation with her – all eyes were invariably on the exuberant Clara, and therefore invariably on him.

An awkward silence stretched between them, before a sourfaced Mitzy stomped back to the table, dragging the recently arrived Lily behind.

'Neville is so naughty,' she moaned. 'He abandoned me almost immediately and is now making doe eyes at some young viscount. It's all very well when we're at the Pink Slipper, but not here. There's undoubtedly press lurking in the shadows. If he makes his tastes too obvious, his father won't be nominated for his coveted peerage anytime soon.'

This was proving to be a decade where the *love that dared not speak its name* was tacitly accepted, particularly amongst the wealthy, who had always been able to flout the laws of the land by mixing with the right people. The law was still the law, however, and occasionally had to be seen to be upheld by those in positions of power. It meant that discretion was the order of the day and it didn't do to flaunt one's preferences. Neville was in imminent danger of getting himself arrested again, if he wasn't careful, often singing his own version of 'All the Nice Girls Love a Sailor' at full volume in the dark streets of the city after consuming too much giggle-water.

'Jackie, you'll dance with me, won't you?' Mitzy pursed her vibrant red lips and fluttered her eyelashes, but Jack had saddled that particular horse before. He'd been engagement number two in her long line of fleeting suitors. She'd notched up and dispensed with number three since then.

'Not tonight. I just want to sit here and admire the view.' He stared at Clara and an uncomfortable feeling started to swell in her belly.

'Why is everyone being such a bore?' asked Mitzy. 'I'm off to powder my nose. Anyone else? Lily? Clara?'

They both shook their heads knowing that *nose* and *powder* were the operative words. Clara had tried it on occasion but didn't like the headaches and bouts of paranoia she invariably suffered from afterwards. Alcohol was preferable; she still got the headaches but it wasn't as riotously expensive, and the jolly feeling lasted much longer. Mitzy was so damned dependent on the stuff that her olfactory receptors had ceased to function properly. As Lily had quite astutely pointed out, a bottle of Guerlain's Shalimar was wasted on her.

'I hear old Philip has rushed the nuptials. Announcement in The Times,' Lily said, changing the subject. 'Wedding is next month. I've RSVP'd. I may not approve of the bride but I couldn't turn down the opportunity to mingle with royalty – however minor.

Not sure how they managed to swing everything so quickly, or why they'd even want to. It's not like there's a bloody war on.'

Clara knew exactly why everything had been rushed – to avoid a scandal – and she was the very reason for it, but she said nothing, trying not to mind, and understanding completely, why she hadn't been invited. She bit hard on her lip and tried to hide her irritation. It was obvious to her now that she'd been a plaything, a last hurrah before Mr and Mrs Philip Highgrove ran into the fiery sunset to begin a life of respectability and marital bliss. Or, at least, give the outside world that impression.

'Why on earth anyone would want to put themselves in the old domestic handcuffs is beyond me.' Lily swiped an olive-bedecked Martini from the tray of a passing hostess, knocking it back in one.

'Love is the reason, dear girl, love.' Jack gave Clara another look that made her stomach roll.

'But Philip of all people?' Lily pulled a face. 'I always thought he was a bit of a birdbrain and, let's face it, he's not much to look at.'

'And yet she has the most splendid chunk of ice on her finger. She could always sell that if it all went down the pan,' Mitzy pointed out. Clara wondered what had happened to the three engagement rings her friend had procured. They'd probably all been snorted up her nose.

Lily put her empty glass on the table as Mitzy snatched up her clutch bag. 'Come on, Lils. You can keep me company on the terrace.' And the pair of them drifted towards the foyer in an alarmingly haphazard fashion.

'Alone at last, Clara, darling,' Jack said, reaching over to take her hand. Alarm bells started to ring in her already buzzing head, and she tried to extricate herself but he had her tight. 'I wanted to talk to you about something...'

'Really, darling, you sound so deadly serious and I want to have fun tonight.'

Jack nodded at a lurking hostess who had a bottle of Ayala protruding from a top hat-shaped ice bucket, and two champagne saucers balanced on a glossy white tray. So like Jack to arrange such an ostentatious display of wealth. Clara eyed the drink suspiciously. It had led her astray before.

'This Philip and Alice caper got me thinking. Let's do it, old thing?' Jack said.

'Do what?'

'Handcuff ourselves together? You really are the pussycat's whiskers, and you know old Jackie-boy likes the best of everything.'

Her heart sank. 'Don't be so utterly ridiculous, darling. I wouldn't make you happy.'

'Perhaps this will change your mind,' he said in a raised voice, and produced a small blue velvet box from his pocket and popped the lid. Inside was a sizeable diamond in a very modern geometric setting. It was an absolute sweetheart of a stone, and her hand twitched, keen to slip it on her finger, just to see how its faces reflected the flickering lights. She liked Jack; he was harmless enough, and he had seen her at her vilest and still came back for more. There were worse chaps a gal could settle down with, but she didn't and never would love him.

She tore her gaze from the ring and noticed how earnest his face was in that moment. A complete change from the flippant Jack that everyone knew. It was a sudden realisation on her part that he probably did love her and she felt bad for him. She reached across to place her hand over his, squeezing his fingers ever so gently.

'Sorry, darling, but no.'

An enthusiastic dancer behind Jack lurched into the back of his chair, lost his balance, and tumbled onto his lap.

'Sincere apologies, old bean,' came the familiar voice of Neville, who completely overplayed the accident and revelled in the moment for far too long, before spotting the abandoned velvet box and leaping back to his feet. 'Oh God, were you proposing? Dreadfully sorry.' He put up his hands and raised his voice. 'Everyone, Jack's manacling himself to our Clara! That's a jolly fine turn up for the books. Bubbles all round – especially for Jackie – he deserves it for taking the old girl on.'

Then he caught Clara's expression. She flashed her eyes wide to signal her horror and the colour drained from his face. He meant well but this was a disaster. People stopped dancing and inane drunken faces grinned in their direction. There was a flutter of applause. If Jack had been the man for her, the moment could not have been more perfect, with silver paper streamers floating around them, tethered black and white balloons bobbing about in the swirling smoke-laden air, and champagne corks popping away in the background. The atmosphere was one of shared joy and celebration.

'See.' Jack shuffled to his feet, emboldened by Neville's apparent support, but clearly annoyed that his grand show hadn't turned out as expected. 'Everyone else thinks it's a splendid idea. Even your father. He all but threw his arms about me when I asked the old chap's permission.'

I'll bet he did, she thought. So desperate to see her safely married, he would gladly have agreed to anyone walking her up the aisle, however unsuitable. How easy it would be in that moment to go along with the game, to agree to be his wife to appease her father. To settle down and have a family. Settle – the word sat uneasily with her. It would be a compromise and one where ultimately neither party would ever be truly happy.

'Sorry and everything but it simply won't work, Jackie, and deep down I think you know I'm right. I love you dearly as a friend but you will never be more than that.'

There was a trickle of mumbles from the gathered crowd, which dried up as two hostesses pushed through the sticky bodies of the pausing revellers with the ordered champagne.

'Ouch, relegated to chum,' Neville said, taking centre stage for which Clara was eternally grateful. 'Whoops-a-daisy. Naughty me – jumping to conclusions. We shall just have to celebrate that this particular eligible bachelor and the most beautiful girl in the room are still on the market. To Clara and Jack – never together and possibly better apart.'

After being given the nod by Mrs Bayswater, the band struck up again, and the music made Clara's feet twitch. On the dance floor, she could forget about complicated affairs of the heart and merely concentrate on the steps. Mitzy had returned from the powdering and was bobbing about like a lunatic, her blonde curls bouncing up and down as she spun about with renewed energy, so Clara squashed her cigarette into the ashtray, and gave Jack a conciliatory smile as Neville sank into the chair next to the jilted man.

'Bad luck, old sport.' He patted the wide-eyed reject on the back.

Poor Jackie. He couldn't possibly understand that it wasn't about the showy proposal and promise of a luxurious lifestyle that might have hooked other girls. Her heart went out to him as she walked over to join a frenetic and insensible Mitzy in a particularly salacious version of the Black Bottom, with arm-waving and bottom-slapping aplenty.

12

The letter Clara received from her father two days later was terse and disapproving. Bad news always travelled faster than good. The ultimatum he presented her with was clear – marry Jack or he would wash his hands of her.

She had no doubt her father would be true to his word, and the thought of being permanently penniless and homeless was alarming. There were some sins, it seemed, he could not forgive. However, Aunt Ag was proof that women could survive without the support and protection of a man. She had sacrificed love for duty and had fared tolerably well. But was she happy? That, decided Clara, was the real question.

From the tall front-facing sash window of her second-floor rooms, she allowed the letter to fall to her side as she observed the bustling activity of the square below. It was another glorious day and the house felt stuffy and airless. Smells of summer drifted in through the open window and a disorientated bumble bee bounced off the windowpane. Everything was sunny and light outside, but dark and claustrophobic inside. She grabbed her lighter and silver cigarette box and headed downstairs, not caring that she was barefoot, feeling frightfully bohemian and revelling in it. A stern-faced gentleman looked up as she closed the front door, horrified by her lack of footwear as he touched his hat and scurried passed. She smiled. It was fun not conforming.

Perched high on the stone steps so that she could admire the view without having to interact with the multitude, she lit her cigarette, just as Jemima, the young mother she'd met previously, walked up the street pushing her pram. There was a basket of groceries balanced on the hood, and her two oldest girls were skipping around her feet like small dogs. With a hundred questions from her eldest daughter and intermittent grumbles from inside the pram, Clara watched her struggle with the gate to the basement.

She jumped up and hastened to help. Aunt Ag had wanted her to start thinking of others and be aware of their needs.

'Here, let me.'

'I can manage.'

'I'm sure, sweetie, but it would be easier if you allowed me to lend a hand.' She took the basket from the hood and guarded the girls. 'Where is your husband?' She tried to sound nonchalant.

Jemima scowled.

'It's Friday. Unlike the entitled men you doubtless fraternise with, he has to earn a living. He's a motorman on the trams for London City Council and works long days. And don't call me "sweetie". It's patronising. Having money doesn't make you better than me.'

Clara raised her eyebrows, not used to being reprimanded by anyone, particularly when she wasn't doing anything wrong. She felt a prickle of heat gallop across her cheeks. There was a tug at her hem and she looked down to find two small rosy faces staring intently up at her.

'Are you a film star?' the oldest daughter asked.

'Only in my head, darling,' she replied.

'Oh.' The little girl looked at Clara's feet. 'You have no shoes on. Are you poor?'

'Not in the sense of needing money, but perhaps needing sympathy. Life can be so dreadfully complicated and people can be beastly for no reason.' She tried not to look at Jemima as she said this, but heard her neighbour tut, as though she couldn't imagine why someone like Clara might possibly need sympathy.

'And it's so dreadfully hard being a woman. One is so terribly reliant on men...' Her comment was a vague allusion to the male-dominated world she constantly found frustrating, but had done little to address. At her words, however, Jemima perked up.

'Absolutely,' the young mum agreed. 'Men decide who runs this country and make the laws – laws which both sexes have to abide by, but neither Miss Goodwin nor I are even allowed to cast a vote.' Lloyd George had given property-owning women over thirty this privilege, but possibly only because the war had forced his hand, and they were still not on equal terms with men.

'But we *will* address this imbalance,' she continued. 'I'm certain of it. What makes a twenty-one-year-old man more qualified to elect a member of parliament than a twenty-one-year-old woman? Most of the young men I know think of nothing beyond their next meal – which they don't even have to prepare themselves. They don't know how to iron a shirt or manage their money without the help of their silent, supportive wives. The skills of men *and* women complement each other but one is not superior to the other.'

Most of the young people Clara knew had neither the practical skills of the worker, nor the domestic skills to run a home – regardless of their sex. Jack had absolutely no idea how much a pound of butter cost or how to get red wine from a dress shirt, but neither could he sharpen a knife nor mend his motor car should it break down. And Neville, whilst he was a genuinely kind soul, was innately selfish when it came to getting what he wanted. His outrageous behaviour would land them all in hot water one day, she was certain. But then, was she any better? She did not do her own laundry, and had never prepared her own food beyond rustling up a sandwich at three o'clock in the morning to deal with her giddy post-party head and spinning stomach. Aunt Ag was right; even delivering Mr Gorski's meals was done half-heartedly.

She suddenly felt ashamed for not having a stronger political or social agenda in support of her own sex. In many ways, she had more power and influence than someone like Jemima, but had done nothing to exercise it. Not once had she used her elevated birth to speak up for her downtrodden sisters. Instead, she bemoaned her financial dependence on her father without considering that she might support herself.

'Then perhaps one should sit an examination in order to vote, man or woman. Only those with a true understanding of what they are voting for would qualify?' she suggested, delighted to have stumbled across a topic that her downstairs neighbour cared about and keen to show solidarity. Surely, the best way to make friends was to find common ground?

'*Everyone* should have a voice,' Jemima snapped, her dark eyes burning brightly again, as she lifted her youngest daughter from the pram. 'Examinations, indeed. And how would the illiterate fare with that, I ask? The intelligent, hard-working masses, who may not be able to quote Socrates but who can skin a rabbit, or mend a broken plough. Far more practical skills. Can you mend a plough?' she challenged.

How interesting, thought Clara, the passions of this abrasive woman were seeping out, but she shook her head. She had very few practical skills. Daddy employed people for all that.

'The war showed the men what we could do, and then they returned from foreign fields and we were relegated back to the kitchen, but now that Pandora's box has been opened, not everything will fit back inside.' Jemima began to descend the steps and Clara herded the older two girls in the same direction.

'Pandora let trouble out into the world, not women – who are, by and large, a good thing.'

'Oh, but we *will* be trouble,' the young mother said, looking back over her shoulder at Clara with fiercely burning eyes. 'We will shake up the old order of things, given half the chance.'

'What a splendid notion,' Clara said, briefly imagining herself campaigning for something, anything, and having a purpose.

'Mummy, please can the pretty lady see my train set?' The young girl was clearly bored by the chatter that she didn't understand.

'How simply divine!' Clara's beaming smile was genuine. 'A train set for a girl. The toys of boys are so much more fun. Don't you agree? I always fancied one but Daddy wouldn't have it.'

The young mum sniffed, seemingly appeased by Clara's enthusiasm for her daughter's request, as she placed her key in the lock of the basement door.

'Nicholas was so convinced Matilda would be a boy, he bought the set before she even came into the world. When she was old enough, I insisted she was still to have it, especially as it had sat on the shelf for years, untouched every time I popped out another girl. Why shouldn't she be allowed to play with trains? Her mind is every bit as curious as that of a boy.'

'Why not indeed?' Clara agreed, amused by this show of passion from the woman who had barely said three words in front of her husband.

Jemima gave a resigned sigh.

'Come and see Tilly's train set if you want. I daresay I could make us both a cup of tea. Be nice to chat to someone other than Matilda for a while... if I'm not stopping you, that is?'

'Not at all. I've nothing better to do.'

'How divine!' Matilda squeaked, echoing Clara's earlier words as she slid her hot sticky fingers into the hand of her new favourite person and gripped tightly. Clara hastily stubbed out her cigarette and regretted her rash acceptance. She would inevitably have to talk to the children. A ripple of apprehension swept across her body. How terribly dull. Or was it simply that she was worried Matilda would see through her? Children could be alarmingly perceptive – something to do with asking the direct questions that adults were too polite to ask.

* * *

Five minutes later Clara sat on the edge of a small sofa peering down at Matilda's eager face as the young girl pulled a chain of brightly coloured wooden carriages around a circular track.

'Choo-choo,' said the youngest sister, who'd had enough of toddling around upright, clinging to the furniture, and had resorted to the far speedier method of crawling on all fours.

Jemima bustled about in the background, putting the groceries away and setting a pale green enamel kettle to boil on the almost matching enamel stove. Clara took in her surroundings. The base-ment was one large room with a kitchen space to the left and some seating near the open fire. A circular dining table to the right and a large sofa divided the room in half, with two doors at the back which Clara assumed led to bedrooms. It was darker than the rest of Burlington Square due to the smaller windows, which were high up as most of the space was below ground, but it felt homely for all that. Colourful knitted blankets sat across the backs of the easy chairs and a bright orange hand-knotted rug was in front of the fire-place. The lingering smells of baked bread hung in the air.

'Your brooch is pretty,' Matilda said.

Clara looked down to where the girl was pointing.

'I'd forgotten I was even wearing it. It's just a silly costume piece. I don't even like the thing.'

It wasn't a bold enough statement for Clara, thin and insignificant. Something Grandmama had passed on and she'd probably worn it to appease the frightful old bird for some family get-together.

Matilda's eyes expanded. 'But it's the most prettiest thing I ever did see. Apart from you,' she added hastily.

'Here, you have it.' She unfastened the brooch and handed it to the girl.

'To keep for ever and ever?'

Clara shrugged. 'If you like.'

'Oh, thank you.' She jumped up, sending the line of carriages flying, and put her arms around her benefactor. Clara was most horrified and looked to Jemima for help.

'Now, now, put the poor woman down, Tilly.' She studied Clara as she slid a steaming hot cup of tea onto the low table beside her. 'You didn't have to do that.'

'I wanted to. Watch her with the pin though. It's sharp.'

'I'll pop it on her smart coat. Thank you.' Her eyes met Clara's, but dipped away almost immediately as the faintest dots of pink flashed briefly on the apples of her cheeks.

She doesn't trust me, Clara thought, and is entirely and utterly wise not to do so.

The women settled down, as the girls played on the floor by their feet, and an awkward silence ensued that stretched fully over five minutes. A hundred topics raced through Clara's head in her efforts to start a conversation, but she wasn't interested in making polite enquiries about domestic life any more than she could imagine Jemima wanted to hear about wild parties or how to mix a Manhattan. Jemima seemed equally at a loss for words. She caught the young mother studying her face, perhaps intrigued by her make-up or even shocked by her bold haircut, but those eyes fell away as soon as she realised Clara had noticed her gaze.

'This isn't going to work,' the young mother eventually said. 'Us trying to forge some kind of friendship. Our worlds are very different.'

Clara considered this for a moment. Surely there was some common ground? They were both of a similar age, after all.

'My friend Joyce likes drawing and knows the names of different flowers from her daddy,' Matilda said, as the silence dragged on. 'And I prefer climbing trees and playing trains.' She had been listening to their stilted conversation (or lack of it) and was chipping in her two penn'orth. 'But we still do things together.'

'How delightfully wise for one so young,' Clara exclaimed. 'The best friendships are between those who can learn from each other.' She thought of how tiresome she was finding Mitzy and Lily. When one's friends were merely reflected images of oneself, the conversation could be so dreadfully dull.

'Tell me something about yourself. What you do in your free time?' she asked.

Jemima coughed. 'Are you trying to be funny? What free time? I'm up with the little one at six and then my life is an ever-revolving cycle of feeding, cooking and cleaning.'

'Surely Nicholas takes you out sometimes? To a dance or a picture house?'

'Every penny my husband earns is accounted for. There aren't spare shillings lying about to spend on frivolous things such as dances. Although... I used to love dancing.' Clara noticed a slight sway of the woman's body as if her body was remembering something her brain wouldn't allow her to revisit. 'But we haven't been since Tilly was born.'

'And yet Agnes told me Nicholas enjoys a pint at the pub most nights.' In her world, the boys and the girls each had their own fun.

Daddy had his club and Mummy had her committees and shopping excursions.

'Don't criticise things you know nothing about. You have no idea of how real people live, do you?' Her eyes narrowed. 'He works. He needs time to unwind.'

'*You* work.' Clara was indignant. This poor woman was on the go from dawn until dusk. 'When do you get to unwind?'

'It changes when you become a mother, and it will change for you, when you have children. Oh no, I forget. You will have a nurse and a nanny, and see the little darlings for half an hour on a Sunday evening. I doubt they will impact on your life much at all.'

Clara wasn't used to being spoken to like this, and certainly not by someone she considered might have reason to be deferential because of her superior education and social standing, yet she rather enjoyed this woman's forthright conversation and penchant to challenge.

'Motherhood isn't for me,' she replied with conviction.

'How lovely to have the choice.'

'Everyone has a choice.' She was vehement in her statement.

'No, they don't,' Jemima said, lowering her voice. 'Some young women, who have dreams of independence and freedom, are forced into unsuitable matches by overbearing families. They are persuaded to marry a man they barely know simply because he has a steady job and a pleasing face.' She was clearly referring to her husband and it was interesting to note that the marriage was not a love match. 'My aunt was a suffragette,' she continued, 'a woman who believed everyone was equal, regardless of their sex, and fought for women to have the same educational and employment opportunities as men. She was the only person who encouraged my dreams, and when she died, shortly after the war, I had no one on my side. You wouldn't know how that feels.' The words were almost spat out and her glare was challenging.

Clara knew *exactly* how that felt, but not wishing to be confrontational, and afraid she might say something she would regret, she slipped down onto the floor and began to replace the carriages on the track. Matilda was delighted that the focus had returned to her, and began a stream of chatter that lasted fully half an hour, where all Clara had to do was nod and occasionally agree. And somehow, in the middle of all the chatter, she found she had promised to take a small six-year-old to the park one Sunday. Just the two of them, for what her ardent admirer has described as *lady time*.

In her delight, Matilda flung her arms about Clara, who froze for a second time, not knowing how to respond to such childlike affection. She'd been spot on with her assessment of the young girl. Matilda Smith was almost as manipulative as she was.

13

THE CUT-GLASS STAMP MOISTENER

Agnes had adored her father unreservedly – a man who brought great joy to the world with his humming and jolly demeanour. She could quite see how her mother had fallen for him, and long after he'd passed away she would smile to herself, remembering how he often referred to things by their function, rather than their proper name. Chairs were 'bottom holders', windows were 'lookey outeys', and the stamp moistener that stood on his imposing study desk became the 'letter licker'.

The letter licker had always fascinated her as a child. She loved the clever way the roller spun through the water as you pushed either your envelope or stamp across it, moistening the glue. It was one of her jobs to refill the reservoir – a task she undertook with all the earnestness of someone caring for and watering a plant. It felt good to be given a responsibility, albeit a small one. If only she'd known what enormous responsibilities were to come.

When Agnes was twelve years old, she sat quietly in the corner of her father's study as he wrote letter after letter. His humming was no more, and the only sound was the distant cry of a newborn baby drifting down the stairs. Agnes didn't like the wet nurse but her father said she would do for the moment, because the sickly Daphne's very survival depended on the woman. He'd not slept for five days, alternately pacing around the front parlour or along the bedside of his dying wife. But his anxious wait was at a tragic end. Now he had heartbreaking letters to write and memorial cards to post.

Agnes took delivery of the black-bordered mourning stationery, and pocketed one of the cards for her scrap album, but seeing the words in print hadn't made it any more real.

In affectionate remembrance of
  HELENA FLORENCE HUMPHRIES
  Who died 21 May 1878
  AGED 35 YEARS
  Daughter, wife and mother

When she was nearly twenty-one, Agnes sat at that same desk and looked out across the back yard. Spring was dancing through the city, and the bare branches of the tree tops now had the tiniest green shoots forming. The anticipation of new life was almost palpable, and yet there would be no new life for her.

Dearest James…

her letter began, and then a flurry of words followed that tore at her like angry cats.

She had two false starts, and crumpled both attempts into tiny balls before dropping them into the tole waste-paper basket at her feet – the painted galleon across the side reminding her that she was putting an end to all chances of foreign travel with her words.

Thirteen years after the heartbreak of that day came the worst heartbreak of all, as she used what was left of the mourning stationery to deliver the news of her father's passing. He had defied all the doctors' predictions with his longevity and this, she had been reassured repeatedly, was entirely down to her patient and gentle nursing.

She struggled to write an adequate tribute. Thomas Humphries had been her everything, a man who'd risen from office clerk to wealthy man of business in ten short years, and then married unusually late. Helena was half his age but twice his match, and their love was absolute. The only tragedy was that he should outlive her. Life can play cruel games and twist the odds, but he'd understood this only too well – being a man whose risky investments had made his fortune.

As the last of the letters was posted, Agnes turned back towards Burlington Square and watched the autumn leaves dance around her feet. Life went on, she reflected, as a stout middle-aged lady in spectacles strode ahead of her with purpose. She's needed somewhere, Agnes thought, perhaps she even has a job. What do I have now? I have nothing.

She returned home and sat for hours in her father's study, the silence of the house bearing down on her. And for want of something to do, she spun the stamp moistener so furiously that it sprayed the desktop blotter with tiny droplets of water.

And, as she watched, the drops evaporated and disappeared, almost as if they'd never been there at all.

14

Clara sauntered downstairs, pleased with herself for rising before midday, and determined to address what she felt was the unjust accusation levelled at her by Jemima that she had no idea how real people lived. Today was laundry day and she had offered to help her aunt.

Agnes looked up from leaning over the copper in the scullery and took in her niece's glamorous attire.

'Are you here to model the linen or help me launder it?' she asked. 'Because it rather looks to me as if you don't know what doing the laundry involves.'

Clara shrugged. 'We have staff to do this back home.'

'Yes, well, Mummy married well and can afford to pay people, but I run this household on my own and I'm getting older now. It's back-breaking work, and I struggle transferring the heavy, wet washing to the zinc tub. I was sorely tempted to rent the rooms to that young widow, because she offered to take on a share of the household duties.'

'I bumped into her the other day, strangely enough. She was visiting the gardens in the square.'

'Mrs Mayweather?' her aunt asked, lifting her eyebrows in surprise, and Clara nodded.

'You were right about her being jumpy, but she seems happy enough in her new lodgings. I might pop into Pemberton's next time I need some new stockings, and say hello. I rather liked her.'

'So did I,' Aunt Ag said, 'so don't make me regret my decision or I'll be visiting Pemberton's myself and recruiting a new lodger. You're young, fit and have plenty of time on your work-shy hands. It's about time you learned something useful.' She gave her niece a knowing look. 'I think it's where I went wrong with Daphne. I felt so sorry for her, being motherless, that I rather spoiled her.'

'Oh, darling, don't try to convince me that understanding the intricacies of starching a collar will make me a better person.' Clara rolled her eyes.

'But it will.' Agnes placed her hands on her wide hips, clearly not having any of Clara's nonsense. 'If you spend the day helping me do this – and it will take us all day, my dear – perhaps the next time you change out of a frock, you will be a little less careless with how you discard it. Besides, you never know what life has in store. We had staff when I was young, but my fortunes changed, and now I find myself cleaning grates and scouring copper pans. It's as well to be prepared.'

Clara knew that she was at a fork in the road. To bow to her father's wishes regarding Jack would ensure her lifestyle continued; to disobey him was to lose all that, but she wanted to remain true to herself. Perhaps starting again, somewhere far away, was the answer, even if she had to do her own laundry.

'Show me what to do, then.' She rolled up the silk sleeves of her orange slip dress. Aunt Ag and Jemima had reminded her what a privileged upbringing she'd had, and there was part of her that felt ashamed for doing nothing with this privilege. She wondered what her friends would make of her now, up to her elbows in sweaty shirts and soiled undergarments. Mitzy would be genuinely horrified, and Neville would joke about her tumbling into the ranks of the proletariat.

'Jack Rigby has asked me to marry him.' There was something about her aunt that invited honesty. Perhaps it was her ability to see both sides of any situation, even if discretion was not her forte. 'He asked me at the Sixty-Three, and put on a great display with champagne in front of a crowd, when I rather think a proposal should be a private affair. He'd clearly spoken to Daddy beforehand and thought my answer was a forgone conclusion...'

'But?' Her aunt knew from her tone that this tale had more to it.

'You'll think me silly and selfish, but I don't want to.' Her shoulders slumped, as she leaned her bottom against the bricks of the copper.

'Daphne mentioned something in her last letter, but I do understand these things are not always straightforward. She thought I was silly to turn down an offer of marriage I once had, yet I did so nonetheless.'

'But you were the one who warned me against becoming an old maid. You said—'

'I was trying to guide you in the direction I thought you wanted to go, but it's quite obvious that what might have suited me, would not suit you.' Her aunt put her hands on her wide hips and stared at her niece. 'I wrongly believed that all the silly behaviour and make-up was about you trying to attract a husband...'

Clara shook her head. 'No, I'm simply drifting along like a pretty little sailing boat, going where the wind blows me, with no coxswain on board to steer my vessel. And Daddy's had enough and is delivering ultimatums. If I don't marry Jack, he's going to cut me off,' she whined.

'Darling Clara, your future is in your own hands. Times have changed since my day and it's acceptable now for girls of your age to find gainful employment. Look at Mrs Mayweather. Perhaps she'll marry again and find purpose in being a wife and mother. Or maybe she will devote herself to her job at the store and end up being in charge of a whole department.' Even Clara understood the poor woman could not do both. 'But she gets to decide either way. What do you *want* to do?'

'Something for myself. Not be dependent on others, even though the prospect scares me.'

'Then forge your own way, darling,' her aunt said, reaching across to stroke her hair in the most heartbreakingly comforting way. No one had touched her like that for years. 'You have a choice. Weigh up your options, listen to advice, but ultimately, it's you, and you alone, who has the live with the consequences.'

As Clara sank into her aunt's comforting arms, she remembered why she loved this forthright woman so completely. She said what she thought, but was always prepared to consider both sides of a situation – unlike her father.

Coming to Burlington Square might just be the best thing that had happened to her.

As they slipped into September and the chill air reminded everyone that summer was being served her notice, Clara found the courage to stand by her decision not to marry Jack. The generous bank of Reginald Goodwin pulled down the shutters for his wayward daughter, but knowing Aunt Ag was on her side made everything bearable.

Wanting to do something useful with her time, she decided to pay the Smith family another visit. There was something about the young mother that fascinated her. Jemima's spirit and her intensity, even though most of that intensity was directed somewhat negatively towards her, made her feel alive and invigorated. For the first time since she was a child, when dragons could be slain and dark mountains scaled, Clara wondered if she could make a difference in the world and fight for what she believed in.

She knocked at the basement with a bundle of frocks over her arm, and the door was opened by a sullen Jemima.

'What can I do for you?' The young mum sounded weary.

'I have some clothes here that I don't want any more.' Perhaps it was a clumsy gesture, but she was convinced that Jemima, with her delicate features, had the potential to be even more beautiful if she would only smile instead of scowling. Everyone felt better when they looked better. At least, that's what Clara had been trying to convince herself for the last decade.

'I don't need your cast-offs.'

'Darling, life would be terribly dull if we only had things we *needed*. We should always make room for things we want – as they will undoubtedly make us happiest of all. Besides, you'd be doing me a favour. Some of these things are simply ghastly.'

Jemima frowned. 'Can you even hear the words that come out of your mouth?'

'Ghastly on me, I mean,' Clara hastily clarified. 'They'd look simply splendid on you. Our colouring is quite different.'

Jemima shook her head in disbelief but pulled the door back, nonetheless, to allow Clara entry, just as the smallest member of the Smith family erupted into tears. The young mother sighed.

'I'll put the kettle on—' she gestured for Clara to deposit the dresses on an empty pine chair '—whilst *you* deal with Frances.' She picked up her youngest daughter from the floor and thrust the child at a horrified Clara. Puce-faced and screaming, the infant's sticky hands began pawing at Clara's face. Jemima stared at her neighbour and placed her hands on her hips, almost challenging Clara to refuse to soothe the fractious child. The eyes of the two women met and held. Clara swallowed and dug deep, clasping Frances closer to her and swaying, imagining herself on a dance floor. The tune to 'If You Knew Susie' began to play through her head as she moved, and Frances seemed suitably soothed. Satisfied, Jemima turned her attention to the kettle and the stove.

'Sorry if I appeared ungrateful for the clothes. There isn't the spare money to buy me nice things, and the girls always come first, so I am appreciative of the gesture. Not that I ever go anywhere to wear such things.'

'Come dancing with me?'

What an absolute scream it would be to take this young woman to a nightclub. They would simply have the best time, and the boys would look after them. Jemima had the potential to turn many a head if she dolled herself up. Clara had a momentary vision of the pair of them holding hands and spinning around in circles, as their peripheral world blurred into unfocused insignificance. But she'd said the wrong thing yet again, and her friend's tone sharpened.

'Married women don't go dancing without their husbands. Certainly not the respectable ones.'

'Then wear the dresses in the house and I'll bring the music to you,' Clara suggested, rather deflated by the refusal but keen to do something to lift the young woman from her domestic drudgery. Neville had a portable gramophone she could borrow. 'I'd like to see you in pretty clothes. You are a very beautiful woman, Jemima, and everyone deserves to be a princess once in a while, even if it's only in the quiet of a dimly lit basement.'

Jemima blushed and put her hand to her cheek, before returning her attention to the tea-making.

'Wouldn't Matilda love to see us all dressed up?' Clara pressed. 'We could pretend we were in the Sixty-Three, young and care-free... Where is the darling child?' She felt guilty at not having spotted the girl's absence until that moment.

'Your most ardent admirer is at school. She's been rather disappointed that you haven't made a return visit.'

'I've been so terribly busy.' There was a pause. 'Erm, Frances has gone very red in the face...' Her charge was now tugging at her hair and pulling a distinctly peculiar face.

'She probably needs winding.' But this meant nothing to Clara, who was horrified as two things then happened in very quick succession: Frances made a most unpleasant noise as she dribbled regurgitated milk down her shoulder, and there was a loud crash as the middle child (whose name she simply couldn't remember) toppled over a plant and the ceramic pot shattered as it hit the wooden floor, sending soil everywhere.

Nicholas chose that exact moment to enter. He focussed on their flustered visitor, immediately removed his cap and ran his hand through his shiny hair. His LCCT uniform, a dark blue double-breasted jacket, with shiny buttons and a peaked cap, made him look rather dashing, and he knew it.

'Well, hello.'

Instead of proving herself capable and alluring (could you be both?) she looked inept and as far from alluring as she could possibly get, with her messed up hair and baby sick across her clothes. Wasn't part of her reason for being in the basement to offer an attractive alternative to this unhappy domestic set up? An escape? To demonstrate that a woman could be something in her own right, not just a wife, mother and drudge? And, if she was brutally honest, to stir up some mischief as well.

'What have we here?' Nicholas said, looking specifically at Clara, who grabbed at a muslin to wipe her shoulder and deposited Frances back on the floor. The child seemed quite content now that she and her milk had parted ways. Clara hastily pinched her own cheeks to give them some colour and smoothed her hair.

'Absolute chaos,' she purred. 'A catastrophe of a quite reckless magnitude. You certainly have some spirited daughters.'

Nicholas smiled. 'Girls can be such a handful.'

'Well, I certainly am,' she agreed, allowing her tongue to brush over her lips.

'Oh, I'll bet you are.'

Jemima stomped between the two of them and scooped up Frances. 'It's time for her nap. Maybe you'd like to put your daughter down?' she snapped. 'Or sweep up the soil? Oh goodness, Ellen's just put some in her mouth...'

'Not likely, love. I've just popped back because I left my lunch behind, but I won't be home until late. A couple of us are stopping at the Mad Hatter after work.'

'But we don't have extra this week, Nick. The rent is overdue already.'

'You stress too much, woman,' he said, as she carried Frances toward the back bedroom. 'Am I right or am I right, Clara? Life is for living. Things always sort themselves out in the end.' He turned to his wife but gestured to their visitor. 'Now, here's a woman who knows how to live. You should be more like her, dear.'

He glanced at his pocket watch and raised his eyebrows. 'I really do have to be getting off. The boss'll skin me if I'm late for the next tram run. Shame,' he said, helping himself to a further appraisal of Clara and her long legs. He grabbed the paper bag of sandwiches and walked out the door. Moments later Jemima returned, Frances now quiet, and with a brush and dustpan in her hands.

'I'd like you to leave.' Her voice was strangely calm.

'But we didn't get to drink our tea,' Clara protested, moving towards her neighbour, hoping to get close enough to absorb the lemony freshness that always lingered around the young woman. Her heart was thumping. This had all gone frightfully wrong and she'd managed to upset Jemima yet again.

'I knew you were trouble from the very first time I laid eyes on you. How dare you flirt with my husband, make wide eyes and twist about before him with your soft exposed skin. I don't need the inevitable comparisons to his dull wife, with her dry hands from soaking pails of endless nappies, her red-rimmed eyes from lack of sleep, her less than perfect body from carrying umpteen offspring. I understand your reasons for befriending me all too well now. How dare you pretend it's me you want to spend time with when it's my husband you're after. There was me thinking I'd found... something... a friend, but your sort are only ever out for yourselves.'

'You're wrong—' Clara tried to explain, but the young mum was having none of it.

'I don't want you in my home, looking down your nose at me and tossing your unwanted clothes in my direction, like I'm some charity case, as you prance about and make doe eyes at my husband. You could get any man you want, so you damn well leave mine alone.'

She engaged Jemima's furious eyes and wondered if the young mother knew how utterly mistaken her assumptions were. Was there a moment, as she stepped towards her, that Jemima realised what was about to happen? Or was she still ignorant and misguided in Clara's real motives for the friendship? The air between them certainly felt electric to Clara. It was thick and heady, and she could almost taste the expectation... like that still moment in the heavy, oppressive skies before the jagged flash of lightning cuts through the dark and illuminates everything. A band tightened across her chest, her thighs trembled, her knees went weak, and a hot pulsing between her legs all left her slightly breathless.

She stepped forward and pressed determined hands on the furiously shaking shoulders of the beautiful woman before her. The woman who had invaded her dreams with her fierce eyes and defiant opinions. The woman she admired, pitied and coveted all at once. Oh, what the hell, she thought, it wasn't as if Daddy could make a fuss about this one. The real scandal of her feelings for Alice was that she was engaged to Philip Highgrove, and Philip Highgrove had a direct, if distant, connection to the monarchy. But Jemima was married to a nobody – and a rather unlikeable one at that.

And without much thought for the consequences, she tipped her head to the side and gently pressed her lips onto Jemima's – the thing she'd fantasised about since their very first meeting – as the brush and dustpan in the young mother's hands clattered to the floor.

15

The slap stung for several minutes, but Clara's regret lasted for hours. Jemima had called her some pretty choice names in the following moments, but she'd heard worse. Usually not directed at her personally, as very few people knew her romantic preferences, but occasionally, at the riotous house parties she'd attended (where there was a certain freedom to express yourself), snide comments had been muttered about those women who openly dressed like men, with short hair swept back over their ears, and challenging, defiant faces.

If only she could pop over to Paris and drop in to Le Monocle to sip cocktails with those who understood, or, even better, live in deliciously liberal Berlin – a city that published magazines, such as *Die Freundin*, catering for women like herself. But no, she was stuck here, with a father who thought she suffered from an illness, in a world where love was regulated, and a beautiful moment between two women who were attracted to each other could be interrupted, judged and treated like a crime. And, really, what does one say in one's defence when one's mother walks in on you cavorting naked on the guest bed with the fiancée of Philip Highgrove? "I mistook this for the bathroom," doesn't fool anyone, and certainly not in your own home. Mummy had actually let out a shriek before her shock turned to anger and condemnation.

Clara had never liked men, not in that way. What had God been thinking sticking such an ugly mass of skin in such an utterly ridiculous place, and giving it the power to do most of the thinking? Further proof, if she needed any, that He didn't exist. Or, and this was rather daring of her, God was actually a She with a curious sense of humour.

There had been no close female friends when she was little, because she preferred the company of boys, and then one intense friendship with a girl she knew through riding when she was about twelve. Too intense, her parents eventually decided. But for a whole glorious year they had written to each other almost daily, able to dance around their feelings on the page in a way that was liberating.

Clara was, undoubtedly, a challenging child, always seeking attention for the wrong things, perhaps to distract from the right things. Initially, girls' toys and pretty dresses didn't interest her much but as an adolescent things changed. She fancied herself in love with beautiful actresses, such as Lily Elsie and Gladys Cooper, and wanted women to feel that way about her too. Mummy was dreadfully relieved when she finally started behaving as her sex demanded and Clara found that, as a particularly attractive woman, she felt powerful for the first time in her hitherto impotent life. Flirting with, and feigning an interest in, men created a smoke-screen behind which she could hide the feelings she was ashamed of and banish the thoughts she knew would inevitably lead to heartbreak.

For Mummy's sake she'd tried to conform, but the sham of the endless play-acting made her unhappy. She partied hard because pretending to be happy was the next best thing to actually being happy. She misbehaved because she wanted to be noticed, to be wanted – even if it was only because the party couldn't possibly start without someone as effervescent as her in attendance. By becoming this stronger personality, she could protect the real Clara – a frightened, confused young lady who didn't know where she belonged and who could not be herself for fear of judgement or retribution.

The world had changed since the war and, as the liberation of the twenties went on, she began to feel a creeping optimism. Perhaps these freedoms would bring about an acceptance, and possibly within her own social set, it had. Stephen Tennant and Cecil Beaton made little effort to hide who they were. Even Neville was tolerated, although perhaps more for entertainment value rather than for his true self.

But now she'd blown it with Jemima – someone she genuinely cared about, and whom she'd been instantly attracted to that first day on the stone steps. The feisty young mother was everything the other women in her life were not. She was passionate, hard-working and principled. Agnes had told her niece how Mrs Smith cared for and sacrificed everything for her daughters, consistently putting herself last on the list in all she undertook. Her small, determined face was not one to be trifled with. Added to this, she had a delicate beauty. One that didn't need rouge and powder to enhance her features. Smiles were fleeting and hard-won but when you were graced by that upturn of her lips, you felt as though you had inherited the world, and your insides spun gloriously and frantically out of control.

And now Clara had spoiled everything. Too impulsive. Too entitled. Simply too damn Clara.

'This week's rent from the Smith family.' She slid an envelope across the pine table towards her aunt, as she entered the kitchen the following morning. After a late night out with Neville, she'd woken up determined to right the wrong. She had money – although with no further allowance from her father, the pot was dwindling by the day – and Jemima didn't, so this was her clumsy first step. 'She asked me to pass it to you when I saw her yesterday.'

'That's kind of her. I know how much that poor family struggles. There have been occasions I've waived the rent when Nicholas has been up against it. He works so hard.'

Yes, and plays hard too, Clara thought, but said nothing. She could bet he'd manipulated her aunt's sympathies with manufactured sob stories, yet she suspected that the landlord of the Mad Hatter was paid promptly.

'Would you be a darling and take this tray up to Mr Gorski when it's ready?' Aunt Ag asked, and then paused. 'Are you all right, love? You look flushed.'

This, Clara knew, was the result of rouging her right cheek to match the slapped left, but she pinned on a bright smile and nodded. Perhaps she would even sit with the old gentleman for a while. Despite herself, she was starting to enjoy their sparring, and had a begrudging respect for anyone who stood up to her – like Jemima. It was part of her issue with Jack; he always let her win.

'I was out late with Neville. I tried to be quiet when I returned.'

After the slap, she'd telephoned Neville and persuaded him to take her to a nightclub. Having never talked about her romantic preferences to him, she figured if anyone would have noticed the clues, it would be her equally anomalous friend, but the topic had never been broached. Not even after Alice. Besides, she felt safe with him and not just because he had no interest in seducing her. It was deeper than that. He, too, was broken and drifting. There was a comfortable companionship in his company, and they had talked of everything and nothing, as they worked their way through gin rickeys, Mary Pickfords and highballs, finishing off with a corpse reviver with a twist of lemon, because Neville simply adored absinthe. She recalled the liquorice smell and her stomach lurched.

'Keep an eye on these eggs for me, there's a dear, whilst I cut the bread. Mr Gorski likes his toast thin.'

Her aunt handed her a wooden spoon that had a flattened side from years of use – another example of her aunt's inability to part with things that held special meaning for her. Clara peered at the yellow gloopy mess nestling in the bottom of an aluminium saucepan.

'Stir them then, for goodness' sake, or we'll end up with an omelette.'

The door to the back yard opened and Jemima walked in, hesitating for the tiniest fraction when she noticed Clara, whose thudding heart immediately accelerated at the memory of the kiss. Everything had felt so right for that infinitesimally small moment of contact, and she felt crushed that this young woman hadn't felt the same magic that had set fire to every nerve ending in her body.

'Here's the outstanding rent.' Jemima stuck out a handful of coins as Agnes frowned.

'Clara has just this minute given me the money you passed to her yesterday.'

The two younger women's eyes met. Clara tried to say so much in one fleeting expression. *I'm sorry, please let me get this, and can we still be friends?* But the look that greeted her was one of simmering anger. Had she made things worse? Jemima was a proud woman and Clara's meddling, however well-intentioned, was rooted in guilt.

'How dare you presume to... aghhh...' The coins fell to the floor and rolled across the tiles, as Jemima bent double, clutching at the back of a pine kitchen chair.

'Oh, my dear girl. Is it the baby?' Agnes put down the bread knife and rushed over to help, stroking her back.

Jemima stood upright again but another wave of pain made her collapse forward and cry out a second time.

'It can't be. It's not due for months.' But everyone in that room knew it was, and that this level of sudden and unexpected pain was not good.

'Get her downstairs and into bed,' Clara said, switching off the gas and feeling suddenly incredibly clear-headed, her hangover dissipating in the hot sticky air of the kitchen. 'I'll ring for the doctor.'

Barely an hour later, and with no sign of the doctor, everyone's worst fears had been realised. Jemima's girls had been bustled next door and Gilbert had volunteered to fetch Nicholas after hearing the commotion; he hoped that he might catch Mr Smith at the depot, or at least, leave word for him there. Clara and Agnes had done the best they could, guided by Jemima herself, as she'd undergone some nursing training before her marriage. The outcome, however, was inevitable and they could only offer soothing words and company.

Clara hadn't realised before, how unbearable it was to watch someone you care about go through such pain. Every agonising cry uttered by Jemima tore through her, and was made worse because there was nothing she could do to alleviate her suffering. Why women all over the world repeatedly put their bodies through such brutal abuse was beyond her, and was part of the reason she was not cut out to be a mother, even though she had enormous respect for all who did.

The tiny form that slipped from Jemima's body was big enough to cup in Clara's hands. The shiny skin was darker than she'd anticipated, the head disproportionate to the body, and the limbs painfully thin. It was a boy and most definitely dead. Agnes handed her a towel and she wrapped it around his doll-like form, exposing the face, eyes still sealed shut, and turned to Jemima, but she shook her head and turned away.

'It's my fault. I willed it out of my body. I never wanted this child and God knew it.'

'There, there, hush now.' Agnes stroked her brow with a damp cloth, as Clara clutched the bundle closer to her chest, worried his soul might be lingering and not wanting him to feel unloved. She was determined to treat him with respect and love, but knew nothing of heaven or the afterlife. Her own faith was shaky but on the off chance this little fellow was still in the room, watching his distraught mother and lingering to say his goodbyes, she didn't mind overriding her beliefs.

They heard the front door open, and moments later Nicholas entered the tiny bedroom. Agnes and Clara both retreated into the shadows.

'They said at the depot you'd started with the baby? That odd lad from upstairs came for me. But I told him it's too early – it's not due until the new year. What's going on?'

'I'm sorry.' Jemima's eyes were full of tears as she told him, without the need for words, the tragic outcome.

'What was it?' Not, 'how are you?' Clara noticed, furious at his insensitivity.

'A boy,' she whispered.

'Jesus, Jemima. Could you not have held on to that one?'

He paused and felt three pairs of eyes bore into him.

'Sorry, sorry – I'm not thinking straight and that came out wrong. Still, at least we know you can make boys now. Let's hope you can carry them. There's always next time, eh?' He looked around the room, noticing Clara still cradling the towel, and recoiled slightly. 'Nothing more I can do here, and you seem chipper enough, sweetheart. I'd best get back to work. Looks like the women have everything in hand.'

Clara glared at him. Did he really think adding the word 'sweetheart' made everything all right? His wife had just lost her baby and all he could think about was the production of the next one. She wanted to walk over to him and shake his shoulders. Of course there was something he could do. He could tell his wife he loved her, that it wasn't her fault and hold her hand, if only for a few minutes.

He slipped quietly from the room and Agnes returned to tend to Jemima.

'There now, that was kind. Popping back from work to check you were all right.' Bless her, thought Clara, for always trying to see the good in people, even when there wasn't an awful lot of good to see.

The room returned to a hushed quiet where no one knew quite what to say. She could hardly do a Neville, pat Jemima on the back and say, 'Dreadfully sorry old girl, but do keep your pecker up.' The pregnancy should have ended with newborn cries, the contented suckling of a feeding babe, or the sound of gentle breathing. But the room was silent and the emptiness of it made her focus on the less pleasant aspects of the situation – the iron-like taste of blood in the air, the slightly sweet smell of broken waters, and a faint hint of sweat from everyone's exertions. She wanted to throw open the curtains and let in light and life, but respected Jemima's wish to shut herself away.

Clara pulled the small bundle even closer and perched on the edge of the low nursing chair, unable to imagine what the poor woman curled up on the bed was going through. Jemima had slunk back under the quilt and was staring at the window, as Agnes bustled about with jugs of hot water, wiping and tidying.

Starting slowly, Clara's thin, nervous voice was barely audible as she struck up the first few notes of 'Baby Face'. Back home, she'd got a record of Benny Davis singing this song, and it was the first thing that came to mind as she studied the perfect little ears, the delicate nose, and closed lids. She carefully pulled back the towel to find one of his tiny hands, barely bigger than her thumbnail, and let the matchstick-like fingers curl over her own, surprised to find that his fragile body was still warm.

There was a knock at the bedroom door and Agnes opened it to Gilbert, but he didn't enter. This was not the time nor the place for menfolk.

'Is there anything else I can do for Mrs Smith?' he whispered.

'You could chase up the doctor,' Agnes said. 'Jemima seems to think there is no more to be done, but neither my niece nor I are medically trained, and I want her seen by a professional.'

'I did but there's a woman on Leopold Street giving birth to twins and it's not going well. He knows the situation and will be along as soon as he can.'

It was right the doctor should focus on babies that stood a chance. Even had he been here from the start, he couldn't have saved Jemima's son.

'Thank you, Gilbert,' her aunt said.

'Not at all. No mother should lose a child.' He bobbed his head and then added mysteriously, 'I've seen the unimaginable damage it can do.'

16

THE DRAWER OF BABY CLOTHES

Agnes had a deep drawer in the bottom of her bow-fronted chest of drawers that was rarely opened but often thought about. It held all Daphne's baby clothes; numerous white cotton dresses, an assortment of lacy bonnets, and a tiny pair of soft pink bootees – amongst other things.

'Our little family is finally complete,' her father said, as he passed his twelve-year-old daughter the red-faced bundle of baby sister. Mummy didn't look well but she smiled at her daughters and gripped her husband's hand. The four of them remained on the large double bed for some time, discussing their future plans, and speculating what sort of child the newborn Daphne might turn out to be.

The late arrival had been a long-desired miracle and, according to her paternal grandmother, granted by a benevolent God. Her mother had never given up hope of conceiving again, although such things weren't openly talked about, and certainly not in front of a child. The young Mrs Humphries had always been a sickly woman and even Agnes's entrance into this world had been traumatic. That benevolent God had his own agenda, however, as Thomas

Humphries' perfect family lasted five short days before his wife passed away, having never fully recovered from the birth.

It was the way of things; in order to bring new life into this world, women frequently sacrificed their own. When Agnes was a child, the high infant mortality and death of the mother were commonplace. Things had improved since the war, but slowly. Even in her prayer book, the service for new mothers began by giving thanks for 'The safe deliverance and preservation from the great dangers of childbirth.' Having babies was a risky business.

Long after Daphne had outgrown them, Agnes kept the baby clothes, moving them to a drawer in the spare room. As a handsome, well-respected professional, albeit in his fifties, there was no reason her father couldn't attract a younger wife of child-bearing age. But Thomas Humphries was as sentimental as Agnes herself. He'd lost his one true love, and as the years went by, she realised there would be no stepmother. He adored his daughters beyond measure and they were enough for him.

From time to time, she went through the drawer, refreshed and refolded the items, and replaced the strong-smelling naphthalene mothballs in the hope the insects would leave these precious garments alone. And when James came into her life, she'd spent an entire evening rearranging the drawer, whispering to the clothes that they might soon be needed, and confident that the years spent caring for her little sister would stand her in good stead. But within months she had to make an impossible choice, and the choice did not include motherhood.

When Daphne became a mother, she turned her nose up at the musty-smelling, old-fashioned garments. She could afford new for baby Clara and the only item she took was the christening robe and matching bonnet – a family heirloom suited to Daphne's newly elevated status.

For over forty years those clothes occupied that deep drawer, and Agnes wondered if they might remain there for another forty. Clara wouldn't want them; the fashions had changed. Boys dressed like little warriors since the war, with military insignia on their button shirts, and girls wore simpler styles in new fabrics, like rayon, with Peter Pan collars. In her heart, she knew the baby clothes wouldn't be needed by anyone else, but the truth was, of course, these precious souvenirs were still needed by her...

Because on those desperately lonely nights, when the house was silent and the walls were draped in shadow, she would slide open that bottom drawer and take out one of the cotton dresses, swaying from side to side in the moonlight, humming a nursery rhyme into the darkness, and wondering to herself: *What if?*

17

A few days after the miscarriage and Clara's sleep was fitful and restless. It was the tiny fingers that invaded her dreams. They were so perfect, like those of a doll, and equally as lifeless. Those hands would never push a wooden train around a track, like Matilda's, and she couldn't shake thoughts of the lost baby from her mind. If the whole episode had distressed her to this degree, she couldn't even begin to imagine what the young mother was going through.

Occasionally, in those fleeting dreams, she would slip her body under the bedcovers next to Jemima and pull the distraught woman close, cover her face in soft kisses and rock her gently, as she had rocked the lifeless child. It was only this image that brought her any peace.

Her advances had been ill thought out, but now was not the time to try and clear the air. Jemima needed space. Equally, there had been no opportunity to gauge the young mother's reaction. Would she keep the incident to herself? Or was she angry enough to reveal Clara's secret? Perhaps it would be prudent to nip this all in the bud and be honest about who she really was with Aunt Ag, if no one else.

'Read me a fairy tale, Aunt, like you used to.'

They were sitting together in the front room, as her aunt drew the curtains across the lookey outeys. She seemed surprised at the request, but shuffled to the bookcase and selected a volume of the Brothers Grimm, stroking Sunny's feathered yellow head as she passed.

'It absolutely must have a happy ending, mind,' Clara said, stretching her legs out along the sofa. The seat was lumpy, but the damn thing was growing on her. It was the memories of snuggling up on it when she was younger, perhaps staying overnight when Mummy took in a show in the West End, or occasionally visiting by herself when she was older in the long summer holiday, that had prompted her request. Familiar equalled comforting, and it was comfort she craved right now.

'Hmmm... then maybe this book is the wrong choice,' said Aunt Ag, sliding the Brothers Grimm back. 'So many end with death. Grimm by name, grim by nature.' She smiled. 'We shall read Andersen.'

Inky entered the room and sniffed at Clara but chose instead the comforting, wide knees of Agnes, as the older woman sat across from her niece and read 'The Princess and the Pea' aloud. When it came to its happy-ever-after ending, they were both silent for a moment. Clara swallowed hard, her chest tightening as she wondered how to best share her difficult truths.

'I want to live my fairy tale, Aunt. I want to be happy.'

'And yet so many of these stories do not have happy endings, but do you know what I love about them, despite this?' Her aunt closed the heavy volume and placed it on the arm of her chair.

Clara shook her head.

'These tales challenge the order of things: princesses are strong, and people who are different triumph. Remember how sometimes the girls save their brothers or their sweethearts? And the magic!'

She clasped her hands together in delight. 'So often I have wished for a flying trunk to take me to far off lands, or a tinderbox to summon giant dogs to do *my* bidding.'

Remembering the tale of 'The Tinderbox', Clara smiled. 'The dogs brought the princess to the soldier in the middle of night, as I recall. If only finding love was that simple...'

'Oh, my darling child, if I had a tinderbox, I'd summon them to fetch you a handsome prince.'

Clara grunted. 'My life is such a terrible muddle, that a touch of magic wouldn't go amiss. As for the prince... it's complicated.'

'I know more than you think. Daphne let slip that the young gentleman you were dallying with was somehow related to Queen Mary. I'm not here to judge, my love – I know things have moved on since my day – but I completely understand your parents not wanting to see you embroiled in a public scandal.'

'No, Aunt,' she said gently, reaching out for the older woman's liver-spotted hand, her heart racing like Jack's Morris Oxford down The Mall at three o'clock in the morning. 'My unforgivable misdemeanour wasn't with Philip. It was with his *fiancée*.' She paused to let her words sink in. 'Men – princes or otherwise – simply aren't for me, I'm afraid. Well, Neville is a total darling and I'm inordinately fond of Jack, but I have no desire to be... intimate with them.'

Aunt Ag hid her shock well. She was of a generation who couldn't contemplate such things, and Clara watched her eyebrows bob up and down her forehead as she tried to reconcile her niece's past behaviour, and details garnered from Daphne, with this surprise announcement. Then, exactly as her sister had done, she tried to explain it all away.

'It's a confusing time, being young. All these silly freedoms are going to your head. Added to the smoking, the drinking, and the late nights... It's just a phase.' Aunt Ag patted the hand of her niece with cautious conviction.

Clara sighed, swung her legs to the floor, reached for the small silver case on the side, and lit a cigarette. 'It's not. In the same way that you don't like tripe, have never liked tripe, and were absolutely certain from a very young age that you never would.' The earnest stare that she gave her beloved Aunt Ag left no doubt about the sincerity of her words. 'I can no more change the way I am than the zebra can peel off its stripes. To the world at large, and for Mummy's sake, I will always have to live a lie, but it's time those close to me knew the truth, whatever they decide to do with that knowledge. I'm heartily sick of pretending.'

Living at Burlington Square had reminded her of the fearless little girl she used to be, and how Aunt Ag, more than anyone, had always been on her side. She still went after the things she wanted in life but, unlike the grown-up Clara, that little girl hadn't been afraid. Now she worried about the cruel judgement of others, hurting those she cared about, and that she would never find love.

For a few moments the older woman processed her niece's declaration. Clara watched her eyes narrow in thought and her forehead crease. Finally, she leaned forward and put her hand out to stroke her niece's knee.

'In many ways, I'm rather relieved. I suspected something was terribly wrong and worried it was your health, or you'd found yourself in the family way. But the thing you carry is a huge burden to carry alone. You should have said something sooner. I may not understand, but I would never judge.'

'I... I thought your faith might put you in an awkward position.'

Aunt Ag snorted and folded her arms.

'The Bible condemns a lot of things. Leviticus certainly gets pretty agitated about the matter, but I also know that Jesus dined with tax collectors and was terribly fond of Mary Magdalene – who I am certain was a woman of dubious morals.

'My faith is important but there are so many contradictions in the Good Book that I have been forced to forge my own path and focus on those tenets that are important to me. Honouring my mother and father, treating others as I wish to be treated, and reserving judgement for God alone. If he forgives the sinner, who am I to convict? Besides, God made all living things, and that includes you, my darling, however imperfect you are. And I can't believe anything He made can be condemned.'

Tears began to tumble down Clara's face, as she furiously tried to blink them away. She should have known that her aunt's heart overruled everything. Just look at her cluttered house. She could not let a lumpy old sofa go because it had been with her for forever. And her tea set had been passed down several generations, even though she had to make it up with odds as pieces got lost or broken. The older woman loved things despite their imperfections, or perhaps even because of them, and fiercely believed that when people or objects were good to you, you must be good to them in return. Aunt Ag was nothing if not loyal.

'I love you so very much, Clara, you are like a daughter to me. Even though I have no comprehension of your situation, I can't bear to see you unhappy.' She sighed. 'As for my faith, I rather feel when I meet St Peter that our negotiations will be long and drawn out. I have harboured many far from perfect souls under my roof over the years – even Mr Blandford had his vices – but I hope that my devotion to Papa, my sacrifices on his behalf, and my efforts to help those less fortunate than myself, will offset the scales against the things I have done wrong. If I am refused entry on the grounds that I loved and supported a poor confused girl like yourself, then so be it. Lucifer will have to set aside a corner for me.'

Clara almost laughed out loud. Aunt Ag still thought of her unorthodox tastes as a state of affairs that her niece must surely be confused about, as if it was something that could be resolved by clear thinking and more sleep. But she was at least trying to understand, and that was something her parents had spectacularly failed to do.

'I... I want you to have this.' Clara stumbled over her words as she untied the aquamarine scarf that she was wearing and placed it around her aunt's neck. It was easier for her to demonstrate her overwhelming gratitude to this magnificent woman, than articulate it. The relief flooding through her body threatened to break her, and she wanted to remain the strong, bold niece her aunt so admired. The older woman flushed pink as Clara kissed both her cheeks. 'It suits you. You should wear more colour.'

'Ah, no one is looking at me any more.'

'Oh, I wouldn't give up entirely. Remember the fairy tales? Anything is possible. Sleeping Beauty had to wait a hundred years, remember? Besides, you'll feel better on the inside, darling. It's why I always make an effort with my appearance – putting up a front to give the impression everything is fine.'

'Yes, although sometimes, you do rather look like a prostitute, dear.'

Clara laughed at the pronouncement. 'Perhaps, and maybe I should address that. We don't want to give men *utterly* the wrong idea, do we?' She winked and then clasped her hands around her aunt's. 'Thank you.'

'For what?'

'For always being honest.'

She had so dreaded confiding in her aunt and yet the dear lady couldn't have been kinder. Clara felt truly supported for the first time in her life, and it gave her the courage she needed. It was time to be equally honest with the world, or at least those in the world who mattered.

18

Clara smiled to herself as she watched Neville throw chunks of stale bread at the disinterested swans and over-fed geese. The curl of his lip and obvious distaste as he studied where to place his feet demonstrated how peeved he was that he'd not been allowed to spend the morning at the Coventry Street Lyon's Corner House, sipping coffee with handsome strangers, but had instead been dragged to Kensington Gardens to feed the waterfowl that gathered at the Round Pond. (The waitresses tended to keep Neville and his sort separate and, as long as they were discreet, no one seemed to mind.)

Clara lifted her face to the early autumn sun and let the chatter of the birds and earthy smells wash over her. The knowledge she had Aunt Ag on her side gave her strength.

'Mid-morning is undoubtedly the best part of the day,' she declared.

'I disagree.' He was still sulky at being dragged to the park. 'That would be somewhere between 5 and 6 a.m., when you have a belly full of giggle-water and a hankering for kippers. It's that moment when you spy the sun rising slowly in the sky like a blazing hot-air balloon, and know that you've had a night well spent.'

'You like the Round Pond,' she reminded him, wondering at the lack of imagination in naming this ornamental lake. Strictly speaking, it wasn't even a circle.

'Only when we're all splashing about naked in it.' She noticed the cheeky sparkle in his eyes.

Neville, she realised, had become an exaggerated version of himself over the years, particularly after a few drinks and with his friends. He was the exact opposite of her. She guarded her real self, whereas he flaunted his. It's like he was testing them all. This is the real me, magnified by a hundred; can you possibly accept it? Perhaps it was a form of self-defence, as much as hers was to act the femme fatale. They were both projecting bold versions of themselves to mask the inadequacy, because she did feel inadequate. She felt as though she'd failed somehow, by not being normal – whatever that was.

'Now, there's a face to wake the gherkin,' Neville whispered, as a handsome stranger sauntered past with a doe-eyed young lady on his arm.

'It's all gherkins with you.' She rolled her eyes.

'Oh, darling, it *really* is.' But he gave a tired smile, because his heart wasn't in it. She understood. One simply couldn't maintain the pretence all the time. He sighed and changed the subject. 'Jackie is hosting an historical, or should I say *hysterical*, Saturday to Monday this week. He wants you to come. Do say you will, darling. It won't be the same without you.'

'I don't feel like partying, Neville. Someone I care about has just lost a baby. It puts everything into perspective.'

'Rotten luck and all that. But that's actually what the bash is about – celebrating life rather than wallowing in death. Amelia Farrington would have been twenty-one on Sunday, only the silly mare got herself killed back in June and everyone's been so terribly glum. Mitzy came up with the theme of tragic historical figures, although poor Amelia will hardly be going down in history. I'm considering going as Caesar – I do so love a toga,' he said.

They were now arm in arm, and heading towards the bridge that divided the gardens from Hyde Park. If they decided to undertake a complete walk about the Serpentine, might it give her enough time to broach the subject she was so desperate to air?

'I barely even knew the girl,' she admitted.

'I only met her on a few occasions, and the last time was the night she died. We were all staying at Alice's pile in the country. Lovely long Saturday to Monday, only the daft cow never even made it to the Sunday morning. Totally squiffy on liquor or drugs – I really couldn't say which.' He shrugged. 'Then she had this frightful row with Alice and stormed off. And she was such a stubborn mule – insisted on driving back to Hampton, even though it was raining stair-rods. I stayed out of it, as she'd proved herself a nasty little cat when provoked. I didn't need name-calling and sly jibes. Ended up wrapped around a streetlamp two miles from home.' He shuddered. 'Not a pretty sight, by all accounts.'

Now that he'd mentioned it, Clara remembered seeing the *Hampshire Heiress Killed in Automobile Accident* headline on a sandwich board.

'But we're all doing it, Neville, living fast and loose, as though we don't have a care in the world. Are we heading this way too? The excesses will take their toll and the consequences could be similarly catastrophic. Mitzy certainly won't make old bones if she carries on like she is.' She wrapped her slender arms around her body and rubbed at her shoulders. The water looked beautiful, despite the greyness of the day.

'But is it really any better to die charging across a muddy field, bayonet fixed and roaring "Long live the king", than to perish as a fractured mess in a motor car?' he pondered.

'It's certainly more noble. And yet, there must be some balance between the quiet sacrifices of Aunt Ag and the wild thing I've become. Marrying Jack is the safe choice and I won't do it.' She looked at him with enquiring eyes. How much did he know? Surely more than most, and definitely more than Jack.

'You know he'll keep asking?' He eyed her sideways and kicked at some loose gravel with his toe.

'Jackie's always been a sweetheart to you, right?' she asked. He nodded. 'Then I shall simply have to tell him the truth.'

'Ah.' There was a silence.

'You know, don't you?'

'Well, you've always been a damn sight nicer to me than some. But do give it some thought, old bean. Once it's out there, people have preconceptions about our lot. Our crowd are more tolerant than most, but even Beaton was thrown in the river last month at Wilton House. When they turn on you, it can be quite unpleasant.' His face suddenly lit up. 'Perhaps we could get shackled? Vita married that Nicholson chap and it got everyone off their backs, and yet the arrangement allows her to have her dalliances. We could dally away in private and conform in public?'

'A kind offer, but no.' She couldn't say it to his face because she loved him dearly, but marriage to Neville would be even worse than marriage to Jack. 'I just want this dreadful charade to stop and so I have finally admitted the truth to my aunt. She may not understand but she loves me. You're right; being honest brings unpleasant whispers and judgement, but knowing that the ones I care about love me regardless, I truly believe I can bear it.'

'Good for you, old thing. And things *are* changing. Look how far we've come since Wilde? They have at least removed the death penalty for our *unnatural* crimes, although I must say, my love has always felt completely natural to me,' he said forlornly. 'They've not hanged any of us for nearly a hundred years. At least your love has never been a criminal act.'

How sad it was, she reflected, that they both believed themselves to be separate from society. 'Our lot' and 'us' marked them as different, not belonging.

'Only because the politicians don't think it's possible and are wary of planting ideas into the uncorrupted minds of young girls.' She was quite indignant now. It was only by stumbling across the poetry of Sappho that she'd even begun to understand herself and sweep up the comforting crumbs of hope that she might not be alone. But there were no novels that recounted her experiences – certainly not any that portrayed those like herself in a positive light. For all Andersen's plucky heroines, she'd never read any stories where the princess got the princess.

'If they don't talk of it, they can convince themselves it doesn't exist,' she concluded. How strange it was that men spent their lives trying to protect women from the real world and yet couldn't face the brutal reality of childbirth or the wearing dependence of a newborn child. Having witnessed Jemima's miscarriage, she knew which was the stronger sex.

'So, you'll tell old Jackie and then what?'

'I thought I might go abroad. Berlin. Maybe Paris. Burlington Square was only ever temporary.'

'Running away, old thing? Unlike you. You always struck me as the sort to stay and fight.'

'Actually, I'm running towards something... an independence and an honesty that I'm beginning to realise are important, Neville. And that's exactly like me...'

* * *

The party at the end of the month began to appeal to Clara. She could tell Jack the truth and make peace with Alice. Loose ends sat uneasily with her, and Alice was certainly one of those. Plans for Berlin were circling around her head. The seed, once planted, had sprouted tiny green shoots that were seeking out sunlight. Cast aside by Alice, and rejected by Jemima, it was only Aunt Ag's understanding that reminded Clara she was worthy of love. Didn't she owe it to herself to find it? Berlin was somewhere she could start again – a country unofficially tolerant of sexual behaviour that was still officially illegal. Even Alice had talked of their provocative, uncensored film industry, daring cabaret and subversive art. As someone who always sought out the most shocking elements of any gathering, Clara was excited by the prospect, but equally nervous at taking such a life-changing step.

Her mind was still wrestling with the logistics of moving abroad as she carried Mr Gorski's tray upstairs. He commented how helpful she was becoming, and wondered if she was perhaps a bee after all.

'Can I not just be a useful butterfly?' she purred. 'Bees are so singularly unattractive.'

'You have clearly never seen one close up. They are most beautiful, but remain a butterfly, if you will. At least you have brought colour to Miss Humphries' life and for that I am happy. She told me the house feels like a home once more.'

There was a stab of guilt to Clara's heart. 'I'm thinking of moving abroad. I have plans.'

'What a great pity. Your aunt will miss you, I'm certain. She's been much cheered by your arrival. Family can be such a blessing.'

'And a curse,' she replied, thinking of her father. He would never accept her. To him, it went against nature. And now Mr Gorski was making her feel guilty for leaving Burlington Square.

She inwardly determined to come back and visit as often as she could.

'Family is something I am short of myself,' he continued. 'I have been widowed for many years, and have never even set eyes on my son.'

Clara frowned. 'I understood your wife couldn't have children.' His eyebrows rose in question. 'Oh, Aunt Ag mentioned something.' She waved her hand dismissively.

'There was a young woman before my wife… and we, how shall I put it? Made hay before the union was sanctified. I didn't know about the child until many years later.'

'How deliciously scandalous,' Clara said. 'A child out of wedlock?'

He shrugged. 'I told you I was not easily shocked, for I have lived a far from perfect life, tinged with regret, and I only wish I'd had the courage of my convictions. I should have married my Alina when we first met, but was persuaded not to do so.' He locked eyes with hers, leaning forward slightly to emphasise his point. 'Never let the opinions of others dictate the path your life should take because, dear child, it is you who lives with the consequences. And now, I fear, my path has come to an end.'

Old people and their obsession with death. She rolled her eyes but turned her face away from his. He'd had little patience with her situation when she'd first arrived, and she had none with his.

'You made your bed, I'm afraid, Mr G. As I have made mine.' Was there part of her that was gleeful that the man who had criticised her behaviour was not in a position to set himself up as judge? 'And I don't envy you confronted by two covetous women in the afterlife.' Not that she believed in it.

'Ah, but it would be Alina every time. She has been waiting for half a century, and that wait is coming to an end. I can feel her calling my name…'

But Clara had no time to indulge his self-pity, or linger any longer to serve up platitudes. He was clearly having a day of feeling sorry for himself, but tomorrow was a fresh start. He'd feel cheerier after a good night's sleep, and she had a million other things on her mind.

'Do say hello from me, darling, and perhaps pop back via the Ouija board to let me know what the host of heavenly angels is like.' She gathered up the tray from earlier and walked towards the door, leaving him with a typically flippant Clara-like remark. 'Although I suspect it is far more likely that we will both be heading south upon our demise. Perhaps I'll see you down there?'

* * *

The following morning, Clara knocked on Mr Gorski's door with the breakfast tray precariously balanced on one arm. The poor fellow had been so melancholy the previous day and she felt guilty for not giving him more of her time, especially as she'd discovered today was his birthday – there was a mixing bowl full of dried fruit soaking on the kitchen table in preparation. She would ask him about his life, listen to his answers and be interested in how he was feeling. Perhaps he could even give her some insights into Berlin, as he'd travelled so widely during his lifetime.

If the last few weeks at Burlington Square had taught her anything, it was that the world simply didn't revolve around her. And she was surprisingly fine with that. Life was less demanding when one didn't have to be witty, alluring and beautiful every moment of the day. Helping others made her feel good. And even the children hadn't proved quite the tiresome creatures she'd imagined.

There was no answer from within, which wasn't unusual as he

fell asleep at odd times, so she rapped louder, called a cheery hello, and swung the door open.

'Mr Gorski? This morning we have a special treat of smoked kippers for your delectation. Would you believe I made the bread myself?' Aunt Ag was determined to see her educated in all aspects of domestic life.

The silence within the room, despite the relentless rain lashing against the windowpanes, was unsettling as she placed the tray on his usual table and went in search of him. Perhaps he wasn't feeling well and had remained in bed. Some mornings he found it harder to rise than others. The arthritis could be unpredictable.

She knocked at the open bedroom door and peered around the frame and into the room. An uneasiness lurked in the shadows, and the absence of sound was surprisingly deafening.

'You should have told me it was your birth—'

The words stuck in her throat the moment she spotted Mr Gorski before her on the bed, eyes closed and face to the ceiling, totally at peace. He seemed smaller, somehow, out of the high-backed leather armchair – like a sleeping child. The wrinkles that belied his years were no longer apparent. There was a blueish tinge to his lips, and his hands were crossed over his chest as though he'd been deliberately arranged. As she moved towards him, she noticed the sepia image of a young woman pressed to his chest.

Her steps slowed. There was no need to check for a pulse.

On his bedside cabinet was the evidence that the decision to reunite with Alina had been his. It wasn't that his path had come to an end, more that he had chosen to deliberately step from it.

There was a catch in her throat as she inhaled, and an audible sob as she let that breath go, but she quickly composed herself. Tears would not bring him back. She hoped that he was running, hand-in-hand with his true love, through carpets of bluebells, or whatever his personal vision of heaven had been. For a moment, she wished she believed in God. And then she remembered that God would not look favourably on the old man's actions, and nor would the neighbours. Neither he nor her aunt deserved that kind of gossip and so she scooped up the empty bottle and dropped it into the low pocket of her dress, before reaching out to cover his ice-cold hands in hers.

'Oh, you silly, darling man. What have you done?' she whispered.

There was nothing to be gained by raising the alarm immediately, so she took these moments to sit with him for a while – something she should have done whilst he was alive – and reflect on her selfishness. She'd been so focussed on herself the previous evening, that she'd heard his words without really listening.

She squeezed his fingers. It was a silly gesture really as the man was dead, but she wanted him to know that she was there, by his side, and that she was sorry. Alexander Gorski had no family left alive, and a failing body that had taken away all the things he loved doing. He felt alone and believed he had nothing left to live for.

If only she'd taken the time to persuade him that was not the case.

The rain continued to beat down, and the shifting clouds cast a greyness about the room, as though the world was grieving for him. The minute hand of the mantel clock worked steadily from the bottom of the face to the top, before she returned downstairs to tell her aunt that Mr Gorski had sadly, and inexplicably, passed away in the night.

19

Aunt Ag took Mr Gorski's death surprisingly well, consoling herself that it was his time. Clara was relieved that no one, including the over-worked and preoccupied doctor, suspected the death was anything other than natural causes. At least her actions had afforded the old man a decent Christian burial, although it was small compensation for her guilt.

'I wrote to Mr Thompson to say rooms had become available,' Agnes told her niece, as they stood in the yard and folded a large linen bedsheet between them the following week. 'He seemed so keen to lodge here, but when I told him of Mr Gorski's sad passing, he lost interest.'

'Perhaps he doesn't want to sleep in a room where someone died?' Clara suggested, quite relieved Mr Thompson wouldn't be moving in. She didn't want any links to Hertfordshire following her to London. She unpegged a pillowslip and folded it into the basket at her feet. Unseasonably dry and gusty, the laundry had dried nicely on the line.

'It didn't seem to bother him when he wanted Mr Blandford's rooms.'

Later that day, Clara got Neville to drop her outside Pemberton's. She didn't have the money to buy anything, but had decided to let Mrs Mayweather know about the first floor now being available. Her aunt had taken to Mercy, and she couldn't help but feel the young woman would benefit from Agnes's love and care, as she herself had done. Alexander's situation reminded her that those who felt alone, could do foolish things.

The bustle inside the large department store was strangely comforting, and Clara did so love a crowd because it made her feel alive and part of something. The building itself was an impressive four storeys high, with an interior to rival any stately home. Before her was a sumptuous spectacle of white Grecian columns, beautiful stucco ceilings, elongated windows and sumptuous lighting, with wafts of expensive fragrances and scented face creams floating in the air. She ambled past the spotless glass cabinets, displaying a myriad of luxurious and perfectly arranged wares, and paused to study a cluster of lifeless mannequins displaying the latest fashions, realising, with a jolt, that before descending on Burlington Square, it was exactly what she'd become – a pretty clothes horse with little purpose other than to display the latest expensive couture.

She located the glove counter, but there was no sign of Mercy. Instead, a sullen redhead greeted her as she approached.

'I'm looking for Mrs Mayweather,' she said.

The young girl huffed.

'She left. All a bit sudden. Family apparently arrived one night at her lodgings and whisked her away. It's left Miss Copely in a right pickle, and she's moved me over from hosiery until they can get someone new in. I liked her right enough, but you knew she was hiding something. Kept herself separate. Reckon she was in some sort of trouble and it caught up with her.' She shrugged.

How sad, thought Clara, certain the unpleasant mother-in-law had tracked down her runaway daughter-in-law and forced her to return to a life she didn't want.

'And no forwarding address?' she asked.

'More like backwarding address, if she was returning home.' The young girl seemed faintly amused at her own joke, and then looked at Clara, remembering her position. 'So, madam, are you requiring gloves or not?'

Clara shook her head and stepped to the side so that the lady to her left might purchase a pair in green capeskin. And, as she walked out the store and headed back to Burlington Square, she realised how lucky she was to have choices, even if those choices were compromises.

* * *

Clara stood her case at the bottom of the front steps in the sultry late September sun. Neville would be with her shortly to drive them both to Somerset, but she had a few minutes to spare and so descended to the basement and knocked, not sure how she would be received. She'd deliberately given Jemima space to heal and time to grieve.

The young mother eventually came to the door and her pale gaze bore into Clara, as the two women stood opposite each other, neither knowing what to say.

The loss of the baby had overshadowed everything, but it was highly possible now the immediate drama had passed that Clara was about to have the door slammed in her face. She knew she'd overstepped the mark – thrust herself upon her friend in a way that she would have found distasteful had it been Jack launching himself on her. In her defence, there had been the thinnest slice of time when she'd believed her attentions might be welcome, but she'd misread Jemima's hesitancy as nervousness rather than shock.

Finally, she put herself in Jack's leather brogues because, looking at the courageous and opinionated woman before her, she knew that this was love, even though there was no hope of reciprocation. Unlike Jack, however, she knew when to step away.

As the seconds ticked by, and Jemima continued to stare at her, making her stomach flip and churn under such intense scrutiny, she allowed herself to hope the young woman might remember the kindness she had tried to show during the loss of the baby. She was trying to be less selfish, but was it too late?

In the end, Clara mumbled a sorry at exactly the moment that Jemima said thank you.

'You and Agnes were very kind,' Jemima continued. 'I was so frightened.' Clara felt relieved this young woman could see beyond her foolish actions and appreciate that her care and concern had been genuine.

'We did our best but I don't think either of us knew what we were doing. You were the one directing us.'

'But if I hadn't come up to see Agnes about the rent, I might have gone through the whole thing alone, or with Tilly as my only help – which would have been unimaginable. So, I mean it when I say thank you.' She started to wring her thin hands together and allowed the baton of conversation to pass to Clara.

'How are you feeling now?'

'Fine. But then I've got to be, haven't I? Nicholas said I needed to stop moping about and get back to normal. It happens to women all the time. Besides, the girls need me.'

Not for the first time, Clara considered that damn husband of hers deserved a good shake.

'Just because other people are going through the same thing as you, it doesn't make your pain any less real. You must take care of yourself or your family will crumble.' Clara considered offering her own services but thought they might be unwelcome at the moment. Everything was too raw – the miscarriage and the kiss.

Matilda appeared by her mother's hip, her face beaming as she realised it was her favourite nearly film star at the door.

'You look very pretty,' the young girl said.

'That's because I'm off to visit some friends who live in a big house in the countryside.'

Jemima snorted, but Matilda was fascinated.

'Can you sleep there?' she asked.

'Absolutely. For two whole nights. And I get to dress up and play games until Monday. Can you even imagine the delicious fun we shall have?'

There was a beat.

'But you said we could go to the park this Sunday,' Matilda whined, and Clara realised with a guilty pang, that she'd completely forgotten her idle promise to a small child who hung on her every word.

'Obviously a better offer has come along, dear,' and, just like that, Jemima's drawbridge was up again. 'Adults are like that. They appear one thing and turn out to be quite another.'

There was a look that passed between the two women, Jemima's one of continued distrust, and Clara's a further silent apology.

'When I'm back, I *absolutely* promise we shall have a picnic in Hyde Park and take a boat out on the Serpentine.'

'Hrmph.' The small child folded her arms. 'You *promised* before.' She stomped her small legs back into the flat.

'Look.' Clara sucked in a deep breath and lowered her voice. 'I'm desperately sorry about what happened before you were... unwell. Take it as a compliment. You are an amazing woman, Jemima, but I made an error of judgement and for that I apologise.'

'I'm not one of those,' she said, 'and I had no idea you were. I thought your kind wore suits, top hats and aspired to look like men.'

Clara sighed. As ever, sweeping generalisations were easy to make. She liked pretty clothes, and she liked being with women in pretty clothes.

'I'm not a man, nor am I pretending to be. I am a woman, like you.'

Jemima shook her head. 'You aren't like me.' Her lips were tight and her head was shaking from side to side.

Clara put her hands up in capitulation. 'I completely understand and it won't happen again. Can we at least be friends?'

'I accept your apology but I don't think friendship is a good idea. We come from different worlds and have little in common. I have my husband and my children, and no time for silly chatter and frivolous things. But I was not brought up to be discourteous or to judge, and Tilly likes you, so I don't mind you calling, especially if you're prepared to roll up your fancy sleeves and offer me some practical help. But next time you promise my daughter something, you stick to it. You are my neighbour; I don't need a friend.'

Clara nodded but she knew Jemima was cutting off her pretty nose to spite her determined face. She appreciated the young mother required time to heal physically, and space to grieve, but everyone needed friends, and isolated mothers more than most. She would try again to pick up her friendships with the Smith family when she returned from Somerset because, despite herself, she was becoming increasingly fond of Matilda, and was determined to win Jemima's trust back.

20

Clara's heart truly belonged to the city – she delighted in the nightclubs and theatres, and revelled in the delectable company of such a cosmopolitan mix of people. But country life also held an appeal, offering shooting and fishing, and a suitable distance from the press. Many of her wealthy friends felt the same, and clung to the pre-war Saturdays to Mondays, trying to convince themselves nothing had changed, partly because these gatherings were an opportunity to flaunt what remained of their wealth, indulge in every available vice and (as a by-product of the uninhibited fraternising) make suitable matches for any unattached offspring.

Jack Rigby's parents were fortunate enough to have an heir who'd been too young to serve in the war, but were now keen to see him married off and the future of their Somerset estate secured. Consequently, he was often allowed to entertain at their large country residence, with the hope that these gatherings would lead to him finding a *suitable* wife. Thankfully, his brief four-day engagement to Mitzy had never reached their ears.

Clara's stomach rolled as Neville whizzed along the Rigby's tree-lined driveway to the magnificent Jacobean manor house Jack would one day inherit. A gardener stood to one side and doffed his cap as they passed. All of this could have been hers, she mused, gardening fellow and all.

They pulled up in front of a ridiculously ostentatious water fountain and staff bled from the house like ants to attend to their every whim. She felt decidedly inferior since Daddy had cut her off. She had no lady's maid with her, a recycled wardrobe, and was genuinely concerned that she might not have enough money to tip staff for the duration of her stay. Aunt Ag had kindly altered some of her dresses to avoid too much scrutiny – changing the trim, adding a touch of beading, and altering the hemlines. Her costume for that evening's extravaganza was that of Eurydice, the tragic wood nymph and wife of Orpheus, chosen because it involved a simple sheet, some tree clippings and a replica snake clutched to her bosom. The reality of her financial situation was starting to bite, and having decided against marriage, the necessity to find employment loomed.

Perhaps it wouldn't be so very terrible. Mitzy said several young women from aristocratic families were in equally dire straits, and had resorted to opening boutiques, turning their hand to journalism, or even dabbling with the stage. It was considered far more acceptable for women to work nowadays – if only Clara could think of a job that was the right fit for her.

She took a deep breath and stepped from the motor car, simultaneously slipping into her captivating Clara persona.

The next few hours proved tolerable enough, although she hated how the women and the men were forced apart during the day, undertaking activities deemed suitable for their sex. She was actually a jolly good shot, but conceded that having access to a gun when she was in close proximity to Alice, who couldn't even bring herself to look Clara's way, was not a good idea.

As the evening's entertainment drew to a close, the assembled historical figures, from Anne Boleyn to Jesus himself, collapsed across armchairs, partook in anachronistic liaisons in the bedrooms (Julius Caesar and Napoleon were an interesting combination), or wandered aimlessly around, wearing substantially less of their costume than when the evening had begun.

It was hurtling towards 4 a.m. when Neville decided it would be an absolute scream to get out the Ouija board.

'Good idea. I'd love to have another word with Great Aunt Elspeth,' Mitzy gushed, her Marie Antoinette wig long since abandoned. 'Finally get the truth about whether her falling down the stairs was really an accident.' She threw a chenille tablecloth over the circular table in the drawing room, and Jack rang the bell to ask the maid for candles and yet more champagne.

'I know some of you think this is all nonsense, but Amelia Farrington's parents have made contact with her,' Alice said, her head in a low cupboard searching for the board and planchette. 'It's helped her mother no end. Everyone was saying the poor woman would end up in an asylum, but she went to a medium and now they have a photograph of Amelia's spirit, apparently. Some chap at a seance caught her on film. Beaky Maitland saw it: Mr and Mrs Farrington clutching each other's hands in their grief, and Amelia floating above them in her cloche hat, holding a champagne coupe. You know how the old gal loved a tipple?'

Clara scoured her mind for the floating dots she was convinced needing joining, but drew a blank. Neville noticed her reticence to join in and patted the chair next to him.

'Come and sit by me, darling, and tell me which much-lamented relative you have a hankering to converse with.'

'I don't want to play a silly parlour game,' she replied, remembering her flippant words to Mr Gorski, and not wanting to afford the old man a chance to reprimand her from beyond the grave. 'I need some air.'

What would Jemima make of such a spectacle? All these entitled young people, up to their silk-gloved elbows in debt, and still
having champagne delivered by the case, whilst they played with
the dead. Death was not a joke, and now that she'd witnessed it
twice first-hand, she was more certain than ever that this was
wrong.

'Play, darling? *Play?* We are not playing, we are communicating
with the dearly departed,' Neville insisted. 'Heeding their warnings
and bathing in their comforting words.'

But she was having none of it and amid the bustle of setting up
this next activity, Clara stepped outside into the gloomy evening, as
ever closely followed by Jack. The nights were chilly now, and she'd
borrowed a small woollen blanket from the window seat and
draped it over her shoulders. Orange oblongs of light from the illuminated windows fell across the terrace and shrieks of laughter
drifted from the house and into the dark.

'Clara... Darling... Been trying to get you alone since you
arrived, old thing. I wanted to ask again, to beg—'

'No, Jack.' She sighed, putting her hand on his elbow as he
hitched up his trousers and prepared to kneel. 'You can ask me a
hundred times but my answer will remain the same.'

'Oh. I thought perhaps when you agreed to come along, you'd
changed your mind.' He frowned. 'Neville, who we both know has
all the discretion of a gossiping housewife, hinted you had something to tell me.'

'Oh, Jackie.' She stepped forward and cupped his face with her
hands. The moon caught his handsome features. 'You don't love
me. You love the idea of me. You don't even know who I really am.'

'I do. You're a fun-loving gal who values her independence, and
that's totally fine with me. We don't have to do the baby thing for
ages. Let's live a little. Perhaps travel. Wouldn't that be fun?'

'And you're a total darling but just not the darling that I want.'

He stepped closer, grabbing her wrists and tugging her to him so that she was forced to look into his eyes.

'Dammit to hell and back on a blasted handcart, Clara. What do you want? Someone taller? Someone with more money? I'll be whoever you damn well want me to be.'

She swallowed hard; her throat dry.

'I want a woman, Jack, and with all the will in the world, even you can't engineer such a transformation. Nor, I suspect, would you want to.'

There was a pause as her words sunk in. Or rather, they cavorted at the entrance to his mind as he watched them dance and spin, not fully appreciating what she was trying to convey.

'You mean you like women in a romantic sense?'

She nodded.

'Not men?'

She shook her head slowly. 'Unlike Neville, I do not have a penchant for gherkins.' She tried to lighten the mood, to offset the enormity of her admission with humour, but the hurt look on Jack's face cut her deeply. A little boy that was told to stop haring around the nursery, and *finally* accepting that Nanny really meant it.

He slumped against the low wall that edged the terrace, resting against the rough bricks and not minding his trousers. She moved towards him and reached out, but he jerked his shoulders away as though he couldn't bear to be touched. It hurt more than she cared to admit. Since when had she become the leper?

'You'd damn well better not be making all this up in some misguided attempt to make a chap feel better about being rejected, because it's in bloody poor taste.'

Her stomach began to swirl as dark currents tugged it in violent directions. This wasn't how it was supposed to go. Jack was a sweetheart. He'd always been so patient with Neville.

'Sometimes,' she said, thinking of the mess she'd made with

Jemima and how her father would never accept her, 'because being true to myself is so dreadfully difficult, I wish I was. But I really am unbalanced, neurotic and decadent – isn't that what people say about girls like me?' She managed a wan smile.

He studied her face for signs that this was an elaborate wind up, but he knew Clara long enough to realise she was in earnest. Although evidently, not long enough to grasp that his winning smile, devoted attentions and gargantuan country estate weren't going to cut the mustard – or as Neville might say, slice the gherkin.

Jack's eyes narrowed.

'My God. All this time you've been luring men to you like some sweetly singing siren, pouting your lips, fluttering your lashes and twisting your ankles, only to laugh as we sail blindly into the jagged rocks. I thought I knew you Clara Goodwin... more to the point, I thought I loved you. I had everything planned...' He tailed off.

Was that what this was really about? Like his previous grand proposal in the Sixty-Three, he'd assumed her acceptance was a foregone conclusion. And now she'd thrown a huge, ugly, incomprehensible spanner in the works – one he couldn't solve with money or emotional manipulation. Clara liked women, and he couldn't bear the feeling of impotence this engendered. He clearly felt tricked and perhaps a little ashamed of his foolishness. She noticed his jaw clench.

'You could have told me this months ago, but instead had me dangling like a puppet, periodically jerking my strings to keep me moving. Does everyone else know? Have you all been whispering behind my back?'

'No one else in our group knows, except Neville. I've only recently faced the reality of who I am.' She decided to keep Alice out of this. She had no wish to perpetrate petty acts of retribution.

'Yes – a Sapphic who toys with the hearts of innocent men.' His tone was sharp.

'Oh, Jackie.' She was weary of his self-pity. 'It's not your heart that's been damaged. It's your pride.'

'So now what? You announce it to everyone and they all have a good laugh about what a fool I've been? You make me sick, Clara,' he said. 'If you were hoping for some understanding, you won't find it here.'

'But you've always been kind to Neville, you come along to the Pink Slipper—'

'Because he mattered to you. Don't you understand? *It was all because of you.*'

She understood only too well; Jack Rigby was as judgemental as her parents.

'You led me on. You toyed with me. Regardless of the reasons behind your behaviour, you should be damnably ashamed of yourself.'

And, as he stormed back into the house, Clara acknowledged that he might have a point.

21

The following morning Clara sat in the large sun-soaked conservatory, sipping lemonade and plucking up the courage to speak with Alice, who was across from her, surrounded by the last flowers of the blousy pink bougainvillea. They were alone and, as she studied her former lover, she realised the young woman's own bloom was fading like that of the flowers. Older by nearly seven years, Alice had partied longer, faster and harder than even Mitzy. Perhaps that was why she was marrying Philip. Nothing lasted forever, and certainly not one's youth.

It was the first time they'd been alone since the scandalous incident, but she knew damn well the woman had been avoiding her. The atmosphere couldn't be frostier if they were sitting underground in the Rigby's Victorian ice house.

Clara compared her companion to Jemima, and the self-obsessed socialite came a poor second. She was attractive on the outside, to be sure, but somewhat lacking on the inside. Everything that came from her mouth was a complaint or a criticism. *Wasn't it all terribly tedious? Weren't they all dreadfully bored? And who gave Neville leave to wear such impertinent shoes?*

'Why the sudden rush to skip up the aisle?' Clara finally broke the silence. After her unpleasant conversation with Jack, she'd been desperate to be back at Burlington Square but had no way of returning to London until Monday. It had been a mistake to come. She longed for the comforting words and wide arms of her aunt.

'I pushed Philip to bring the date forward. Really, Clara, darling, when one has made one's mind up, there is no point in dilly-dallying. Besides, the weather in Cairo is splendid this time of year, and Philip promised me pyramids.'

'But you don't love him.'

'I don't love you either, if that's where this is heading. It was a bit of fun and awfully liberating but not where my tastes lie. When I was a child, I behaved like a child, but now that I am a woman I must put such childish things away,' Alice said, slightly misquoting Corinthians. 'I'm afraid that includes you, Clara dearest. Back in the box you must go. Please let's not speak of it again.' She put her ivory cigarette holder to her perfect rosebud lips and took a long drag.

She was drawing a line under the whole affair and the rejection didn't hurt as much as Clara had anticipated.

'I absolutely can't have Philip getting wind of this nonsense.'

'Of course not, sweetie.' Clara narrowed her eyes. All Alice was concerned about was her meal ticket. 'It would be such a disaster for your father if he called off the wedding.'

The two women exchanged a look.

'Are you threatening me, Clara Goodwin?'

'Not at all. I don't believe you were the one for me, and I shall move on. You run into Philip's arms, if that's truly what makes you happy, but I won't settle for a second-best because I'm worth more than that. I *will* find true love.' She dropped her voice a fraction. 'And *she* and I will be happy. I value myself far too much to compromise with either my relationships or my aspirations. I shall achieve things by my own merits and be remembered for them – maybe start a business or do something wild and adventurous, like drive across the desert in a motor car.' Not that she was seriously contemplating such folly, but it was as good an example as any. 'Too many women are content to go down in the history books as the wife of the prime minister, or the mistress of a king. I want to be an Edith Cavell, a Marie Curie or a Lillie Langtry—'

Alice laughed.

'You're proving my point. Lillie will be remembered for her affairs, not her acting. If you want to own a hat shop and sleep in a garret, be my guest. Quite frankly, I'd rather Philip showered me with gifts and tucked me away in his glorious country pile, where I lived a boring and un-noteworthy life, than resorted to trade—' her face wrinkled in disdain '—just to prove some ridiculous point about independence.'

Alice crossed and uncrossed her legs in a manner Clara knew full well was designed to be seductive. Then she lit another cigarette, her eyes never leaving Clara's.

'Besides, what could you do, darling? Your only skills are looking beautiful and attracting beautiful people. If you truly want to be happy, you should be surrounded by the things that make your soul sing.'

Clara thought then of Mrs Bayswater, who owned the Sixty-Three. Her evenings were spent sipping champagne and talking to the rich and the famous. She had a comfortable residence in Chelsea, a small cottage in Devon, and both her daughters had been married off to minor nobility who had patronised her clubs. Clara's mind raced. She'd already determined to experience the freedoms of Berlin, but an absolute cat's meow of an idea had occurred to her. If Mrs Bayswater could do it, so could she.

And, yes, that's what she would call her nightclub. The Cat's Meow.

22

September heard October creeping up behind, and it gracefully stepped to one side, opening the door to the darker evenings and falling leaves, frost-covered lawns and hearty stews. The knowledge that she'd let Matilda down gnawed away at Clara, and so when she ventured to the basement the following Sunday afternoon, she felt relieved that although it was a grey day, it was at least a dry one.

'Here for the picnic, as promised,' she announced, as Jemima's pale face poked around the door frame.

Clara gestured to the wicker basket Aunt Ag had magicked out of nowhere. It was far too late in the year for outside dining, and there would certainly be no lettuce sandwiches or strawberries, but her aunt had helped her rustle up some bread and butter, hard-boiled eggs and a pineapple upside-down cake – thank heavens for canned fruit. As quite an adventurous child in her time, she was certain that anyone who played with trains would also be up for an unseasonal caper.

'Thank you for *actually* turning up this time. I don't think Tilly could deal with more disappointment. Her father has already upset her this morning, and you letting her down would be too much. Excuse the mess; we've just had lunch.'

Clara stepped over the threshold and inhaled the faint lemony smell in the air between them, almost making her knees buckle. Jemima had no idea of the power she still held over her, and Clara engineered the slightest brush of arms as she passed into the room. The young mother moved her hand to her skimmed elbow but let it drop almost immediately.

There was a colourful vase of flowers on the mantel and it was heartening to see something so cheery after a situation so joyless.

'He's trying,' Jemima said in a low voice, following her eyes and ushering her into the room.

Her husband was in an armchair, reading the paper, and the two youngest girls were at his feet. The table in the corner was strewn with the remnants of their meal, and glorious smells of roasted meat hung in the air, making Clara feel guilty for disturbing their family afternoon. Nicholas noticed their guest and ran his hand through his hair, hopping to his feet and offering her a chair.

'Make a brew, there's a love,' he said to his wife.

'Terribly thoughtful, darling, but I shan't stop. I've only come for Matilda.'

'She stormed off earlier, sulking like a child,' he mumbled, and neither woman felt they could point out the obvious.

Jemima called for her daughter, who reluctantly shuffled from one of the back rooms with red-rimmed eyes and a sulky expression. Used to being greeted by a beaming smile, it was heartbreaking for Clara to see her so glum. She wasn't at all maternal but this little creature had grown on her.

'Why so sad?' She ruffled Matilda's hair.

'Daddy took my brooch. He gave me sixpence for it. But I didn't want the sixpence. I wanted the brooch. He said it was too grown up for a little girl but I wanted to wear it today.'

Clara's eyes darted over to Nicholas, who shuffled uncomfortably in his seat, rustling the newspaper but not taking his eyes from the page. Even Jemima stopped counting spoons of tea into the pot and turned to look at her husband in surprise, obviously unaware of the details of the quarrel.

'I was worried about the sharp pin. Besides, it was gold,' he said, from behind the paper, as though that explained everything. 'Far too sophisticated for her.'

'Was it?' Clara shrugged. She had absolutely no idea. 'Then lucky Matilda. But I gave it to her because she liked it and I didn't. It could have been encrusted with diamonds and rubies for all I cared.'

'How nice not to have to worry about money like that,' Jemima muttered under her breath as the kettle began to whistle.

'Exactly,' Nicholas agreed and dropped his arms to look over at her. 'It's all very well for you, swanning around in your fancy clothes, and partying all night on champagne and oysters...'

Clara hated oysters; they were slimy, salty little things, but that wasn't the point. And the assumption that she had money was almost laughable; her funds were diminishing by the day. She didn't defend herself though and instead stared at Nicholas because a slow churning in her stomach warned her where this was heading.

'Tilly didn't need a fancy brooch. She's six years old, for Christ sake.' He shook the newspaper again and pretended to return to it, but he was rattled and defensive.

'She didn't *need* it, but she wanted it, and it was a gift. Return it to her, Nicholas. You had no right to take it,' Jemima chimed in. 'We don't need a sulky child for the rest of the day.' Matilda was glaring at her father, her small arms crossed and her face red.

But Clara was one step ahead. 'How much did you get for it?'

'You've never sold it?' his wife gasped, coming to a halt in the middle of the room, holding the hot enamel teapot.

'Oh, for God's sake, woman. Don't look at me like that. Here we are scrabbling around for money to pay the rent and our six-year-old daughter has more money pinned to the lapel of her wool coat than I earn in a week.'

'If the flowers came from selling something that wasn't yours to sell, then I want nothing to do with you for the remainder of the day.' His wife's face was fierce and she took a step away from her husband. If looks could kill, Nicholas would be in the plot next to Mr Gorski.

'Fine by me,' Nicholas said, abandoning the newspaper and walking to the door, snatching up his jacket and cap. He'd been caught out and he knew it. 'I'm not staying around to be judged in my own home. I'll see you later.'

An uncomfortable atmosphere swirled around the room, and Jemima looked on the verge of tears. Clara couldn't leave her alone with the two smallest Smith girls, whilst she and Matilda swanned around Hyde Park having a riotous time.

'Let's make this a girl's trip,' she suggested. 'We should all go. I'm sure that between us we can rustle up some more picnic food.'

Matilda sighed.

'I did want it to be just me and you, but I know Mummy is unhappy,' the little girl said. 'She cries a lot, so I guess it's all right for her to come—'

'Tilly!' Jemima was embarrassed by her daughter's disclosure.

'Do we have to take Frances though? Her stupid pram slows things down.'

'We do, I'm afraid, but thank you for being so kind,' Clara said, avoiding Jemima's eyes. Instead, she tried to soften the blow for Matilda, who would no longer get her film star-like friend all to herself. 'And as a reward, you shall get an even bigger brooch that no one can ever take away.'

'Truly?' The little girl's eyes were saucer-wide.

'Truly,' she confirmed.

'No,' Jemima said, 'this was Tilly's treat. I'm not up to making small talk with people or plastering a smile on my face for the world right now.'

But Clara was having none of it and had already scooped up Frances. She sat the chubby-faced infant in the large pram, pleased to see Matilda was on her side and thrusting a variety of random objects into a small wicker basket. She moved swiftly to Ellen and wriggled a pair of scuffed red T-bar shoes on her agitated feet, scanning the room to see if she'd forgotten anything or, more importantly, anyone. If she took control and led the way, surely Jemima would follow?

She spun the pram around to drag it backwards out the door and finally the young mother made a move.

'Honestly, what do you think you're doing? You can't put Frances inside until you've got to the top of the steps or the poor child will be tipped out and bounce all the way to the bottom. Really Clara, you have no idea.' She removed her daughter from the pram but her words were said with mock-severity because her eyes were twinkling. 'I wouldn't trust you with a teddy bear.'

'I'm trying,' Clara whined.

'Yes, you *really* are.' Their eyes met and neither woman could prevent the laughter that flowed as naturally as water from a spring. Even Matilda joined in, although Clara wasn't convinced the young girl knew what they were giggling about. To be honest, after a few minutes neither was she. Tears began to stream from Jemima's eyes and it took a while for Clara to realise her friend's mood had morphed from joy to sadness. Tentatively she put her hand out to the young mother's shoulder, expecting her to freeze or pull away, but instead she leaned into the proffered arm, still holding her youngest daughter, and let her head fall against the glamorously attired figure of her taller friend. Her body started to shake, racked with sobs, which took a few moments to subside. The embrace was savoured by them both – perhaps for different reasons – before Clara rallied.

'Right, girls, we're going to the park,' she said. 'And we're going to invite a special guest.'

23

'Well, isn't this simply lovely?' Aunt Ag said, as she sat on a bench, lifting her face to the sun, with Clara, Jemima and the oldest two girls at her feet on an old blanket. They'd found a picnic spot in the short grass of Kensington Gardens, Jemima not wanting Ellen to be too close to the Serpentine lest she fell in. To anyone who didn't know them, it was a scene of blissful family life, where Agnes was with her two daughters and a scattering of grandchildren, enjoying a sunny afternoon at the park.

A heavily pregnant woman sauntered past, walking a small dog, and Clara noticed how Jemima's hand went to her stomach, but there was nothing helpful she could say that would ease the pain.

'I think Matilda wants you,' she whispered to her aunt.

'What do I know about entertaining children?' Her aunt's worried face turned to her niece, as the little girl repeatedly asked for someone to play with her.

Clara whispered back conspiratorially, 'I know even less. But you practically brought Mummy up so I'm sure your parenting skills are better than mine. Besides, with Matilda, you won't have to do much talking.'

Aunt Ag's eyes crinkled in delight. She heaved her wide self up from the bench and toddled towards Matilda who was now throwing, but spectacularly failing to catch, a large red rubber ball. Frances was sound asleep and Ellen trailed after Matilda, always keen to be involved in whatever her big sister was doing, largely worried that she'd miss out on something.

A few minutes of contemplation followed as the younger women watched the happy scene before them. Agnes, despite her knees, managed to repeatedly toss the ball to the laughing girls, whose limbs were still insufficiently coordinated to be able to catch it, but enjoyed the chase nonetheless.

'She's so happy. Look at her beaming face,' Clara said, leaning back and stretching her long legs in front of her.

'Doesn't take much to make Tilly smile.'

'I meant my aunt.'

Jemima tilted her head towards Clara. 'It was kind of you to think of including her. I feel bad that I've never really had much to do with Agnes before now, apart from the occasional babysitting in an emergency. She's been good to me this past couple of years.'

'Yes, she's an amazing woman, although quite lonely, I think, despite having a houseful.'

'I misjudged you. I thought you were selfish but you're not.'

Jemima's words took her by surprise, and warmed her heart, all at once. She'd tried so hard to be a better person, and that it had been noticed, specifically by the young mother, meant the world.

'I was when I landed here back in August but things are changing.' Clara was astute enough to recognise her own faults. '*I'm* changing. Moving to Burlington Square, reconnecting with my aunt, meeting you...'

There was a pause.

'Do you think my baby knew he wasn't wanted?' Jemima couldn't meet her eyes.

'Don't beat yourself up about something that was beyond your control. You're a good wife and loving mother. It's natural you felt resentment toward this baby – for goodness' sake, you've practically been pregnant since your honeymoon. Your body needs a break. I guess, with what my father refers to as my unfortunate illness, I can at least guarantee never to be in such a position.'

She let the statement hang in the air, like the linen line of laundry her aunt so often strung across the kitchen fireplace. After a few moments, she risked resting her hand on Jemima's arm, and was relieved it was not immediately shrugged away. There was another prolonged pause, before Jemima finally slid her arm out from under Clara's fingers.

'You make me uncomfortable. Every time I'm near you, I feel inadequate and on edge...'

'That's not my intention. I've put my feelings for you aside and want nothing but friendship. The chap that visits me in the red motor car proposed to me back in the summer, but how can I be angry at him for feelings he can't help? Even though they aren't reciprocated.'

Jack remained cross about her declaration and hadn't been in touch since the party, but he was a good sort, and would soon get over his wounded pride, she was certain.

A wave of emotions swept across the young mother's face. Clara tried to read them but she'd spent the last few years being so focussed on herself that she couldn't always gauge the feelings of those around her. That's what made Aunt Ag so special. Her earnest grey eyes studied everyone as they stared out from above her round pink cheeks, and she consistently put others first. Clara was glad she'd taken the time to talk to, and ultimately trust in, her aunt.

'It would be good to resume our friendship,' Jemima finally said.

Clara's heart gave a little skip. She liked having this forthright woman in her life. It was unlike the fake friendships she had with so many of her rich acquaintances, and instead was based on real, earthy things. Things that mattered – not the cut of your dress or who was seen out with whom and when. Even the girls were starting to matter, especially Matilda. The joy and adoration that sweet child had for her was worth more than a hedonistic night out with Mitzy.

'Despite the way I make you feel?'

'Maybe because of it.' Jemima shrugged.

There was a shared smile between the two women, which made Clara's heart beat faster, her mouth dry, and her thighs tighten. But she knew she was misreading the situation, hoping for more in those lingering looks than Jemima could ever give, and revelling in the accidental brushes of the young mother's skin on her own. How was it that the scent of a simple shop-bought soap could be so intoxicating, and the fall of a shapeless cotton blouse could tease at the curves beneath? This was one of the few occasions in her life when she couldn't have what she wanted, and for Clara, it was both frustrating and deliciously sobering.

After a while, her aunt and the girls returned to the bench.

'I have another brooch for you,' Clara said, holding out a crescent of teal blue rhinestones to Matilda, which sparkled as they caught the light. She'd run upstairs to find it before they'd set off, and it was worth very little, but it had never been about the material value for the young girl. The piece had been given to her by a relative many years ago, but Clara wasn't the sentimental sort. Her aunt wore that mantle for the whole family.

Matilda's eyes nearly popped out and rolled onto the grass at her feet.

'And Daddy can't take this one away?'

'Absolutely not.'

'I think I like it betterer than the first one. Thank you.' The little girl threw her arms around Clara, and this time, instead of remaining stiff and aloof, she returned the embrace.

'Let's pin it on then, and you can wear it whilst we row around the Serpentine. Aunt Ag and Mummy will prepare the picnic, whilst we go boating.'

'So, we do get alone time together, after all?' The young girl was beside herself.

'Absolutely,' Clara confirmed. 'And you can ask me anything you like.'

Matilda reached up to grip the nearly film star's hand.

'Oh goody, because I've been wondering for such a long time where exactly babies do come from...'

24

Clara stood in her aunt's kitchen at the wooden ironing board, wrestling with an embroidered cotton blouse. The time-consuming nature of her task gave her a chance to think, and her head – which had been the most dreadful muddle when she'd arrived at Burlington Square – was slowly clearing, like the dissipating smoke before her eyes every time she had a cigarette. Opportunities and dreams had slipped away from so many of the people that lived in the house, and she was determined not to follow in their footsteps.

Neither Jemima nor Alice had romantic feelings for her, that much was clear; but there would be someone who would love and cherish her, and moving to Berlin and embracing a new life might just be the best way to find the love she deserved. She'd already started to make enquiries and had even written to Mrs Bayswater, hoping the nightclub owner might share some of her business insights.

As she left her aunt's kitchen with the neatly pressed clothes hanging over her arm and a degree of optimism in her heart, she bumped into Nicholas.

He locked eyes as soon as he noticed her, and ran his hand through his hair, as was his way.

'I know what's going on, you know. Why you've been hanging around the house and popping in on our Jemima all the time.'

'You do?' Clara's heart quickened. What had Jemima told him? And how would he feel about someone like her associating with his wife?

He leaned casually against the wall, preventing her from continuing, and she caught the citrus scent of a cologne she recognised: 4711. Neville wore it from time to time, and like this man before her, he was rather heavy-handed with its application. She also noticed that his hair was Brilliantined to within an inch of its life, as he rubbed at his recently shaven chin.

'Yeah. I mean, it's obvious really.'

He slid towards her in one swift movement and was suddenly barely inches from her face. Ah, now she realised where he was coming from.

'It's been tough for me since the baby thing...'

Baby thing? Clara tried not to let her horror show. Was that really how he was going to sum up the utter heart-aching tragedy of his wife's miscarriage?

'She's become even more distant, and she was never exactly what you'd call a willing woman...'

'I don't want to hear this—'

'No, no, of course not. I get that you're her friend and everything. But we can be discreet...'

'Right...' She processed his words. 'So, you're suggesting I book us a hotel room, away from the neighbourhood...'

His eyes lit up. 'Absolutely ideal. I would pay but things are tight right now, but yeah, yeah, away from it all. A separate thing.'

'Because you think I find you attractive and will willingly satiate my desires without the necessity of a commitment from either party?' This time Clara's shock was clearly etched across her face, as she stared at the man in disbelief.

There was a twinge of guilt that flittered across Clara's conflicted conscience. She had flirted with him when they first met in her attempts to make Jemima jealous, so there was no moral high ground she could stand on and look down at his dishonourable actions. In her heart, she wanted the same things he did – intimate relations with one half of a married couple. Adultery was still adultery.

Nicholas's eyes narrowed and there was the first flicker of uncertainty.

She shook her head. 'You've got this all wrong. Jemima is my friend, and Matilda, come to that. I spend time with them because I want to. Not to be near you.'

'I see.' He narrowed his eyes. 'So, you were playing with me? Trying to trap me? And now you go running back to Jemima telling tales?'

'I'm not interested in causing trouble.'

His top lip curled into a snarl.

'Bloody rich, entitled cow – you're all the same. Stepping on the little people. Well, our time is coming. Enjoy the high life while you can, lady, because the workers of the world *will* unite, and perhaps we'll ship over some guillotines whilst we're at it.' He moved his face menacingly close to hers. 'You wouldn't recognise an honest day's work if it danced around you, waving ribbons.'

And you wouldn't recognise a smart but unfulfilled wife and three beautiful daughters who are every bit as worthy as sons if they were standing right in front of you, she thought, but said nothing as he stepped to the side, and she continued on her way.

* * *

Clara and her aunt began to spend more time with Jemima and the Smith girls. Although the steps to the basement were just as troublesome as the stairs in the house, Aunt Ag convinced herself that her knees were improving and nipping down to the basement was no trouble at all. Perhaps they were. The mind was a powerful thing, and the joy on the older lady's face from something as simple as an exhausted Frances falling asleep across her lap was obvious to all.

Returning from one such visit, the telephone rang as the pair stepped through the front door, so Clara left her aunt to it and sauntered up to her rooms, collapsing onto her bed. Barely five minutes passed before there was a knock at her door. She called for her aunt to enter and the older woman came to find her, with a pained expression across her face.

'It was your mother on the phone,' she explained. 'Warning you that Lady Rigby has been gossiping, and has let the cat out of the bag, so to speak.'

'The cat that curls up with other queen cats, rather than the toms?' Clara asked, shuffling to her elbows.

'Oh, darling, was it that lovely Jack, do you think? He seemed like such a nice man.'

Clara realised that Jack had finally delivered his revenge, and she must bring her plans for Berlin forward. She'd always known he liked to be in charge, even if that meant controlling damaging information about another, but he hadn't behaved this way when Mitzy had ended their engagement. Perhaps the truth was he'd never loved Mitzy but had, in fact, genuinely fallen for her.

She finally admitted her plans for The Cat's Meow to her darling aunt.

'A nightclub?' Aunt Ag looked sceptical and slumped onto the foot of Clara's bed. 'How about a nice café or small hotel? Far more respectable.'

'But nowhere near as much fun.' Clara laughed. 'And, as soon as I'm making money, I shall pay for you to visit.'

'But I've never been abroad.'

'Exactly. And I shall buy you the most outrageous hat I can afford. I might even make you wear a touch of lipstick, too.'

Her aunt smiled at the thought.

'So, you must teach me everything you know about running a house before I leave, so that I will be fully prepared. I'm going to make a success of this, Aunt.'

'Of that, dear child, I have no doubt.'

25

THE BATTERED SOFA

Agnes's favourite sofa was a duck-egg blue Chesterfield. It was far too pale to be practical, but had stood for years along the side wall of the front room, affording a good view of Burlington Square, and all its comings and goings. In many ways, it was the furniture equivalent of herself – overstuffed and worn, with bulging arms and shabby fabric, making it somewhat of a bulky and unsightly object. It had two deep indentations where bottoms had repeatedly sat during its long life, and the front cushions now bowed so low that they almost touched the floor.

Daphne had offered her a replacement sofa a couple of years ago, when she'd redecorated her morning room, and wondered if her older sister might make use of her cast-off furniture. When Agnes declined, Daphne couldn't understand her sister's refusal – the bright floral fabric would lift the room. What was Agnes thinking?

But Agnes was thinking of the times she had curled up on that sofa as a young child. How when Mummy was sick, as she often was, she had tucked herself below the big arm and tried to overhear what the doctor was telling her father in the hallway. And how, when her mother had passed away, it became a place to be near the people of the household and yet not have to talk to any of them.

She was thinking that when Daphne's newborn cries became overwhelming, she'd escaped downstairs in the middle of the night, and curled up in its soft creases, closed her eyes, and pretended that her mother was sitting in one of the fireside chairs. If she focussed hard enough, she imagined she could hear the soft strains of 'Nearer, My God, to Thee' drifting across the room. As the singing became harder to detect, the ethereal tune lost in the sounds of her own breathing and the ticking clock, she would be forced to accept that her mother was no longer with her, but instead seated at the feet of the Lord, perhaps showing Him her embroidery (she imagined embroidery being how her mother would while away her hours in the afterlife) and that the words of the song had come true: she *was* now nearer to God.

She remembered how she'd slept on that sofa for seven weeks when her father had neared his end. Not able to mount the stairs, his bed had been moved to the front room so that he could look out over the square and watch the russet leaves curl and loop in the breeze, until the branches of the trees were bare. He had called for his oldest child, clutching at her hand and in a rare moment of lucidity, embracing the winter of his own life and repeating over and over again the words, 'I love you, my darling daughter...' She consoled herself that he had at least known who she was at the end.

After refusing Daphne's offer, Agnes sat on the lumpy sofa and thought of all these things, rubbing her thumb over the bumps and dips of the fabric, and repeatedly tracing circles around the button edges. *This is where my tears fell,* she thought. *Where I cried for my mother, my sweetheart and my father. Those tears seeped into the horsehair and tufting, and remain there still, as much a part of this furniture as my blood is a part of my body.*

And I simply will not part with my tears.

26

Clara, wrapped in a high collar fur coat and kidskin gloves, tripped down the stairs to meet Mrs Bayswater. The nightclub owner had been most forthcoming with her advice, and even offered to introduce her to a contact from Berlin who might be able to help with premises. A flustered Jemima almost crashed into Clara as she turned on the half landing, heading up as she headed down.

'Agnes told me this morning you're moving abroad.' It wasn't a question so Clara didn't respond, but in not denying the statement she was indeed confirming it. 'I... I wanted to... There are things I haven't...' Flustered, which was most unlike the straight-talking woman, she finally managed to form a sentence. She looked as fierce as she ever had. 'Were you even going to say goodbye?'

Goodness gracious. Her aunt didn't hang about with news.

'I'm not leaving today, darling. I may be up against it, but I do own more than just the coat on my back.' She spread wide her hands. 'Look – no suitcases. I haven't even started packing. As if I'd leave without speaking to Matilda. I'm rather fond of your dear daughter.'

'And me?'

Clara wasn't quite sure what she was asking.

'You know how I feel about you.' Jemima was part of the reason for her departure but she couldn't tell her that. If being with her wasn't an option, being around her would be difficult – the smell of lemons was becoming quite unbearable. Perhaps when the whispers from Jack's gossip had died down, popping back for jolly visits and slipping into devil-may-care Clara for a few hours might be more manageable. She could periodically return to Burlington Square, shower everyone with gifts, remind them all how simply marvellous she was, and then return to her new life. She'd already decided she would write regularly to Matilda, who would be beyond thrilled to have a penfriend in Germany, of all places.

'I am leaving soon though. Jack's been absolutely ghastly, telling tales, and I don't want things to become uncomfortable for Mummy. I'll write, and be back to see Aunt Ag, naturally, but I have plans to make a name for myself, to earn my own money, and to live as honestly as I dare.'

'You surely can't be thinking of admitting to your... tastes?' Jemima paled. 'People will be unkind. I wouldn't want that for you.'

'I hardly see the point in pretending any more. It's out there now, and that's probably for the best,' she acknowledged. 'People like me spend our lives believing our inversion is a tragedy, we are pitied and sent off to medical professionals to be examined like museum curiosities. I certainly won't be putting an announcement in The Times, but unfortunately the silly boy has forced my hand.' Jack's revenge for her perceived transgressions would always hurt. She'd thought him better than that. 'Besides, in these last few weeks I've become stronger and refuse to be one of the thousands living in constant fear of being held up as an example... and all because I love outside the bounds of what is considered acceptable. My dear friend Neville, as a man, lives daily with the very real possibility of jail. At least I am spared that. But in Berlin, I might find a level of acceptance.'

Jemima's eyes flashed with something Clara couldn't determine. Surprise? Panic? And then the young woman composed herself, running her tongue across her pale lips before meeting, and holding, Clara's eye.

'Love between women was tolerated so much more last century, so perhaps one day it will be again?' she offered. 'Women like the Ladies of Llangollen were ultimately accepted by their community when they realised they posed no threat.'

'Well, there you go then, darling. Perhaps there is hope for me, after all.' Bless her for trying to understand something she had no desire to experience, Clara thought.

'You do realise that those in power only taint lives such as theirs because they are frightened...'

Jemima stood straighter and Clara recognised the spark of passion igniting in her friend again. The young mother did so love the opportunity to give voice to her opinions. Had she been born twenty years earlier, Clara could quite imagine her chained to the railings outside Downing Street, fighting for the vote. She was preparing herself to say more. Clara could sense it.

'These men – for those in power are *all* men – are scared of our possible economic independence. They squirm at the thought we might not need them any more, that we will overthrow the established social order if we have jobs and do not rely on them financially. And the thought that some women may not even need them sexually is a consideration they cannot even *bear* to contemplate.'

Jemima actually understood what she was up against, Clara realised, even if it had taken a while to swallow her distaste. God, how she loved the fierce woman before her. What a force they could have been in another lifetime. What a difference they could have made. So small, she mused, but so mighty.

'I can quite see why you have chosen Germany,' Jemima continued, rubbing her hands nervously over and over each other, still refusing to let Clara pass. 'They lost the war and yet have embraced the worth of women more than our own victorious nation. The Weimar constitution asserts that *all* Germans are equal before the law, and their women have the same voting rights as men.'

Clara yet again felt ashamed of her ignorance. Perhaps she should have researched the politics of her chosen destination, instead of focussing on the hedonistic advantages.

'And one in ten of the seats in the Reichstag are held by women. Can you even imagine?' Jemima's face lit up, before she self-consciously dipped her eyes. 'You are exactly the sort of woman who will bloom in such an empowering environment.'

'Too jolly right, darling. I'd certainly drink to that, if I wasn't heading out.' She raised an imaginary glass in the air.

'Here's to female solidarity.' Jemima chinked an invisible glass in return.

'With shiny brass knobs on. Thank you for being my friend and opening my eyes to so much of this. I am a better person since meeting you.'

'I think you've always been a good person, Clara. Just a little lost, that's all. I will never forget how you sang to my baby.'

'Not perhaps the most appropriate song...'

'No, but it reminded me that he was real, and that I needed to see his face, even if just once. And after you'd left, I picked him up from where you'd laid him so tenderly in the drawer, and cradled him. Thank you for that. I was so very angry at the time.' She swallowed. 'I believed I was being punished.'

'We talked about this. It's natural to resent a child you hadn't planned.'

'No, I don't mean being punished for wishing the baby dead.

For another sin. Thoughts I'd been struggling with for a while, something darker...'

Was there anything darker than wishing to erase the existence of a human soul?

Jemima's forehead pulled itself into a frown as she took her time before elaborating on her statement. Whatever she had to say was clearly difficult for her to admit.

'For wanting you.' She couldn't look at Clara, and turned her head away to focus on the banister rail, her words almost a whisper. 'For wanting your body in the way Nicholas wants mine.'

At that moment every nerve ending in Clara's body tingled, and an icy wave washed over her. Not of fear, but of hope. *Was Jemima suggesting that her affections were reciprocated?*

'You have feelings for me?' It took a lot to shock the thoroughly modern Clara, but her head jerked in disbelief. There had been no clues, just snappy comments and awkward looks.

Jemima turned back to face her but cast her eyes down, unsure of herself and nervous. The outspoken crusader of moments before was now a bundle of anxiety and doubt.

'I never really wanted Nicholas. Not in that way. But I wrongly assumed women didn't feel things in their bodies the way men did. I remember my granny telling my mother that it wasn't something you were expected to find pleasure in. "Make a shopping list in your head or plan the menus for the week, and before you know it the whole unpleasantness is over." I never had any expectation that it was a thing I would enjoy. But my body felt more alive, more sensual, from your kiss than anything I've experienced as a married woman.'

Clara allowed her mouth to drop open. Was that why Jemima had been so unkind? Because she was fighting her own demons and struggling to accept the truth about herself?

Both women were breathing heavily now, and there was a creak of the stair as Jemima moved almost imperceptibly closer. The warm breath of her friend caressed Clara's shoulder. Each time she inhaled, Clara's chest tightened and her head felt giddy. She was desperate to reach out, but this was Jemima's moment. She had to make the first move. And how delectable it was to let someone else take control.

She took two steps down, without breaking eye contact, making herself smaller than Jemima and pressing her shoulders back into the wall. She tipped her chin upwards and waited. Jemima's lips parted and wobbled slightly as she tried to form difficult words.

'You have to understand that this can't be. It can *never* be. I have a husband whom I promised to love and obey, and I won't do anything that would hurt my girls. But I wanted you to know before you left that I will carry you in my heart always. That if things had been different, or we had met years ago, I might have found the courage to be with you.'

Clara briefly toyed with outing Nicholas to his wife, as a way of persuading her to leave him, but it was a tit-for-tat game she had no interest in playing. Besides, the infidelities of men were acceptable; those of women were not.

'The memory of that kiss hasn't left me for one second since it happened.' Jemima swallowed hard. 'I may have fought it at the time, but inside I've always known the truth. Perhaps if I can share one pure moment with you, it will be something I can carry with me always. Kiss me again.' She bent forward to bring her face level to her friend's.

Clara reached up to cup Jemima's pale face in her neatly manicured hands, and studied this constantly surprising woman. There was a strength in her Clara hadn't seen in anyone else. A woman who dutifully fulfilled her obligations even though she knew that life held so much more. Could she be persuaded to fight for those things? Might she finally be allowed to blossom? But the tears that were building in the beautiful grey eyes before her signalled that gut-wrenching truth that theirs was a love that could never be. Both women closed their eyes as their heads moved slowly towards each other until their lips finally bumped together.

And this time there was no slap.

Eventually, Jemima broke away, breathless but smiling, despite her wet cheeks. There was no need for words, explanations or attempts to make promises neither could keep. She turned and slipped back down the stairs, returning to her family. Clara allowed her hand to brush her own lips, salty from tears, to prove to herself the kiss had been real, but as she started to descend the stairs to keep her appointment with Mrs Bayswater, she saw a figure on the landing above. Gilbert looked down at her and she knew he'd seen and heard everything that had passed between them.

Three days passed but Gilbert said nothing to Clara, and she couldn't help but wonder when he would strike. Would it be outright blackmail or snide comments to revel in her discomfort? She was beyond caring about her own reputation, but she would do whatever was necessary to protect the woman she loved, and those dear girls. Was Gilbert about to take a vicious swipe at her Achilles heel? Things had become very complicated, surprisingly quickly.

On the fourth day she could bear it no longer and knocked at the attic door. He eventually answered and she pushed imperiously past him, strutting up the wooden stairs, as he mumbled his irritation to the back of her head.

'What do you want, Clara?' he asked, in a weary yet guarded tone. 'I'm in the middle of developing some photographs so please be brief.' He nodded to the closed door at the back of the attics, which she guessed must be his darkroom.

'I know you saw me the other day with Jemima...' She tailed off, not knowing what to say, and suddenly noticing the curious proliferation of objects that graced his room. Apart from the obvious links to his photography, spread across a side table were an assortment of tools, scissors, a fishing rod and, rather curiously, a tambourine.

'And what? You expected me to extort large sums of money from you? Or run to a journalist to sell an exclusive?'

She looked uncomfortably at her feet, because that was exactly what she was expecting.

'I have no need of your money and firmly believe people are entitled to have secrets. My business is not your business, and vice versa. Live and let live is a very underrated sentiment. And we certainly should not condemn one another for feelings we cannot control.'

'Wait...' Clara paused, as a thought suddenly occurred to her. 'Are you... are you also guilty of the love that dare not speak its name?' Her voice had dropped to a whisper. Neville and she chose to put on a confident, extroverted front in order to cope, but she knew others who sank into the shadows. Perhaps Gilbert was trying to blend into the background to avoid close scrutiny. Her vanity also allowed the fleeting realisation that he'd never shown any romantic interest in her.

'Sorry to disappoint but it's girls all the way for me – I just don't believe in judging others, that's all.'

'So, you're not going to tell anyone about Jemima?'

'Of course not. You don't have a very high opinion of me, do you? You seem to have cast me as some sort of villain when I'm not convinced I deserve such an accolade.'

Clara felt distinctly uncomfortable. Here was someone on her side, or at least, not prepared to condemn her for something she genuinely had no more control over than an autumn apple could fight gravity. And yet he left her with an uneasy feeling. She looked about the sparse space, and remembered the roll of banknotes he'd pulled from his pocket. His photography clearly paid well, yet there was no apparent excess in either his dress or furnishings. He doubtless had some dirty habit to fund – drugs, by the look of him. Perhaps gambling. Maybe even prostitutes. One never could tell. She tugged at her painted thumbnail between her teeth. But he was right; it wasn't her business, and she needed to keep him on side.

'Thank you,' she said. 'For being understanding.'

He shrugged. 'I only wish I could say the same.'

28

Clara was enjoying a brisk walk with Jemima, through a blustery Hyde Park, wrapped up in winter woollens to combat the cold air. It was the day before she was due to sail from Dover and there was an unspoken desire to spend as much time together as possible before her departure. Matilda was at school, and Aunt Ag had offered to mind the youngest two, allowing the women a rare opportunity to be alone.

Mrs Bayswater's contact had found Clara suitable premises and Neville had made a sizeable investment in her venture, allowing the wheels to turn with alacrity. She could hardly believe that the keys to the premises in Berlin-Mitte would be in her hands by the very next day, but she remained in turmoil as she walked beside her friend, afraid to touch her, yet afraid that if she didn't these final moments would slip though her fingers. Not being allowed to have the thing she wanted was an unpleasant novelty. Still amazed Jemima had feelings for her, she was almost more distraught that they could not be together than she was when she believed her love was not reciprocated.

'Come to Germany with me?' It was a silly request. If only it were that simple.

'Cannot the fact I have feelings for you be enough? I'm married and you are about to embark on a great adventure. I will always be grateful to you for opening my eyes to who I really am, but I'm not as brave as you, Clara. I could not suffer the unkind whispers, nor could I put my girls through such a thing.'

'But you don't love him. Can you not get a divorce? I have friends who have unchained themselves from unsuitable spouses. It can be done, you know, darling. Times are changing.' Yet again, she stopped short of revealing Nicholas's advances. Her friend didn't need proof that the marriage was a sham; that had been clearly established.

Jemima sighed.

'You still don't understand my world, do you? Your friends can divorce because they have money. It's a preserve of the wealthy. Most of them actively court the press anyway, and the shame of such a thing doesn't seem to bother them. You also do not seem to understand that my daughters could be taken from me. I cannot allow that to happen.'

'But you, and they, deserve more. Help me set up this nightclub in Berlin? We can start a new life together. I've always known that I would have no need of a husband, but it's entirely possible I have need of a wife. You'd be invaluable in my ventures, and financially independent, giving the girls far more opportunities. I *know* I can make this work. For the first time, I've applied myself to something, done the sums and the research—'

'It's just a silly dream.' Jemima cut through her friend and came to a standstill. 'A lovely one, but a dream nonetheless.'

They had turned from the Serpentine and entered a cluster of trees, away from the enquiring glances of elderly ladies parked on the rows of wooden benches that faced the water. They stood under the shadow of the thinning tree canopies, fire-coloured leaves strewn at their feet, crisp breezes whipping at their cheeks. But Clara was desperate to prove the worth of her plans.

'I've secured suitable premises, and plan to call it The Cat's Meow; it will be full of beautiful things and beautiful people. I know how much money these clubs take and we'll be turning over hundreds a week by the end of next year.' She grabbed Jemima's hands. 'The girls will have the very best of everything. They will quickly pick up the language and then think of the opportunities open to them? I want the best for Matilda – you know how fond I've become of the little poppet. And you and I will be together, which is the most important thing. We can be as secretive or open as you like. Pretend you're my sister? Or just tell the world and to hell with everyone. It's up to you. But whatever you decide, know that I love you – really love you – and I'd help you to bring up the girls as though they were my own.'

Jemima laughed then. 'But you're hopeless with children and have never wanted any of your own.'

'I love yours because they are a part of you, and I know I might not be great at the nurturing thing, but I can learn, and I have other skills. Matilda likes me,' she finished, in her defence.

There was a pause. Clara's stomach spun the carousel of nervous expectation. This woman before her was everything. She'd taught her so much – that she didn't need money or nice clothes. That women, in many ways, were stronger than the men they were forced to rely on, and that she was more capable than she had ever realised.

'I'm sorry. Nicholas isn't perfect but he loves me. I can't do it to him.'

Was this going to end like the Alice situation? Finally, she had found someone she knew she could be happy with and, yet again, a man was in the way. Alice didn't love Philip any more than Jemima loved Nicholas. Both women did, however, love her – despite Alice's protestations. But losing Jemima was so much worse. She had made Clara a better person; Alice had merely indulged her.

She put her hand out to Jemima's cheek. She would say nothing of Nicholas's proposition because Clara Goodwin was learning to put others before herself. And, at that moment, under those copper-coloured trees, she finally accepted that what she wanted and what was best for her, was not necessarily aligned with Jemima's wants or needs.

As the pair walked back to Burlington Square, she reflected on the sorrows and joys of her short time at the house. She knew she was doing the right thing by leaving. Whilst her stay had brought great happiness to her aunt, she knew that in her absence the Smith family would take the older lady under their wing. Life was precious and she had a duty not to waste hers. She'd witnessed two deaths in her time at Burlington Square; one at the very start of a life and one at the very end. It was proof that you never knew how long you'd got left – look at poor old Amelia Farrington. Clara determined to make something of herself before it was too late.

She looked across at her friend and determined not to give up on her. Everything had happened too quickly, and the more she thought about it, the more she realised it was unrealistic to expect Jemima to skip off into the German sunset with her three small children in tow. Some things, like a petite, feisty, beautiful woman, were worth waiting for. Surely Nicholas's true colours would eventually be pinned to the mast, and his wife would recognise him for the cheat he undoubtedly was.

Clara would make a roaring success of her nightclub and then she would return.

29

BERLIN, FOUR MONTHS LATER.

Clara was surprised by a knock at her apartment door. She glanced at her wristwatch, thinking Frau Müller was early. A shrewd woman who had swallowed her distaste for the British because renting the young Miss Goodwin her dilapidated former furniture store – which had now been transformed into a glamorous nightclub – had seen a reversal of her fortunes. Although not enamoured of the young Englishwoman, she was happy to take money for whatever services Clara would pay for, and teaching her German three evenings a week was one of these services.

'*Frau Müller, du bist sehr früh...*' she called across the room. Or was it *Sie sind*? The language was so jolly confusing but, like everything she'd undertaken in the last few months, she was giving it her all.

Her modern flat was a product of this defeated nation rebuilding the shattered lives of its disheartened population, and Clara loved the clean lines, curved walls and geometric shapes that now surrounded her. Living alone, for the first time in her life, she found it uncomfortably quiet but, thanks to her aunt's tutoring, she was at least on top of the housework. After Burlington Square and all Aunt Ag's clutter, she was embracing the futuristic and some-what eccentric Bauhaus style. Now that her business venture had started to reap rewards, she'd purchased a few pieces of elegant but simple furniture, and there was not a stuffed canary or fancy china ornament in sight.

She swung open the front door and froze.

There on the doorstep stood Jemima, her eyes as fierce as ever, and that determined up-tilt of the chin proof that her indefatigable spirit still burned brightly within. The familiar smell of lemons and washing powder drifted across the gap between them and made Clara's heart ache that little bit more.

'Why didn't you tell me?' Jemima's voice was accusatory, and there was no hello, or explanation for her appearance seven hundred miles away from home.

'Tell you what?' Clara had been in trouble so frequently with the young mother that she couldn't think what misdemeanour she'd possibly committed on this occasion, and certainly not one so great that her friend would travel across Europe to reprimand her for it.

'That Nicholas tried to bed you?'

Clara was confused. Jemima had finally uncovered her husband's attempt at infidelity but *she* was the villain?

'It wasn't important. How did you find out?'

'It came out in an argument last month. He returned late from the Mad Hatter, worse for wear, and I said I'd received a letter from you, and that we needed a serious talk.'

Clara had taken a while to write to her friend. Aunt Ag she had kept regularly updated, and she'd sent Matilda several postcards of the city because a cheery sentence was enough to fill the small blank correspondence space, but finding the right words for Jemima had been difficult. What could she say that wouldn't come across as emotional blackmail, when all she wanted to write was *I ache without you* a thousand times over, across the page? Instead, she waited until the club was up and running so that she could at least talk about that.

'Funny what guilt does to a man,' Jemima continued, 'because he began to rant about how I shouldn't believe anything you said. He assumed you'd told me and tried to back-pedal so fast when he realised I knew nothing about it and he'd slit his own throat.'

'Ah...'

Clara gestured her inside, not wanting this conversation to be conducted in a communal hallway. Frau Müller had impeccable English and might enter the building at any point. The young mother stepped over the threshold and closed the door behind her, but she still clutched at her handbag like a shield.

'Four months without you, wondering what I had sacrificed to remain with a man who had so little respect for me, he tried to seduce his landlady's niece. The worst of it was he tried to shift the blame – told me you had practically seduced him in Agnes's hallway... And I was so torn between anger and amusement that I told him the truth. How his lies had tripped him up because any schemes he'd planned in order to bed you, would never have worked.'

'You told him about me?' Clara's eyes flashed wide.

'Yes, and how I felt about you. He was so shocked he collapsed into a chair before launching into a diatribe about what a dirty little whore I was – an unfit mother and deviant. He was torn between despising me, his morbid curiosity, and not wanting to admit the truth of it all. And then he started to panic that other people would find out, because somehow that makes him less of a man – the fact he married a Sapphic and didn't know – as if he couldn't attract someone normal.'

Clara flinched at her choice of language, but felt she needed to be honest about her part in Nicholas's advances.

'He approached me, it's true, but I'm guilty for making eyes at him before. Some misguided attempt to make you jealous. You must realise that none of us in this tangled triangle are blameless.'

'That is *exactly* my point – we are all as bad as each other. I felt so awful, you see, for being the one who wanted to escape the marriage, and was trying to make everything right because I thought *I* was the one at fault, but I have to ask myself whether this was the first time he'd wandered.'

Again, Clara said nothing. Nicholas's wanderings weren't her concern.

'Neither of us are probably fit parents in the eyes of the Church,' she continued, 'but I suddenly knew with absolute certainty that I'd do a damn sight better job bringing up the girls than him. The last month has been hell, but at the end of the day, all he wants is for this mess to go away and to start again, even if it means losing his daughters. Perhaps he can find someone to bear him the son he is so desperate for, but it won't be me. I'm done with all that. I'm done with him.'

Clara's head was in a spin. Was Jemima here to stay? Had she left her good-for-nothing husband and travelled all this way so they could be together?

Jemima took a step forward. 'I eventually suggested a divorce, and to my surprise, he's agreed. He's even offered to hire a woman and stage the necessary photos, because he'd rather be labelled an adulterer than let the world know about his wife. I doubt he'll even miss the girls.'

Clara suspected Nicholas wasn't quite as cold-hearted as his wife painted him. He did love his daughters; he just wasn't prepared to fight for them. They were simply the noisy creatures who gave him sleepless nights and cost him money that he didn't have to spare.

'Where are they?' Clara suddenly remembered that they were part of this equation. 'You surely haven't left them with him?'

'Sitting in a taxi downstairs, having been dragged across Europe on what I have promised will be the greatest adventure of their lives. Uprooted from everything and everyone they know.' There was a moment of realisation as she heard her own words spoken out loud. 'I'm totally insane, aren't I?' Her hand went to her mouth. 'I didn't even write to let you know I was coming. You might be with someone else. Do you even want me?'

'How could you doubt it?' Clara said, sweeping her into her arms and kissing the top of her head. 'You are no more insane than me, running off to a foreign country to start a nightclub with only a vision and pocket full of change. I will always be fighting a world that thinks I'm different and challenging, but that's what makes me, me.'

'And why I love you.' Jemima tipped her head up to Clara's and the women exchanged a look that said everything.

'Here's to non-conformity.' Clara raised an imaginary glass, and Jemima chinked it with one of her own.

A few minutes later and the three Smith girls were in the hallway, the older two clutching brown cardboard suitcases, and Frances wedged firmly on Jemima's hip. Goodness, she'd grown so much in the past few months, Clara realised.

Matilda held Ellen's free hand and gave the broadest grin, the blue crescent brooch pinned at a wonky angle on the lapel of her brown wool coat. The paste gems caught the light as she walked towards the flat, her small chin tilted upwards, like a miniature version of her mother. Clara's heart lifted and panicked all at once. This little one's entire world is about to change, she thought, because of me. I cannot let Matilda down. I cannot let Jemima down. I cannot let any of them down. They are my family now.

'Isn't this a splendid adventure?' Matilda said. 'Just like the ones Miss Humphries read to me from her big book.'

'Absolutely, sweetie,' Clara said, grabbing Ellen's suitcase and leading them into the modest flat that would be a squash for five, but would, at least, no longer be silent.

Ellen and Matilda raced off to explore the flat and Clara turned to their mother.

'Are you sure about this?' Clara had to check.

'Bit late to change my mind now, but I'm pretty sure this time around I'll have an equal say.'

'You really will,' Clara agreed.

She reached out for Jemima's hand. Had Frances not been in her mother's arms, she would have kissed her then. Tasted her lips and revelled in her scent. This should be the most romantic moment of their lives – the moment that they committed to each other. But their love could not be openly celebrated and this is how it would be from now on, she realised. Snatched moments and secret looks. But as the warmth of Jemima's hand seeped into her own, and she felt an almost imperceptible squeeze of her fingers, her body reacted with a thousand tiny fizzes and throbs. No, this was even better, she decided, as she had a vision of them standing across a dance floor from each other, after a successful evening as hostesses of their nightclub, exchanging a knowing look.

Perhaps, she mused, as they stepped over the pile of abandoned suitcases, they would be buried together in fifty years' time, like the Ladies of Llangollen. And perhaps, in fifty years' time, the world would be a place where their secret was no longer one they had to hide...

PART II

STEPHEN THOMPSON

30

FRIDAY, 5TH AUGUST 1927

Agnes dipped the nib of her pen into the pewter inkwell and began to write.

Dear Mr Thompson

Further to your interview, and subject to your references proving satisfactory, I am pleased to offer you the rooms at 23 Burlington Square. As discussed, you do not require any meals at the present time, just laundry services for your shirts, but should that change in the future I would be happy to accommodate you.

It will be a delight to have a professional man, such as yourself, at the house, and I look forward to your arrival. Any time from Sunday afternoon would suit.

Yours truly,

Agnes Humphries.

She felt inordinately proud of herself for basing the decision on logic rather than sentiment. Daphne would be cross that she'd not given the rooms to Clara, but Mr Gorski would be pleased with her choice. Mr Thompson was a respectable man with a solid profession. He would be nothing but an asset to the house, and indeed the neighbourhood. She loved Clara dearly, but the thought that whatever scandal had erupted in Hertfordshire might follow her niece to this quiet and respectable part of west London worried her. At the end of the day, that girl was more self-assured and wayward than she had ever been. Like the cream in the bottles delivered to her doorstep every morning, Clara Goodwin would always rise to the top.

Declining the timid young woman from Suffolk unsettled her more. Now there was someone who wore her fear and disquiet like a shroud. A part of her had been pulled to Mercy – an inexplicable desire to offer the frightened widow a refuge and show her a little kindness – but ultimately, she was inviting more trouble to the house. That girl was hiding something, she was certain. Later today she would write to her and recommend Mrs Johnson's boarding house two streets down. Perhaps she could mention that she still needed help with laundry and cooking. If Mercy took up the boarding house, Burlington Square was on the way to Pemberton's and she might yet consider Agnes's offer of the extra work. It would certainly alleviate some of the guilt she felt.

The letter to Mr Thompson was quick to write and she heard Gilbert coming down the stairs just as she sealed the envelope and dabbed the stamp on the roller of the little cut-glass moistener. It had stood on her father's desk for as long as she could remember, although the desk had been far less cluttered back then. Nowadays there was barely space to lay a sheet of writing paper.

'Gilbert?' she called, and his dark, sullen eyes appeared at the doorway. He didn't say anything – words were just not his thing – but he looked over to her expectantly.

'Could you pop this in a postbox for me?' she asked. 'Save my legs.'

He nodded and hastily retrieved the letter, before exiting just as swiftly and closing the front door gently behind him. The lad was like a ghost, she thought, drifting about the house and not interacting with anyone.

Relieved that the decision had finally been made, she could go about her day now. Perhaps she'd sleep better tonight. Choosing a lodger should be straightforward but, as she caught the omniscient eyes of Sunny, she wondered why it felt as though she was playing God with these people's lives.

31

Stephen Thompson stood on the stone steps of 23 Burlington Square five days later, rested the antiquated suitcase by his feet, and rang the bell. He fiddled nervously with his tie, conscious it was important to appear professional and to impress. This was a fresh start, a new beginning. All he wanted was to put the past behind him and start again. Surely everyone deserved a second chance?

It took a few moments for the door to be answered, and then it was swung back by his new landlady, Agnes Humphries. She was slightly out of breath but had the broadest smile across her round face, and a cheery yellow pinny around her ample middle. This kindly lady reminded him of a particularly benevolent school-teacher he'd had as a child, which lifted his flagging spirits. As did the wholesome smell of baking bread and the strong aroma of cinnamon.

'Come in, come in. You're earlier than I expected but I've just made a fresh batch of cinnamon biscuits – one of Mr Gorski's favourites – and I'm sure I can spare a couple. Think of them as a welcome to your new home gift.'

'How very kind.' His tummy rumbled in eager anticipation and he returned the smile. It wasn't a facial expression he'd had much practice at of late, but somehow the simple act of lifting his cheeks to form a grin also lifted his heart, even though he felt there was little to be glad about.

He picked up the case and heaved it over the threshold, catching his foot at the last minute, which sent him tumbling to the floor.

'Oh, my dear man, are you hurt?'

Stephen's hands stung where they had hit the cold yellow and burgundy Minton tiles, but it was his pride that had suffered the most damage. Why was it that everything seemed stacked against him? Far from creating a good impression with his new landlady, here he was sprawled across her hallway, his hands stinging and his knees badly bruised. Was his life to be one of constant humiliation?

He struggled to his feet and assured her he was fine. Leaving his case in the cluttered hallway, he followed her, noticing a top hat on the hall stand as he passed and wondering if she had a visitor. But it was only the two of them as he entered the kitchen, which proved just as cluttered as the rest of the ground floor. He realised this bustling woman's love for curious knick-knacks and ornaments extended everywhere. Old-fashioned wallpaper was obscured by a proliferation of hanging souvenir plates from a variety of seaside destinations, and copper pots and pans, and yet more china ornaments, were squashed together on narrow pine shelves that reached to the ceiling. Streaming sunlight came from a large sash window over the sink and wholesome aromas lingered in the air. He'd missed this kind of homely atmosphere so badly over the last few years, and was temporarily hit by a wave of homesickness. Everyone needed to feel they belonged somewhere, and he hadn't belonged for so very long. Perhaps Burlington Square would be his refuge.

'Pull up a chair and I'll make a fresh pot of tea. I'll pop the water hotter on to boil.'

'Sorry?' He frowned. 'Water hotter?'

'Oh, it was something my dear, departed father used to say.' She smiled to herself. 'I've just taken up Mr Gorski's tray – although don't my knees know it?' She gestured to her legs and rolled her eyes. 'But he does so love a little something in the afternoon.'

A mangy black one-eared cat, that had been curled up on the chair at the end of the table, leapt down as he scraped the nearest pine chair towards himself. He reached out his hand in an attempt to pet the creature but the feline hissed, lifted up its tatty head and strode out the room in that indignant way that cats excelled at. The baking smells made his stomach clench and he hoped Miss Humphries couldn't hear the grizzling protestations coming from his abdomen. He'd had nothing but a piece of bread and lard all day. It was important to make economies where you could, and food was fairly low down on his list of priorities at the moment.

'When will the rest of your belongings be arriving?' She proffered a small plate of pale brown biscuits. He could quite happily eat them all but politely took two.

'Oh, erm, there is nothing else.'

His new landlady slid a dainty cup and saucer in front of him, full of steaming hot and slightly stewed tea. The only good thing about his brief time serving in the war had been the standard issue decent-sized brown enamel mugs. The cup before him held barely enough to satisfy a gnat and he downed it in two gulps.

'Goodness me. You can't honestly tell me that everything you own can be bundled up into one suitcase?' She looked about her and perhaps considered how many suitcases she would need for her possessions. It didn't bear thinking about.

'I've been living abroad – I thought I'd mentioned it at the interview. And I always think it's wise to travel light, especially when you move around a lot. Besides, the key to a good life isn't owning an abundance of possessions, but treating people well and being treated well in return.'

'Very true, Mr Thompson.' She nodded, almost to herself. 'I should very much have liked to have travelled.' She looked momentarily wistful. 'In my youth, my father often took my sister and I on short trips to Margate and Brighton,' she said, pointing to the plates. 'But I always had a fancy to see the world beyond these shores; the Americas or the deserts of Africa. I've read plenty about them but you really can't get the sense of a thing from a photograph or a painting.'

'True enough,' Stephen agreed, his eyes darting back to the biscuit plate.

'There is a delightful watercolour of a coffee plantation hanging to the right of my fireplace, I'll show it to you sometime. I always feel the heat of the day positively emanates from the picture. It must be all the vibrant sunburnt oranges in the sky.' She peered at him, leaning over the table slightly. 'But you surely can't have been anywhere hot, you're as pale as the moon.'

Stephen remembered from their previous meeting that Miss Humphries said what was on her mind. She'd been less than discreet about the other residents last week, and he'd quickly recognised that this was not a lady to confide one's secrets in. He knew he was to share this house with a young man who was 'somewhat of an oddity and looks as though he might have risen from the mortuary slab', an elderly Polish man who was 'unusually personable for a foreigner but has some peculiar ways', and a young family in the basement where 'the poor mother has been in the family way since they moved in four years ago'. What might she say about him to the others, he wondered, given time?

'Very little sun for me, I'm afraid. I was inside buildings most of the time. The travel was connected to my work, you understand.'

Indeed, his time away had been directly as a result of his previous source of income.

'Ah, inside a fancy bank in some far-away city. Marble counter-tops and wooden panelling?' Stephen chose not to correct her assumption and let her prattle on. 'I've barely left London as an adult, apart from visits to my sister in Hertfordshire. It would have been lovely to see a bit of the world but the opportunities presented to me were... impossible to undertake.'

She sighed and then offered him the remaining biscuits, which he took with grateful thanks.

'I expect you're keen to unpack and make yourself at home so I won't hold you up. Any problems, just pop down. I must get on with the dinner for my other gentlemen – rabbit pie for Mr Gorski and bean stew for young Gilbert.'

Stephen inwardly salivated and nearly dribbled onto the table before him. Perhaps she noticed his wistful look.

'And you're sure you don't want to pay extra for meals?' He shook his head. 'Ah, you undoubtedly dine at gentlemen's clubs or chop-houses with friends,' she incorrectly surmised. 'Or perhaps your lunch is provided by the bank? Like Hoares. Now there's an establishment that knows how to look after its staff.'

'Yes,' he replied. 'Exactly that. They lay on such magnificent fare that I find I want very little of an evening.'

'And my food is very basic, but Mr Gorski has a delicate stomach and has expressed a wish for me to avoid too many fancy spices or overly strong flavours. Here are your keys. The largest one is for the front door, and the smaller is to your rooms. I'll see you in the morning then. I expect you have to be up at the crack of dawn for work?'

'Yes, it's always an early start for me, and then a long day filling in transfer ledgers and checking, and double-checking, endless rows of figures. The bank opens at nine so I'll endeavour to leave at eight, as punctuality is vital in my profession.'

But Stephen Thompson didn't have to be anywhere on Monday morning because Stephen did not, in fact, work in a bank.

Stephen had lied.

32

THE SMALL PAINTING OF A COFFEE PLANTATION

Agnes often thought back to the year she'd acquired the painting. A flier pasted on the wall outside the greengrocer's had advertised a small exhibition at a private gallery in Bayswater, and she so rarely did things for herself. *Art of the Empire* would enable the visitor to 'view a multitude of far-away countries through the eyes of the artist'. The lure of enormous and colourful canvasses was immense.

With Daphne now school-age, Agnes had finally reclaimed some precious free time and begun to work her way through her father's numerous bookshelves. But it wasn't novels or poetry that she turned to. The former were often frivolous and would add nothing to her learning (what did she need to know of pretty dresses, trembling lips and beating hearts?), and with the latter she always felt she was missing something, hidden behind the imagery and in the rhythm of the words. Instead, it was the travel guides and journals, detailing far-off places, unusual clothing and surprising customs, that truly held her attention. She was particularly drawn to those written by women; writers such as Isabella Bird, with her *An Englishwoman in America*, or works by Mrs Trollope. So, an exhibition that would bring these far-off places further to life was appealing, giving her hope that a woman's lot was not always that of housewife, mother and carer. She'd been running the house for her father and acting as a substitute mother for Daphne for nearly eight years, and hoped these obligations would soon be discharged, enabling her to explore the world beyond Burlington Square.

She kissed her father goodbye as he asked for the third time that day where she was going, and it was with great effort that she stopped her expression betraying her increasing concerns regarding his memory. The day was bright, which lifted her spirits, and the forty-five-minute walk was a balm to her troubled soul.

Inside the gallery, the large gilt-framed artworks hung on the dark red walls in clusters, rather than at regimented heights, and were grouped into works, not by artist, but by continent and country. A tall gentleman, wearing a top hat and frock coat, stood before the wall of paintings from India – landscapes with waving palm trees and emaciated cattle, temples with onion-shaped domes, and people in colourful turbans and saris. She placed herself a little way from him so as not to intrude, and stood silently for a while, awed by the vibrancy of the art. He was examining a large depiction of a market scene, and stood so close to the picture that she couldn't see the whole, and yet she was intrigued by the edge that she could see – bustling crowds in front of wide baskets of fruit and vegetables piled into high pyramids. Some of the produce she recognised, some she did not. But, oh, the colours!

Surreptitiously, she studied the side of the gentleman's earnest face. He wasn't handsome by any measure you might employ, but Agnes decided he looked kind. With blond curls poking out from beneath the hat, and ears that protruded like teacup handles, there was something slightly comical about him. But his body language drew her in. She moved closer.

'You are very tall, which I'm sure is a lovely thing for you, but when you stand so near to the canvases, smaller people like me do not have an adequate view.'

'I do apologise, miss,' he said, doffing his hat and moving to the side. 'Have you been to India?'

'I have not travelled beyond the shores of England,' she admitted.

'Then you are an art lover? Perhaps an artist yourself?'

Agnes giggled at that. She could no more paint a landscape than sing an aria. Her skills were practical not creative. Bed-making, cake-baking and clothes-mending.

'Not one jot. Anything I attempted would resemble the handiwork of a drunken monkey. Possibly one holding the brush between his toes.' The gentleman smiled at her remark, making his eyes crinkle and his cheeks lift. She couldn't help smiling back. 'I am merely an admirer – and even at that, I am an amateur.'

'Have you visited the National Gallery?' he asked.

'Yes, several times.'

'And your favourite works of art?'

'Certainly not the stuffy portraits of wealthy people – often only worthy of such canvasses because they have money, and not because they have done anything kind or noteworthy. And, as beautiful as they are, the altarpiece scenes, with their gold paint and fine detail, do begin to look alike. There's only so much martyrdom I can stomach.'

The man smiled again, but did not interrupt her escalating flow of words.

'So, I would probably choose Canaletto's scenes of Venice. Anything that takes me to a place I've not visited before. I so long to travel but instead, I console myself with pictures in books or paintings that capture a foreign landscape, a different people, or architecture that is alien to me. Perhaps in another life I should have been an explorer... only I do worry whether I could cope with actual travelling.' She shook her head. 'I was terribly seasick on the one occasion I took a pleasure cruise up the Thames. Perhaps I should stick to reading about these places, and viewing their treasures in museums and galleries.'

'Ah, as Charles Kingsley so wisely said of picture-galleries, "In the space of a single room, the townsman may take his country walk… beyond the grim city-world of stone and iron, smoky chimneys, and roaring wheels, into the world of beautiful things". But there are beautiful things all about us, and we do not always have to look for magnificence in the small square of daubed paint in the fancy frame. The view across an open field, or the sight of a majestic building is, after all, the thing the artist is trying to capture with his brush. The original is always preferable to the copy.' He paused. 'Such as the face of an enchanting woman.'

So certain he couldn't possibly be referring to her, she didn't even blush but continued with her train of thought.

'And things don't have to be beautiful to be fascinating, do they?' She tipped her head to one side. 'You are hardly attractive and yet I noticed your kind eyes. Oh, and the ears. They suit you somehow, even though on another they might look ridiculous.'

The man coughed in surprise, but it quickly became a laugh. 'Do you always say aloud what you are thinking in your head?'

This time Agnes did blush, fully aware she should not have been so forthright.

'Yes.'

They both turned back to the paintings as the conversation dried up, and Agnes squinted at a smaller insignificant work labelled, 'Plantation Workers, Coorg'.

'What a charming little scene,' she said to no one in particular.

'Isn't it? The artist has somehow cleverly captured the heat of the day. I've been to those very hills because the company I work for has offices in that province,' the gentleman explained. 'We import coffee, cardamoms and cinchona – the latter vital in our ongoing fight against malaria – and all of which are grown on the hillsides there. See how lush and evergreen the land is? Far from what many imagine of India. This painting shows the harvesting of the fruit that contains the coffee beans.'

Agnes noticed the large baskets full of bright red cherries on the backs of the workers.

'That is coffee?' she exclaimed, and then sighed. 'Oh, I know so little of what I'm looking at. Book learning can only teach you so much.'

'Then without agenda or wishing to intrude, but in the spirit of friendship and education, let me be your guide. I have travelled widely and have more than a passing interest in art,' he added, as if to prove his credentials.

'That would be most welcome.'

'James Garrison Hunt Esq., at your service.' He bowed.

'Miss Agnes Humphries.'

The gallery was only two rooms and Agnes found herself wishing it was more, that perhaps one day he might accompany her to the National Gallery, or the more daring Grosvenor Gallery, and educate her further, but she was grateful for his time and over the following hour she did indeed learn much from him.

'Have you just two moments, Miss Humphries, before you depart? I have purchased the small plantation painting for you as a souvenir. If you would be so kind as to supply the gallery owner with your address, it will be delivered after the exhibition.'

'I can't accept such a gift,' she exclaimed. Would this somehow make her indebted to him? Although that wasn't an altogether unpleasant notion.

He shrugged. 'The young artist who painted it will be able to afford his lodgings this week, and perhaps buy some more oils, and you will be able to escape to India whenever you look at it. I've made two people happy for a relatively small sum.' He bowed his head. 'A pleasure to meet you, Miss Humphries. I do so hope you get to travel one day and that you don't forget the strange fellow who accosted you one sunny April afternoon.'

He bowed to take his leave and then walked up the High Street, his black top hat bobbing into the distance above the crowds, as Agnes whispered under her breath, 'Never.'

33

Stephen's first week at Burlington Square was relatively uneventful. He settled in well and largely kept in his rooms, recognising it was important not to force himself upon his fellow lodgers. Friendships were not his forte; he'd always been a loner, even though he'd grown up in a large household. Besides, he didn't want intrusive questions about his past or his fictional employment.

Not, in fact, working for a bank, the first order of the day was to travel to some part of the city where he was less likely to encounter people he knew. Sometimes he walked for a couple of hours to places like Hackney or Streatham. If the funds were available, he might even take a train further afield. When the weather was fair, he sought out nature and spent the first part of the morning in one of the parks, watching the birds start their day, and this quiet, reflective time was when he was at his most content. Growing up in the countryside had given him a deep love of nature, and bird-watching had been one of his few pleasures. He'd even collected and blown eggs for a while, but his modest yet impressive collection had been sold when money got tight.

His days were then spent either walking the streets, trying to engage with passers-by, or frequenting public houses during their daytime licensing hours, chancing his luck with the regulars. Most establishments started serving alcohol at half eleven, and his enterprises generally worked better with the more amenable and slightly intoxicated individuals.

He was not a big drinker himself, having grown up in a household where drink was considered almost certain to pave the way to hell. One of their neighbours had been rather too fond of strong liquor, and his love affair with gin brought disrepute and poverty upon his family. Stephen noticed that the more alcohol the neighbour consumed, the more talkative and less observant he became. His scheming wife took advantage of this to conduct an affair with the cooper, and unscrupulous shopkeepers often rounded up their bills, certain that he wouldn't notice. Drunk people were far too free with their tongue and far too removed from their common sense, and he'd quickly learned to use this to his advantage.

Turning his hand to a few pub tricks that he'd picked up over the years (as long as he had a pack of cards and some loose coins, he could earn a few bob), Stephen began to put the rent money aside for Agnes. Paying his landlady promptly and in full was his priority because moving to Burlington Square was the start of good things for him – he could feel it in his weary bones.

Every evening, he returned to his rooms at a time he deemed appropriate for a bank clerk to be coming home from an honest day's work. Sometimes he was greeted by a bustling Agnes, always free with her opinions but kind with her ministrations, and tried not to salivate as the wonderful smells of cooking food drifted up the stairs alongside him. The delicious aromas of roasting meat and steaming puddings were particularly tantalizing as, more often than not, he settled down to a supper of bread and butter.

He hadn't formally met any of the other lodgers yet but one evening he came across a harassed-looking young mother on the pavements, surrounded by several small children. Her expression advised him to steer clear, but he smiled, only for her to glare at him, perhaps mistaking his attempt at friendship as humour over the tantrumming child at her feet.

He glanced at his watch, from embarrassment more than necessity, and spun away as he heard the squeak of the gate leading to the basement. But as he climbed up the steps to the front door he felt a tug at his coat, and he spun round to see a small, rosy face looking up at him.

'You dropped this, mister,' the young girl said, handing him a pocket-watch.

'Thank you.' He hastily shoved the watch into his suit jacket before the little girl had a chance to comment on the engraved initials *G.K.* across the case front. The person who had owned the timepiece that morning had been a Mr King – a man who had believed himself to be better at cards than Stephen and had wagered his pocket-watch on this conviction. He wondered how Mr King would explain the loss of such a valuable heirloom to his wife that evening. Ah, one of the few benefits of being a bachelor – Stephen did not have to justify his actions to anyone. But he also did not have the pleasure of returning to a home-cooked meal after a long day, or the warm arms of a woman to crawl into at night.

'Matilda!' a voice called. 'Get in here this instant.'

He ruffled the young girl's hair and wished he had a spare penny to pass to her as thanks, but instead complimented her on her beautiful blonde curls, like sunshine, he said – which to a child meant much more.

They exchanged a smile and Stephen felt his heart lift a fraction. Miss Humphries had assured him that the residents of 23 Burlington Square were kind people. He dearly hoped so.

* * *

At the end of the first week, Stephen was woken in the middle of the night to the sound of someone rapping repeatedly on the front door below. He'd not slept particularly well, as his room was sticky and airless, and Mr King's watch informed him that it was one o'clock. Visitors at this time could only mean trouble and so he got out of bed and moved to the front window to look down at the street below. The lamplighter wouldn't be round for hours to extinguish the street lamps, and they gave off sufficient light for him to spy a semi-clad man (possibly in some sort of loin-cloth) lolling about in the back of a saloon motor car. The hood was down and Stephen could see a bottle in his hand.

Not the police then. Far from it.

The noises continued, but more muted than the knocking, as giggles and whispers floated in the hallway and swirled around outside his door. After a few minutes, he gathered his cheap terrycloth robe, to make himself more presentable should he encounter anyone, and stepped out onto the landing to investigate the commotion. Animated voices drifted up the stairs.

'... Because I was hoping for some appropriate items to complete my costume, darling, and I simply knew you'd be able to help me out. I have none of the necessary paraphernalia with me at the hotel, and the staff will hardly have a child's rattle about their person. We were this side of town to collect Neville, and you have rather hoarded things over the years, so I just knew there would be toys of Mummy's tucked away somewhere...'

'No, Clara, you are not to take her. She's too precious.' Stephen recognised Miss Humphries' voice.

There was a loud rendering of 'Three O'clock in the Morning' that was decidedly off-key, even to Stephen's non-musical ear, followed by an enormous crash and a loud groan.

'Jackie! You silly thing. Now look what you've done!'

'Will you please keep the noise down,' Stephen heard his landlady reprimand. 'You will wake my gentlemen.' There was a further pause and then a vibration up the walls as the front door was opened. 'Is that man in the motor car wearing a *baby napkin*?' The incredulous voice of Miss Humphries, whilst in more hushed tones than those of the intruders, was still loud enough for Stephen to hear, as he crept nearer to the bannisters, intrigued by the drama down below.

'Don't be such a spoilsport, dear woman,' came a well-spoken male voice. 'If you'd ever been to the old Chelsea Arts Club shebang at New Year, you would know that this is just what we do. And we do it damnably well. If you think Neville is a shocker, you should see Lily. She's dressed as some Shakespearian wet nurse and chasing people around, exposing her—'

'Jackie!' the female voice reprimanded for the second time.

Toot toot.

The cheery motor car horn was a reminder that a further member of their party was still outside.

'Frightfully sorry to get you out of bed, Aunt Ag. Must dash though. Nothing really gets going until we turn up.'

Ah, this was the wayward niece that Miss Humphries had mentioned, who had also hoped to take the rooms. Some entitled young madam, playing at life, whilst the rest of the population held down demanding jobs for little pay. He wondered what the old man in the rooms below him thought of all this noise and nonsense, and could quite see why his landlady had decided he was the preferable option.

'You may borrow the spinning top but *please* put Lady Winifred down,' Miss Humphries pleaded. 'I demand that she remains here with me.'

Stephen wondered at the nature of her niece's companions. Lady Winifred, he assumed, was as intoxicated as the rest of them.

34

Stephen finally met the young man who lived in the attics the very next morning. As he descended the final run of stairs, a pale-faced lad with sunken eyes headed up the hallway, carrying a large wooden tray. Miss Humphries had referred to him as a walking corpse on a previous occasion, and he could see what she meant.

They merely nodded in acknowledgement of each other, neither of them keen to start a conversation. Poor chap had doubtless been through the war. You somehow recognised it in others, even though Stephen had only been involved towards the end. He was in his forties by the time he was called up – the government so desperate in the last few months that they'd raised the conscription age to fifty-one – but he'd seen very little action. This chap, however, carried a look about him that suggested a mind altered by unspeakable sights. He was certainly haunted by something. Unless you'd been through it, Stephen acknowledged, you couldn't hope to understand how it crystallized the doubts you'd held before, made you want to grab life and live it – and to hell with the consequences.

He located his landlady in the kitchen and passed over his rent. She thanked him and slipped the envelope into her apron pocket.

'I must apologise for the disturbance last night,' she said. 'My niece was thrown out by her friend and is now staying at some hotel. I feel guilty for not offering her the rooms but you heard how noisy she was? She's far too wild for our little lot.'

Stephen nodded in agreement. He had no connection to the girl, but he was learning that when you showed interest in the people that others care about, they start to care about you.

'I was not overly troubled, and the sounds I heard were all jolly. What it is to be young, eh?' He smiled. 'Perhaps she will take time to consider why you didn't take her on and adjust her behaviour accordingly.'

Miss Humphries sniffed.

'I very much doubt it, but then she always was a handful, almost as though from the off she thought the world was against her and she had something to prove. Sometimes, I think those who demand attention, unwittingly courting closer scrutiny, are the ones with the most to hide.' Agnes shook her head and looked somewhat melancholy. 'Take Mr Blandford. Such an engaging fellow, but he would corner you when you had a hundred and one things to do, unaware that he was outstaying his welcome, simply because he was so desperately lonely. Drank like a parched fish – never aggressive with it, mind. But then we all have our faults, Mr Thompson, and I'm fully aware I'm too free with my opinions. I think a thing and it just comes out before I can stop it.'

'I'm afraid I don't have much time for those who consume excessive amounts of alcohol for it's a self-destructive path, but I am sorry that you lost Mr Blandford. Will he be missed by a great many people?' He was genuinely curious to know more about the man whose rooms he now occupied.

'There were no relatives to speak of, but those who knew him thought of him kindly. Generous to a fault. Whatever money he had, he either spent on drink or gave away. Although, the tragedy of his death is that I do believe he'd turned a corner. I'd made some unfortunate remark to his face a couple of months ago and an earnest conversation ensued, where he decided he would try to give up the demon liquor. Mr Gorski even put his cut-glass decanters out of sight and insisted their afternoons were conducted over a pot of tea – somewhat of a sacrifice on his part. So, I truly believe the poor man was trying to step off that path you mentioned and turn himself about.'

'Then it wasn't the drink that got him in the end?'

'I'm not sure it helped. He'd been to the Mad Hatter one evening and some generous fellow started buying him drinks. Before you could blink, he rolled clean off the sobriety wagon. When he came home that night, more pickled than a jar of walnuts, his hand was bandaged up and I remember being surprised that he'd been involved in a brawl – he really wasn't the sort. "Far from it, dear lady," he'd explained, "a complete accident". He didn't want a fuss. That was his personality – always convinced things would turn out sunny. Sadly, a nasty rash developed. Shut himself up in a darkened room and started to run a terrible fever. I tried a tincture of iodine, and eventually called the doctor out but it was too late. Blood poisoning. I hardly think the dear man knew much about it. It was over so quickly.'

Stephen was pleased Mr Blandford had not suffered for too long and deftly changed the subject; he could see Miss Humphries was struggling with painful memories.

'I've just encountered Gilbert in the hallway but I am keen to make Mr Gorski's acquaintance. Then I will have met you all. Do you think I might call on him at some point?'

The smile that spread across his landlady's face lit up her eyes and lifted the apples of her pink-tinged cheeks.

'I'm sure he'd be delighted. His mobility is poor now, due to the arthritis, and I'm always so busy, but I would happily make you both up a little tray of tea and cakes, if you could see your way to spending a bit of time with him on the occasional Sunday afternoon?'

What an unexpected bonus. Stephen had been keen to meet the man regardless, but now he was to be fed as well.

As he walked towards the front door, he wondered if his fortunes were finally reversing, and caught an unexpected tear from the corner of his eye with the back of his hand. Things had been unbearable for far too long, but his move to Burlington Square was the turning point. He just knew it.

* * *

'If you can correctly point out the ace of spades, you win the sixpence,' Stephen said with a flourish, as he dealt out five cards.

The old gentleman had previously won a penny from him for doing exactly this, and was confident in his selection, pointing to the middle card. Stephen flipped it over, knowing the man couldn't possibly win, as the ace had been dropped into his pocket moments before.

'Mine, I believe,' he said, collecting the sixpence, before nodding and taking his leave. The old man grumbled into his pint.

It was getting late and he'd had an unusually lucrative day but decided not to catch a tram back, and instead settled on walking, as the weather was so pleasant. He would treat himself to a beef pie at the public house and beg a glass of water. Three streets away from Burlington Square, and with quite the thirst on him, he stepped into the Mad Hatter.

Leaning on the bar top and eagerly awaiting his food, he caught his reflection in a large mirror that hung on the wall behind a row of brightly coloured spirits. The grey around his temples was advancing fast and he felt much older than his fifty-two years. He acknowledged how different his life might be had he fallen in love and had a family: returning home to boisterous children and a willing woman. Instead, he found himself in a backstreet pub, where the unloved and lost congregated, looking for the answers to life in the depths of their half-empty glasses.

This is where the lonely people come, he thought to himself. Several gentlemen, and fellows one might not choose to attach that label to, sat alone at shadow-draped tables, or were lined up against the bar, like himself. The landlord, engaged in conversation with a ruddy-nosed man whose shoulders bore the weight of a thousand troubles, reached out his hand to the fellow's arm in a conciliatory fashion. Even the public-house drunk has someone to share his woes with. Stephen realised he had no one.

His pie was carelessly deposited in front of him by a dour-faced woman. He scooped up the plate, but as he made for the snug he recognised Gilbert sitting at a table near the backdoor talking to a young lad. Stephen tipped his hat forward over his eyes to avoid recognition and pulled back to observe the interchange.

It was a furtive meeting. Gilbert's head was low and their voices were whispers. Occasionally, his sunken eyes scanned the room and, finally, he slipped some coins across the table before the young lad disappeared out the back. Gilbert downed what was left of his drink and stood up, making his way to the main door, and Stephen turned his face away so as not to be spotted by his fellow lodger.

Interesting, because the boy was Charlie Taylor and he was known for petty theft. Whatever Gilbert was up to with Charlie, he certainly wasn't discussing the merits of last Sunday's sermon.

35

A day of relentless rain meant Stephen returned to Burlington Square smelling of wet dog. He was glad he paid Miss Humphries to launder his shirts, even though it was money he could ill-afford. Food he could skimp on; his appearance, he could not.

He noticed a rain-spattered black umbrella with a pretty enamelled handle in the hallstand, water puddling in the metal drip tray beneath, and walked towards the kitchen, only slowing down when he heard voices.

'... If only you'd let me take the rooms, instead of some pompous banker fellow who has absolutely no connection to you or your family.'

'Mr Thompson isn't pompous – a little strange perhaps, but he's very down to earth and hardly any trouble at all. He's out all day and is as silent as the grave when he's here. I had no complaint from him when you woke everyone up in the middle of the night. Mr Gorski and Gilbert both had words with me the following day. And just look at the state of you now, Clara. You tell me you've only been up since lunchtime and I wonder how that would have gone down here. I can't have my other residents disturbed by your comings and goings. I do love you, very much, but I don't think your—' Miss Humphries paused to find the right word '—habits would be compatible with my gentlemen.'

Ah, the troublesome niece whose late-night antics had woken the household. Stephen had deliberately not complained to his landlady, being a firm believer that you should not judge others, lest you be judged yourself, and he was certainly in no place to throw stones.

'You don't understand, darling, the hotel is costing an absolute fortune. Daddy has threatened to cut me off until I toe the line, and whilst I'm not destitute, I don't have limitless funds.'

There was a deep sigh from the older woman, and Stephen heard the sound of a kitchen chair being scraped across the floor.

'Tell me what this is really all about, eh, love? I'm a good listener.'

There was a pause.

'I simply can't.'

He was curious now so shuffled silently closer to the kitchen. He could see into the room, but the table was off to the left, so he had no view of the women, just the butler sink and wooden draining board.

'I'm struggling, Aunt,' the niece said. 'The hotel has told me to be out by tomorrow as they have prior bookings, and I don't think I can face finding another. Mummy was awfully disappointed that you didn't take me in. She wanted me to be with family. The only offer I've had is from Jack Rigby.'

'You can't cohabit with a gentleman!' Miss Humphries was obviously scandalised by the notion.

There was a dry laugh. 'I'm not quite *that* daring – whatever people might think. No, the offer was to move in with a maiden aunt of his but I simply couldn't face forced conversation with some overweight, meddling, dreary old spinster with nothing better to do with her day than mind the business of others. And I certainly don't wish to be beholden to Jack.'

'If you'd come to Burlington Square, you'd still have been living with an overweight, meddling, dreary old spinster. There are a lot of us about...'

'You are not dreary,' Clara insisted, eliminating only one of the adjectives, and Stephen had to swallow a laugh.

There was silence for a while, perhaps as Miss Humphries considered her niece's perception of herself.

'It's a generous offer and Jack is a lovely young man... when he's sober. You can tell he's aristocracy – good breeding always shows – and Daphne said he's sweet on you. His father sits at the Lords, Clara, and I've been told they have a lovely estate in Somerset. Maybe it's time to settle down, get married and have some babies? I'd love to be a great aunt. And it would solve all your problems – money, housing and boredom.'

'Boredom?'

'Surely all this gallivanting about is proof that you struggle to settle to anything? You have parents wealthy enough for you not to work, and a strange determination not to marry, but running a home would give your days purpose.'

'Eurgh...'

Stephen heard the young woman groan, and assumed she'd collapsed forward on the table in her frustration as her next words were muffled. 'I knew you wouldn't understand. No one does.'

There was a further scrape of the chair and Stephen receded into the shadows as a rather glamorous slim figure sauntered across the tiled kitchen floor and collected a glass from the draining rack to fill under the tap.

'Oh, Clara Ann Goodwin, what are we to do with you?' the older woman said.

Stephen's eyes flashed wide. The sauntering figure hadn't

looked familiar but he'd known that name for much of his adult life. Surely not? She'd been perhaps twelve when he'd seen her last, but he studied her profile as she gulped back the water, and realised he knew her. The same defiant chin, the same haughty expression, and seemingly the same annoying sense of entitlement. And here he was again, facing the unjustness of a society where the accident of your birth determined your status in the world. What made this young woman more worthy of a fine house filled with servants than so many of the kind souls he'd come across in his life who'd been forced to commit desperate acts to feed their starving children or pay for the funeral of a loved one?

But it undoubtedly *was* Clara Goodwin and this was an absolute catastrophe. He clenched and unclenched his fists, and then turned around and retreated up the hallway.

Why did he feel as though every time he advanced in life, something or someone was there to push him back? Fate was a fickle mistress to resurrect someone from his past – a past he was desperately trying to leave behind. It was imperative that he never, *ever* came into contact with Agnes Humphries' niece whilst he lived at this house, or all his secrets would come spilling out and he would be well and truly undone.

36

It wasn't until the following Sunday that Stephen decided to broach the subject of Clara with his landlady. Since he'd overheard her talking to Agnes, he'd either kept himself to his rooms, or been out and about in the city, trying to earn money and pretending to hold down his fictitious banking job. He scanned the hall stand for signs of a visitor, specifically those of the young lady who might be his undoing, and wondered not for the first time who owned the abandoned top hat. When he was certain Miss Humphries was alone, he tapped on the door to the kitchens.

'Mr Thompson – how wonderful of you to pop down.'

She was sitting at the heavily scrubbed pine table, a large ceramic bowl on her wide lap, full of bright green runner beans – August was indeed a bountiful month. Each one, once relieved of its strings, was deftly sliced between the knife and her sturdy thumb, before being dropped into an aluminium saucepan on the table beside her. The almost unbearably divine smell of roasting meat drifted from the oven.

'Good afternoon, Miss Humphries. I trust you had a pleasant time at church this morning?'

'Yes, thank you, and I've been meaning to catch you to say that the young widow who also applied for the rooms is to start helping me out next week. She stopped by yesterday and I introduced her to Mr Gorski. Within ten minutes she'd got him playing that gramophone of his again – wonderful what a sweet smile and a bit of gentle persuasion can do.' Agnes gestured for Stephen to sit. 'She has lodgings nearby now, and I asked her if she still wanted to earn some extra money. The stairs are my biggest enemy at the moment. It's my knees, see?' She obligingly lifted the hems of her mid-calf skirts to display a pair of sturdy legs and swollen knees. Stephen nodded sympathetically. 'That and the laundry are starting to defeat me, but I don't want to stop offering it as it's all money. Poor Mr Gorski couldn't possibly manage if I didn't.'

It was always 'poor' Mr Gorski, he noticed. A man who had led an interesting life, by all accounts and, more than anyone else at the house, the person he was most looking forward to meeting.

'Can the young man from the attics not help? He doesn't appear to have a regular job.' He paused. 'What *exactly* does he do for a living?'

His landlady's face scrunched into a frown.

'Something to do with cameras, but it's all a mystery to me. He's taken the train to Surrey today to see a Mr and Mrs Farrington, which I understand is something to do with his work. I assume he takes portraits, but one can hardly make a living from that, especially without a studio. All he has is a dark room at the top of the house. I opened the door once and got snapped at because he was developing a film. Honestly, that boy will end up covered in mushrooms. He spends far too much time in the dark.'

'Well, if there is ever anything I can do to assist, just ask.'

'That's so kind,' she gushed. 'Perhaps you could take the tray up for Mr Gorski when I've prepared his lunch? You're a true Christian, Mr Thompson. Gilbert owns to having no faith but is a likeable lad for all that, and I hope he shall eventually come to the fold. Where do you worship? I, myself, attend All Saints.'

'St Peter's. It was closer to my previous lodgings, but I continue to attend.' He smiled.

There was something quite calming about church services, as long as the vicar wasn't one of the fire and brimstone sort. The peace and tranquillity of the setting, and the trusting and caring nature of the congregation, were a balm. He'd found a church as soon as he'd arrived in London, and a young family had invited him for afternoon tea when they'd discovered his interest in ornithology. He'd been treated to the most pleasant cakes and sandwiches, in the equally pleasant company of those who shared his bird-watching passion, but had found conversation awkward, not used to such socialising. He knew that making friends was key, even though it was not something that came naturally to him, and given that he was pretty certain God didn't exist. But he felt it was worth backing that particular horse, though – just in case.

Stephen, however, was not in Miss Humphries' kitchen to make small talk, even though his next question was dressed up as such.

'Did I see a young lady visiting the house a few days ago? Glamorous article if ever I saw one. I wondered if she might be an actress or some such? She certainly had that look about her.'

'Oh, that was my niece, Clara. The one I told you about. My sister Daphne did rather well for herself and married a wealthy landowner who has latterly become a politician. They have a modest country estate in Hexton – just outside Hitchin. Do you know Hertfordshire at all?'

Stephen shrugged without answering. Somehow it was easier than the outright lie, and he wanted to be as honest as possible with Miss Humphries from now on in. Yes, he'd deceived her regarding his profession but only because he was trying to better himself.

Some people, like Clara Goodwin, were born with more than their fair share of luck; others, like himself, were born with none.

'Beautiful views across the Chiltern Hills. I don't get to visit as often as I would like, running this place.' She swept her hand across the room. 'And my knees really aren't up to the travel.'

'And how is she? Clara, I mean. Did she find somewhere to live in the end?' He tried to steer her towards the information he sought.

Agnes Humphries sighed and returned to stringing her beans.

'She moved into a hotel, of all things, until it proved too expensive. And now she's staying with some elderly aunt of a friend, so my sister tells me, in the middle of nowhere. Can't see her lasting long sipping sedate cups of afternoon tea with some dour old lady. Still not allowed back home, and still refusing to repent her sins.'

'Oh?'

Agnes leaned forward, conspiratorially.

'I gather she was being a bit too free with some young man, if you know what I mean, and her parents discovered them together. Scandalous, really. In my day you couldn't so much as nod at someone without consequences.'

The older lady looked lost for a moment, perhaps reflecting on some young man in her own past, but soon shook herself from her reverie and whizzed her knife down each side of a bean before slicing it into the saucepan.

'That's good then, isn't it? Perhaps time away from the temptations of London will calm her down and, after a while, she can return home. For those lucky enough to possess one, family can be such a blessing.' He smiled encouragingly and tried not to look too relieved that Clara was out of the equation.

'Yes,' she agreed. 'Family is important, but I can't help but wonder if sometimes it's a mistake to put them above all else. I came very close to giving your rooms to Clara for that reason, but

I'm not sure it would have been in her interests to do so, and certainly not those of your fellow residents. Like you say, it's probably for the best. Daphne – Clara's mother – seems to think there will be an engagement soon, so my niece's life is about to take a wonderful turn.'

Stephen now had the information he sought and felt a weight lift from his troubled shoulders. Everyone deserved a second chance, and his own would be in jeopardy if Miss Goodwin was on the scene. The vicar had preached forgiveness from his pulpit that morning, and it's what he liked best about the idea of a god – that he would always be forgiven his sins. In return, he tried not to judge others, lest he be judged and found severely wanting.

Because Stephen Thompson had an awful lot of sins to forgive.

37

'Please, come in,' a heavily accented voice called through the door, and Stephen pushed it open with his free hand, balancing a tray of Sunday lunch in the other. Pleasant strains of piano and violin came from the gramophone.

He was greeted by the seated figure of an elderly man, white clouds of hair either side of his face and unnervingly sharp, almost unnaturally blue, eyes. For a moment, under this intense scrutiny, he felt that the old man knew everything. That he could see every misdeed and scheme Stephen had ever executed. But then realised how ridiculous he was being.

'Mr Gorski,' he said with a smile, 'I'm your new neighbour from the floor above, Mr Thompson.' He placed the tray on the small table.

'Pleased to meet you, young man.' A misshapen hand was stretched across the table to shake his own.

'Not so very young any more,' he joked. Stephen felt his years keenly. Most men his age were long since married, with grown up children of their own, but life hadn't worked out quite how he'd hoped. Being away for the last four years, however, had given him time to reflect. He ached for an uncomplicated life, perhaps a little house in the suburbs. Numerous housing developments were springing up on the outskirts of London. Take Welwyn Garden City, a completely new town designed to combine the advantages of urban and rural, and dispensing with the disadvantages. He'd seen pictures in magazines and newspapers of the tidy squares of lawn and uniform windows. Real communities away from the rotten stench and dishonesty of the capital. At first it had seemed an impossible dream, but during his time away he'd decided self-belief was key. When you had a plan, however unattainable it was, there was at least something to strive for. And Stephen was a quick thinker, an opportunity grabber. Unlucky, yes – but not stupid. He would put in the necessary work and it would pay off. Even the possibility of a family wasn't entirely out of the question, if he could secure a younger wife.

'Young to me,' Mr Gorski replied. 'When you get to my age, even the old seem young.' He sighed. 'Ah, to outlive all those I once knew, it is such a great pity. There is no one left from my childhood now. A shame for I have long dreamed of returning to Warsaw, to see my homeland finally independent of other nations.'

The accent was Slavic – a rather more melodic version of Russian. Stephen's ability to recognise birdsong was also useful in identifying accents, and he hoped his keen ear would stand him in good stead when he endeavoured to learn more about music from this cultured gentleman.

'What a delightful melody,' he said, gesturing to the gramophone. 'What is it?'

'Tchaikovsky. Are you a lover of the greats?'

'To be honest, sir, I know very little about such things.'

'The gentleman who had the rooms before you, God rest his soul, used to listen to my records with me every Sunday afternoon. Well, I say *listen* but the truth is more came from his mouth than entered his ears. An odd fellow but a kind one. I have never known someone hold forth for so long without taking a breath, as I rather thought that was a skill females excelled at. But I didn't mind listening to him, nor him to me. It can be quite pleasant to chat at length with someone over a glass or two of something, with the delightful strains of Beethoven in the background.'

Stephen saw his opportunity to make a new friend.

'I currently find myself without company on Sunday afternoons. I attend church in the morning but would happily join you on occasion. The company would benefit me as I am new to the area and have few friends hereabouts.'

'Do you play any instrument, Mr Thompson?' The old man looked animated all of a sudden and leaned forward in his chair.

'I do not, I'm afraid. The opportunity was denied me as a child, although it is strange how my dreams are so often flooded with pianos and sheet music, as if it were my destiny. And do call me Stephen, especially if we are to become friends.'

'Then you must call me Alexander.'

The two men shook hands and Stephen grinned from ear to ear. This was the start of something fabulous. He could feel it in his bones.

That Wednesday evening, Stephen stepped back through the door at Burlington Square after a frustrating day plying his dubious trade in Greenwich, and heard happy chatter drift down the long corridor. Miss Humphries appeared from the kitchen clutching a bottle of cheap sherry. 'Oh, Mr Thompson!' she exclaimed. 'Do come and join us. I've had a telephone call this afternoon from my sister with the news that Clara and her young man, Jack Rigby, are officially engaged. Apparently, he proposed in a nightclub, of all places. Isn't it simply wonderful?'

She disappeared into the front room, and he placed his small case by the door to take her up on the invitation. One small glass wouldn't hurt as he'd been on his feet all day, with very little financial reward for his endeavours.

'My heartiest congratulations,' he said, following her in, and hoping the impending life of marital bliss would keep the young woman away from Burlington Square, busy with babies and house-keeping.

Miss Humphries began rummaging in the long oak sideboard and he noticed Gilbert, the pale-faced lad from the attics, and a woman he could only assume was the widowed help, were also present, seated on opposite sides of the room. They were both looking awkwardly at their feet, and both doubtless ushered unwillingly into the room by an enthusiastic Miss Humphries.

'Mr Thompson, meet Mrs Mayweather – the unfortunate lady I told you about.' The pair nodded politely at each other, both embarrassed by Miss Humphries' chosen adjective.

'Mr Blandford was always partial to an afternoon sherry,' their landlady continued, going off on a tangent, 'although he only ever had the one in front of me. Most of his drinking was done at The Mad Hatter—'

'That's where I know you from,' said Gilbert, surprising everyone by speaking up. 'I knew I'd seen you somewhere before.'

'I'm not a drinker, but it is possible,' Stephen acknowledged, wondering what exactly the young man had seen, and surprised that he should own to being in the public house. He surely had more to hide. 'It was close to my previous lodgings and they do an acceptable pie.'

'Perhaps you came across Mr Blandford then?' Miss Humphries suggested. 'Jovial fellow with a head like an egg. Always wore a waistcoat in a cheery colour – red, green or a lovely mustard. Paid me several times to replace missing buttons, as the velvet often struggled with the job of securing the two sides across his expansive middle.'

'Possibly.' He rubbed at his chin. 'Now I come to think of it, it was a fellow in a burgundy waistcoat who suggested I look for lodgings in this area. He was extolling the virtues of the neighbourhood, and its convenient location not far from the parks. How strange that would be if I am now in his rooms.'

Gilbert narrowed his eyes but Agnes finally located the glasses and the conversation moved on.

'These were my mother's.' She briefly held two aloft. 'I was only twelve when she died, but I always remember her as a happy lady, and feel connected to her when I use the things she owned. Perhaps she even celebrated her own engagement with these very ones.' She smiled to herself as the cork came out with a pop. The dark brown sherry was poured into four of the delicate trumpet-shaped glasses and handed around.

A pink flush came to Gilbert's cheeks as he mumbled something about being certain she was in the room, watching over them all. Miss Humphries, somewhat mollified, beamed and lifted her glass aloft.

'To Clara and Jack,' she said, as everyone else raised their glasses accordingly. 'And to marriage. May that poor lost girl finally be happy.'

'To marriage,' Stephen toasted in reply. Whilst he had never taken a wife himself, he did not doubt it was a perfectly reasonable thing to do, should one be so inclined.

'To *happy* marriage,' Mrs Mayweather muttered, adding a qualifier to the toast, and not meeting the eye of anyone else in the room.

'Daphne informs me there is to be a celebration in Hertfordshire this coming weekend. You were indeed correct, Mr Thompson

– a brief period of reflection has done wonders. Clara has been welcomed back to the bosom of her family and all her sins forgiven.'

'How wonderful. Shall you go?' he asked.

'Me? Oh no, I couldn't possibly leave Mr Gorski.'

'We can look after him,' Gilbert said, from across the room. 'You *should* go. You never get the chance to go anywhere.'

Miss Humphries shook her head, as though brushing the ridiculous notion aside, and Stephen realised the poor woman was tied to Burlington Square and wondered if she ever had the opportunity to leave.

'It would be my pleasure to spend time with him in the evenings,' he offered.

'And I can cook the meals. You know I'm a competent cook,' Mrs Mayweather said.

'Perhaps just for the one night...' Everyone in the room could see she was wavering.

'Please,' Stephen put his hand out to her shoulder. 'Let us do this for you. Be with your family and celebrate your niece's engagement. I feel certain we can pull together and keep things running.'

He looked to the others for support, and they both nodded in agreement. These *were* nice people, he realised. Strange and definitely hiding things, just like himself, but nice, and he liked being surrounded by kindness. It had been missing from his life for so long. Besides, it would give him the chance to bond with his fellow housemates, and even the young widow.

'I must remember to keep today's newspaper,' Miss Humphries said, slumping down onto the old sofa with a contented look across her face. 'The date of Clara's engagement is certainly a day I want to remember.'

38

THE PILE OF DUSTY NEWSPAPERS

Thomas Humphries took The Times every day, which pleased his oldest daughter, as she liked to keep up with world events, even if she was not much a part of anything outside her front door.

'Let's see what's going on in the printed pages today, Aggie,' he would say, before shaking the newspaper and peering at the tiny lettering through his spectacles.

For Agnes, like all women whose days were filled with the monotony of cooking, cleaning and laundry, any diversion was welcome, be it snatches of gossip from the neighbour over the railings, or the salacious scandals printed in The Times. Yesterday's news was then either used to light fires or, as money became increasingly tight, torn into squares, threaded together in a bundle, and hung on a hook in the outside privy. She was all for making economies where they could, especially if it meant Daphne didn't have to go without.

But Agnes kept certain editions back, in a pile next to the mirror of her dressing table. She liked the idea that notable national and international events were happening in the wider world beyond her doorstep on the days that she wanted to remember for personal reasons. Yes, it may have been the day the philosopher Karl Marx passed away, but it was also the day that a wobbly eighteen-month-old Daphne took her first steps.

A few weeks after her trip to the Bayswater gallery, she decided to skim through the morning newspaper at the kitchen table, before setting it on the tray with her father's soft-boiled eggs and cold herring. Inadvertently, she stumbled across a James Hunt Esq. of Palmer and Drayton's listed amongst the guests at a lavish charity ball held the previous weekend. Immediately, she knew this was *her* James – hers in her head alone since he'd gifted her the painting, even though she doubted that he'd given the strange outspoken girl another thought after their parting. She recalled his kind manner, extensive knowledge of the world, and those endearing ears. Seldom given the opportunity to associate with young men, their afternoon together had been somewhat of a novelty for her and she dearly wished to repeat the experience. The company of her elderly father and demanding eight-year-old sister could be trying at the best of times – regardless of how much she loved them both.

Palmer and Drayton's, she discovered, were based in Leadenhall Street, which was quite some distance from home, but on a couple of occasions she took buses to that part of the city in the hope he might be found conveniently walking into the building as she passed. But, of course, he never was.

It was, in fact, nearly four months later, when she'd dragged a complaining Daphne to the National Gallery, for want of something better to do on a rainy November afternoon, that *he* found *her*. She was sitting on one of the wooden chairs, supplied for the viewing comfort of the public, admiring the *Arnolfini Portrait*. Daphne was beside her, complaining that her feet hurt. If only Mr Hunt were here, Agnes mused, he could explain the significance of the dog, the oranges on the windowsill and the solitary burning candle on the chandelier – for she was certain there was a hidden meaning behind these items. As though her thoughts had summoned him, she heard her name called from across the room.

'Miss Humphries!'

Not one for the giddy foolishness of her contemporaries, she was alarmed to find her heart did indeed flutter and a breathlessness came over her that she really couldn't explain.

'Oh, my goodness. It's the kind man with the ears,' she exclaimed, without thinking, and then immediately clasped her hand to her mouth.

He grinned in response. 'Do you know so very many men unfortunate enough not to have a pair of these auditory appendages, then?' he asked.

She smiled back. 'I think you understood my meaning well enough. Apologies though, I'm not blessed with the gift of circumspection, but I'm thrilled our paths have crossed again.' The smile across her face could not have been more effusive. 'I have been looking out for you since we met, and even saw a report of you in the newspaper, and established that you work for the importer Palmer and Drayton.'

Daphne shoved her big sister in the shoulder and muttered under her breath, 'Don't own to that, you silly goose. It makes it look as though you were hunting him down.' She was consistently mortified by Agnes's embarrassing frankness, and had even refused to have playmates to the house after her sister had commented that her friend Vera was a singularly churlish girl. To her face.

'I was though, wasn't I?' Agnes replied, true to form. 'And now I've found him.' And she turned to Mr Hunt. 'I was so touched by the gift of the coffee plantation painting that I—'

'Please, there's no need to explain. I was a fool not to ask for an address so I could call on you, or leave you my card and arrange another meeting, but sometimes these things can come across as indelicate, and my future was unsettled at the time. Instead, I have been visiting local exhibitions and the National Gallery – avoiding the stuffy portraits and altarpieces, naturally—' he grinned at her '—in the hope of bumping into you once more. So, I have also been hunting, Miss Daphne.' He smiled at the young girl by Agnes's side. 'Although I seem to have been more successful than your sister...'

Agnes kept the newspaper from that day, with its unfortunate headline about the Whitechapel murders, because after a lengthy tour of the gallery, Mr James Garrison Hunt Esq. asked Agnes if she would step out with him. And Agnes had willingly agreed.

39

In the end, Agnes Humphries travelled up to her sister's for two nights. Although reluctant at first to accept the help of others, (as kind people often were, Stephen noticed in his long and troubled life), when the decision had finally been made, she had a spring in her step and a twinkle about her eyes. Even her knees began to behave themselves.

The people at 23 Burlington Square all took to their respective roles in earnest. The young widow made sure Alexander had trays delivered to his room three times a day, laden with good home-cooked food. Because she was working shifts at Pemberton's, Gilbert took him up sandwiches for lunch, although with conversation not his forte, Stephen understood he didn't stay for long. Stephen then spent his evenings with the old man, listening to the gramophone and learning about a world of music and privilege he could only dream of.

On the Sunday, the young widow knocked on Alexander's doors with a roast lunch, not long after Stephen had arrived to check on him. (Apparently, she'd also made some sort of nut cutlet for Gilbert, such was her kindness.) He gestured for the old man to eat, and received a grateful nod in return. Mercy, who had now insisted Stephen call her by her Christian name, had thoughtfully cut the meal up for his new friend, he noticed.

'I do so hope Miss Humphries is making the most of her nights away,' Alexander said.

'She seems mightily relieved her niece is settling down at last. The timing was never right for me to marry, but perhaps it's not too late. We shall see,' Stephen mused.

Mercy collected a napkin from a freshly laundered pile on the sideboard.

'I understand you lost your husband?' he ventured. He guessed that she was in her late twenties, and was a very attractive woman, if somewhat skinny. She still wore her wedding band, but so many women continued to wear their rings after losing husbands in the war. At the mention of marriage, a petrified look flashed across her delicate features.

'Yes, I lost him on a battlefield in 1918...' Mercy said, choosing her words carefully. She looked uncomfortable and he instantly regretted being so nosy.

'I'm sorry.'

'Not at all. We lived on neighbouring farms and it was always assumed by both sets of parents that we would wed and combine the lands, merrily producing offspring for generations to come. But I have been grieving too long for things that will never be, so decided a fresh start was best. It was all so very... cruel,' she finished.

'You're young. You could marry again?' Stephen said.

'No.' Her head shook firmly from side to side, and she cast her eyes to her clasped hands. 'No, that won't happen.'

'Oh, what a tragedy.' Alexander joined in the conversation between mouthfuls. 'You have such a good heart – I can sense these things. I thought I would never get over my first love, but I found another. It wasn't the same, but it was a love of sorts. And it is better to be with someone, than to spend a lifetime alone.'

She shook her head. 'It takes time to work through grief, and I have done that now. Since coming to London, I can truly say that I am the happiest I've been in many years. I want nothing more from life, and certainly not another husband.' There was such a determined look on her face that Stephen thought she must have loved him very much.

'How sad, then, that you did not have children,' Alexander continued. 'They would have been a blessing at least. My wife was not able to conceive and carried that burden always, even though I never felt any resentment towards her because of it.'

With the old man's words, Mercy burst into tears and took a step back towards the door. 'I'm so sorry. Please excuse me.' She almost ran from the room, leaving them both slightly embarrassed.

'Oh, goodness. I should not have said anything. I am an old fool who does not know when to keep quiet.'

Stephen patted his knotted hand.

'It's not your fault. You were trying to help, but I guess there's a tale in there somewhere. We shouldn't have pushed her. Perhaps she lost a baby, or they weren't together long enough. Sad though, I believe she would have made an excellent mother.'

'I agree.' The old man nodded.

'And you would have made an excellent father. I feel sure of that, too.'

There was an awkward pause and Stephen regretted his words for the second time. It had been a natural continuation of the conversation, but it was wrong of him to talk in such a familiar way when their friendship was so new.

'I am a father,' Alexander said, 'but I think I will very much be needing a glass of something stronger than tea to tell that story. If you can spare the time, and do not mind if I continue to eat, I will share my sorry tale.'

Stephen nodded, so the old man waved his hand at the walnut sideboard where two bulbous decanters stood, side by side, the glass etched with ferns. Both had silver labels hanging around the bottlenecks on chains – one proclaimed Madeira and the other port.

'Pour two glasses of the Madeira, if you will. The glasses are in the cupboard underneath. I can remember a time when it was very much the done thing to offer a gentleman a sherry and a biscuit when they called at your home, and I rather acquired a taste for it, even though everyone expects me to prefer the vodka of my homeland.'

'I am not really a drinker, so just a small one for me.'

'You are not a club man?'

'Although my profession might suggest such, I was not born into the gentleman class. I am not from money and do not have the necessary connections.'

'Ah, but I know many gentlemen. I could make the necessary introductions for you?'

'Perhaps,' Stephen said, non-committally, as he found two small glasses and placed them on a silver tray. The stopper clinked as he removed it, followed by a satisfying *glug, glug, glug* as the rich, amber-coloured liquid streamed from the decanter. A sweet scent lingered in the air. He wasn't used to such luxuries, but was certainly not adverse to experiencing them in moderation. One small glass would not hurt any more than the communion wine he took of a Sunday. He handed Alexander his sherry and copied the old man's actions, swirling the liquid around and inhaling the aroma, even though he didn't know what exactly it was his olfactory senses were seeking.

'And what hits the nose for you?' Alexander asked in his slightly broken English.

'Coffee?' he hazarded. 'Caramel?'

He copied Alexander again and took a sip.

'And for the mouth?'

Stephen focussed. Would he make himself look ignorant if he gave the wrong answer? Was there a wrong answer? He closed his eyes and tried to pick out the subtle flavours.

'Maybe chocolate? Dates?'

'Excellent. Excellent. You have a fine palate, sir.' A small smile rested across Alexander's lips. Stephen was pleased to see him happy. He knew that pain was a constant companion for his new friend so to distract him from that for a moment was an achievement. 'Now, where were we?' He gestured for Stephen to return to his seat.

'Talking about children, but I should not have made such a personal observation,' he said, settling back into his chair.

'Not at all. I did have a child, and I think about him often, especially now the years are slipping away. I wonder what he might look like, and what he has done with his life, and I am sad that I never got to meet him.'

'But, I thought you said your wife—'

'The child was from before my marriage. The mother was someone I knew when I was younger. Someone I was not married to. Does that shock you?'

Stephen shook his head. It happened all the time. It wasn't talked about. But it happened.

'It was long before I found fame with my music, when I was just a student in Germany. We were young and in love, and simply got carried away without a thought for the consequences.' He chuckled. 'You know how it is when blood runs hot and the head is ignored? Ah—' he waved a dismissive hand '—we knew it was wrong but the plan was always to marry. She was my first and, I truly believed, would be my only.'

Stephen took a sip from his glass and adjusted himself in the chair.

'This isn't something you must feel obliged to share. I didn't intend to pry.'

Alexander shrugged. 'I find myself wanting to talk about it more in recent years. I shut it away for too long. My wife knew about the child, but it was not something she was ever prepared to discuss. When she died, however, I unlocked the door to those memories.'

Alexander knocked back his drink in one and carefully placed his empty glass on the low table before him, hindered by his misshapen hands. Stephen then watched as he struggled to chase a piece of roast potato around the plate with his spoon.

'The girl's name was Alina, and she had a twin sister, Erna. They were not alike at all in either looks or temperament, but very close. I met them towards the end of my studies in Leipzig as the family owned a café I frequented in the city. Alina was the quieter of the two, and the one who captured my heart with her shy smile. I knew her social class and nationality would be difficult for my family to accept, and I was shortly to tour Europe for a year with an orchestra, so we delayed any engagement but promised to remain true to each other during my absence.'

He paused for a moment, and they were both aware the tale was to take a more melancholy turn.

'We decided not to correspond, as I would be constantly on the move, and a year did not seem so very long. I would have more money upon my return, my career would be secure, and we could marry. But when I finally returned, I could not find my Alina. The café had changed hands and the family had moved. Neighbours told me that one of the sisters had died abroad, yet I knew nothing of them travelling. It didn't make sense. No one was certain which sister had passed away and I prayed, rather unfairly, that it was Erna. But later found out it was not. It was Alina. And she had died alone in London.'

The pain across the old man's face left Stephen at a loss at what to do or say. Comforting others was not his strength. Was this a moment for a conciliatory pat of his companion's arm? Or a time to offer platitudes? He was unsure and so did neither, hoping his expression conveyed his sympathies.

'To cope with the grief, I threw myself into my career and toured the world, giving concerts and composing pieces. I let the pain of losing her come through my music – perhaps it even made me a better player.' He shrugged. 'And then, because of my growing fame, Erna was able to track me down. She confronted me several years later, shaking with anger, to ask why I'd abandoned Alina in her time of need. Why had I ignored her sister's letter, she asked, written to tell me she was coming to England? I was shocked. I had received no such correspondence, and do not know to this day what happened to it.'

He shuffled uncomfortably in his high-back chair, his wrinkled face scrunching up and his bright eyes misting over.

'She had missed me by two weeks apparently, and yet I *still* did not understand her desire to seek me out, until her sister turned my world upside down and told me there had been a child. Frightened of her family's judgement, I can only think my poor Alina was hoping to legitimise our union, but the child came early and there were complications. She survived for only two days after the birth…'

Alexander's intensity was overwhelming to Stephen. He felt awkward around emotional people, and rubbed his hands nervously together, able to understand his companion's distress but not able to alleviate it. He had decided to befriend this vulnerable old man, hoping his companionship might offer Alexander some compensation for the loss of Mr Blandford, but the level of intimacy required for such a friendship was alien to him.

'I'm sorry,' was all he could muster.

'No, I'm a silly old man to keep dredging this up. I can't change the past by talking about it. The Polish are a proud people and my father would have seen this as weakness, but age and loneliness break down defences.' Alexander wiped wet cheeks with his twisted knuckles and a few moments of reflection for both the men followed. 'Tell me about your family?'

Stephen shook his head. It would take time before he told his story – he needed to know his companion better. There was a definite order to these things.

'I will tell you about them another day. For now, let us lose ourselves in beautiful music. Miss Humphries says there are gramophone records of you playing the piano from before the war?'

The old man smiled, his melancholy temporarily forgotten, his twinkle restored.

'Ah, yes, at Maiden Lane, Covent Garden. I visited there several times. On the turntable is a disc of me playing a Grieg piano concerto – a little fast to the trained ear, but we had to fit the entire performance on one wax disc, so we often upped the tempo. You will have steadier hands to change the needle. It is such a fiddly task for my useless fingers.' He gestured to the large wooden gramophone near the window and they settled down to a pleasant afternoon together, where the old man offered to teach him cribbage.

Stephen was pleased Alexander had trusted him. Soon he would share his tale and he was both nervous and excited by the prospect.

40

Miss Humphries returned to Burlington Square late on the Sunday and told Stephen that she was planning a thank you meal the following evening, should he be free, for all at the house who had kept things ticking over during her absence.

'I'll get a nice piece of brisket from the butcher, and I shall cook it long and slow. Mercy suggested the recipe. She's a good cook, that woman, and has even pepped up some of my vegetarian recipes for Gilbert. Mr Gorski has my father's large mahogany dining table in his rooms, and has said we may all eat there. Meeting you and the young Mercy – who I rather think he's taken a shine to – has perked him up no end since the death of Mr Blandford. I hope you can make it. It will be like a real family gathering.'

The thought of the brisket made his mouth water, but his pockets feel empty. However, appearances were important.

'How lovely. I should be delighted to attend and to hear all about your visit. Add it to my bill and I will have a modest lunch at the bank so as not to spoil my appetite.'

'I wouldn't dream of it,' Agnes said. 'After everything you did for me, enabling me to celebrate such an auspicious occasion with my sister. There will be plenty and I appreciate the time you're spending with Mr Gorski. It's lovely to hear his music drifting down the stairs again.'

Everyone duly gathered Monday evening at seven o'clock on the first floor, although Miss Humphries passed on Gilbert's apologies. He was to eat in his rooms. He was shy, she said, and particularly so if there was to be an attractive young lady present. Mercy went quite pink and studied her cutlery in undue detail.

'Don't be embarrassed, dear,' Agnes said, patting her hand. 'Nine years is a long time to be on your own and you have such a pleasing face. I know it's difficult to get more than two sentences out of him, unless you want to hear about cameras and exposure times, but he does have lovely manners. He is only two years your junior. Age is no barrier to love.'

It was, Stephen thought, rather a jump on his landlady's part to matchmake these two quiet people, based purely on their age. Mercy was running her hands nervously around the edge of the table as light from the long sash window fell across its highly polished surface, catching the wisps of rising steam from the tureens of vegetables. He could barely contain the saliva in his mouth.

'How did you find your niece?' Stephen asked, to change the conversation and spare the poor girl further blushes.

'Surprisingly subdued.' Miss Humphries lumped herself down in her chair now that the meat had been distributed. 'I appreciate none of you know her, but she is usually quite the social butterfly. Perhaps she's finally ready to settle down. Still smoking like a chimney, mind, but none of her usual *joie de vivre*, and did not come across as an excited fiancée. That young man of hers, on the other hand, looked like the cat that got the cream, and talked non-stop about his plans for the future. Bit of a show-off to my mind, but when you have money, I suppose you're entitled to flaunt it.' She shrugged. 'Everyone should have someone in their life who looks adoringly at them like young Jack looks at our Clara.' She paused. 'And yet the whole thing doesn't sit right with me somehow. The light has gone out of her.'

'Marriage can do that to people,' Mercy said, her voice barely audible. 'I'm glad for her that she had some time to enjoy her youth. I married far too young. It is only now that I'm beginning to realise what I want from life.'

'They do say marry in haste, repent at your leisure,' Stephen chimed in, scooping up mouthful after mouthful of the most delicious food, and wondering if he could reach for more carrots without appearing greedy. He must be careful with all this rich food after so many years of such simple fare.

'Oh, I don't know,' Miss Humphries said, 'I've been able to do what I choose without the need to consult with a husband for decades now and it's not always a blessing. Sometimes it would have been nice to have decisions taken out of my hands or, at least, someone to share the decision-making with.'

'And yet,' Alexander said, 'I will regret to my dying day, that I decided to wait before marrying. The reasons were sound but the outcome most tragic.'

Everyone was silent for a moment, even Mercy, who if she hadn't heard Alexander's tale from his own lips had likely heard a version of it from Miss Humphries.

'Will it be a long engagement?' Stephen finally asked, to break the silence.

'Reginald, my brother-in-law, is pushing for a Christmas wedding, but Clara seems in no hurry.' She shook her head. 'The Rigbys may be rich beyond my imagination, but I don't believe that matters a jot to Clara. If only I believed she was marrying for love. Happiness is far more important than wealth.'

He felt a surge of momentary sympathy for his landlady. Her

sister had made a fortuitous match and elevated herself socially and financially, and the subsequent privileged lifestyle was all the niece had ever known. But poor Miss Humphries was alone and struggling to make ends meet. His beginnings were even more humble and he was beginning to doubt that he would ever escape his background. How was that fair?

'Clara's side of the church will be quite bare. We are such a small family. Do you have family, Mr Thompson?' She was understandably curious as to her new lodger and put down her cutlery.

'Not real family. Perhaps there is something about blood ties that bind you tighter, make you more forgiving and loving to another person, because the people who brought me up were strict and not particularly kind. As for a wife, there were a few ladies before the war but I was concentrating on my profession, thinking I had plenty of time, and then other things got in the way.'

Buoyed by the good company and learning to relax and enjoy the moment, Stephen realised that he liked being part of this disparate group of people. He had connected with them in order to improve his circumstances, but found when you let others in, good things happened.

An idea occurred to him. September was almost upon them and the forecast for the next few days was fine.

'I will not be at the bank from tomorrow until next Saturday. Their holiday allocation is most generous so I have taken four days' leave, and I have no plans to travel anywhere so wondered if I could be of any assistance to you at Burlington Square, or take Mr Gorski on some walks hereabouts?' He reverted to the older man's surname because his deferential landlady always addressed him as such.

'There are some tea chests that need moving in the spare room,' Miss Humphries ventured.

'And I should be delighted to get outside again,' said Alexander.

'I have felt myself stagnating, trapped between these four walls, and I rather think it has been affecting my mood.'

'Excellent,' Stephen said, nodding his head and reached for the carrots, 'then I will be at your disposal.'

* * *

The last day of August was a bright sunny day and Stephen flung back his curtains to a splendid vista. Higher than the treetops, he had a beautiful panoramic view of their tiny part of London and knew he was lucky to be at Burlington Square; he'd never lived anywhere this grand in his life. The rich architectural history of the capital was somehow easier to appreciate from above, as there was never the space to stand back far enough when one was scuttling along the crowded pavements.

The thing that he loved most about this view was the trees; a solitary ash, rows of sturdy plane trees and occasional willowy silver-barked birches. Homes to his most favourite of creatures – the birds. They were the only animal that truly had no boundaries, transcending the sea and the land. Even wild horses were confined by the landscape – the rivers and seas. Ever since he was a small boy, he'd had an overwhelming desire to escape, and towards the heavens was the only direction he desired to go.

It was the red-breasted robin that Stephen related to most. Solitary and territorial, it was an adaptable bird, making its nest wherever it could. He recalled a pair of robins raising their brood in an abandoned boot in the yard when he was young. How many times had he set up a new nest in his own life? Burlington Square was where he would roost for now, but who knew what the future held.

Ten minutes later he was wrestling Alexander down the stairs, as Miss Humphries stood in the hallway, wringing her hands and muttering 'careful' under her breath. The arthritis made walking any distance almost impossible for the old man, although he managed to potter about his rooms, clutching the backs of chairs, or occasionally using a walking cane. Some days were better than others, with the cold, wet weather seemingly increasing the pain and swelling. (Miss Humphries had once mentioned that Mr Gorski could predict coming storms in his joints.) The gentle heat of the late summer day was therefore in their favour, and finally, he was settled into the wicker Bath chair that Stephen had parked on the pavement outside. Their landlady tucked a thin blanket over his knees, insisting that despite the temperatures, Alexander needed to be mindful of chills.

Alexander put a twisted hand up to his eyes to shield them from the sun. They paused for a channel green coupe to whizz past, overflowing with drunken partygoers in an assortment of costumes.

'In many ways it only seems like yesterday that I was gallivanting about Europe, perhaps not with the same gay abandon as these Bright Young Things, but avant-garde in my way. My music was surprisingly daring for its time.' Alexander watched the motor car disappear around the corner.

Stephen had read about this privileged set of people who were always in the press for their increasingly outrageous – and occasionally illegal – revelry. The public could not get enough of their wild night-time treasure hunts through the city and the scandals that followed. He understood from Miss Humphries that Clara Goodwin was hanging on the coat-tails of these people, although he suspected that her activities had been curtailed since the engagement.

'I imagine you have travelled widely and mixed with some interesting people?' he said to his elderly friend.

'Indeed. There was a time when I was in a different European city every month, but I eventually settled in London because Alina was buried here. Later, I married an Englishwoman, and travelled the world with my music until my body started to let me down. Now I find myself alone again, and all I leave behind are my melodies.'

'That's more than I will leave behind. Your music will live on after your death.'

Alexander chuckled. 'And yet my father never approved. He wanted me to become a doctor, like him, but my mother was musical and persuaded him to let me follow my dream. Did you know that my most successful composition was a popular Christmas carol?'

He started to hum a tune Stephen instantly recognised.

'You wrote that?' he asked in awe. 'It's beautiful.'

Stephen gently lowered the wheels of the chair down the kerbstone and crossed to the gardens.

'Beautiful and surprisingly lucrative. Ah, wealth is all very well but when you have no one to share it with, it's of little consequence. Because my wife and I were not blessed with children and were never extravagant people, much of it still remains. Nathaniel Blandford and I had been discussing the merits of various charitable establishments when...' His voice tailed off. 'A weak man to let the drink control him so, but I do miss him terribly.'

'Money isn't everything,' Stephen ventured.

'I agree. Music was my *rację bytu* – the reason for my existence.'

'I'm not musical but I appreciate the melodies found in nature. My favourite being birdsong.'

'Ah, yes, many of us have taken inspiration from birds. Take Beethoven's Sixth. The flute as the piping nightingale, the plucky cuckoo from the clarinets, and the oboe delivering a delightful rendition of the quail.'

Alexander started to hum a tune under his breath and wave his hands in the air. All Stephen could see from his vantage point behind the chair, as his friend conducted an imaginary orchestra, was the balding head of the old man, wisps of beard from his cheeks, and the two misshapen hands fluttering about before him, like autumn leaves toyed by the breeze. He couldn't see Mr Gorski's face, but he just knew his eyes would be closed.

They entered the gardens and passed an elderly couple seated on one of the wooden benches to their left. Stephen nodded a hello. They smiled as their eyes followed the pianist's gesticulations, and he smiled too. One person's happiness was surprisingly infectious and the following hour he spent in the old man's company was one of the most pleasant mornings he'd had for some considerable time. His heart was full of hope for a brighter future. God had surely pardoned his sins and his slate had been washed clean. It was now a shiny black and ready for him to take up the chalk and make his mark.

But as he left the gates of the gardens and crossed the road back towards the house, he noticed a figure standing on the corner of the Square. The man tipped his hat forward to shield his eyes, but it was too late. Stephen was almost certain that he recognised him, and that meant they were watching.

41

THE TAXIDERMY CANARY

Agnes was perhaps only three or four when her father brought Sunny the canary home. Her mother had been unwell for months, often laying across the sofa in the front room during the day as her daughter amused herself on the floor. The distraction of the bright yellow bird, with his feverish song, gave them both something to focus on, and Agnes a companion to talk to when her mother fell asleep – as she often did.

Sunny had the most melodious voice. A Norfolk canary, her father said, with his distinctive stocky shape and large head. He was kept near the front room window and spent all of his nine years looking out over Burlington Square, yet was never allowed to soar into its clear blue skies. Agnes wondered if he could see his fellow feathered friends flitting from tree to tree and ached to join them. Did he even realise his liberty had been denied him? Or was he content in his ornate mahogany cage – a pretty prison that kept him safe from predators but limited his freedom? But then Burlington Square had become her cage in many ways, and she had not minded either.

'Sunny is lonely,' Agnes announced, when she was eight years old. 'He needs another canary to play with.'

'They are solitary birds,' her father said. 'If I was to give him a companion, they would fight. He has your mother.' But Agnes could not imagine how any creature on God's earth could be content without a companion of its own kind. And yet her mother had an undeniable bond with him. She could call him to sit on her finger, and he would swoop down and tip his tiny lemon head to one side, as if he was hanging on her every word.

Barely a year after her mother had passed away, Agnes entered the front room to find a small bundle of feathers on the bottom of the cage. Pieces of her mother were drifting away from her and she couldn't bear it, so her father took the tiny body to a local taxidermist, even though Agnes was never sure she liked the idea of preserving a corpse. The inanimate eyes were made of glass and followed her about the room, seeing everything from that moment on – how a young Daphne would snap at her sister for perfectly reasonable requests, and how hard Agnes would cry afterwards. How an exhausted Agnes would flop across the sofa of an evening, sometimes too tired to even mount the stairs. How her father returned from work, gently kissed his sleeping daughter, and carried her up to bed.

Those shiny black beads also witnessed the late November day Mr James Hunt Esq. called at Burlington Square to formally introduce himself to Thomas Humphries. They noticed the acceleration of Agnes's heartbeat as she studied the engaging young man opposite, how her cheeks flushed pink when her darling father referred to her as his rock, and how James studied the earnest and open face of the forthright young girl sitting across from him, as though she were the most interesting and beautiful thing in the world.

'You want to walk out with Agnes?' her father repeated, leaning forward slightly aggressively. 'Confound it man, she's barely eleven years old.' He turned to his daughter. 'Honestly, Helena, I should chase the fellow from the house with a walking cane.'

She held his shaking hands in hers, understanding that his mind increasingly took him to a time when his wife was alive, and was grateful that these fleeting visits were to happy moments in his life, if nothing else. After a few sips of his tea, she knew he would come back to her, and it would be as though his mind had never strayed. But these muddled moments were concerning and she knew that it was time to get a physician involved – with or without his approval.

When it was time for James to leave, her father escorted him out to the hallway. Agnes remained behind, her heart fit to burst, and moved to the window, in anticipation of watching her young man depart, when the door to the room was swung open again.

'I forgot my—'

'I love you,' she said, as though she had realised this irrefutable fact at just that moment and saw no point in pretending her feelings were otherwise.

'I know,' he said, his eyes never leaving hers, as he took four long strides across the room and swept her into his arms. There was a moment when neither of them moved. His eyes pinned her as surely as the lepidopterist pins the small tortoiseshell to his board, and her hands, draped over his high shoulders, carried a current of warmth from her fingertips to her toes, stopping at every station in between, and firing up parts of her body with such intense heat, she thought she might combust.

Eventually their lips moved closer, quarter of an inch at a time, until she allowed his mouth to press against hers, boldly, briefly and unbelievably intensely.

And Sunny witnessed that too.

42

_____

After so many years away, both as a consequence of the war and then circumstances beyond his control, Stephen had returned to his childhood home and tried to slot back in, but had quickly realised he no longer belonged with these people. He was different to them; a loner – a carrion crow. Intelligent yet solitary, he scavenged to survive, until London beckoned – not because the streets were paved with gold, but because the people on those streets wouldn't recognise him. He could reinvent himself. Start again. Stephen Thompson could be anyone he wanted – even a bank clerk.

There had been few people in his life who had really mattered, and he was starting to wonder if he'd missed out by separating himself from others. The friendship with Alexander, for example, was becoming increasingly important, even though he worried the old man might not have many years left. The walk they'd shared around the square together had been more enjoyable than he'd anticipated and he desperately wanted to further befriend the heartbroken, world-famous pianist, whose life was so empty now, and whose joys were few. What might make the old man happy? he considered. Something that reminded him of his homeland? A meal out in a fancy restaurant? A music-related experience?

'Do you still get the opportunity to attend concerts?' he asked, on the second outing they undertook, later that same week, as September elbowed her way in and he continued the pretence that he was on holiday from his fictional employment.

He'd wheeled Alexander further afield this time, venturing out into the neighbourhood, which the old man seemed to enjoy, as he pointed to various front doors claiming to know the residents. Pianists, it seemed, often got invited to dinner – or at least they had when their legs had worked properly.

'Ah, not for many years. When I first came to Burlington Square I persuaded Miss Humphries to accompany me to one or two local recitals, but it's impossible to undertake such a journey now. Instead, I have the pleasure of my records, and recently acquired some of the London Symphony Orchestra's recordings.' He sighed. 'But it is not the same as being in a concert hall. There are the subtlest of differences each time a work is performed, and I take great pleasure in listening out for them.'

'Classical music isn't something I know very much about,' Stephen admitted. 'Although I look back on my life now and realise there has always been an invisible force pulling me to the musical over, for example, the written word. Hearing an uplifting melody does something to your very soul, doesn't it?'

'It *is* my very soul,' Alexander answered. 'As essential to me as my heartbeat.'

'Perhaps if I had been brought up in a more musical family... Ah, who knows,' Stephen lamented.

'It is never too late to start an appreciation of music. The joy of being at a concert cannot be counted in pounds, shillings or pence. Your heart rate slows and your worries ebb away. I firmly believe I feel the pain of my arthritis a little less when Chopin or Beethoven are in the room with me – their melodies flowing through my veins. Music is a very healing thing.'

Stephen understood completely.

'This is exactly how I feel about my birds. Observing them flit from tree to tree, wade about in a lake, or glimpsing a silhouette soar in the sky above me, I feel more at peace. Look... sparrows.'

He stopped the Bath chair, and both men had a moment of silent contemplation, observing the scene ahead of them. The nearest of the plane trees that lined the street they were on had a host of sparrows gathered on the lower branches.

'Tell me something of them?' Alexander asked.

'They are a communal bird,' Stephen said. 'And quite a pretty one, with all those shades of brown. Their vilification has always seemed unjust to me, with sparrow clubs awarding annual prizes to those who can kill the most, just because they are so prevalent.'

He'd understood little of his friend's musical talk, but birdlife was a topic he was sure of. His polite interest in music was now being reciprocated – a verbal game of tennis. Alexander Gorski was clearly a man who knew how to make friends. Stephen began to push the chair forward and the birds dispersed.

'We are rather lucky to see these sparrows because many have flown to areas with hedges and farmland to feast on the glut of seeds and grains by now. August was a month for recovery and recouperation in the bird world, especially for the autumn migrants, who have many thousands of miles of flight ahead of them.'

'What a shame we do not extend this courtesy to our own species. I gather the poor woman in the basement is expecting again, and Miss Humphries has been quite free with her opinions in this regard.'

The men exchanged a look, Alexander twisting in his chair and looking up at Stephen – a definite twinkle in his eye.

'She's also decided that the young widow and Gilbert will make a good match, contriving of reasons to push them together. No good will come of her interfering. But she is a caring soul,' the older man clarified. 'She would never see anyone starve or unfairly treated.'

'I suspected as much but am delighted to have it confirmed.' The generous nature of his landlady was indeed a bonus, and he was already starting to look kindly upon his fellow house-members. He had chosen well, lodging at Burlington Square, and was eternally grateful that he had been selected above the other applicants. How different everything would be had the wayward niece moved in, with her entitled gallivanting about. He was only nervous that his own troubles would follow him there. Troubles with fierce eyes and big fists.

By the time Stephen turned back into Burlington Square, a great number of topics had been covered, and the pair were chuckling together like old friends.

'It is my birthday soon and I shall be seventy-two,' Alexander said, as the chair was brought to a halt at the bottom of the stone steps outside the house. 'Usually, Miss Humphries bakes me a small fruit cake and we celebrate quietly with a glass of sherry, but I feel a renewed energy in recent days. I've heard it has become increasingly fashionable to dine out, and there are some quite splendid places to eat in St James's now. Perhaps you would accompany me to a French restaurant? Some of the best food I ever had was in Paris. Or perhaps Italian? My motive, naturally, is selfish. I could not hope to get there without assistance and you have proved more than capable of manoeuvring my dilapidated body into this cumbersome chair. If we get a cab, and with your strong right arm, I think I might even manage without it. What do you say?'

Stephen immediately felt nervous of the foreign menus and proper etiquette for such a place. There would be, he was certain, a language of eating and drinking that was alien to him. He knew to work from the outside in with his cutlery – he'd learnt that much from books – but his diet nowadays was plain fare indeed, and during his time away, even more so. Would his poor stomach either cope with or, indeed, appreciate the nature of such fine dining? However, this was an opportunity he knew to embrace.

'I should be delighted to accept.'

'Excellent.' A flush of colour swept over Alexander's cheeks, and the eyes, often so melancholy and lost, danced in his silver-haired head. 'We can eat, drink and make merry.'

'Leave all the arrangements to me,' Stephen said, knowing how he could make the day even more special for the old man.

43

On the Saturday, Stephen left the house early and headed out to make some money. It was all very well spending time with Alexander, but he needed funds more than ever, particularly if he was to make the old man's birthday memorable. Returning several hours later, he became aware how silent the house was. Usually, he could hear Agnes bustling about in her kitchen, and she'd got into the habit of popping into the hallway to greet him. But his landlady was nowhere to be seen.

He climbed the stairs feeling despondent. There would be no kettle 'just coming to the boil', or freshly baked biscuits for him to sample that day.

As he reached his rooms and took the key from his pocket, he heard footsteps from above. Moments later, Gilbert appeared on the landing.

'The mother in the basement has lost her baby,' he said, with his usual brevity and charm.

Stephen narrowed his eyes, confused by the statement. Did this quiet man think he'd stolen the child? Or might know where she'd wandered off to?

'I don't have it,' he said, frowning. 'Have you called the police?'

'No, she went into labour earlier this morning. Miscarriage.'

Finally, he understood.

'Is there anything I can do?' he asked, keen to make himself useful.

Gilbert shook his head. 'Short of instilling a bit more compassion into her husband – no. Miss Humphries is with her. Just thought you should know.' He turned back to the staircase and returned to his rooms. Neither man had anything else to say to the other, and certainly not on such an unpalatable matter that they did not feel either inclined or sufficiently qualified to discuss.

* * *

Stephen had spent his life being suspicious of people and reluctant to make close friends. Even his liaisons with ladies had been fraught and awkward. But something inside was changing – something he hadn't anticipated. He enjoyed Alexander's company, but also often sought out Miss Humphries after returning from his day, and not only in the hope she would offer him biscuits. His landlady seemed equally as comfortable with him and had recently insisted he called her Agnes.

They had sat together on her battered sofa one evening, as he lamented the way his life had turned out, and she had insisted that he was still young enough for wonderful things to happen. Anything was possible, she announced – her childhood books of fairy tales had taught her that. Friends, he was discovering, could teach you so much. Perhaps he should get to know Gilbert better, and the husband from the basement. Apparently, he worked on the trams and Agnes said he liked a flutter. And a drink.

He decided to make positive things happen by taking positive action, and embraced Agnes's optimism.

'Some flowers for you,' he said, depositing a small bouquet on his landlady's pine kitchen table. He'd stopped at a flower-seller that afternoon, thinking of poor Mrs Smith, but had grabbed a second bouquet for Miss Humphries on a whim.

'Oh, how kind. No one has bought me flowers for so many years,' she said, and promptly burst into tears. Not quite the reaction he'd expected, but he knew those pink, lilac and pale yellow dahlias had been a wise investment, shoring up the shift in their relationship. In exchange for a few minutes of his time, some pertinent questions and interested noises, he was shown kindness. All she wanted was company as she busied about the kitchen, stirring an array of aluminium saucepans with a lop-sided wooden spoon, keen to hear about his day. So, he fabricated tales of his life at the bank, inventing a couple of characters to keep her amused, or took pains to notice things he saw about the city that he could report back; details of the flora and fauna, the latest headline on the sandwich boards or the changing fashions, particularly the hats – Agnes loved to hear about hats. This friendship business was easy; it was a reciprocal thing. Now that Stephen had grasped that, it was plain sailing.

He then knocked on the basement door with a larger bunch of chrysanthemums. Flowers had worked wonders with Agnes and, from what he could gather, Mrs Smith could certainly do with a similar lift of her spirits. He was surprised that it was the young mother who answered, but then with little ones, she would not have the luxury of a recovery period – time for her physical injuries to heal or to reflect upon her grief. With her husband out at work and no local family, if she was not up and about, there was no one to look after her daughters. Miss Humphries was apparently checking in on her regularly, but everyone had busy lives and no spare time to care for three small girls.

The woman looked pale and her grief was etched across her face.

'Yes?'

'These are for you. I'm sorry about... what happened.' He thrust the flowers forward just as her husband appeared at her shoulder, with narrowed eyes.

'Why are you giving my wife flowers?'

'They're from all of us,' Stephen blustered, not wanting the aggressive-looking husband to have cause to doubt his motives. Here was someone who looked as if he might solve things with his fists, and Stephen suddenly had no desire to get to know him better. 'We had a whip-round and wanted her to know we were thinking of her.'

'Huh. What good are bloody flowers? We can't eat them. All they do is look pretty for a couple of days. The pennies would have been more useful.' He huffed and wandered off.

'He's feeling guilty because he didn't think to buy me any,' Jemima said in hushed tones, taking the bouquet. 'Thank you. I shall put them in water.'

'My— Our pleasure. Right.' Stephen pulled out his pocket-watch and glanced at it. 'I promised Alexander a game of cribbage and the time is ticking on.'

* * *

'I need more money.'

Stephen stood before the intimidating Bill Sikes of a man. He wasn't a registered money lender; there was nothing legitimate about his business. Down a dirty backstreet of Golders Green, they were behind a door that didn't advertise any of the services offered within. He'd followed a gruff Irish lad down a long corridor, and waited as he gave four knocks before the door swung inward.

Becker sat behind a large circular table that Stephen could imagine was the scene of many an illicit card game, made more sinister by the flickering overhead light.

'You ain't paid back the last loan yet.' The man rubbed at his greasy beard, wondering if his client was good for the money.

'I'm meeting all the payments. Things are looking up for me. I've moved into new lodgings.'

'We know. We've been following you. Nice-looking place. The interest is a penny in the shilling, like last time. How much do you need?'

Stephen had worked out how much it would cost to give Alexander a birthday to remember and requested the appropriate amount. The sooner he got out of this place, the better.

Becker growled – a noise Stephen gathered was merely his brain processing the request. 'I'm not sure about this. You know we'll come knocking if there's any problems?'

He nodded his understanding but Stephen didn't want trouble for Burlington Square. It was his home. The first one he'd had for many a year.

'Don't worry, I'll come good. Business is a bit slow at the moment. People are starting to think about putting money aside for winter fuel and Christmas, but it will pick up. This is a short-term loan for something specific.'

'Isn't it always?'

'Ah, but this is an investment.' And Stephen tapped the side of his nose in a manner that made Becker grin.

'All right,' he said, leaning forward. 'Let's talk...'

* * *

Alexander's birthday proved to be a relentlessly wet day. Stephen spent the morning filling the coal scuttles from the bunker to help his landlady, and the afternoon up in Alexander's rooms. There would be no birds to observe in the park that day. The rain kept everyone inside and confined the birds to the trees.

He told the old man that he'd taken another day of holiday and it was not questioned. As the two men sat together drinking tea, Stephen was surprised by the number of people who popped by to pass on their regards to his friend. Every member of the household visited the first floor at some point – Gilbert with a surprisingly expensive bottle of Madeira, Miss Humphries with a cake, and Mrs Smith and her girls with a picture of something Stephen couldn't determine drawn by the eldest child, but it was enthusiastically received. There were also visits from musical acquaintances, members of the Polish community and an assortment of friends Alexander had made in his long and interesting life. In contrast, no one had remembered Stephen's last birthday and he'd spent it alone.

Later that evening, the pair of them arrived at the restaurant Stephen had booked after seeing it advertised in the newspaper. He felt tiny beads of perspiration forming on his brow as they waited to be seated by the maître d'. Could the judgemental eyes of the man see through his charade? Did he know that Stephen was not used to such fine dining?

When ordering his food, Stephen stuck to items he recognised and that weren't too expensive: the thick kidney soup, grilled sole, lamb cutlets for the entrée, and finished with a peach Melba. In all things, he was guided by Alexander, watching his every move and mirroring his actions, from which glass to use to where he placed his linen napkin. And when he realised his friend was struggling with the cutlery, he discreetly assisted him by cutting up his meat, as he'd witnessed Mercy do.

As the meal progressed, the old man retold the tragedy of his first love, his reserve eroded by the wine. It was sad that he could not shake the guilt, which seemed greater every time they spoke.

'We must not allow mistakes from our past to consume us,' Stephen said, kindly. Something he was learning himself.

'I appreciate your attempt to shake me out of my self-pity, my son,' Alexander said, leaning forward and patting Stephen's hand with his own. The term son was not to be taken literally, and he'd heard the old man use it on several occasions to refer to anyone younger than himself, but it bought a lump to Stephen's throat nonetheless. 'And I thank you for your friendship. I was quite at sea when Mr Blandford died. There is a difference between a man who calls on you once a year to pass on birthday wishes, and a man who gives up every Sunday to make your life a little less lonely.' He paused, his eyes misting over, as he stared beyond Stephen. 'Nathaniel was someone who loved people. The sort to strike up a conversation with a stranger on a bus or man standing next to him in a bar. He talked to excess but I rather enjoyed his company. A sunny personality. "Don't look for problems, Mr G," he would say. "Look for solutions." The only problem was that in his eagerness to engage with others, he sometimes forgot to let them participate.' He grinned. 'Not everyone has the luxury of time, like myself, and I rather suspect people avoided him rather than get drawn into a long conversation that it was difficult to excuse themselves from. But he was the sort who never took offence.' Alexander smiled, as he scooped potato onto his fork. 'I liked that about him very much. He became like family.'

Stephen thought it might be the right time to open up to his friend more. The natural pause in the conversation allowed him to change topic.

'I had a difficult upbringing. It wasn't just our reduced circumstances; it was the lack of love in the household. Children know when they are loved and when they are not, and I felt keenly that I was not. The truth was I never quite fitted in. I guess your Mr Blandford would have looked for the positives – I was fed and had a roof over my head. There are people in the world who have neither food nor shelter. And, of course, I witnessed men younger and better than I lose their lives during the war, so I should not complain. I was proud to serve my homeland.'

'At least you have a homeland – one that meets the sea and marks its boundaries. Prior to the war, Poland was just a memory. We had been carved up by Russia, Germany and Austro-Hungary – like a cake split between three hungry men. The country of my fore-bears was handed down to the generations of my family in legend that no one alive could remember – wiped from the map for a century. But it lived on in our hearts.' The old man lifted his twisted hand to his chest and thumped it repeatedly. 'And now it exists once more, even if we are still quarrelling over borders.'

'Do you plan to return?' Stephen asked, but Alexander shook his head.

'I think perhaps a part of my heart will always belong to the Vistula – the arteries of which unite its people and shape its land-scape, economy and very soul. I played on the sandy beaches as a child and have fond memories of the many gothic castles and palaces along its banks... but there is no one left who remembers me now, and I have spent more years in this country than any other. If home is truly where the heart is, then perhaps my home is here. Those that have meant the most to me over the years are buried in English soil – my wife, my first love, and possibly even my child.'

'At least you have somewhere you feel you belong. You know your roots. Mine,' said Stephen, 'are unlikely to ever be known. My real mother either didn't want me or was unable to provide for me, and left me to the care of others.'

Alexander almost choked on his caramel custard. 'You were an abandoned baby?'

Stephen nodded. 'I didn't say anything before because I didn't want to open up wounds for you, but yes.'

'Then this gives me hope,' his companion said, 'that my own child may be out in the world, like you, and living a good life. Despite your unenviable beginnings, you are in a respectable profession, and a kind and thoughtful man.' He smiled and dabbed at the corner of his mouth with the enormous linen napkin. 'What a delightful meal. I will not hear a word said against dear Miss Humphries' cooking, but this was on a level unsurpassed.'

'I'm so glad you enjoyed it but the night is not over.' Stephen finally understood how the anticipation of giving a gift could outweigh the thrill of receiving one yourself. Since organising his friend's birthday surprise, he'd almost been unable to sleep with anticipation.

'It's not?' the old man queried.

'No, we are off to a concert.'

There was a look of genuine surprise, quickly followed by disbelief, and ultimately delight. This, Stephen acknowledged, was what material wealth could do. You could transform the day, or even the life, of someone you cared about. The joy on Alexander's face was worth the risks associated with adding to his debt.

They hailed a cab further out of the city centre and Stephen escorted his friend into the local assembly-rooms. The building was neoclassical, Alexander informed him, as they stood in the central octagonal entrance hall admiring the architecture that surrounded them. It was buzzing with eager guests; ladies waving fans and gentlemen in dinner jackets. Stephen had used some of the loan to purchase such a jacket for himself, considering it a necessary investment for the future, when he hoped there would be many similar evenings in Alexander's company.

'I could not secure tickets for anywhere grand, like the Royal Albert Hall, but this quartet was highly recommended.' He'd done his research, and for the funds he had, this should be a pleasurable enough experience for the old man.

'Not at all. As beautiful as the Royal Albert is, that domed ceiling gives an unfortunate echo that no one has yet resolved. Biggest is not always best,' Alexander said, as he was handed a programme. 'A piano quartet. How charming. For chamber music is surely the music of friends.'

Stephen felt relieved his offering was acceptable.

Eight pieces were played in all, including several by Mendelssohn and Beethoven – who Stephen had at least heard of. He enjoyed the evening, even though he was fully aware he didn't understand the subtleties of what he was listening to. But Alexander was enraptured, not, as it turned out, because the ensemble was particularly proficient ('the pianist was too anxious and it came through in his performance') but because he was in a hall again, and could see the musicians caressing their instruments, and *feel* the sound as it travelled around the room.

'With my gramophone, the crackle of the needle running along the groove sadly becomes part of the piece,' he reflected, as Stephen held his arm whilst they waited to hail a cab home. 'And the acoustics of a first-floor bedroom do not lend themselves to such depth of sound. But tonight... Tonight, I closed my eyes and I was part of it all once more.' He turned to his companion. 'I cannot thank you enough. You have made an old man very happy.'

'I'm just sorry it was on such a small scale.'

'My dear fellow, I would be delighted to hear a fiddler play folk music in the street.' He chuckled to himself. 'You got me out of the house and into the world once more. Your thoughtfulness is unsurpassed.'

'Not at all. It makes me happy to see you happy.'

'Oh, look, there's Carmichael. He's a manager at one of the

larger merchant banks. Let's see if we can catch him. You may well know some of the same people. What bank are you with again?'

Stephen turned his face away, mumbled something and then feigned an issue with his shoelaces. By the time he was upright again, the gentleman had disappeared from view. It was a close call because Stephen would have been rumbled had he been part of any banking conversation, and the thought that Alexander would have cause to be disappointed in him made his heart thump in his heavy chest.

And this was why, even though he'd tried to do a kind thing, it was not a good idea for him to be out and about with other people, particularly Alexander, who seemed to know so many people.

He simply could not allow kindness to be his undoing.

44

Things were finally starting to come together, Stephen thought, as he left Burlington Square the following morning. Even with the extra loan hanging over him, he had enough money to meet his repayments and give Agnes the rent early. She was forever slipping him food, enabling him to save pennies that he would otherwise have spent at a chop house or in a tea room. He was also earning well from the drunk and cocksure in the pubs. Unusually for him, he plied his trade in the centre of the city that day, wanting to walk back through Hatton Garden and visit a gentleman on Greville Street. He now had in his possession a triple ruby and diamond cluster ring, which he knew had substantial value, even though the original owner had not.

He stopped at a jeweller's recommended to him by someone he'd encountered during his years away. Since arriving in London, the proprietor occasionally brought pocket watches and the like from him – items Stephen had acquired when people gambled them unsuccessfully on the outcome of his tricks. The pair struck an unusual deal over the ring, with Stephen taking less than its true value and stipulating that the ring was not to be sold on for six months, allowing him to buy it back at an inflated price should he come into sufficient funds in the meantime. He felt uncomfortable having it in his possession and intended to use it only to secure temporary funds.

This creeping tender-heartedness was new to him, because he would dearly love to reunite the ring with its original owner. Making people happy was not a drug he had expected to become dependent on. But the undeniable truth was that the residents of 23 Burlington Square had wriggled their way into his empty, but surprisingly spacious, heart. As a consequence, he cared. He cared about everyone and everything, from the stray cats scavenging scraps in the streets, to the one-legged veteran begging on the corner at Covent Garden. He'd even chucked a penny into the poor man's cap – at least Stephen had a roof over his head, and both legs.

Perhaps it was the extra bounce in his step, or perhaps he'd been careless taking the bundle of notes from his pocket as he'd paid for a tongue and tomato salad at the Lyons Corner House, but whatever it was, as he walked along the streets not many minutes from Burlington Square, that early October evening, he knew that he was being followed.

He crossed to the opposite pavement and sure enough, a slim man in a wool suit and flat cap, crossed with him. Pausing outside a shoe shop, he pretended to study the footwear within, but was able to look behind and assess the man hanging back in doorways and avoiding his eye.

It was only as he headed down a narrow passageway, one he often used as a shortcut back to Burlington Square, that he saw another, broader man standing at the exit. Also in a woollen flat cap, and also avoiding his eye, he realised too late that the men were working together. All his money was about his person. If they took it, he would have nothing. He slowed his steps but could hear those of his shadow continue to advance behind him, so he spun around and locked eyes with the man. Although he was taller than both of them, he was considerably older and, as the first man approached, he saw him slip a poker from his jacket. Was he really about to be assaulted by such a banal household item.

'Come on, gentlemen,' he pleaded. 'Do you really want to do this?'

His answer came in the form of a swift blow to his stomach from the second man, who was suddenly right next to him.

'Come into some money, old man?' one of them said, 'How about sharing your good fortune with us, hey?'

But neither gentleman was interested in Stephen's reply, because a flurry of blows rained down on his curled-up body, followed by a sly kick in the groin, until they were certain he would offer no resistance, and then Stephen and his good fortune parted definite and permanent ways.

45

THE BLUE SILK DRESS

It hung at the back of her enormous Victorian wardrobe, and was yet another thing that Agnes was most anxious the moths should not get to. A blue silk dress with brocade details on the bodice and underskirt, and a bustle at the back so ridiculous that you could practically set out an entire tea service on it. How she had detested clambering into the crinolines back then. She smiled. Dresses nowadays were so much more practical, and decidedly less fussy.

She lifted the wooden hanger and slid it out, hanging it on the cornice, and looking between the dress and her own reflection in the mirrored door panel.

Of course, she had been a young girl back then, and whilst never a slim thing, she was certainly not as plump as she was now. Daphne couldn't understand why she would keep something so hideous that no longer fitted and, as she'd so brutally pointed out, never would again. Weight had always been Agnes's enemy and perhaps over the years she'd eaten as a way to comfort herself. Stuck at home with her father and not able to go out much, one of her few pleasures in life was food. She enjoyed baking, although she was hardly patisserie standard, and had a soft spot for cheese and pastry. And, despite his appetite diminishing towards the end, food was one way she'd connected with her father and his wandering mind. He was often alarmed and bemused by the world around him, but when she could get him to sit down and eat, there were moments of lucidity and genuine contentment.

After he passed, it was a habit she couldn't shake off – a late night supper in the quiet of her large house with only her travel guides and a stuffed canary for company. And as the lodgers began to swell in number, her baking skills were once again required and, more importantly, appreciated. She knew now why her father had always joked that you would never come across a thin cook.

It wasn't until James entered her life that Agnes began to care about anything as frivolous as pretty clothes. She removed the dress from its hanger and held it to her body, the width of it barely covering half her girth. Those damn corsets had done their best to give her the fashionably miniscule waist but, even then, it was asking a lot of several cotton panels, a bit of boning and the sturdy lacing. She squinted and tried to merge the image before her into a memory of herself nearly forty years previously.

She had taken a stroll around the city with James, arm in arm, and they found themselves walking past a drapers, where her eye was caught by a beautiful blue silk dress adorning a mannequin in the window, and James noticed her longing looks.

'I can imagine you wearing a dress of such luxurious fabric,' he said, looking between her and the window display. 'Shall we go inside and enquire?'

'Oh no. Such fine silk is far too sophisticated for the day, and I rarely go out at night.'

'Then we shall address that. Such an enchanting young lady deserves to lead an enchanting life. To be taken to balls and theatre shows. To be courted properly.'

Agnes shook her head. She was hardly enchanting. Her propensity to say what she thought without a filter was amusing at best, and inappropriate on the majority of occasions. He was teasing.

'I can't leave my father for long periods. He's not well. Any such outings could only be possible if I could find someone to sit with Father.'

'Then I shall take that as an acceptance, on the condition that you allow me to purchase several yards of the silk and commission a similar dress. Everyone should own beautiful things, from artworks to frivolous clothing. We need to embrace sources of joy in our lives.'

She was both thrilled and terrified by this new world James was introducing her to. He'd talked of the circles he moved in, the events he attended and the exotic lands he had visited. And now it appeared she was to be a part of it.

Once she had found a suitable dressmaker, and the gown had been completed, Agnes Humphries was treated to a performance of a West End play in James's company. The last time she'd had such an experience had been with her father, but he'd not been in a position to escort his daughter to such things of late.

They left the theatre and stood in the lamplight of a chill December evening, as their misty breaths merged together in the limited space between them, and a robust gentleman approached.

'Hunt!' he exclaimed. 'Is this the young lady that's got you all of a-tither?' He looked her up and down and his eyes twinkled like the stars above their heads. No clouds meant a frosty night and she was increasingly worried how her family would fare financially through a bitter winter. 'Why, the fellow can barely concentrate on his work of late, such is the spell you've cast over him, young lady.'

Agnes blushed, but noticed with satisfaction that James did not. He was embarrassed by very little; certainly not the outspoken and forthright nature of his female companion. Sometimes she wondered if he only spent time with her because she amused him.

There had been no further kisses since the day she'd recklessly thrown herself at him in the front room of Burlington Square, despite him asking her to step out with him.

'Indeed. May I introduce Miss Agnes Humphries. Mr George Palmer.'

It took her a moment to remember that James worked for Palmer and Drayton's.

'A pleasure,' the gentleman said, taking her hand and nodding. 'I would love to talk longer but I fear I am being summoned.' He raised his hand to a woman across the way. As he began to take his leave, he gestured to James that he wanted a quiet word. The pair of them turned from her and Mr Palmer lowered his voice, although it remained loud enough for her to catch his words.

'And remember, Hunt, I need a decision on the Indian posting by the month end,' he said, before striding over to the woman Agnes assumed was his wife.

Was this the truth of it, then? He was shortly to be posted abroad and was using her to idle away the weeks until he began a new life on another continent? James, who often didn't feel the need to explain every detail of his inner thoughts, unlike Agnes, said nothing further on the subject, but there was a slow churning of her insides.

Once safely inside the cab, James looked across at her and reached for her hand. Not one for silly romance novels, she wasn't used to such an intimate gesture, so when he leaned closer, she wasn't certain what was happening.

'You look utterly enchanting in that dress,' he said, serious for a moment. 'I knew you would.'

'It has been quite a thrill to have such an opportunity to wear it. I haven't been to the theatre for several years and, even though I found parts of the performance tonight quite confusing, I can only thank you for—'

'Agnes Humphries, will you stop talking and let me engage those strangely enticing lips of yours in a far more important activity.' He looked mock-serious and her heart finally flipped. He was going to kiss her again. Still with her mouth slightly agape from her chatterings, she froze, as he tilted his head, slid his hand around her blue silk waist, and swooped in to prevent her from talking for fully a whole minute.

Which for Agnes was quite the achievement.

46

What Stephen didn't know, as he sat bemused in the alley, propped up against a dirty wall in considerable pain, was whether the attack had been Becker's men reminding him they were watching his every move, or a random mugging because he'd been careless concealing his present wealth. What he *did* know with certainty was that if he couldn't raise the funds to start the repayments, he'd be in for another beating, and the next one might involve a damn sight more than a few cracked ribs and a kick in the groin.

'I forgive you,' he muttered under his breath to the retreating backs of the men. He was not sure he meant it, but was trying so hard to be a better man. They'd seen a quick way to make a killing and not hesitated. He'd done the same so many times in his past, albeit without the violence. 'May God do the same.'

Stephen's relationship with religion was peculiar. St Peter's had been the first place to offer him any comfort for many years, and he found, to his surprise, that religion suited him. He wasn't entirely sure there was a God but, as a gambling man, decided to bet both ways. And so, just in case there was a heavenly entity keeping score, Stephen kept a ledger in his head of all the good and bad things he'd done in his life, utterly convinced that as long as the good column outweighed the bad, he would be forgiven. In other words, for every sin he committed, atonement was achievable. Perhaps by forgiving the thugs, he could offset some small sin of his own.

After a while, Stephen realised he had no choice but to return to his lodgings, although with what he suspected was a broken rib, smudges of crimson blood across his white shirt and a hat now fit for nothing but a scarecrow, how would he explain his injuries to Agnes?

She heard the door and, as had become her habit of late, she called to him that there was tea in the pot.

'Not today. I'll retire to my rooms. I'm feeling a bit—'

But Agnes had waddled out from the kitchen with a plate of biscuits. 'I have the most unhappy news... Oh, Mr Thompson,' she gasped. 'Whatever has happened?'

By this point, he was clutching at the newel post and bent nearly double. His landlady abandoned the plate on the long sideboard, squashing up the ornaments and clothes brushes to make room on the edge, and rushed towards him.

'Have you been attacked?' she asked, the most obvious explanation being the correct one.

'Set upon and robbed,' he finally admitted.

'Then we must call the police,' and she started to turn towards the front room and the telephone.

Stephen panicked and reached for her arm. He didn't want unwelcome truths spilling out, which they inevitably would if the police were involved.

'No. Please.' He had to think quickly. What reason could he possibly give for keeping this quiet? 'The bank mustn't hear of this.

There was a horse running and the name reminded me of a former sweetheart and, even though I'm not a man prone to gambling, I couldn't resist. It won me a tidy sum.'

'Oh, you poor man. A moment of weakness, a lucky win, and now you've had your good fortune snatched away.'

It was ironic that his landlady had warmed to him even more now that he admitted to being less than perfect. But that was Agnes all over – she loved things despite their imperfections.

'My bruises will heal, even though I am disappointed that the things I had planned for my winnings – sweets for Jemima's girls, perhaps a new hat for you and further excursions for Mr Gorski – won't now happen. But I can't have my employer thinking I suffer from such a weakness – even though it was just the once. Oh, such folly.' He groaned. 'Please don't mention it to anyone.'

Although he had fabricated the reasons for having such a large sum about his person, his plans for the money were true. He had borrowed from Becker to treat Alexander and his friends at Burlington Square, not himself, and the proceeds from the sale of the ring would have covered the first repayment. Life was so unfair, and it wasn't as though he'd idly pissed the loan up against the wall, like many.

But his landlady was having none of it. 'It makes my blood boil that there are those in this world who would violently steal from another rather than earn money of their own from an honest day's work. And I really don't like the look of that eye. Let me call the doctor at least. After what happened to dear Mr Blandford, it would be remiss of me not to have your injuries properly tended to.'

'No, really, I don't want a fuss.' He hadn't been aware of any injury to his eye but as he felt along his brow, the swelling was apparent.

'Then Jemima Smith must look at it. She's good with such things.'

Agnes helped him into the front room and onto her sofa, reassuring him that a bit of blood on the fabric was the last thing she was concerned about, and wincing at his swollen face.

'I do so worry about you, Mr Thompson, with no family to care for you.'

'It's not the lack of family that I mind,' he said, as he tried to settle between the lumps and bumps of the upholstery. 'It's that everything was *finally* coming together for me.' He looked up to his stout landlady, whose building tears of sympathy matched his own. His father had always told him that such emotions were a weakness, but he had reached the end of the line. All these months trying to scrabble out of a desperate situation and better himself, snatched away by a couple of street thugs. He'd found genuine friendship at Burlington Square, but it was now likely he'd have to walk away from these dear people. 'Perhaps my sort of person just isn't meant to succeed in life.'

Agnes reached for his shoulder, her touch gentle, mindful of his injuries.

'Life can surprise you. Sometimes it deals harsh blows, but equally it can delight and amaze. My life hasn't always played out as I imagined, but I like to think good things are waiting just around the corner. Think of Catherine the First of Russia, born to a family of Lithuanian peasants, and that Dickens fellow, who drew on his deprived childhood in his novels. They didn't do too badly in the end.' She smiled. 'Don't be too downhearted, Mr Thompson. I feel certain that there are brighter things to come. Perhaps for both of us.'

She left to fetch Jemima, who appeared at the door a few minutes later, and then retreated to the kitchen to make a nice pot of tea that she was convinced would aid his recovery.

'Miss Humphries said you had a nasty injury.' The young mother looked across at him. 'Ooo.' She sucked in a breath. 'She wasn't wrong. Let me take a look. I underwent some basic nurse training, back in the days when I had hopes of a career.'

He wrestled to stand, as manners dictated, but she waved him back down.

'No need to stand for me. Nicholas never does. Not any more.'

'I appreciate your time. I seem to have got myself into a bit of a scrape but must be thankful that the poker they were brandishing was only used to threaten, and most of the damage was done with fists... although there was a particularly brutal parting kick once I was down.'

'A poker?' Jemima repeated, looking pale. 'Dear sweet Lord. Why must men be so violent? I find I am less and less inclined to think favourably of your sex, Mr Thompson. That is not to say there are not rotten apples amongst us, but women rarely turn to fists to solve their problems. Or drink...' she added, forlornly.

She knelt by his feet and raised her eyebrows as if to ask permission to examine him. He nodded.

'Thank you again for the flowers. Miss Humphries said they were from you, not the household.'

He flinched at her touch, but knew if he'd cracked a rib, there was little to be done.

'It was nothing. We all know mothers who have lost children, but just because it happens all the time, doesn't mean it isn't a terrible and heartbreaking thing.'

She squeezed his hand and gave a weak smile.

'I'll doubtless be going through it all again. Nicholas wants a son – something I have so far failed to give him. But then I chose the path of motherhood, so I must make the best of it.' She shook her head as though she'd only just realised she was being too open with this relative stranger. 'Excuse my frankness; my emotions are all over the place. I've been spending too much time with Agnes.

She came to sit with me and the girls today, distraught that the young widow has returned to Suffolk.'

Ah, perhaps this was the unhappy news his landlady had referred to when he'd come through the door.

'When she didn't arrive to help this morning, Agnes rang the lodging house and was told that family had turned up for her late last night and taken her back home. The poor thing didn't want to go, apparently, and was weeping the whole time. Miss Humphries has been inconsolable, saying she should have done more to help her. Poor Gilbert doesn't know yet. I think he was sweet on her.'

She sat back on her heels and locked eyes with him.

'Perhaps we all have our secrets, here at Burlington Square. I know I do. Gilbert shuffles around in those attics, never open about anything. Mr Gorski is wracked with guilt about his behaviour in the past, and I wonder if you have secrets too, especially not wanting a doctor out.' Her left eyebrow rose in a knowing manner. 'The only person within these four walls with nothing to hide is Miss Humphries who, even had she murdered someone, would have told us all by now.'

They both smiled, and Stephen didn't challenge her truth. He knew he was hiding the biggest secrets of all.

* * *

After a week of rest and recuperation (and intermittent bowls of Miss Humphries' beef broth), Stephen took himself back to Golders Green. It was not a call he wanted to make but his first loan instalment was due, and if he didn't go, Becker (or worse still, his men) would come to him. Perhaps if he was just honest... if he could explain about the assault...

It was a chilly night, with hunched figures scuttling about in doorways, and painted women stepping from the shadows as he

passed to offer services he could not afford. The walk took two
hours and the exertion of it all hurt his chest like hell, but he had
no money for the electric tram or a bus. He consoled himself with
the magnificent view of the heavens. The stars were out, twinkling
glimmers of light and hope in a black blanket of emptiness. And as
he left the Thames far behind him, the stench became less, too.

'I've come to see Becker,' he said to the Irish lad.

He was led down the dark corridor again. The man gave the
usual four knocks and Becker was behind the table, this time with a
woman on his lap, who leapt up and disappeared into the darkness
as the door opened.

'You have my money?' he asked.

'No, but I came to explain—'

'I don't care for explanations. Either you pay me, or you speak to
my men.' He reached for the whisky tumbler in front of him. 'Liam,
take him outside.'

And that was the end of the meeting, it appeared, as he was
yanked by the collar back into the corridor.

'But I was attacked.' Stephen's eyes were wide and his voice
squeaky. 'Two men set about me the night before last and took
everything. I had Becker's money, and more besides, and now it's all
gone. Can you not see the bruises? I was practically left for dead.'

'Bruises could be from the wife, for all we know,' the lad scoffed.
'Heard more creative excuses, if I'm honest.'

'You know damn well I'm not married.' But any protestations
were useless. These men were not going to listen to reason.

'You think the beating you got when you were robbed was bad –
we'll make you *wish* that was all you had to worry about,' a second
fellow chipped in, his eyes serious and his voice a low growl.
'Becker don't care what happened to you, he cares about your
agreement. Either you get that money to him by the end of next
week, or we'll be paying you a visit at your lodgings.' He tapped at

the Webley revolver in his waistband. 'And we're adding another two shillings for the inconvenience.'

'Come on, gentlemen. I'm really no use to you dead.'

'No, but I'm reckoning to Becker's mind, he won't have so many welchers if they get to hear of the consequences of not paying.'

Oh, great, so he was to be made an example of. Stephen sighed. Of all the rotten luck, to get attacked when things had been coming together nicely, and now he could feel himself slipping back down into the pit he'd so painstakingly clawed his way out of.

And with that disturbing thought, the two men manhandled him out the door, which was slammed firmly in his face, leaving him to acknowledge that he was fast running out of options.

47

Stephen absolutely could not allow bad people to do bad things that would put those at Burlington Square in jeopardy. He must leave to keep them safe, and start again, somewhere else. It would need to be a big city – perhaps Manchester, where he could be anonymous but still earn a wage. Despite all his weeks of careful preparation, he knew when to quit.

What surprised him the most, having made the decision, was how much he would genuinely miss Agnes and Alexander. These people had shown him such kindness, and had awoken unexpected feelings of compassion within him. Buying the flowers for Agnes and Jemima had made him feel inexplicably good, and Alexander's obvious joy in his company was equally uplifting. These alien feelings flooding through him – the stimulation from the old man's company, the lump in his throat when his landlady patted his arm, even Jemima's gentle ministrations – he hadn't expected any of it, and it would be a wrench to leave. But leave he must.

He began to pack his meagre possessions and decided to execute a moonlit flit on the Sunday night. It would be easier than fabricating a reason for his sudden departure, but the truth he wouldn't acknowledge was that face-to-face partings would be too emotionally overwhelming. He did, however, owe Alexander a goodbye, even if the old man didn't know his final afternoon visit was exactly that.

'What's all this I hear about you being attacked?' Alexander said, as they listened to a concerto on the gramophone. 'You said the eye was a stray cricket ball in the park when I asked you in the week, and now I find it was not that at all.'

His fellow churchgoers had queried the yellow bruises above his eye and been told the same thing – a small boy with a careless aim. He sighed, feeling he owed the old man a degree of honesty and suspecting he knew some of the truth anyway.

'I was robbed. Two men set about me in an alley and took all that I had – even my pocket watch. But I asked Miss Humphries not to say anything. It is rather embarrassing to admit one was not able to defend oneself.' It did not take a genius to work out the source of the Polish gentleman's information.

'Have the police no leads?' Alexander asked. 'It's doubtless someone from one of these criminal gangs. They're becoming a real menace around here, I understand, intimidating shopkeepers and running gambling clubs.'

'I haven't reported it,' Stephen admitted. 'I don't want the bank knowing.'

'Miss Humphries said you had rather a large sum of money on you?'

'My own foolishness, and I must have been careless concealing that. I was followed from the ale house where I stopped for some supper, after a long day at work. They did for me in an alley – blocked my escape and set about me with their fists. I suppose I should be thankful it was not worse.'

Stephen paused as he thought on Agnes's earlier words. Might better things be just around the corner? Perhaps he should be honest with his new friend about his circumstances. If he was imminently to bolt anyway, he had nothing to lose by exploring this new avenue. He swallowed hard.

'The truth is,' he admitted, 'I am not in the healthy financial situation I had hoped. I found it so hard after the war, only securing the clerk's position through someone I had done a kindness for. Losing the money has been a bitter blow.'

'Yes, Miss Humphries and I suspected as much. Your clothes were a giveaway – a little worn and dated.'

How clever he thought he'd been, but this wily pair had known all was not quite as he presented it to be – and yet... and yet, the thought that he was less successful than he pretended, that he was living with a degree of dishonesty, had somehow endeared him to them more. People really were strange.

'I want you to have this.' Alexander passed over a thick cream envelope. Stephen lifted the flap and pulled out a bundle of folded black and white notes, staring at the paper between his fingers, open-mouthed, and genuinely overcome. In all the scenarios he played out in his head, he had not foreseen this.

Alexander noticed his stunned expression.

'Miss Humphries said you had a substantial sum on you. Does that not cover it?'

He flicked through the money, bemused at the old man's actions. Everyone at the house was being so kind and he could hardly bear it.

'I can't take this,' he muttered. Even Stephen could not believe the words coming from his own mouth. Burlington Square had worked its magic a little too well.

'Nonsense. Pay me back, if you want – I understand a man has his pride. You have a respectable job and I know that you are good for the money. I'm not doing anything with it and I can't see a kind man like yourself suffer because some lowlifes took what wasn't theirs by force. You were so generous for my birthday, and wouldn't let me pay.' He shrugged. 'Now it is my turn to be kind to you. But I honestly do not care if I never see a penny of it again. Good deeds are remembered.'

Still in shock, Stephen had not expected this degree of generosity with such a short acquaintance. Agnes had been quite correct to describe Mr Gorski as the very best of men. Perhaps there was a God after all and, having noticed how desperately hard Stephen had striven to get his life back on track. He was rewarding him for his kindness to Alexander.

'Then I can't thank you enough. And I will return every penny when my circumstances improve. You have my word.'

'That is your decision, but I feel you have already paid me back by giving me your time and your friendship. To a lonely old man like me, that is worth more than money. I have no family left that I am aware of, so you must join me in a drink and let us toast friendship instead – which is surely the next best thing?'

He pointed to the sideboard, and Stephen knew the drill. He stood to pour them both a port and returned to the old man's side. Mere moments ago, he'd been contemplating his midnight flit, his heart sinking at the need to secure new accommodation, create another backstory, and begin again. Now all his problems were solved, and all because he'd shown an old man a little kindness.

'You do not realise,' Alexander continued, 'what you have done for me. I don't mind admitting to some very dark thoughts of late, and had even considered that my birthday might be a good time to bow out. Now, suddenly, I am reminded that I have friends and a reason to live.'

Stephen decided if ever there was a time to share his story, it was now. He had thought it too soon, not worth the risk, but Alexander was proving almost as sentimental as Agnes.

'To friendship,' he said, clinking their glasses together. 'Because, like you, I have no family and so your friendship is of equal importance to me.' He cleared his throat. 'As you know, I was a foundling, given up for reasons I shall never know, with no knowledge of my parents or my heritage. The fact that it should have been on Christmas Day, of all days, somehow makes it all the more poignant...'

Alexander's glass remained in the air, the contents wobbling from the tremor in his hand. His face registered shock at this new piece of information.

Stephen frowned.

'But you knew I was abandoned? Despite my desperate wish not to stir up memories of your own child, and for you not to think less of me, I was always honest about my origins. It's an uncomfortable coincidence, but there are many of us about.'

'Christmas Day?' the old man repeated.

'Yes, although I was not entrusted to a foundling hospital but instead left on the doorstep of a smart London house, apparently.' Stephen half-laughed. 'Those hospitals always struggle to keep up with admissions – there are hundreds of babies born out of wedlock every week. Perhaps my mother knew of their high mortality rates and hoped for something better for me. I like to think so, even though my life has not been what she might have wished.'

Still, Alexander stared at him, open-mouthed. The untouched glass of port was now resting in his lap, but he was leaning forward as if to catch his words a fraction sooner.

'What exactly were you told of your abandonment, if you don't mind me asking?'

Stephen rubbed at his forehead with his free hand and slid into his usual chair. 'It's difficult to talk about. You must excuse my emotions, and I know very little except although I was abandoned in London on Christmas Day it is highly likely I was born a day or two before. There was nothing to identify me, and it was assumed I was left there by my mother. Any token she may have included in the blanket I was wrapped in, has never been disclosed to me, but it could easily have been lost or stolen. I was not told of any note. I was given no name, to my knowledge.'

Alexander had become increasingly agitated as he relayed the information, wriggling in his seat and an unreadable expression across his face.

'And the year?' The old man's voice was cracking and barely audible.

'1877. I am soon to be fifty,' Stephen acknowledged, but moved swiftly on with his tale. 'If my mother had hoped I might be adopted by the wealthy owners, she was sorely mistaken. They had no interest in taking in a child of unknown parentage, but they did at least re-home me. By the January, I'd been found a home in the Hertfordshire countryside, with a childless farming couple, who I suspect saw me as a source of labour and someone to pass the land on to. They were not particularly loving, nor were they overly cruel, and had not fate intervened, I might have been tolerably happy.'

He sighed and took a quick sip of his port. All this talking was making his mouth dry.

'And then when I was five, my mother conceived the child she thought she would never have, and I was suddenly surplus to requirements. I wasn't blood, as I was constantly reminded, and over the years my position in the household became unbearable. Their natural child resented me and, in the end, I cut all ties. I have made my own way in the world ever since, and have been fortunate enough to make a career from my love of numbers.'

By this point, Alexander was openly weeping. One of his hands was outstretched, as if he was reaching for Stephen.

'What have I said? What's wrong?' Stephen placed his glass on the side table and walked over to the old man, kneeling at his feet.

Alexander's hand rested on his shoulder, and he struggled for breath as the colour drained from his wrinkled face. Was he about to have a heart attack? For a few moments, Stephen was panicking. Surely, he wasn't about to die? Could he foolishly have killed the old man with his tale?

'What you are saying is so incredible, I can hardly believe your words. Alina followed me to England, unaware I had moved on to Paris, but the child came a month early and she gave birth alone, abandoning him on the steps of a large house. Perhaps her last act on this earth was to write to her sister and confess everything, telling her that all hope was lost. She passed away shortly afterwards at a cheap boarding house in Stepney, but her child... my son... was left on the doorstep of an anonymous house in London on Christmas Day, 1877.'

48

There was a moment of silence which hung heavy in the room. Stephen's heart was racing as fast as Alexander's surely was. He knew that his whole world was about to change in the most dramatic fashion, even before his friend spoke again.

'Could it be... could it possibly be... that you are my son?' the old man said, watery eyes flickering in both disbelief and an effort to stop the tears spilling out. 'The similarities in our stories are surely too many for this to be a coincidence. I can hardly believe you are standing before me. To think that of all the lodging houses in London, you should end up here. The chances must be so microscopically small that a power greater than we can comprehend must have drawn us together. It is nothing short of miraculous.'

He lifted his eyes to the heavens and muttered under his breath, 'Dzięki Bogu!', as he reached out for the younger man.

Stephen moved towards his friend and let himself be embraced. There was surprising strength in those frail arms, even though the hands were next to useless, and a dampness seeped into Stephen's collar as the old man rested his weeping face against his bowed neck. He allowed tears of his own to flow. A man not particularly given to emotion, he knew if there was ever a time in his life when he should cry, surely it was now.

He pulled back and shook his head. 'You have no proof. I have no proof. Just a shared date and a similar story. I cannot tell you the address of the house, nor even approach my foster parents for further information, for they have long since died and I have no contact with the child they bore after they took me in.'

'Do you need proof?' the old man asked. 'Can you not see God's hand in this? Do you not feel it in your soul?'

Stephen sank back to his knees. 'Perhaps. The way music has always called to me, my connection with you since our paths first crossed.' He shook his head. 'Maybe these things are in my blood. But if this is indeed true... Father...' He tried the word out and it sounded strange on his tongue, although not altogether unpleasant. 'You must know that I have lived a far from perfect life—'

'Hush,' Alexander said. 'We are none of us perfect, and you have done well to elevate yourself from your humble beginnings. I am proud of you, son. It is not necessary to talk of these things. That you have survived, that you are here, is enough. We are neither of us alone in this world any more. When I think how futile my life seemed a few short weeks ago, that I now have something to live for...' He was barely able to speak, so choked was he by emotion. 'My son has been returned to me; God's in his heaven, and all's right with the world.'

* * *

'Well, bless my soul and praise the Lord, indeed,' Agnes had said, when the news was shared. So astonished was she, that she'd collapsed into a kitchen chair, nearly squashing a sleeping Inky as she did so. 'Had I not chosen you to come and live at Burlington Square, Mr Thompson, you may never have found each other.'

Things moved quickly after that, and the remarkable similarities between his sad story and the details Erna had passed on regarding her sister all those years ago, convinced Alexander that his lost child had been returned to him. Stephen's debts were settled and the improvement in Alexander's health was quite remarkable, as the man he now called Father prepared to make amends, both financially and emotionally, to his son.

Not everyone was elated by the news, however, and Stephen overheard Gilbert interrogating Agnes in her kitchen a few days later, questioning whether she had passed on details of Alina's tragic story, but this was vehemently denied. 'Mr Blandford was the only one he truly confided in,' she had stressed. 'I think he felt more comfortable opening up to men about his premarital exploits. I was only told there had been a child conceived out of wedlock, and that the mother had died.'

'I find the whole thing an unbelievable coincidence,' Gilbert huffed. He remained suspicious and Stephen could hardly blame him. 'And I'm always wary of coincidence.'

'And yet,' said Agnes, 'coincidences do happen. Take the "unsinkable" Violet Jessop, surviving disasters on the sister ships the Olympic, Titanic and Britannic. Or Mark Twain's birth *and* death coinciding with the appearance of Halley's Comet. Explain these away, if you can...'

Stephen was thankful Agnes was on his side, but he could well imagine his own good fortune would be resented by the pale young man who had nothing in his life but glass plates and developing solution. He felt sorry for the fellow; his landlady confided that the joy had gone out of him since Mercy had disappeared. Stephen wanted to ask 'What joy?' but kept his uncharitable thoughts to himself. The lad had clearly been sweet on the young widow, but there was no need for him to take his failure in matters of the heart out on him.

Alexander and Stephen spent several nights talking into the early hours. As desperate as young lovers to learn every detail they could about the other, they shared their life stories. Stephen wanted a fresh start, away from Becker, the untruth of his employment, and the possibility of bumping into unsavoury characters from his past. He knew that returning to Poland would make Alexander happy, and it would suit him also, to start completely afresh. Besides, for the first time in years, he genuinely cared about the happiness of another. They made arrangements to rent an apartment on the outskirts of Warsaw, much to Agnes's distress.

'I shall have to advertise the rooms again, which unsettles me. It was a hard enough decision this time around, but the first *and* second floors will be vacant. You will be sorely missed, Mr Gorski. You've been here for so long.'

They were seated around Alexander's dining table again, Gilbert reluctantly joining them for this last supper.

'And yet you still won't call me by my Christian name,' Alexander said, smiling. 'However, we insist that you come and visit when we are settled. After all, you have always wanted to travel.'

'There is a part of me that longs to try the sheep's cheese of Zakopane, sit on the beaches of the Vistula or visit the many beautiful castles,' she admitted, 'but I'm not sure my knees are up to it any more. Send me plenty of postcards, though, and I can add them to my scrap albums. Everything is too topsy-turvy here for me to be thinking of going abroad, what with Mercy disappearing as well.'

Three pairs of eyes flicked to Gilbert, who was picking at the embroidery on his linen napkin and actively avoiding eye contact with everyone around the table.

'I asked Jemima if she might like to help me with the laundry and cooking,' Agnes continued, 'as I shall still offer these services to my new lodgers. To be honest, I don't know why I didn't think of her before – maybe because she was always in the family way, and her tongue can be a little sharp. But she seems so increasingly unhappy, and I wondered if it is because she's starved of adult company. It's only a temporary solution as I'm sure it won't be long until she's expecting again...' She sighed. 'Perhaps Nicholas will finally get his son. But it will be wonderful to have the girls up here in the kitchen. The boundless energy of the young almost makes you forget your aches and pains.'

'With a December wedding, it's likely your niece will be expecting by the spring,' Alexander said, leaning over his plate and bringing a spoonful of leek and potato soup to his lips. 'That will be something to look forward to.'

'I'm convinced motherhood will be the making of Clara. She's desperately searching for something, but I'm not sure she knows what it is. I wish we'd had more time to talk. I always felt there were things she wanted to share but didn't quite know how to put them into words.'

'Such a shame I never got to meet her,' Stephen said.

'She'll be in London next week, making preparations for the wedding with her mother, and I have asked them both to supper on the Tuesday. Daphne is keen to show me the catalogue they used for her trousseau. You would be most welcome to pop in and say hello?'

Stephen cleared his throat. 'How kind, although I'm afraid I have plans that evening. There is so much to organise before my father and I leave these shores. Such a pity. I should so have liked to meet her.'

'To family,' Alexander toasted from the head of the table, as he raised his glass. 'And to Agnes, who has shared her home with us all, and fashioned us into a family of sorts.'

'To family,' they all replied.

For one brief moment, Stephen Thompson thought of his real family: the mother, father and four brothers who lived in Hexton,

Hertfordshire, on the estate of Reginald Goodwin. Then he put them out of his mind, because they didn't deserve his time. They'd all disowned him when he'd been sent to prison, and cut him from their lives completely. Yet, here he was, having the last laugh, because he was brighter than the lot of them, and when an opportunity had come his way, he'd grabbed it. A snatched conversation with an overly talkative drunkard in the Mad Hatter, and enough brains to remove the stupid man from the equation, slip into Mr Blandford's former lodgings, and become the cuckoo in the unexpectedly comfortable nest.

He smiled at the gullible old man across the table, who had enough money, and sufficient guilt, not to pursue the truth. Alexander Gorski saw what he wanted to see and, in fairness, was all the happier for it.

Agnes had always said, happiness was more important than wealth.

Soon he would have plenty of both.

PART III

MERCY MAYWEATHER

49

FRIDAY, 5TH AUGUST 1927

Agnes dipped the nib of her pen into the pewter inkwell and began to write. Daphne always told her sister that her kind heart would be her downfall, and she accepted that it had indeed led to a share of heartache, but over the years it had also brought her great joy. Look at Inky. He had turned up on her doorstep one morning, half-starved, with a broken leg, a missing ear, and riddled with fleas. The neighbour had offered to put him out of his misery, as the odds of survival were next to nothing, but Agnes couldn't let that happen. She had to give the poor thing a chance, even though her horrified sister had offered to buy her a Pekinese should she be that desperate for company – an animal considered eminently more suitable than a mangy flea-ridden cat. But Agnes stood firm, and gave Inky a home, because her heart ruled her head.

Her head told her to offer the rooms to the bank clerk. He was respectable and churchgoing. The rent would always be paid on time and she was certain no scandal would follow him. But, sentimental fool that she was, she couldn't help an affinity with her own sex. She may now have the vote but many young women didn't. Men would always be all right in the world.

Her strong sense of family would have her give the rooms to her niece, but time and time again, Agnes questioned who would look out for that young widow if she didn't take her in? Mr Thompson would find adequate lodgings wherever he went. Clara had her parents and a large group of wealthy friends to fall back on. All the nonsense over her niece's silly indiscretion would soon blow over. But Agnes just knew that Mrs Mayweather was scared and alone, and it was the alone part that bothered her.

'You liked her, didn't you, Inky?' she asked the cat, curled up on the battered sofa. Clara was indifferent to animals, and Inky was indifferent to Mr Thompson. However, he had taken a particular liking to Mrs Mayweather, and Agnes believed that animals had a sixth sense when it came to people. She looked across at the curled up black bundle on the sofa, his missing ear apparent, and his black fur never quite as glossy as she would have liked.

'This is for you,' she said to the sleeping feline.

Dear Mrs Mayweather

I am delighted to offer you the rooms at Burlington Square, to take up at your earliest convenience. As discussed, I should also be pleased to offer you a few hours' employment in the house, helping me with the laundry and meals, and will deduct the wages from our agreed rent.

Yours truly,

Agnes Humphries

As she ran the envelope over the letter licker, she heard Gilbert coming down the stairs so she called out to him.

'Would you mind dreadfully popping this into the postbox for me and saving my legs?' She repeated the action with the stamp and fixed it to the envelope.

He nodded, as wordless as ever.

'Mr Blandford's rooms are shortly to be taken up by a young widow. Quiet thing, rather like yourself, but she is going to help me with the running of the place, so I will ask her to bring your trays up when she takes the rooms, as she will be serving Mr Gorski his meals.'

Gilbert looked faintly alarmed. 'Thank you but I'd rather not be disturbed.'

'As you wish.' Agnes shrugged.

She could never quite make her youngest lodger out. He was secretive, not very good at conversation, and seemed to have merely a passing acquaintance with daylight. She knew he tinkered about with cameras but didn't have a studio, and so could not easily offer portrait services or the like. And yet, he appeared to have a steady source of income; his rent was paid on time, his clothes were new, and he always had the money for a cab on the few occasions he ventured outside of Burlington Square – often with a large suitcase and his tripod camera. He was not ostentatious with his money, nor did he appear to have a limitless supply, but enough to live on, and live in relative comfort, even if she felt that as a solitary twenty-five-year-old man, he was really not living at all.

The unstoppable matchmaker in her considered two lost, lonely and shy people who would soon be living only a floor apart, and she couldn't help but wonder if the company of a nice young lady might lift him from the constant melancholy that he carried around with him.

Perhaps she would insist that Mercy took Gilbert's trays up, regardless of his protestations...

50

Mercy stood in the middle of her new rooms and spun around three times. She could hardly believe her luck. In truth, it had been foolhardy to apply for them because they would stretch her financially, but the gardens in the square were so pretty, and the area felt more salubrious than her previous lodgings. In her haste to secure accommodation in London, she had chosen badly, and she'd begun to feel increasingly unsafe in some of the streets she had to walk through to get to work. Men loitered in the doorways, and with the shorter days, it wouldn't be long before she was walking home in the dark. Burlington Square was a far more respectable neighbourhood, and half the distance to Pemberton's.

She threw her dated straw hat onto the bed and wished she had a more fashionable wardrobe. Working at the department store, she could only gaze wistfully at the stylish cloche hats and the glamorous beaded drop-waisted evening dresses, but then farm life had never leant itself to fashion. Practical, hard-wearing clothing had always been the order of the day.

There had been no plan when she'd arrived on that late-night train at Liverpool Street, with only one small suitcase of possessions and a decade of misery draped across her thin shoulders. She had very little money to her name, but a heart full of hope, believing that here she could find a little respite, and that nothing she encountered in the city could possibly be worse than what she'd endured back home. Her mother-in-law had always treated her badly, blaming Mercy for what had happened to her son in the war, the poor financial state of the farm, and the fact she would never be a grandmother.

'You ungrateful little chit,' she'd shouted at her. 'Made him so miserable that he had little to live for, and so distracted that he hadn't seen the danger. Toying with him all that time and then going off the boil like that.' Hardly fair, but then Mercy had believed everything was her fault for so many years. Only recently had she realised the woman just needed someone to blame, and her unassuming daughter-in-law was the perfect scapegoat. She could hardly lay the fault at the feet of her son, and the Kaiser was too far away to shout at, so Mercy became the whipping-boy.

She sat on the edge of the bed and took her coin purse from her handbag. A few months of putting aside what little was left of the housekeeping, and a loan from the schoolteacher's wife, (her only true friend in the world) had been enough to buy her train ticket with a few pounds left over to start a new life. She'd secured the job at the department store with a reference supplied by her friend, and was just about getting by. That much of what she told Miss Humphries was true. The pinch-faced woman, a Miss Copely, who'd interviewed her at Pemberton's had recognised Mercy was well-spoken, bright and would surely be an asset to the glove counter. When quizzed about her marital status, Mercy informed her that she'd lost her husband in the war. That, combined with the fact that she was twenty-seven, seemed to secure her appointment; the woman had muttered something about her being less likely to scamper off and get married within five minutes of taking up her post.

Shop work was still not considered entirely respectable, but Mercy quite enjoyed it. Besides, there wasn't much else open to a country girl with a limited education in the big city. At least, on the glove counter, she was mostly selling to other women, and her hours were much reduced compared to those of farm life – although it was astonishing how exhausting standing on your feet all day and making small talk to potential customers could be.

The sartorial elegance of gloves had not struck her before acquiring the job. They were purely a practical item on the farm, to protect hands from the rough nature of the work, and for warmth in the bitterly cold winter months. Naturally, she'd owned a smart pair for church, but the array of styles, lengths, colours and fabrics for sale at such a fancy establishment was utterly bewildering. She was actively encouraged to push the customer towards the most expensive designs, and instructed that the fit was everything. One's social status was defined by one's gloves, and the hitherto poor fit of store-bought pairs was an issue Pemberton's was striving to address.

During her short time at the department store, her eyes had been opened to so many things, not least of which was that it was possible to be rewarded for hard work by suitable financial remuneration and kind words. She'd had little of either up until now.

This led her thoughts down the inevitable path to Roland, the young man she had married when she was barely eighteen. He was tall, self-assured and undeniably good-looking. Even in the schoolroom, he could have had any girl he wanted, but when the time had come to choose a sweetheart, he'd chosen her. Mercy Lummis – the small, quiet girl with wide blue eyes and long fair hair. She twisted the gold band on her ring finger and a tear fell from the corner of her eye, dribbling a hot, wet path to her chin.

Running away had been a foolhardy move. Her only trump card

was that no one had seen it coming, although she knew Mrs Mayweather senior would not rest until she had tracked her ungrateful daughter-in-law down. But as she stretched out across the wide bed at Burlington Square, for the first time since she'd made her mad dash down to London, she felt as though she might actually get away with it.

* * *

On the Monday, up two whole hours before she was needed to smile at customers and arrange gloves in glass cabinets, Mercy began her duties with Miss Humphries in earnest.

Skipping down the stairs then heading towards the kitchen, she heard a knock as she passed the front door. To save Agnes's legs, she opened it and cautiously peered around the door frame to see a suited middle-aged man wearing a bowler hat, his greying temples just visible above his ears.

'Would it be possible to see Miss Humphries?' he enquired.

'Certainly. May I say who's calling?'

'Mr Thompson.'

Mercy turned to find Agnes but she was already coming up the hallway, wiping damp hands on the edge of her floral apron.

'Oh dear, did you not get my letter? I've given the rooms to Mrs Mayweather.' She pointed to Mercy.

'Yes, yes, but I wanted to let you know that I'm still interested should the young lady move on or any of the other rooms here become available. It really is such a delightful part of the city. I cannot express in words the affinity I had with this charming house and the beautiful square opposite. I remain at my current lodgings but do entreat you to contact me should anything else become available.'

'Of course. I still have your details.'

Mr Thompson nodded to show his understanding but seemed reluctant to leave, only stepping back down the steps and returning to the street when the silence became awkward.

As Miss Humphries closed the door, she turned to Mercy.

'Unusually keen,' she said. 'I'm very fond of Burlington Square myself, but there are plenty of similar lodgings available. It must be my natural charm,' she joked. 'Or my cat. Although, Inky wasn't particularly keen on our Mr Thompson, as I recall. But then cats can be inexplicably fussy.'

Mercy followed her landlady into the kitchen and set about helping with the breakfasts. She'd done most of the cooking at Home Farm and knew her way around a frying pan. Miss Humphries was impressed.

'It's taken you half the time it takes me,' she said. 'I'm exhausted just watching you whizz about like a spinning top. Thank you so much. When you've delivered the breakfasts, you must eat something yourself. You have plenty of time. It will only take fifteen minutes to walk to Pemberton's from here. I'll scramble you some eggs whilst you take up the trays.'

Mercy tried not to look too overcome by the older woman's thoughtfulness. She couldn't remember the last time someone had thanked her back home, let alone offered to cook for her, or suggest that she took the weight off her feet.

Mercy collected the first wooden tray, laid out with black pudding, bacon and kidneys, with a pot of tea and a sturdy mug, and headed back down the hall.

She knocked on Mr Gorski's door until she heard a voice command her to enter. Trying not to drop the tray, she opened the door to be greeted by a kindly-looking white-haired old man seated in a high-backed leather armchair.

'Not only a delightfully arranged tray for my breakfast, but also something beautiful to look at,' he said, with a smile. 'You must be the new girl Miss Humphries mentioned.'

'Mercy Mayweather.' She stuck out her hand and gave a nervous bob of the head. The gentleman before her was the most famous person she had ever encountered, apart from catching a glimpse of Lucy Baldwin, the prime minister's wife, drifting through the department store – and even then, it was only because the other girls were whispering her name that she'd even looked up.

'Alexander Gorski – the grumpy foreigner Miss Humphries has undoubtedly warned you is overly melancholy and long since past his prime. Ah, but time catches up with us all eventually.'

Mercy offered to open his curtains and plumped some cushions, and they exchanged impersonal pleasantries before she returned to the ground floor to collect the tray for the gentleman who lived in the attics. This breakfast was much smaller, just a soft-boiled egg and some soldiers. Apparently, the gentleman in question didn't have much of an appetite and was quite particular about his diet.

'Fancy ideas about not eating flesh,' Agnes tutted. 'Like those Hindu fellows that live on vegetables and believe the cow is a sacred animal. Not sure I could live without roast beef. But he says if it was good enough for Percy Shelley, it's good enough for him. He feels eating animals is akin to cannibalism.' She rolled her eyes.

'Still, he's a nice enough lad,' Agnes continued, 'so I do my best, although I can't deny that a bit of lard finds its way into things sometimes, but let's keep that between us, eh? He needs building up and I don't think potatoes and turnips are up to the job, however fancy I cook them.'

Mercy smiled as she picked up the second tray. There was something about this woman that reminded her of her dear old dad. He had always called a spade by its name and had no time for anyone who deigned to give it a fancier term.

Three flights of stairs confronted her this time, and she could understand why Miss Humphries was finding it increasingly difficult to manage them.

She tapped at the narrow door that separated the final flight from the remainder of the house and heard the patter of feet down the wooden treads. The door opened outward and the startled face of a man about her age greeted her. She hadn't expected him to be quite so young and it unnerved her. He looked surprised and embarrassed all at once, and his pale face flushed slightly pink.

There was an uncomfortable silence as they both stared at each other.

'Your breakfast,' she finally said, and raised the tray to him. He was on the bottom step so higher than her, although he didn't strike her as a particularly tall man.

'Agnes knows I prefer to collect it, but thank you.' He nodded as he took it from her. There was another silence until he eventually turned and headed back to the attics. She closed the door and returned downstairs, thinking Miss Humphries had been right. He didn't say much. In fact, their entire conversation had consisted of only twelve words.

51

Mercy quickly settled into a comforting routine. Used to being up with the lark, she sorted breakfast for Agnes's gentlemen of a morning, and then undertook the brisk walk to Pemberton's for a long day on her feet, smiling and extolling the virtues of the soft kidskin, or enticing the customer with fancy embroidered cuffs. She preferred to spend her lunch hour alone for, whilst she craved company, the highly animated chatter of her excitable work colleagues was sometimes too much. They talked about things she had no experience of, like jazz music, screen idols and drinking cocktails, and she wasn't bold enough to offer her opinions, even when she had them.

At the end of each day, she returned to Burlington Square, looking forward to more time in the company of her landlady, who was fast becoming a firm friend. Yes, she was opinionated, but she was also kind, and cared about Mercy in her mother hen way. It was a new and pleasant feeling. Her inconsequential chit-chat as they both moved around the kitchen doing various jobs, or stood together heaving laundry from the copper, was calming and uplifting, and before long Mercy knew everything about her fellow lodgers that she could possibly need to know – and several things she most definitely didn't.

'I'm talking far too much,' Agnes apologised. 'It's like having a conversation with young Gilbert – he barely contributes, much like yourself. You must describe farm life to me, and tell me about Suffolk. It's not a county I have ever visited.'

They were sitting together in the front room, Mercy happy to spend her evenings with this motherly old lady. She sat on the shabby pale blue sofa, her legs curled under her slender body. It was a bit lumpy but Mercy rather liked it. If only it could talk, she pondered, it would be able to tell all manner of tales.

'Oh, I'm not the chatty type,' Mercy said, dipping her eyes. 'My past holds too many painful memories. I'd rather move on from it all.'

Agnes nodded her understanding, as she petted Inky's lopsided head. He stretched out his two front paws, and then rolled onto his back to allow her to stroke his tummy. The trust that cat had in his owner gave Mercy immeasurable comfort.

'I understand completely, my dear. You came to London to see the bright lights, meet new people and make wonderful memories.'

Why *had* she come to London? Perhaps simply because all roads led there and she had no connections anywhere else. Mercy had hoped such a bustling city would offer anonymity and employment opportunities, but had not considered that there might be new and exciting experiences open to her. From the moment she'd disembarked at Liverpool Street station the previous month, she'd known time was against her. Constantly looking over her shoulder, expecting to be tracked down and shamed into returning to her old life, there was a part of her that accepted the inevitability of her situation.

'Life doesn't always turn out the way we imagined when we were young,' Agnes lamented. 'But we must embrace every aspect of it whilst we can. I firmly believe that anything is possible, even when you believe all hope is lost. God will see that the righteous are rewarded.'

Mercy didn't hold with the older lady's belief that God had everything under control. The decision to flee had been hers alone, but perhaps Agnes had a point. The righteous certainly *deserved* to be rewarded, even if they had to take matters into their own hands.

'There is much to see and do, and so many interesting people hereabouts,' her landlady continued. 'The city is a veritable melting pot of cultures and social classes. I so longed to travel when I was your age, but I have consoled myself with the realisation that in many ways, the world has come to me...'

And as Agnes embarked on another verbal ramble, ruing that any chance of globe-trotting adventures had passed her by, Mercy made a promise to herself. It was inevitable that she would be tracked down, the only uncertainty was when. But in the meantime, she should embrace every aspect of her new-found freedoms. She should live every day as if it was her last, take chances and savour every moment.

* * *

On the Friday night of her first week, Mercy was woken from her slumbers by a loud crash. She'd been dreaming of when the handsome young Roland had walked with her down to the south meadow and asked if he might kiss her. Mercy's sixteen-year-old heart had soared with the swallows above. It was one of her happiest memories and it often came to her when she least expected it – taunting her with what could have been.

As Roland's lips were about to bump into her own, her eyes flew open at the noise, which was followed by shouts and banging doors, echoing up the staircase and filtering through the thin walls into her rooms. Alarmed at first, she thought perhaps she'd been found, that they were here to take her back to Suffolk, but as she lay in the dark, clutching the counterpane tightly to her chest, she realised these were happy sounds – laughing and singing.

She grabbed her cotton dressing gown and walked to the long window overlooking the square. The soft glow of the gas lamps illuminated an open-topped motor car below, with a largely naked figure sprawled across the back seat. No one she knew owned a motor car, and so she crept to the doorway and opened it up just a crack to hear the bossy tones of a young woman drifting up the stairs.

Pulling her dressing gown cord tighter around her body she ventured into the hallway and was both horrified and relieved to bump into a topless Gilbert, who almost collided with her as he rounded the corner from the attics. (Yes, it was a warm August evening but the proliferation of semi-naked young men was alarming.) There was a moment as he looked down at her attire and she up at him. His thin, pale body, whilst lacking the broad shoulders and firm muscles of Roland (who had spent a lifetime lifting, ploughing and hoeing) was still unmistakably that of a man, and the sight of it affected her in ways she couldn't control. Dark hairs were arranged in a triangle under his collar bone and, more disconcertingly, leading from his navel to somewhere beyond the drawstring waistband of his striped pyjama trousers. Her chest tightened as the tips of the fingers on her right hand involuntarily traced a slow path down her throat.

'Damn. I'd forgotten about you,' he said, suddenly conscious that he was naked from the waist up.

She pulled her eyes away from the mesmeric sight and back into the moment. It was, she acknowledged, reassuring to have him nearby when there was such a commotion below, but she chastised herself for the places her libidinous thoughts were leading her. It wasn't as though she hadn't seen such a sight before, but she ached to be touched, to have a man hover above her, his arms either side of her body, and lean down to kiss her. She day-dreamed of that moment a lover entered her body with his – for two sticky, fumbling figures to unite in glorious and mutual desire. Sometimes, much to her own embarrassment, it was all she could think of when she encountered an attractive young man, and she was certain that her flushed cheeks would give her away every time.

'No, Clara, you are *not* to take Lady Winifred.' Agnes's indignant voice drifted up the stairs. From what Mercy could gather, some young people had turned up to the house on their way to a party, and Lady Winifred was part of the group, but it was obvious that Agnes knew these people, alleviating her fear that drunkards had accessed the house for high jinks, or thieves were ransacking the rooms below. Their polished speech reeked of money, as did their total disregard for those in the house. She'd heard of the Bright Young Things and their increasingly unpalatable, occasionally illegal, escapades in the streets of London at night. What must it be like to have enough wealth not to care what people thought about your behaviour?

Gilbert sighed and began to descend the stairs, closely followed by Mercy, anxiously clutching the two sides of her gown, and wishing she looked more respectable.

As they rounded the final landing, they were spotted by the most vocal of the intruders.

'Goodness, darlings, have we woken you all up? Terribly sorry and all that.' A glamorous young woman wearing the high-hemmed dress of a little girl and a huge yellow ribbon in her extremely modish shingled hair, blinked apologetic eyes up at the pair of them.

'I can only apologise,' she purred. 'Especially as it appears we have disturbed your little midnight tryst. Scurry back up to bed and we shan't say a word.' She put a painted fingernail to her lips. 'Even though Aunt Ag really doesn't condone that sort of thing under her roof.'

Mercy's face coloured up faster than a recently stoked furnace, and their landlady chose that moment to reappear at that end of the hallway, also in her nightwear. She looked up at Mercy and Gilbert, before returning her glare to the young lady.

'We weren't... I didn't—' Mercy began, but Gilbert had already spun on his heels, stomping back up the staircase and grinding his teeth, too angry to respond.

'You've disturbed my lodgers. It really won't do, Clara. Mrs Mayweather is a respectable widow who helps me with the house. And Gilbert, well, I'm not really sure girls are his thing,' she said, and turned her face upwards to Mercy. 'I can only apologise for the unruly behaviour of my niece, who is just leaving,' she finished, pointedly.

Mercy noticed for the first time a handsome gentleman loitering near the hall stand, dressed like a schoolboy, and clearly embarrassed by the uproar they'd caused.

'There's no need to pick on the staff, Clara.' He nodded up at Mercy. 'I'm terribly sorry, Miss H. I fear we've rather made a nuisance of ourselves. Come on, old thing, you know the party can't possibly start without us.'

And the disturbance ended as abruptly as it had begun, as he whisked the young woman through the front door and out into the sticky night.

* * *

Every time Mercy stepped from the front door at Burlington Square her heart was filled at once with both joy and fear. The late summer weather was proving unduly oppressive, and being greeted by the uplifting sight of such a green patch of garden in the middle of the city made her long for home. It was a very different landscape to the flat open fields and wide expanse of sky that surrounded them in Suffolk, but it was undeniably a beautiful part of London. Extravagant Georgian houses surrounded the square and there was a beauty to the grand architecture, peppered with large trees and small tubs of flowers.

All that mattered to her was her freedom. No one demanded to know where she was going, or scolded her for her tardiness and ingratitude. Living at Home Farm she had been made to carry the weight of everyone else's pain, and bear the brunt of their frustrations. But those who resided at Burlington Square had, so far, been kind to her. Even Gilbert, whose words were few, never complained or berated her for any perceived transgression. There was a familial feel to the household despite the lack of blood ties, and Agnes was maternal in her care and generous with her time.

But each step of her journey to Pemberton's was taken in trepidation, and she studiously avoided eye-contact with passers-by, should they prove to be someone from home. She kept her head down and allowed her wide-brimmed unfashionable hat to shield her face until she arrived at work, hoping that such a place would never be frequented by simple farming folk from Suffolk – even those hunting her down.

She enjoyed her job but shop work was almost as tiring as the labours involved in milking cows, washing heavy laundry and digging over vegetable patches. Gloves were not the most exciting things to sell but it was certainly a cleaner occupation than mucking out pigs or plucking fowl. Miss Copely was forever telling her to be more confident with the customers – especially the men – and that she must make an effort to smile at them more. They occasionally approached her counter to buy gloves as gifts and she found these interchanges awkward. The only males she'd really spoken to in her life were family or itinerant labourers – and to be honest, these conversations largely revolved around food and whether the privy was free. In fact, with her movements so closely monitored in recent years, she hardly interacted with anyone outside the farm.

Her exchanges with Gilbert were proving equally awkward. He was clearly unhappy that Agnes had employed her and insisted on collecting his trays from the kitchen. She assumed this was because he was shy, like her, but during her second week she witnessed a confident side to him that surprised her. The man from the basement appeared when both she and Gilbert were in the kitchens, to offer excuses for the non-payment of his rent to Agnes.

'We're a bit short again this week and I wondered if you could see your way to looking kindly on us, maybe taking a bit under, or giving me more time? You wouldn't want the little 'uns going without...'

'Well, no but —'

'Pay up,' Gilbert said, leaning nonchalantly on the door frame, rolling a cigarette between his fingers, his eyes not lifting from his task. 'Miss Humphries is a good sort and doesn't charge enough rent as it is. If you can't afford her rates, find cheaper rooms. She'll not have a problem getting in others who can.'

'Keep out of this. You don't know anything about our situation. Times are hard – for some of us, at any rate.'

'Not so hard you can't stop off at the Mad Hatter. I've seen you there. If times are that hard, stick to cups of tea.'

The look Mr Smith shot across the room at Gilbert was murderous, but Gilbert seemed strangely unthreatened. Apparently only shy twenty-seven-year-old widows had the power to reduce him to a nervous wreck. The man left the kitchen with a scowl.

'But I don't want the kiddies to go without,' Agnes whispered, as the backdoor closed.

'They won't.' Gilbert stood up straight, tucked the cigarette behind his ear and snatched up his tray. 'I'll see to that.'

'Do stop a while, Gilbert,' she said. 'It's hardly as though you have anywhere to be. And young Mercy here is new to London and about your age. Perhaps you could show her some of the sights? You can surely spare us both a few minutes to chat about your day? I can quite easily pop the kettle on the stove and we can sit around the table and have a nice cup of—'

'Sorry, things to do,' The tips of his ears went beetroot red and he nodded at Mercy before making a hasty retreat. Tiny prickles danced up her arms as she stared hard at the eggs she was whisking for Mr Gorski. He was leaving because of her and she wasn't sure why. Probably Agnes's ill-judged attempt to matchmake.

However uncomfortable it made her, she knew her landlady's interference was kindly meant, but after several days of similar such comments from an increasingly unsubtle Agnes, Gilbert decided that it was easier to confront Mercy briefly at the bottom of the attic steps, without Agnes's overseeing eye, than suffer such humiliation, and allowed her to take up his trays.

'Um, I don't suppose you'd pose for me?' he asked her one evening, as she handed over a steaming bowl of macaroni and cheese.

'Absolutely not.' She was quite scandalised and suddenly a little afraid. What was he up to in those attics? And what could he possibly want with a photograph of her?

'Sorry, no, that sounds dreadful... It's not what you think. I'll pay.' He scrunched up his face and put his hand to his forehead. 'Oh God, that sounds worse. Forget I said anything. Sorry.'

She nodded at his apology and retreated back downstairs as he offered a further 'Sorry' which followed her along the landing.

However, she realised with a degree of amusement, he was now at least able to communicate with her in whole sentences.

52

Just before Mercy left for home after a long day at Pemberton's, Miss Copely pulled her aside again to chastise her for her shyness.

'Gloves aren't selling like they used to so we cannot afford to lose potential sales through your reluctance to speak up. They want you to have opinions,' she stressed, 'for you to tell them which gloves they must buy, and these are, naturally, our more expensive ranges...'

Mercy wasn't used to anyone caring about her opinion, so hadn't felt qualified to offer it, but realised she would have to try harder if she were to keep her job. She was trying to be bolder, and had made a real effort with her colleagues during her lunchbreak. They had invited her to the picture house and she'd accepted, determined to make positive memories during her time in London after her conversation with Agnes. They might be the only thing keeping her spirits up in the lonely years ahead.

As she rounded the corner into Burlington Square, looking forward to an evening of peace and quiet, she recognised the smart young lady who had caused such an uproar in the house the week before. Miss Humphries' niece was sitting on the stone steps, with her elegant legs stretched out before her.

'Oh, darling,' Clara said, as she approached. 'I've been here for forever. There's no answer and I'm absolutely gasping for a cup of tea.'

'Your aunt must be out shopping,' Mercy said. 'I'm sure she won't be long. Mercy Mayweather.' She stuck out her hand.

'Oh, the widow,' Clara said, putting a cigarette to her lips, making smoking look the most elegant of activities. She blew a wispy stream of intoxicating vapour from her red lips, and Mercy was almost tempted to ask if she could try one. 'Who works at the department store?' Mercy nodded. 'I thought you were a *friend* of the corpse boy when you appeared the other night. I do apologise but the pair of you appeared together and I just assumed...'

Mercy didn't like the way she said 'friend', or her unkind description of Gilbert, but didn't comment.

'I'll let you inside. My key is here somewhere...' She fiddled with the clasp of her crocodile handbag.

'Sit with me a moment first,' Clara said, patting the step next to her. 'I need to talk to someone, and came to bend dear Aunt Ag's ear, but you'll do.'

Charming, she thought, but obediently sat next to the elegant woman. Mercy tended to do as she was told.

'So, here is a jolly fine to-do. The young man you saw me with the other evening proposed to me last night. His parents are eye-wateringly rich and have a sizeable estate in Somerset. He simply adores me and has promised me the heavens, the earth and everything in between.'

She paused, clearly expecting Mercy to congratulate her, and raised a curious eyebrow when she did not get the anticipated response.

'Do you love him?'

'Interesting.' Clara narrowed her eyes and Mercy felt unnecessarily scrutinised. 'No one else has asked me that, as though the money eclipses all other considerations. Yet, you were married – surely you would recommend such a noble institution?'

'It's a legally binding contract,' she replied. 'Don't do it for the wrong reasons.'

'I tend to agree, darling, but when your beastly father makes it clear that you will be left penniless and homeless if you dare to refuse, it rather puts one in a tight spot.'

Mercy wondered if she should confide that her own marriage had also been at the behest of her parents (it appeared even money and privilege did not enable a woman to be truly independent), but they were interrupted before she had the courage to speak.

'Mummy, why are there so many ladies sitting on our house?' a small girl of about six asked her harassed-looking parent, as a row of curious eyes stopped at 23 Burlington Square, and stared up at the pair of them. This must be Jemima and her children, Mercy surmised.

'Some people don't have jobs, children, or husbands, and all the time in the world to fritter away on doorsteps, smoking cigarettes and contentedly watching the world go by.' Both women heard Jemima's disgruntled reply, as she struggled to manoeuvre a large black pram through the gate to the basement. There was a sleeping infant within, and a girl of perhaps three or four sitting on top.

'Let me help,' offered Mercy, jumping to her feet.

'I'm fine, and am sure I don't wish to disturb you *busy* ladies.'

'Mrs Mayweather has no doubt worked an extremely long day at Pemberton's,' Clara interjected, 'on her feet for the whole day, listening to the moans of selfish over-indulged customers like myself, so don't be so hasty to judge. I, on the other hand, am exactly what you imagine, but I wouldn't describe myself as contented – far from it.'

'Then I apologise, Mrs Mayweather. Agnes told me about you, but we haven't met.' She nodded at Mercy, who was lifting the middle daughter from the top of the pram, having anticipated the next stage of Jemima's manoeuvres.

The pair of them wrestled the three small children and an unwieldy pram through the gate as Clara wittered on.

'I, darlings, am at a junction in my life. A crossroads, if you will. A lucrative offer of marriage has been dangled before me, that my father insists I accept, but my heart isn't in it.'

'For the love of God, do *not* get married,' Jemima said, lodging the pram safely at the top of the steps and making eye contact with Clara for the first time. 'I'd rather be hanged for murder. Considerably less painful and the awfulness over so much faster.'

Clara muttered to herself something about wishing she could murder an Alice, but the drab colours of prison uniform really didn't go with her complexion. There was a pause before Mercy started to giggle at the comments made by the two women. Almost immediately Clara joined in with a throaty, infectious laugh, and Jemima promptly followed.

Sometimes all it takes is one defining moment in time and you just know. You look at someone across a crowded room and your heart assures you they are your soulmate. You set eyes on your newborn baby, confident that the love that binds you to that child is absolute. Or you share a joke with two relative strangers and realise you're set to be the very best of friends.

Mercy looked at the two women before her – one as prickly as hedgehog and the other so entitled it was almost embarrassing, acknowledging that she also had her faults, not least that she was shy and unworldly. Busy farm life ensured she'd never had close girlfriends, but perhaps this was a benefit she could reap from her grand adventure. Might they even correspond after her London life came to an end? Surely her mother-in-law couldn't deny her that – she'd denied her all else.

Determined to win these disparate women over, she wondered how to engineer further encounters. Would Agnes mind her arranging an afternoon tea party in her rooms? It was a curious mix but then the chickens quite happily shared the paddock at Home Farm with the cows and the goats. Creatures did not have to be the same to get along.

'Mummy, can I show these ladies my train set?' the oldest of the three girls asked.

'A train set. How lovely,' Mercy said, leaping on the opportunity presented by Jemima's daughter. 'Do you have brothers?'

Jemima tutted, but the hardness around her eyes had softened since their shared joke. Clara elegantly dismounted the steps, brushing down her skirt and stubbing out her cigarette. 'Darling, girls can have train sets too,' she said. 'I always hankered after the boys' toys – when I wasn't riding my horse, that is.'

'How very la-di-da,' Jemima mocked. 'Owning a horse.' She turned to her eldest daughter. 'Don't you be getting ideas, Matilda. The only horse you're likely to ride on will be an upside-down mop, with buttons for eyes.' She grabbed the hand of the middle child and descended the basement steps to her front door. 'But you may invite the ladies in for a cup of tea, if the posh one doesn't mind slumming it in our tiny basement.'

Mercy's heart lifted.

'I can ride,' she volunteered. 'But my horse pulled a cart and sometimes a plough. I lived on a working farm.'

'Oh, goodness!' said Matilda, her eyes as wide as saucers, as crying noises started up from the depths of the pram. 'Now I don't know who to play with – the farming lady or the film star.'

Clara, realising that she was the latter, smiled. 'Play with the farm lady. I'm so much better at making grown-up conversation and drinking tea.' She swept past the crying child and down the steps into the basement.

Mercy sighed and picked up the little girl, who was getting more agitated by the second. It felt natural to sway, so she placed the infant on her hip and rocked her. The crying subsided and a pair of chubby hands began to explore her face and pull at her hair. The biggest, gurgliest laugh came from the child and Mercy had a hard job keeping her emotions in check.

'Come on, farming lady, I have four carriages and a shiny red engine.' Matilda pulled at her dress and Mercy realised that being friends with these two women was going to be hard work, for so many different reasons, but was inexplicably certain it would be worth it in the end.

53

The hour spent with Jemima and Clara was everything Mercy could have hoped for. She spent most of that time on the floor with the children, happily listening to Jemima hold forth about equality for all, regardless of social standing or sex. This woman had a drum and was determined to bang it as loud as she could. Clara deliberately teased the young mother, and sparks flew, but as a bystander, Mercy could see both women enjoyed the lively discussion. When the time came to leave – or rather when Mr Smith arrived home after a long day on the trams and not best pleased to find his house full of strangers – Clara insisted they should meet up again when she was next visiting her aunt, and the women had all agreed. But then Clara had a way of getting people to do what she wanted, Mercy noticed, and even Mr Smith's mood had improved by the time they left.

With her limited funds, Mercy went to the pictures one evening with two of the girls from haberdashery. The film starred Ivor Novello and his dark looks and brooding expressions were worth every hard-earned penny of her ticket price. She also persuaded Agnes to accompany her to afternoon tea at a Lyon's Corner House and, as they nibbled on finger sandwiches and scones, they admired the smart uniforms of the nippies. But these things, lovely as they were, cost money, so she also made memories that were free, wandering around the landmarks of the city and visiting museums. The British Museum was first on her list and it totally enthralled her, although she was decidedly unsettled by the Egyptian Hall, and not only because the statues made her feel so tiny.

Along with Agnes's encouragement to embrace life, came an overwhelming desire to carry out small acts of kindness, almost to offset the unkind things she would be returning to. It wasn't as though her mother-in-law beat her – nothing so barbaric – but Mercy was treated like an unpaid scullery maid and farm labourer rolled into one. The bitter old woman was making her pay for a crime she had not committed, and from the moment she'd married Roland, her identity, her farm and her independence had all been stripped from her. So, after nine years of being at the beck and call of Mrs Mayweather senior, she was determined to be regarded kindly by those at Burlington Square, and maybe even remembered, after she'd moved on.

She didn't have long to spend with Mr Gorski before work, but chatting to her landlady soon realised how unhappy he was, so made sure to spend extra time with him in the evenings, when she had nowhere else to be. Her first success was persuading him to listen to his music again after Agnes confided that she hadn't heard his records since Mr Blandford passed away. At Mercy's insistence, he directed her to a favourite recording of Chopin, and instructed her on the operation of the gramophone.

She noticed his fingers twitching along with the music. How he must long to dance them across the ivory keys and produce the music himself, she thought. He raised his hands into the air as the music swelled, and swayed them gently from side to side. It was then she noticed the abandoned piano in the back corner, dust across the closed lid, and she could hardly look at the poor man without welling up.

'You must understand,' he explained, as the sonata he'd selected came to an end, 'that the recording of the piano is not very satisfactory, offering greater difficulties than the recording of almost any other instrument in the orchestra, but to listen to my records is better than not hearing any music at all.'

'Tell me about your life? I have lived such a small existence, I should be interested to hear of one bigger than mine,' she asked, as she lifted the needle from the spinning disc and switched the turntable off.

'And yet I shall die such a tiny death.' He sighed. 'I have no children to mourn me. Only my music is left behind.'

'But what a fantastic legacy. I will leave no children, nor anything of significance when I pass away.' She sighed at the truth of this. 'Did you always know that the piano was your destiny?'

And so, he told her of his childhood, his musical training, and his international career, and she was in awe of his achievements and global adventures.

'I have lived everywhere but my homeland since I was a young man. As I got older, however, and my body began to betray me, I travelled less and earned my living from gramophone recordings, teaching, and even composed a Christmas carol, which still earns me a surprising amount.'

He began to hum the tune and Mercy recognised it immediately.

'You wrote that?' she asked. 'You are so clever.'

'Mr Thompson said much the same. I am feeling quite flattered by all this attention of late.'

'Mr Thompson?' The name meant nothing to her.

'The gentleman who applied for the rooms you now occupy, but who, having heard about me from Miss Humphries, expressed a particular desire to meet. We had the most pleasant afternoon yesterday discussing music and birds. He has offered to take me to the park before the weather turns.'

'How kind,' she said, now remembering him calling by on her first week, and pleased that there were still people in this world who would put themselves out for others with no thought for themselves.

54

'Here's the rent we owe and I can only apologise that it's late... again.'

It was almost a month into her time at Burlington Square. Mercy had taken the gentlemen up their breakfast trays and was just preparing to leave for work when the backdoor to the kitchen opened and Jemima appeared.

'Nonsense,' said Agnes. 'I know it's tough at the moment and, what with another on the way, I'm sure pennies are tight. But thank you.' She took the coins from Mrs Smith.

The young mother flinched slightly, frowned and then rested her hand protectively over her slightly rounded stomach. Mercy wondered what it must feel like to grow another person inside yourself – to feel them move within and to know that they will soon be part of the wider world and dependent on you for everything. How did you cope with such an onerous duty of care? And do so until such time as you must inevitably set them free? Because that's what you did when you truly loved someone – you set them free.

'I assume you never had children?' Jemima said, noticing

Mercy's gaze. 'I didn't think to ask you the other day, too busy being free with my opinions.' She smiled by way of an apology.

'No, we didn't have children.'

'I'm sorry, but p'raps it's for the best if you're on your own now. I do love them but they are exhausting.'

She swallowed. 'Actually, I should have liked children very much.'

'There's still time. How old are you?'

'Twenty-seven.'

'There you go then. Childbearing until we are forty – though God help me if that proves the case. And you can always help me with this one—' she moved her hand in a circular motion around her stomach '—if you'd like some practice?'

Mercy smiled. She loved babies but would it be harder to be around them when she knew it wasn't something she could ever have? She would never meet anyone else. The duration of her fertility was irrelevant.

'Perhaps,' she replied.

'Actually, you can have my Nicholas,' Jemima said, without a smile. Mercy wasn't sure if she was joking or not. She noticed the young mother study her face, as though trying to decide whether passing on her husband was a realistic option. 'Apologies, I don't mean to make light of your grief. I do understand that some people find that one perfect love and no one else will ever measure up.' Which rather implied she had not found that with her husband.

Mercy remained silent. She had been tricked into her union and it had not been love. Perhaps at first, when she'd been young and innocent, but it hadn't taken long for her to realise the truth.

'That reminds me, ladies,' Agnes said. 'My sister Daphne rang first thing this morning to say Clara is engaged to Jack Rigby. Isn't that simply wonderful news?'

The two younger women exchanged a look that said anything but, and Mercy thought it rather sad that Clara had felt she'd had no option but to accept a proposal from a man she clearly didn't love. She also realised that an impending marriage was likely to be the end of their burgeoning friendship. A grand home in Somerset and the inevitable offspring would make visits to London difficult.

'There was talk of an engagement party but Clara has apparently put her foot down. Such a shame. Not that I would have been able to attend but family events are always such a delight—'

There was a sudden groan from Jemima, as she reached out for the back of the kitchen chair.

'Oh, my dear girl,' Agnes exclaimed. 'The baby?'

'It can't be.'

But even Mercy had seen enough farm animals to understand the process. She glanced up at the clock, thinking she should be leaving for work, but there was another cry of pain and she knew Jemima was more important.

'I'll get Gilbert to fetch the doctor. He's lived here longer than me, and he'll be faster than either of us,' she said to Agnes, and raced from the room, dashing up the stairs to the attics.

When Gilbert finally answered his door, clutching a bundle of papers, he looked most alarmed to see Mercy.

'It's Saturday. You work.' His conversation was as terse as ever.

'I think Jemima's baby is coming, and it's far too early. Can you fetch a doctor?'

'Of course.' The remaining colour drained from his already pale face and he patted his waistcoat pocket for his key. He stepped out onto the landing without pause for thought, thrusting the papers he was holding at her, and before she knew it, he'd leapt down the stairs, two at a time, and disappeared from view.

And Mercy couldn't help but notice, as she placed the papers on the floor by his door for his return, that it was a quantity of leaflets advertising the personal services of Gilbert Adams – medium and spirit photographer – who for a very reasonable sum, could help alleviate your grief by contacting your dearly departed.

55

Nothing could be done for Jemima, except offer comforting words and deal with the distasteful elements no one wished to dwell on. Her girls had been hastily despatched to the lady at number 22, and shortly afterwards, their tiny baby brother had slipped into this world, never to take a breath of air. With Jemima guiding them and Mercy having delivered a variety of animal offspring in her life, they managed a clean and hygienic delivery, even though the tragedy of the outcome was inevitable. The babe was always going to be too tiny to survive and was almost certainly dead well before Jemima's body rejected it.

Gilbert came to the basement to tell them that the doctor was delayed by a tricky twin delivery on Leopold Street, but everyone knew his presence would have made little difference. Nicholas arrived as the ladies were clearing up, grunted when he established the child had been a son, and said very little else before leaving.

'Thank you for thinking to fetch Nicholas,' Mercy said to Gilbert, as she took a bundle of cloths out to the yard to burn. He was leaning against the wall, cupping one hand around a flickering match as he tried to light a cigarette.

'I don't like the man, but I thought he should be told. Thought he might be of comfort to his wife.'

'He wasn't, but that's not your fault.'

'He doesn't understand death, and particularly how it affects a mother. Can you imagine being responsible for the miracle of birth, and having that cruelly snatched from you? It is the natural order of things that a child outlives its parents. The grief will eat at Jemima and never leave.'

His pamphlets from earlier had alarmed her. She was certain that spiritualism was all a sham and wondered how he could stand there, pretending to have compassion for the bereaved, when he was profiteering from their misery. Not that she'd had much time to make an informed judgement about the young man before her, but there had been something about his eyes when they'd first met that had led her to believe he was honest. More fool her. She'd made that mistake before.

'I wouldn't know,' she replied, feeling indignant and trying not to let her emotions overwhelm her. 'Never having been blessed with children.' Her tone was bitter and he sensed it. She spun on her heels and returned to the basement to offer what little comfort and consolation she could to her new friend, at a time when there were no words powerful enough to ease the pain, and left Gilbert stuttering out an apology to the back of her head.

'I'm not sure what I said to offend you earlier, but I'm sorry,' Gilbert said.

Mercy stood at the bottom of the attic stairs with him, having hastily rustled up some sandwiches for the gentlemen. Agnes was still with Jemima but had suddenly realised her lodgers needed to be fed, and the young woman had willingly obliged, wanting to feel useful in a futile situation.

'No, I'm sorry. Look,' she said, feeling brave, and fed up with Gilbert scampering up the attic steps moments after she'd handed over his food. Nurturing environments did that to you; they made you feel safer, stronger and a little bolder. 'I don't know why you seem so reluctant to engage with me, but I'm only trying to be friendly and certainly have no designs on you. Have you not noticed the ring on my finger?'

She held out her hand, knowing that she did have designs, but they were faintly erotic and merely fantasy. She would not act on them. His virtue was safe.

'Yes, but a widow, and Miss Humphries is hardly subtle when she talks of your being alone for nearly a decade, and how your biological clock must be ticking.'

Mercy fiddled with the dull gold band.

'Why is it everyone thinks they know what's best for me? I'm perfectly happy on my own. I've been married once and that is enough. I can't bear the heartbreak it brings. However, I like people, and we are living in the same house, so it would be easier if we could get along. I don't have many friends.'

'Nor me,' he admitted, dropping his gaze to his toes. 'I think people find my fascination with death disconcerting.'

She couldn't bring herself to mention the pamphlets, and was certain that Agnes knew nothing about his dubious activities.

'Were you in the war?' His age was difficult to pin down, and she wondered if this was why he was so withdrawn. Perhaps he'd witnessed similar unimaginable horrors to those her own husband had been through.

'Too young, thankfully. I'm not sure I could bring myself to kill another man and would probably have been a conscientious objector and the recipient of the dreaded white feathers. I've seen too much of death to go out looking for it.'

She gave him a questioning look, not wanting to ask directly what he was referring to.

'I lost my younger brother and it was not pleasant. He took seven hours to die,' he finally said. 'Lye poisoning. Mistook the white solution for milk. Vomiting blood from a mouth that was red raw with burns and blisters. His tiny body racked with convulsions as we stood by, unable to do anything to ease his suffering.'

She noticed how his pale eyes sank even further into his head and he scrunched up his fists into tight white balls as he leaned back on the wall. She didn't want to hear the disturbing details, but perhaps it was important for him to talk about them. He noticed her wince.

'I'm sorry,' he said. 'It wasn't kind of me to lay that on you without warning.'

'Not at all. I've seen my fair share of unpleasant injuries and deaths, working on a farm,' she admitted. 'I had to dress a leg that had been exposed to the very bone with a scythe, and comfort a man caught in a harrow who did not live beyond an hour, when all I could do was make sure he didn't die alone.'

Gilbert nodded. 'I still can't decide which is worse – the suffering of the victim or the suffering of those left behind. My mother blamed herself, but it wasn't her fault. Billy climbed up and took it from a shelf no one thought he could reach. And I felt guilty because I should have noticed he was missing. I'd been playing with him all day.'

'How old were you?' Mercy asked, gently.

'Eight.'

'Then you know that it wasn't your fault either?'

'I know that when a thing is preventable, and you didn't prevent it, you'll spend a lifetime thinking *what if* regardless of blame.'

They both silently acknowledged this truth, before she nodded and he looked down at the plate of sandwiches that was still in his hand.

'But no one could have prevented Jemima's loss. Please pass on my regards when you see her next.'

'I will.' She took this as the end of the conversation and turned back to the stairs, realising that the usually monosyllabic Gilbert had spoken to her more in the last few minutes than in all the time she'd known him.

56

Agnes had talked to Mercy with great enthusiasm of the National Gallery – a place where one could view magnificent artworks not only from across time, but also from across the globe, for free. To see a Van Gogh, a Botticelli or a Constable would be another memory that she could take back to Suffolk with her. She doubted her mother-in-law even knew what a Botticelli was, probably assuming it was some sort of infectious disease, and that amusing thought alone lifted her spirits.

Consequently, she walked back via Trafalgar Square on her next afternoon off and lost herself for an hour amongst the treasures that hung on its walls. A painting of two lovers by Paris Bordone had held her attention for longer than she'd intended, but there was something hypnotic about two people so clearly together as one. This was how love should be, she knew, and the tiny spark of resentment that had caught on the tinder of her unhappiness began to glow brighter.

The brilliant sunshine and cooler air were most welcome as she stepped outside and headed for Nelson's Column. She had an overwhelming desire to lay her hands on the paw of one of the imposing bronze lions at the base of the monument, but as she neared them, she felt herself being watched. Icy panic turned to relief when she met Gilbert's startled eyes, which dipped away as soon as hers made contact. He was sitting on the steps between two of the magnificent plinth-mounted beasts, facing the gallery and clutching his camera.

She walked up to him, shielding the sun from her eyes, torn between the attraction she felt and her distaste over the pamphlets, but more at ease in his company since their recent candid conversation.

His pale cheeks coloured and he immediately leapt to his feet. 'Mrs Mayweather. Please, take a seat... well, a step.' He waited for her to settle before perching next to her.

'What brings you to this part of the city?' she asked, curious about this jittery man and what he might be taking photographs of in the open air, in the middle of the afternoon. Surely there were no recently departed souls floating thereabouts. His dubious spiritual services were still weighing on her mind.

'I'm observing the world around me, but with the discerning eye of a photographer, looking for interesting things to capture on film.'

'The gallery?' she surmised. It was surely the only thing worthy of a photograph ahead of them.

'Is that all you see?' he asked. 'I fear you've blocked out the things you think don't matter. Before us is a wonderful bustling snapshot of modern London.'

She looked again, trying to focus on the whole scene, and not just the impressive architecture in the distance.

'Close your eyes.'

'Sorry?'

'Close your eyes,' he repeated gently, so she did as he bid.

'What can you remember of the view? Be as specific as you can.'

'Erm... the white splendour of the National Gallery, with its pretty dome and row of fluted columns under the portico. The two fountains, and the road busy with omnibuses and the odd motor car...'

'What else?'

She shrugged. 'People milling about.'

'Details?' he pressed. 'Smaller details.'

'Oh, I don't know. Pigeons?' What did he want her to say? Her frustration was apparent in the tone of her voice.

'Open your eyes and search out the minutiae. Look at how the sun catches the iridescent plumage on the necks of the pigeons. See that tramp in the overcoat that is too big for him? It is missing two buttons, and the cane he carries is little more than a blackthorn stick. How sad he looks. I wonder if he's had a decent meal in the last week. Over there is a small boy holding a lollipop, his face so full of wonder and joy. His front teeth are missing, making his smile somehow even more endearing. And the lovers – for surely they must be lovers – sitting together on the edge of the fountain. His eyes are boring into hers, but she is anxious. Look how restless her hands are. Do her parents disapprove, I wonder? But their eyes speak of shared secrets, and the camera would pick up all these things. Capture that moment in time and preserve it like a colourful salad set in aspic.'

'But without the colour,' she pointed out.

'True, and that is why the artist remains so important, but photographs, for all their lack of colour, capture a moment in time, and they capture *everything*. All the things our brain doesn't have time to pick up on – the *mise en scène*, if you will. Even the artist doesn't see all, or chooses not to include unpalatable or irrelevant details. But the camera records the dirty, manure-covered street below the beautiful building or the clutter on a mantelpiece in the background of a family photograph.'

'Which is why they say the camera never lies,' she said, challenging him to own to his distasteful occupation. He couldn't bring himself to look at her and he stared into the middle distance, remaining silent, but she pushed him further. 'Agnes said you make your living from taking photographs. Are they portraits?'

'Mostly,' he said, non-committally, and then he forced himself to face her. 'I... I should very much like to take your portrait, if you would allow me.' He swallowed, his gaze suddenly very intense and his voice serious. 'You are very beautiful.' It was a bold statement for such an unassuming man.

Mercy was momentarily stunned. Where had this come from? Her heart flipped at the thought that he admired her in such a way. This really set the cat amongst the iridescent-necked pigeons. It was one thing for her to secretly lust over him when her idle fancy could do no harm, but quite another to find there might be a reciprocal attraction. This was wrong for so many reasons, not least her rippling unease about his distasteful occupation – something he still wouldn't own to.

'I must get back to Burlington Square to help Agnes.' She got to her feet, refusing to address his comment and desperate to retreat to the only place she felt safe.

'I... I'm sorry. I didn't mean to embarrass you.'

'Not at all, but I offered to help Agnes make some chutney and she'll be wondering where I am.'

'Then I'll accompany you.' She could hardly refuse since it was his home also.

They walked through the busy streets together, saying very little on the journey. She was aware of his body every step she took, barely two feet from her own, and torn between wanting to reach for his arm and wishing he was anywhere else but so close. Occasionally, she threw him a glance and, in turn, she felt his face turn to hers when he thought she wasn't looking, but they exchanged few words. It seemed Gilbert Adams was a man who was either gushing with conversation, or unable to think of a single thing to say.

But then, if he was going to make such unsettling and unexpected proclamations out of nowhere, perhaps it was best he remained silent.

57

THE PRESSED FLOWER

It was February and there were already hints of spring in the air. The gardens at Burlington Square were promising growth and colour, but there had been precious little colour in Agnes's life over a bleak winter. James had been abroad since before Christmas – her fears that he was about to disappear from her life forever allayed when he told her he was being sent to manage a project in India for two months and would return in the new year. The days dragged like months, but she was patient, knowing his return was imminent, and was rewarded when he called on her the day after his ship docked. Cook reluctantly agreed to keep an eye on her sleeping father, and Agnes suggested they walked to the river, as James was curious to see how the building of the new Battersea Bridge was coming along.

As they stepped from the house, he looped his arm through hers, as though re-establishing ownership, but things between them were complicated. She had overplayed her hand by declaring her love too soon – she knew that – and was at a loss to know where they stood. She'd hoped for clarification, and would even have been bold enough to ask, had he not been suddenly shipped out to oversee the construction of new offices in some city she had never heard of (but had subsequently investigated). A realistic girl, she suspected he saw her as a companion to fill his time until he should be posted abroad again. And in a funny way, she could accept that. If only it were more seemly for her to be direct and ask him outright what his intentions were.

'It's terribly frustrating being a woman,' she said, inadvertently voicing her thoughts aloud.

'Ah, you are one of those ladies who believe women should have the vote?'

Agnes was horrified.

'Certainly not. What a notion. We would be guided by the candidates' manners and dress sense – not his politics.'

James smiled at her with genuine affection in his eyes. She was still convinced he only looked on her in a sisterly way, despite the kisses. But then, she had rather put the poor fellow in an awkward situation by so rashly declaring her love.

'And yet, I think you would be guided by your heart and would be sure to vote for the kindest fellow, and I fervently believe we need kinder politicians.'

They continued to walk, arm in arm, until they happened across a small patch of primroses under a cluster of trees. James bent down to pick a single bloom and tucked it behind her ear. She felt self-conscious and silly, but did not try to stop him.

'Beautiful,' he said.

'Yes, such a sunny yellow. A delicate and cheery flower.'

'Not the flower,' he replied, suddenly serious, and bent towards her, pausing for a fraction, before swooping down on her lips. It was different from the first kiss, but more powerful than the second. He was in charge and had a much better idea of what he was doing. Her insides told her so.

Perhaps not so much of a sister, after all.

'I'm returning to India at the start of May,' he said, as they reluctantly pulled apart, and Agnes floated contentedly back to earth.

'More building works?' She tried to hide her disappointment that he should be off again in just a few short weeks.

He let his hand drop from her waist and his head dipped.

'No, I'm to head up the very offices I have overseen the construction of. The company is to run a warehouse from Cochin, a city on the south-west coast of the country, two hundred miles south of the painting I gave you. The position is permanent. I expect to be there for some years.'

Neither spoke for several moments, until she was able to utter an inadequate, 'Oh'. Her heart sank to the bottom of her stomach. That was it, then. He really was leaving.

'I wish you well, James, and hope that we might perhaps correspond? I will be most interested to hear about your new life. It will be like receiving a serialised travel journal.'

James, rather disconcertingly, started to laugh.

'You silly, adorable, bemusing little thing. I'm building up the courage to ask you to accompany me as my wife.'

'Your wife?'

'Why else do you think I've been calling on you? I spent *weeks* tracking you down after we met in the Bayswater gallery, Agnes Humphries. I knew that I'd found the woman I wanted to spend the rest of my life with – even if I was too much of a blockhead to do anything about it at the time.'

Agnes couldn't slow her rapidly spinning brain down enough to analyse any one element of what she was being confronted with in any detail.

'I should warn you that the climate is often unbearably humid,' he continued, 'and the monsoon season lasts six months. But we shall have an extensive house and a full complement of staff – all of whom you may personally secure—'

'But my father...'

'There will be plenty of room for him, and young Daphne. Think of the experiences she shall have?' It seems he had considered everything.

'The journey will kill him,' she said, shaking her head. 'Everything that is familiar is already slipping away from him. To take him from the memories of his precious wife would be beyond cruel.'

James, who had been smiling and so full of enthusiasm for what lay ahead, suddenly realised what she was saying.

'And you would not leave him.' It was not a question.

Her silence answered for her, nonetheless.

'We *will* find a way to make this work,' he said firmly, and they turned to walk back to Burlington Square. 'Because I love you, and love conquers all.'

She loved him too but could not match his blind faith that a solution could be found.

The primrose from that day was kept between the pages of her King James Bible, and it occasionally fluttered out, falling to the ground when she opened the pages too quickly. And every time it did, she wondered what might have been.

58

Mercy visited Jemima twice that following week. On the first occasion, Clara stopped by for a fleeting visit, initially unaware of the desperate sadness that hung about the Smith household as she talked about her visit to an exclusive London jeweller to get her eye-wateringly expensive engagement ring resized. But even the self-obsessed socialite soon picked up on the atmosphere, and her compassion for Jemima's tragic situation was plain for all to see. The three women drank tea and said very little, but somehow that was enough. There was a solidarity in their togetherness, and Mercy suspected that they were all nursing silent worries, but with the miscarriage so raw, it was not the time to air them.

On the second occasion, Mercy entertained the children and let their exhausted mother lie across the long sofa and rest. She correctly surmised that practical help would be more important than inadequate words, and only returned upstairs when it was time to help Agnes with the meals. As she walked past the spare bedroom to the kitchens, a shadow caught her eye. She popped her head around the door and saw the back of a man hovering by the window. He spun about, looking faintly alarmed, as he heard her

enter and she recognised Mr Thompson, the man she now understood was regularly visiting Mr Gorski.

'Can I help?'

'Oh, good day. I was looking for Miss Humphries. I've just spent
a pleasant afternoon in the park with Alexander and I wanted to let
her know he was now back, as she's probably anxious to serve
dinner.'

Mercy frowned. 'I expect she'll be in the kitchen...'

'Of course, silly me.' He stepped into the narrow hallway. 'Such
a fascinating man, don't you think? And such a tragedy that he can
no longer play the piano.'

Mercy nodded her agreement. 'Yes, I have listened to some of
his recordings. He was extremely talented. It's kind of you to spend
time with him. I know he appreciates it.'

'Not at all. But it is most certainly not all one way. I'm sure
spending time with Mr Gorski will enrich me in so many ways...'

Agnes appeared at the kitchen doorway, perhaps drawn to their
voices.

'Ah, Mr Thompson, you're back. Did you have a nice time?'

'The very best. I took him round the square and then we
ventured a little further afield because the weather was so agree-
able. He has invited me to play cribbage with him on Sunday afternoon, so you will see me again.'

'Then I shall rustle up some cheese scones and a pot of tea
when you come.'

'That would be most kind. I've returned the wicker Bath chair to
the hallway, but must be off now.' He glanced at an expensive-
looking gold pocket-watch and bowed his head, before leaving the
ladies alone.

'What a charming man,' Agnes said, as they heard the front
door close. 'I seemed to have managed to secure the best of both
worlds. You have the rooms and are an invaluable help to me, and

Mr Thompson has formed a friendship with Mr Gorski who, I can'
lie, I have been extremely worried about of late.' She wiped her we
hands on the pretty floral apron. 'How did you find Jemima? She
insists she's fine but she's the sort who looks stronger than she is.'

'Tired, but these things take time. I'm more worried abou
Clara, if I'm honest.'

'Really?' Agnes looked surprised, but the conversation Mercy
had shared with the young woman on the front steps kept replaying
in her mind.

'You must know she isn't happy? There's something off abou
this engagement. I can sense it. She may have raved about the
Somerset estate, but I didn't hear any such adulation about her
fiancé.' Perhaps it took one unhappy woman to recognise another
or indeed, another two. Jemima was going through the motions o
life, not living it. Maybe that was why Mercy was so convinced the
three of them would bond – they shared a cynical view of the world
and were certainly all disillusioned with the institution of marriage
for one reason or another.

Agnes absent-mindedly fiddled with the ornaments on the bow-
fronted sideboard and looked momentarily lost in thought.

'Goodness. I think you might be right and I've only this moment
realised it. My insides were telling me something was wrong but
I've been so swept up with Daphne's enthusiasm over the forthcoming nuptials, and relief that Clara is reconciled with her father,
that I've failed to give my darling niece the attention she deserves.
I'll have to invite her down again, I barely saw her the other day
and see if she won't open up to her dear old Aunt Ag.'

Did Agnes regret not giving the rooms to her? she wondered
Even though they didn't see each other very often, it was apparent
to Mercy that there was a special bond between these two women
You could see it in Clara's eyes when she looked at her aunt, for all
her pretence of being in control.

'Gilbert's tray is ready, if you wouldn't mind?' Agnes returned to the matters in hand, and began to walk back towards the kitchen. 'I've used that recipe of yours for stuffed celery and fried cauliflower, and it's under the saucepan lid on the table. You know what a little tinker Inky can be when food is left out...'

* * *

Several minutes later, Mercy was knocking on Gilbert's doors, depositing his tray and about to return downstairs when he surprised her by asking if she'd like to see his darkroom.

'If this is about the photograph, I don't feel comfortable—'

'The darkroom is where I develop my photographs, not where I take them. I thought you might be interested in the process. Perhaps you misunderstood my request last week. You have a beautiful face, like St Paul's Cathedral is a beautiful building.' He shrugged. 'I was merely appreciating the symmetry and delicacy of your features, as the artist appreciates a sweeping landscape.'

Mercy felt her cheeks colour. Had she jumped to the foolish conclusion that Gilbert was trying to woo her, when his words had merely been a dispassionate appraisal of her looks?

'I want to show you something in my rooms,' he pressed.

She laughed then. 'Do you realise how inappropriate that sounds?'

He frowned. It was obvious that communication was not one of his strengths, and it clearly frustrated him.

'Look, I know you saw the pamphlets the other day,' he finally said. It wasn't a question so she didn't reply. 'I want to explain.'

There was something in the air between them that she couldn't quite define. She noticed him glance at her mouth and then quickly look away. Her heart beat a little faster and Gilbert shuffled from foot to foot, awaiting her response.

'All right.' She was curious to learn more about him, even if being in close proximity to him was asking for trouble. 'But Miss Humphries won't like it – two young people of the opposite sex unchaperoned in a dark attic.'

Gilbert raised his left eyebrow. 'Unfortunately, I think she would like it rather too much, but *we* know there is no romantic interest on either side...'

'Absolutely,' she agreed, as his shuttered expression gave nothing further away. It seemed she was the only one with unfulfilled sexual longing racing through her veins.

'So, you'll come?' She nodded. 'There's no hurry. When you've eaten and had a chance to unwind after your busy day, knock on my door.'

His words made her realise how thoughtful everyone at Burlington Square was. For the first time in many years, people were considering how she might be feeling – tired, hungry, or that she might have an opinion and that they would be interested to hear it. And, as she walked back downstairs, she adjusted her hair and wondered where she'd put her tiny bottle of lavender water.

* * *

An hour later and the pair of them stood in Gilbert's small garret bedroom under the sloping ceilings. There was a door at the back, which she assumed was his darkroom, and the main space contained his bed, a large, cluttered table, a bookcase packed with books, a small wardrobe and a washstand.

They stood opposite each other in the same shy manner they always did, and Mercy yet again questioned what it was about this young man that tipped her insides upside down. Perhaps it was his endearing awkwardness or his gentle quietness. Or perhaps it was something more animal than that, because every time she caught his scent or his serious eyes bored into hers, her body began a slow fizz that she had absolutely no control over.

She stepped towards the table and picked up a tambourine, looking questioningly at him.

He sucked in a deep breath. 'Do you know anything about spiritualism?' he asked.

'A little, but do please enlighten me.'

He sighed, which she thought was an unusual way to begin an explanation. After all, she hadn't pushed to find out about his enterprises; he'd invited her to his rooms.

'It is based on the belief that the spirits of those who have passed continue to exist in another realm. That they have the ability to communicate with the living through gifted individuals, such as spirit mediums, who reach out to them through seances.'

He pulled out a hoop-backed chair, plumped up the cushion and gestured for her to sit. She returned the tambourine to the table, sank into the seat and rested her hands nervously on her knees.

'It grew in popularity after the American civil war – relatives desperate to communicate with those loved ones who did not return. I'm sure you can appreciate the Great War led to a similar surge of grief...'

Despite the earnestness in his pale face, Mercy felt her stomach begin a slow churn. She didn't like where this conversation was heading, and hoped he was not about to suggest contacting her husband.

'Mediums connect with the dead in a variety of ways. Often, they go into a trance-like state and the deceased soul speaks through them to the living. Usually, some quite astonishing sights follow that defy explanation – proof that the departed are present and wish to make contact. The moving of the planchette across a Ouija board, the banging of a tambourine, the apparent unaided levitation of a body, a pencil held by a detached luminous hand, writing across a sheet of paper... Surely, you've read about seances in newspapers and magazines?'

She shrugged. Yes, she had gleaned a little of these practices from the newspapers, but had always found the whole thing rather distasteful.

'I don't understand *why* you would want to speak to those who have passed. Let the dead rest.'

'These are desperate people, Mercy, who crave solace at a time when they have little comfort in life. To hear that your child has found peace, that they are happy in some other realm, brings the grieving mother immeasurable joy.'

Mercy felt her body tense. She couldn't keep her opinion to herself any longer.

'But it's nonsense – all of it – an elaborate charade, executed with trickery to exact money from vulnerable people. Conan Doyle remains convinced his dead son has spoken to him on several occasions, and yet I read somewhere that Houdini wrote a book denouncing it all as nonsense. After the escapologist's tragic death last year, you would have thought that if any spirit was going to return, it would be his – if only to apologise.' She was being slightly flippant but the sentiment was real.

'Oh yes.' He gave a resigned nod. 'I firmly believe that once you are dead, you simply cease to exist. I don't even believe in God. Spiritualism, and all the mysticism that surrounds it, is absolute twaddle.'

59

Mercy, mouth agape, stared at Gilbert.

'But you... I thought you were a...'

He sighed. 'It's how I make my living, but I don't believe any of it. You're absolutely correct; it's all a sham. Educated guesses, some research beforehand, and careful manipulation of the client to reveal the thing they are most desperate to hear. Or see. I once took a photograph of what appeared to be my brother's floating spirit and it's now my mother's most treasured possession. The production of such images is something I've worked hard to perfect, even though they are either an extension of Schröpfer's smoke and mirror trickery or double exposures.'

Mercy couldn't bring herself to say anything. Why was he standing before her, suddenly being so candid? Admitting to being a fraud, to taking money from grief-stricken and vulnerable people. And doing so without any obvious remorse or guilt.

'Sometimes I hire private rooms, sometimes I am invited to a person's home. I summon the spirit, who then knocks in reply, or moves things in the room, to let us know they are with us. Then during the seance the deceased passes on comforting words, _healing_ *words*, and I take a photograph that captures their presence. I know a young lad, Charlie – of dubious morals but genuine and heart-breaking financial need – who often secures previous images of the dead relative for me. When this isn't possible, I employ a model who resembles the person in question. That is my first exposure. A chap in a uniform, a doll swaddled like a newborn, or a veiled bride, and people are easily convinced, particularly if the image is blurry and out of focus.' He had a strangely resigned look on his face, almost as if he was explaining something as mundane as how to make a pot of tea to her.

'Charlie occasionally operates the camera for me, once I have everything set up. And those poor bereaved relatives have an ever-lasting keepsake of their loved one and proof that they still exist in some higher form, in some other unworldly plane, content and finally at peace, watching over those they loved on earth.'

Mercy shook her head. 'And the knocking? The ghostly mani-festations? How are these engineered?'

'Why do you think seances are performed in the dark? Why the clients are asked to remain seated at a table, holding hands, unable to move or investigate the truth of the strange phenomenon around them? Because,' he said, answering his own question, 'bells are tied to my feet, mechanical tricks make objects move around the room, I pull strings to bang tambourines and items are dangled from fishing rods.'

'How can you be part of such an underhand venture and still sleep at night?' Mercy was appalled that this man she had formed a tentative friendship with, not to mention found herself attracted to, could be so calculating. 'Profit from people's grief like that?'

He pulled a second chair out from under the table and collapsed into it, running his hand repeatedly through his hair.

'Because however immoral you think this all is, I have seen the good it can do. You bandage a flesh wound; why not apply a balm to one of the mind?' he said. 'So much of death is brutal, unjust and under horrific circumstances. Many of us have watched people – good people – die awful deaths. Billy never even made it to his fifth birthday.'

He paused to take in a slow breath and steadily exhaled it, perhaps trying to push raw emotions aside, but Mercy was shocked. Her hand had involuntarily gone to her chest. She remembered the lye. It was a terrible and agonising way to go. But she felt in her heart that what Gilbert was doing was wrong. A feeling of nausea washed over her as he continued.

'My mother lost several babies after having me, often before you could even determine their sex. Her body repeatedly rejecting the tiny creatures, disappointment after disappointment, and then finally a little brother...' He didn't need to finish.

The building anger she had felt towards him only moments ago now edged towards pity and she was confused at how quickly her emotions had lurched in another direction. The stark truth of his questionable behaviour was cast in a new light if real people and their suffering was somehow alleviated by his actions. She decided to hear him out.

'My mother never had any more children after Billy, and the relationship between my parents completely broke down after he died. I often heard her cry out in the night and, as time went on, she became more and more withdrawn, and consequently she showed less interest in me. I couldn't understand it; after all, the accident wasn't completely my fault—'

'Not your fault at all,' Mercy corrected, beginning to understand how the trauma of losing his brother had shaped his relationship with his mother.

He jumped to his feet, unable to settle, and ran his hands through his hair again, inadvertently allowing tufts of it to stick up, as he began to pace back and forth.

'It's not like I planned any of this. I was just desperate to see her smile again. And then the war came along and made everything worse – not because we lost anyone close, for I was a child and father was exempt. But suddenly she wasn't the only mother grieving for her son. Others were now losing sons in equally brutal ways, and had the right to feel the way she did. In a funny way, I think she resented that.' He stopped pacing and slipped back onto the chair, flicking his eyes periodically across to her. It seemed to Mercy that he was particularly anxious that she should understand.

'After the war, with so many bereaved families looking to ease their suffering, the spiritualist movement took off again and she was persuaded to go to a seance by my father. To be honest, I think he just wanted to get her out of the house. She'd languished in her grief for too long.'

'And she heard from your brother?' Mercy guessed. 'He came through and spoke to her?'

He nodded and then gave a quick shrug of his thin shoulders.

'I wasn't there, but she was convinced Billy had contacted her, and he told her to move on and be happy for him. Of course, his death had been in the papers and was widely known about in our town. It was easy enough to find out the details, so I felt cross that she'd been tricked by some charlatan into parting with money we didn't have to spare, and was all set to confront the woman concerned and expose her as a dangerous fraud. But the change in my mother was almost immediate. Believing she had made contact with him, that he was watching out for her and looking down on us as a family, lifted that soul-crushing grief from her shoulders.'

'So, you rustled up some photographs of your brother to give her further proof?' Her tone was sharper than she intended.

'It wasn't like that.' He'd avoided eye contact for much of their interchange but now met her bright eyes with his own. 'You weren't there, living for years with a mother who could barely function.' He leaned forward, willing her to understand. 'I kept quiet because my mother was coming back to me. She started to take an interest in what I was doing. So, when my uncle gave me a Box Brownie for my fifteenth birthday, I took some photos of her. We sat together in the front parlour, closer than we'd been for years, even talking about Billy, and remembering the naughty things he used to get up to. "Can you hear us, Billy?" I joked into the air. "You were such a mischief, I wonder that you didn't burn the house down or set all the hens loose from the coop." I managed to catch her smiling, forgetting that the last time I'd used the camera was to take a photograph of Billy's picture on the mantelpiece – wanting one of my own to remember him by and wondering how well such an image might come out...'

Mercy saw where this was leading before he finished his tale.

'Only when I developed the film did I realise that I hadn't wound it on and the blurry image of my brother was hovering above my smiling mother. A double exposure that made Billy seem ethereal and ghostly.'

'And she believed the camera had caught his spirit?'

'Worse than that. She thought that by talking about him I had somehow summoned him. That I had a... a gift, that I was... special.' His deep-set eyes became watery and he began to stumble over his words. 'It was the undisputable proof that her faith in the afterlife was justified. And then it all spiralled out of control when she told the neighbours I had gifts, but I was able to figure out how to replicate similar images and manufacture a few heartfelt messages from the fallen. I quickly realised that, besides the odd sixpence these people handed me, I was doing something magical – I was easing their pain.'

'But it's still lies, Gilbert.' She frowned, conflicting emotions tumbling inside her.

His briefly open and honest face returned to the shuttered and cynical one of earlier.

'Some would say that of religion, but that doesn't stop the Church from stripping people of their wealth, making them feel guilty for not only sins in deed but also in thought, and promising a heavenly afterlife that enables them to face the miseries of this one.' He noticed her shocked expression and changed tack. 'There are lots of instances when lies are told with altruistic motives. Doctors selling pills of starch to ease conditions that are more of the mind than the body, or parents soothing the anxious child with a little white lie – those times when the truth will do more harm than good...'

'But you are charging people for these words, Gilbert. What you are doing is wrong.'

'Until you've lived with someone so consumed by grief that they can't perform the simplest of tasks, I don't think you're in a place to judge. I got my mother back, Mercy. She began to live again, to love and laugh once more. Yes, I charge for my services, but I have materials to purchase and rent to pay. I think you'll find I make very little profit and am extremely discerning in my choice of client. Oftentimes, when it is obvious to me that they do not have sufficient funds, I don't even take payment.'

It was all very confusing and her head was spinning. In recent years she'd learnt that the rights and wrongs of a situation were often morally ambiguous, and she was trying hard to see the whole situation from his point of view. Ultimately, however, she could not tell him she approved of what he was doing.

'I'm sorry, but I think it is cruel and wrong. You told me that photography was all about truth, and yet your photographs are the biggest lies of all. I need to go.'

She stood up to leave, no longer interested in the darkroom. She didn't want to see where he prepared his hoax photographs. He jumped up with her and for a moment they were almost chest to chest. He had a powerful smell about him – soap and chemicals. She tipped her head up to his and felt a strange thudding beneath her ribcage.

'Why did you feel the need to tell me all this, Gilbert?' she asked.

'You really don't know?' His eyes fell to her lips. 'I want you to know everything about me. And I want to know everything about you...'

They stood in perfect silence for a moment and the electricity that coursed around her body from his unexpected and candid words surprised her. She could feign ignorance but it was obvious what he meant. Only half an hour before she'd had similar thoughts about him, but his admission had made her cross. His occupation was morally questionable and it sat uneasily with her. Briefly, she allowed herself to wonder *what if?* Both bodies swayed forwards a fraction as she glanced up at his mouth. There *was* something that pulled her to this strange young man, however much she tried to fight it, and it would be so easy to lean in to him and let his lips brush against her own. But she honestly believed if that were allowed to happen she would not be able to stop herself from wanting more. In recent years, for someone who'd been denied the opportunity to engage in any form of marital relations, she'd become increasingly consumed by carnal thoughts. Perhaps that was why. When you are starved of a thing, you desire it so much more. And she suddenly knew, whatever she must now let Gilbert believe, that she did desire him – for all his vulnerability, darkness and deceit, he was like a magnet pulling her soul towards his. His intoxicating smell, his intense eyes, even his awkwardness was endearing. It would be so very different to Roland, and so much more. He would be respectful, cautious and... at the thought of those eyes boring into hers should they ever be together in that most intimate of ways, a shiver ran up her spine.

'No. This cannot be allowed to happen.' She took a step backwards.

'I don't understand why you're fighting this. It's obvious that you like me as much as I like you.'

'You're mistaken,' she lied. 'I am lonely, and have been for many years, but a casual dalliance to satisfy desires of the flesh is not the answer.'

Gilbert's dark eyes expanded. 'Is that what you think I'm after?'

'Isn't it?'

His exasperated face said it all, as his eyes narrowed and his patience finally deserted him.

'Of course – it must be the never-ending stream of young ladies going up and down the stairs to my rooms that have persuaded you I am some sort of Lothario.' His words dripped with sarcasm. 'Perhaps if I were a more discerning gentleman, more socially awkward and perhaps a little shy, you might believe that I took my romantic aspirations seriously. You might perhaps be convinced that I would never dream of pursuing you unless I had honourable and ardent feelings. The sort who would only ever make himself this vulnerable in front of someone if he had hopes it might lead to something more lasting.'

His words were both what she longed to hear, and what she was desperately afraid of. He didn't want to use her body and then abandon her. He wanted to keep her, cherish her, love her.

And that simply wasn't possible.

'I'm afraid I don't feel the same way about you,' she said, knowing that it was better to lie to him and let him go, than string him along and break his embarrassingly sincere but fragile heart.

His head dropped but he made no further move to pursue his

romantic intentions. She turned towards the door, but he grabbed her hand at the last moment and twisted her back to face him.

'So...'

'So, what?'

'Are you going to expose me? Tell Agnes how I make my living?'

'I simply don't know,' she said and shook her hand free of his. The warmth of his touch lingered on her skin all the way back down to her room, where she closed her door, collapsed against it and cried non-stop for fully an hour.

60

'Come on. Let's go for a walk and you can show me some of the sights.'

Mercy stood at Jemima's door on her afternoon off, determined to get the poor woman out into the fresh air and away from her grief. It would also do Mercy good to focus on something other than Gilbert. He was invading her dreams now, and their conversations at the bottom of the attic stairs had reverted to the brief, awkward interchanges of before – barely a handful of words but a veritable torrent of emotions gushing around the small space between them. He bolted up the steps within seconds of her handing over his meals, finally accepting that she was not interested but possibly under the belief that she'd led him on. Perhaps she had.

'Not today,' Jemima replied. 'I'm behind with everything and don't have the energy.'

'Nonsense. The housework can wait. We can do it together when we return. There's so much I want to see before... the weather changes.' How long did she have left before she was found?

Her motives for dragging Jemima out were twofold; this was a small act of kindness that would benefit her new friend and distract her from her sorrow, and Mercy would get to see some more of the spectacles that the city had to offer without doing so alone.

It took some cajoling but eventually Jemima was persuaded to leave the house, and the pair, with Ellen and Frances in tow, walked to Buckingham Palace in the September sunshine. Mercy had long since had a hankering to see where the king lived, and was totally overcome by its sheer size and splendour. The Victoria Memorial alone was a breathtaking spectacle for a simple farm girl from the countryside to behold. Then, after wrestling the pram aboard, they took a bus to the Tower of London. As they walked across Tower Green, Mercy felt a shiver run through her, thinking of Anne Boleyn and Catherine Howard meeting their end in this secluded open space, and decided everything was relative. Should she be found and returned to Suffolk, there were worse fates. And she knew, if this was to be her destiny, that she was a stronger woman now for her time at Burlington Square.

'I appreciate your friendship,' she said to Jemima. 'I've never had someone of my age to talk to.' They were making their way back home. Frances was sound asleep and Ellen, who had become increasingly fractious in the last hour, was now contentedly sucking on a toffee apple, allowing the women a chance to talk. They had covered a variety of topics, from politics to farm life, and found much common ground – perhaps not in life experience, but certainly in their opinions.

The young mum looked surprised. 'No girls from school or neighbours?'

Mercy shook her head. 'Since moving to London, I've started to make friends with some of the ladies I work with, but I was kept very busy on the farm, and going into town was not encouraged. My only friend was the schoolmaster's wife, Mrs Donnington, who was

considerably older than me. Not someone I could talk to about...
delicate matters.'

'Sex?' said Jemima, so matter-of-factly that Mercy nearly choked
on her own tongue. She'd planned a circuitous route to this conversation, but her friend's directness bypassed the need for such an
unnecessary preamble. The young mum's chin was stuck defiantly
up in the air and she didn't make eye contact. 'It's not all it's cracked
up to be, is it?'

Mercy didn't answer at first. What could she possibly reply?
That despite having married, she'd never once had sexual relations
with her husband. With anyone.

'I think about it more than I should,' she finally admitted. 'I look
at handsome men in the street and cannot help but wonder what
they look like beneath their clothes, how it might feel to have them
touch me. Sometimes... sometimes, I feel so aroused by these
thoughts that I think I can't be normal.'

'Your husband has been dead a long time. I suppose it's natural.'

'Do you think about men other than Nicholas?' Mercy dared to
ask, not addressing her words directly. 'Or am I some sort of
aberration?'

It was Jemima's turn to take a long time to answer. 'Perhaps we
are all aberrations in our own way.'

There was a further prolonged silence, both women lost in
private thoughts.

'What do you think of Clara's engagement?' Mercy decided to
steer the conversation in a slightly different direction.

'I think it's a mistake, and she can't say we didn't warn her, but
ultimately she's a self-obsessed, spoilt woman who would not
survive five minutes in the real world if she were not cushioned
with money. Of course she's accepted him – he's wealthy. Her world
is far removed from ours.'

'I like her,' Mercy said, worried that her hopes for the three of them forming a lasting friendship were unfounded. 'I think she puts on a front but is desperately unhappy underneath. We all need friends, however much we pretend to the outside world that we're in control.' She paused to allow her words to sink in. Jemima was too spiky for her own good, but Mercy was letting her know that she was there for her. 'And she's exceedingly glamorous.'

'Yes,' Jemima begrudgingly admitted. 'Clara is an attractive woman.'

They arrived in front of the house and Jemima parked the pram so that she could open the gate to the basement. She turned to Mercy.

'Things are changing. For all that I find women like Clara irritating and entitled, they are pushing for an equality long overdue for our sex. Her smoking, lipstick and undoubtedly loose morals are, if not embraced, at least tolerated now. Such behaviour would have been obscene before the war.' She paused. 'The infidelities of men have long been acceptable. Why not those of women? I would go for it, if I were you.'

'Go for what?'

'Gilbert Adams. Why shouldn't you have some fun? Agnes keeps wittering on about the intense attraction between you both – discretion not being her forte. I know people think he's odd, and I've certainly heard some curious things about him, but he's a good man. I can't tell you how many times he's bought gifts for the girls, how he pays for the medical treatment of one of our elderly neighbours, and how he insisted on purchasing Agnes's new stove when the last one packed up in the spring. He begged her not to tell anyone, particularly given the sum of money involved, but you know Agnes.' She rolled her eyes. 'Plus, I think there must be something innately good about a person who can't even bring himself to eat the flesh of an animal. Don't you?' Mercy nodded mutely. 'Well, like I say, Agnes is convinced there's something going on between you two, and if there isn't, she's desperately hoping there will be soon. It's blatantly obvious to everyone that you like him.'

Mercy blushed a deep red, as she opened her bag to retrieve her key, and wondered both at Jemima's words and her own transparency.

* * *

Mercy spent the following evening with Mr Gorski. The whole day had been grey and overcast, the heavens finally opening as she walked back from work, soaking through her wool coat to her cotton blouse, and ruining a good pair of stockings. She'd made them both some cocoa, conscious that summer was slipping away, and the nights would soon be drawing in. As the September rain lashed at the window panes, and cast the room in an eerie and belligerent light, her mind was jittery and her stomach unsettled, as though the elements were warning her of dark days to come.

'Alina is calling me,' the old man said, after a pause in their inconsequential chatter. 'She has been weaving her way into my thoughts of late. Tomorrow is my birthday and with each year, my frail body lets me down further.' He sighed. 'And I ask myself do I wish to see another year come and go? I am no use to anyone any more.'

'That's nonsense.' She attempted to jolly him out of his glum mood. 'I, too, have had periods of unhappiness, but things change. Yes, people are taken from us and sometimes we feel that we can't go on, but then we make new friends, fall in love again and have new experiences. Learning about your beautiful music has certainly lifted me. You must know that Agnes is particularly fond of you, and that lovely Mr Thompson goes out of his way to visit on a Sunday, or pop by after working at the bank. Please don't think that you have no purpose, Mr Gorski. It's simply not true.'

'My dear child, you must call me Alexander.'

'Only if you stop this silly talk and have brighter thoughts.' She put her mug down and took his withered hands in hers. 'Don't talk as if you don't matter – you truly do.'

A tiny, clear tear swelled over his lower eyelid and trickled down his wrinkled cheek.

'I have found hope since coming here,' she continued, squeezing his fingers. 'Although we were the victorious nation, the devastation caused by the war still ripples through the lives of many, including mine. But even from the most desperate of situations, joy can flow. Take the mill owner's son from my village back in Suffolk. A strapping young man of twenty-three, blinded by gas in the trenches and condemned to a life of everlasting darkness. Instead of giving up and taking his resentment out on others, he chose a better path. He used his amazing baritone voice to forge a successful singing career. He tours the country giving performances and feels that his blindness has opened up his world, not closed it down.'

This was the rub. The mill owner's son, who had every right to be angry at the world, had not allowed himself to become the victim, nor had he blamed anyone for his situation. Thinking of those back at Home Farm, it rather seemed to her that it was all too easy for unkind people to use the bad things that had happened to them as an excuse for their unpleasantness.

'Perhaps your son didn't die but is alive and well, and your paths will cross. Perhaps they won't. But imagine if he tracked you down and found that you'd passed on? He'd be so disappointed. Without hope, there is nothing.' She raised his fingers to her lips and gently kissed them.

He smiled.

'You are very wise for one so young.'

'Not wise, just confident that there are better days ahead.'

Their eyes met and an understanding passed between them. He reached his misshapen hand out to hers and squeezed it.

'Thank you. Your words have done more than you will ever know.'

When Mercy returned from work a few days later, she discovered Clara sitting with her aunt in the kitchen. Agnes was bustling about at the stove, looking every inch the charwoman. In contrast, everything about her glamorous niece was sparkle – from the crystal choker around her neck, to the rhinestone details on the sleeves of her dress. But not the eyes, Mercy noticed. There was no sparkle there.

'Oh, Mercy!' her friend exclaimed, clapping her hands in excitement. 'How simply thrilling to see you again. We've set a date, I have the ring now and it's all terribly real. Mrs Jack Rigby has quite an air about it, don't you think?'

She stuck out her manicured fingers to show off the biggest sparkle of all – an enormous square-cut diamond mounted on a gold ring, tilting her hand to allow the light to bounce off the numerous reflective faces.

'It's lovely,' Mercy said of the ring, but making no further comment.

'We've been down to show Jemima,' Agnes said. 'I took the last of Mr Gorski's birthday cake for the girls, but all Matilda could focus on was the diamond. As if she didn't think Clara was practically royalty before, I'm convinced the size of that stone made her believe she's a real-life princess. I've got a paste ruby cluster dress ring in the spare room which I might pass to her if I can lay my hands on it. It will be far too big for her tiny fingers but I'm becoming fond of that little girl, and she does so love fancy jewellery.'

'Jemima still didn't seem particularly pleased for me.' Clara's face was sulky. 'The reaction from you both last week was decidedly muted. I understand the loss of the baby overshadowed everything, but surely you wish me well?' she challenged.

The new, braver Mercy, however, crossed her arms and sighed. 'I would if I thought it was what you wanted.'

'What on earth can you mean? It's simply marvellous and I'm a very lucky girl. Daddy is beyond thrilled and Mummy is in a total flap, absolutely drowning in preparations, but secretly relishing every moment.'

'You don't love him.'

Clara picked at a thread on her pleated skirt.

'Mummy didn't marry for love. Those with money aren't expected to.' She put out her hand again and stared intently at her ring, but her eyes seemed unfocused. 'People marry for a variety of perfectly acceptable reasons that are far more practical than emotional, and that doesn't make the decision any less valid. You were doubtless terribly in love, and there were hearts and flowers all around, but it's not like that for everyone.'

Meek and mild Mercy decided someone had to challenge Clara and her rash assumptions, and it might as well be her. Why should this young woman be the only one to shock?

'I may have thought myself in love with Roland when I was younger but I can assure you that by the time of our marriage I most certainly was not. I was tricked into becoming his wife.'

Agnes was serving up two bowls of vegetable soup for Gilbert and Mr Gorski, and froze with her ladle mid-air, as Clara's pretty eyes flashed wide. It was time for Mercy to share this part of her story. The deceit was weighing heavy, even though she had never technically told an outright lie.

'My father owned a small farm – barely fifty acres of arable land – and I was the only child. Roland was the only son of the neighbouring farm. It was... expedient to marry us off.'

'Ah, land. It's the same thing.' Clara studied the young woman beside her, waving a dismissive hand.

'But I was forced into it to please others. Made to feel guilty about even thinking of refusal. There was always something selfish and manipulative about Roland, and that's exactly what he did – manipulated me.'

'Oh, sweetie, and now you feel awfully guilty because he died a noble death and everyone thinks he was some sort of hero?' Clara surmised, finally granting Mercy some sympathy.

Mercy didn't respond. She backed down from making yet another shock announcement. There was only so much bravery she could find on an overcast Wednesday night.

'It rather seems to me,' Agnes said, putting in her two penn'orth as she buttered several thick slices of homemade bread, 'that we need to consider the vast divide between love and duty. Duty is a cold word. It means something you feel obliged to do rather than something done for pleasure. By implication it is an unhappy choice – a sacrifice. Mercy felt it was her duty to secure the future of the farm, and her poor husband did his duty and now lies buried in some foreign land. Is this what you're doing too, Clara? Because I have never seen you look so miserable. Daphne must know this and yet does nothing, whereas I don't think I could stand by and let you make, what I now believe to be, a terrible mistake, if you were my daughter.' Niece and aunt exchanged a look and Mercy saw genuine affection between the two women.

Clara bit at her bottom lip and wriggled in her seat, looking uncomfortable for the first time in the conversation. 'But you did your duty by looking after Grandfather, even though Mummy tells me you sacrificed your own happiness in order to do so.'

'No, my darling, what I did for your grandfather, I did for love, and that is the difference. *Everything* you do should be driven by love.'

At her aunt's words, Clara finally crumbled. Any pretence that she was in control evaporated as her head fell into her hands. Agnes was quick to come to her side of the kitchen table and place her arm around the sobbing young woman.

'You have to talk to me, Clara,' she begged.

'Oh, Aunt Ag, I just don't know if I can...'

Mercy recognised at once this was a private conversation, and she was the intruder. She somehow managed to scoop up both trays, made her excuses and left the room to deliver Gilbert and Mr Gorski their meals.

And, although she was not privy to any details of the following interchange – which Agnes hinted went on until the early hours – when she appeared downstairs to help with the breakfast the next morning, her landlady told her that Clara was heading down to Somerset to break off her engagement.

61

THE RUBY AND DIAMOND CLUSTER RING

Agnes wasn't a great one for housework, but open fires necessitated that dusting must be undertaken at least weekly, and there was something soothing about working around a room, starting to the left of the door, whipping her little feather duster over all her knick-knacks until she returned, full circle, to the door once more – now all the richer for embracing the memories each item offered up as she encountered it.

It was how she noticed that the ring was missing. There was a pretty blue velvet jewellery box on the walnut chest in the spare room. It was left permanently open, with an assortment of costume pieces within; paste necklaces, bracelets made from coloured glass beads, and a large imitation ruby and diamond cluster ring, that was surely too gaudy to be valuable. It sat in one of three cushioned slits in the top tray, half-concealed under a jumble of beads and hat pins. Agnes frowned and rummaged around in the necklaces to find it. She was of a mind to pass it on to the oldest Smith girl, already imagining how her young face would light up on receiving such a garish gift. But it was not there.

Her father had presented it to her not long after she'd met

James, insisting it was extremely valuable and might make a suitable engagement ring. The truth was that, by then, reality and fantasy were becoming increasingly intertwined for him. There was a distant male cousin on her mother's side – an actor who had lived and died a bachelor – and the family had inherited some of his possessions after his death, including a trunk filled with theatrical props. She'd always assumed the ring came from there.

Agnes felt uncomfortable that it was missing. The only people who came down to the kitchen past this room were her lodgers or her family – people she trusted. Had Clara borrowed it for one of her ridiculous fancy dress parties? Or had poor Mercy taken it? Lord knows, that poor girl was scared of something. Mr Gorski never came down this corridor, and besides, he had money. But that Nicholas was always short of a bob or two. She frowned. She didn't like to think ill of anyone, but he'd done himself no favours when his wife had lost the baby.

Agnes shrugged. Perhaps she was simply getting old and had moved it herself but forgotten. Besides, what did it matter? She was sad because she remembered playing with it as a child, but it was hardly valuable...

62

Agnes caught Mercy as she walked through the door that Saturday. Her landlady's face was positively beaming.

'God's plans for us all are a wonder to behold,' she said, waddling up the hallway. 'I have today been told the most extraordinary news. Sometimes, He makes us wait, but God does indeed reward the righteous.'

Mercy gave her a questioning glance as she wiped her shoes on the doormat, wondering if God might get around to rewarding her after all. She'd only been waiting nine years.

'Tomorrow afternoon we are having a celebratory tea in Mr Gorski's rooms and you must attend.'

'To celebrate what exactly?' Mercy was confused. Alexander's birthday was last week.

'Although I'm about to burst with excitement, I feel it only right that you should hear everything from the dear man himself.'

So, Mercy climbed the stairs and knocked on the old man's door, brimming with curiosity.

'My darling girl. Has Agnes told you my news? I am the happiest I have been in so many years. You were so right to talk of better days to come, and I can hardly contain my disbelief or my joy.'

He gestured to the armchair across from him and Mercy took a seat, delighted to see him radiate such happiness.

'Mr Thompson, who currently has some days of holiday from the bank, took me to Hyde Park this afternoon, and in the meandering way that conversations often take, he began to tell me of his sad start in the world. I found myself astonished to learn that he was abandoned as a baby on the doorstep of a large London house on Christmas Day, fifty years ago, with no knowledge of his parentage.'

'I'm not sure I follow.'

'Forgive me. You do not know, perhaps, details of my own tragic tale...'

She knew that Alina had been his one great love, and that she'd died young, but when Alexander explained about their son, Mercy's astonishment at the unbelievable coincidence matched his own.

'Goodness me. For you both to have had similar experiences is indeed extraordinary.'

'No, my dear, don't you see it is more than that? *He is my son.* He must be.'

Mercy's mouth formed a perfect O.

'I can hardly believe he has come back to me. What are the odds? Recently, as you know, I was at a point when I had almost given up on life and, I'm ashamed to say, was even considering departing this world by my own hand, when your kind words gave me cause for reflection. I was relaying all this to Stephen on our walk. Shortly afterwards his own tale came out. To think how foolish I could have been...'

'That's wonderful. I'm so happy for you both.' And she genuinely was, even though she felt guilty that the old man had been considering something so dark without her realising.

'Do come up and say hello when he visits this evening,' Alexander said. 'I am eagerly counting the minutes until he returns. After all, we have fifty years to catch up on...'

As she left, she couldn't help but notice the tears of joy building in his eyes.

* * *

Exhausted from a long week at the department store, Mercy had hoped for a quiet night with a book, but as she returned downstairs after taking up the dinner trays, Agnes wanted to chat further about the exciting revelation, and persuaded her into the front room. When Mr Thompson arrived shortly afterwards to visit his father, her landlady threw her arms about the poor man and kept him talking fully half an hour before he politely made his excuses and went up to the first floor.

It wasn't many minutes after that that Clara descended on them, and any hopes Mercy had of an early night, drifted up the stairs without her.

'Darlings, I have a bottle of bubbles and you must both help me sink the thing. I know you have some delightful little coupes in here somewhere,' she said, rummaging through the sideboard.

'What exactly are we celebrating?' Mercy asked, bewildered by the appearance of a bottle of champagne, never having tasted such a thing in her life and mildly curious.

'My freedom, naturally, darling. But perhaps also commiserating my abandonment. All my chums headed to Somerset today for a Saturday to Monday at the Rigbys', and it would be frightfully awkward if I put in an appearance – even though there was some unfinished business with a young woman that I wanted to put to rest, but hey ho.' Clara exchanged a knowing look with her aunt, as she started to hand out the promised drinks.

'To following your heart,' she toasted, and the other two ladies sipped at their champagne. Mercy found herself undecided about its appeal – the bubbles tickled and it had a sour taste she couldn't quite reconcile herself to. Clara, however, knocked her first glass back alarmingly quickly and poured a second.

'So, are *you* going to follow your heart, Mercy?' she asked. 'We're all simply desperate to find out if Gilbert really is a case of still waters running deep. Agnes tells me the air is positively electric whenever the two of you are in the same room.'

Mercy swallowed hard. It appeared she and Gilbert wore their attraction like enormous placards.

'Oh, yes,' said Agnes, leaning forward. 'I've always thought you would be perfect together.'

Before Mercy had a chance to interject with a futile denial, there was a knock and Mr Thompson popped his head around the door frame.

'I'm off now. My father is quite tired and I don't want to wear him out for our celebration tea. This whole thing has been quite a shock for us both, as wonderful as it is.'

'Of course,' Agnes said. 'We shall see you tomorrow.'

His head disappeared and, as they heard the front door close, Clara leapt from the battered sofa to peer out the window at the departing visitor.

'What on earth was Stephen Thompson doing here?' Her eyes were wide.

'Oh, that's Mr Gorski's son,' her aunt explained. 'Isn't it marvellous? They became friends quite by chance and through the strange and inexplicable way the universe seems to operate, have made the most incredible discovery. He was abandoned as a baby on Christmas Day, and has now found out that Mr Gorski is the father he had never known. It's unbelievable that they should both be drawn to Burlington Square – like something you might find in a Dickens novel.' Agnes clasped her hands together and beamed.

'Unbelievable is about right,' Clara said, scowling. 'Stephen Thompson is a lying, good-for-nothing petty thief who has been detained at His Majesty's pleasure for the last four years. He is no more Mr Gorski's son than I am.'

63

Mercy and Agnes stared at Clara for a few seconds, before Agnes downed her champagne in one and gave an astonished cough.

'But he—'

'Long lost son, my eyes.' Clara tutted in disgust. 'He's one of five brothers who are every bit as alike as peas in the proverbial pod. In fact, Stephen looked so like his younger brother Oliver that people in the village used to confuse them as children, even though they were born three years apart. The Thompson family have lived in Hexton for generations and farmed the land on our estate all that time. Daddy remembers the boys as children, as they were a similar age. I think he was born the same year as the eldest brother, although they obviously didn't have much to do with each other.'

'Obviously,' echoed Mercy, struggling to take in the shock news that Stephen was an imposter and trying not to mind Clara's snobbery by implying that the mixing of social classes was undesirable and generally to be avoided.

'He's always been trouble.' Her eyes narrowed and she returned to her seat. 'And the last one living at home as I recall – although I was still a child when he left for the war. And yet he's claiming to be a foundling baby, abandoned at birth?'

Agnes nodded, her face creased in a worried frown.

'If you don't mind me curling up on this old thing tonight, Aunt, I think I should rather like to be a part of this celebration tea tomorrow. Perhaps my visit shall be every bit as entertaining as the undoubted high jinks I'm missing out on in Somerset. All we shall be lacking is the fancy dress.'

* * *

The total bewilderment across Stephen's face the following day when he entered Alexander's rooms, only to find himself confronted by a crowd and no obvious tea party, was plain to see. Gilbert moved swiftly behind him and stood in front of the door. There was a room full of people wanting answers and, centre-stage, a particularly distraught Alexander who had been told of their suspicions the night before. Stephen's face took on a wary expression as he noted the hostile gazes and folded arms of the unwelcoming welcome party.

'Stephen,' Alexander said, 'do come in and make yourself comfortable. There seems to be some confusion about your revelation and we have some questions for you.'

Mercy noticed the old man's countenance. Despite the overwhelming evidence, he was still holding on to the wisp of hope that somehow Clara had got everything wrong and that this man was truly his son. She felt for him. A miracle had been presented to him that offered atonement for a life of regret and remorse, and now it was about to be snatched away.

'What's this about?' Stephen asked, and Mercy noticed him wipe his palms on his trousers as his head turned slightly, establishing Gilbert was indeed blocking the exit. Any hopes she had that Clara might be mistaken were rapidly diminishing, because, like Agnes, she generally preferred to believe the best of people.

His eyes darted from person to person, until they finally rested on a composed Clara and he frowned as she shrugged her elegant shoulders, as if to say, 'You're on your own here'.

'The jig is up, darling. You're not Mr Gorski's son,' she said, uncrossing her long legs and reaching forward for her silver cigarette case, as though she were settling down for a matinee.

'Do I know you?' he asked, clearly struggling to place her and wondering why this attractive stranger was in the room.

'Clara Goodwin.' She smiled and waited for the penny to drop, placing a cigarette between her lips and flicking the wheel of her enamelled Tutankhamun-inspired lighter.

'Reginald Goodwin's daughter?' He scrunched up his eyes, as if the name meant something but the face did not quite fit.

'Absolutely, darling. The very same. And *you*, despite what you might have told this dear old gentleman, are the third son of Mr and Mrs Thompson, who live in one of the tied cottages on my father's estate in Hertfordshire. Not, in fact, a baby abandoned on the steps of a large anonymous London house fifty years ago by an unwed German mother.'

'Is what she says true?' Alexander asked quietly, from the leather armchair in the corner. Stephen couldn't meet his eyes and instead continued to stare at his accuser.

His hesitation was enough for everyone in the room to shift from doubt to absolute certainty that Clara's claims were correct. Stephen had realised that the jig was indeed up.

'And *you* are a spoilt, arrogant young lady born into a world of privilege who has never gone hungry or done a backbreaking day's work for inadequate pay. You know nothing of what it's like to be born into poverty, to watch how the random nature of your arrival in the world determines *everything*. The obstacles that are in your way and the prejudices you face when you have nothing. Your birth opened doors by magic wherever your dainty, silk-slippered feet went, and you have led a privileged life because Daddy is a wealthy landowner and high-ranking politician. Tell me how you would fare if you were born in reduced circumstances? Consider what lengths you might go to redress this imbalance.'

'I would not have lied to a kind and vulnerable elderly gentleman in the hopes of falsely securing a fortune that was not mine.'

'No, your kind make ill-advised and loveless marriages to that end.' Clara winced but didn't bite. 'Besides, I said that I could not prove that I was your son...' He turned to Alexander. '... and you said it didn't make a difference.'

'You lied to me,' was all Alexander could say. His blue button eyes narrowed. 'I do not understand how you came to know so much about me but it was extremely cleverly done.'

Perhaps flattered by the indirect compliment, Stephen decided to elucidate.

'That was the beautiful thing about all of this. No name, no records, no birth certificate, no idea what the child even looked like or if it had survived.'

'But you work in a bank,' Agnes said, still confused by the whole affair. 'And you go to church.' Because in her world, these two facts alone meant he couldn't possibly be guilty of any crime. It was a naive assumption, Mercy thought. In her own experience, church-going folk were some of the meanest she had come across.

'There's no way he works in a bank,' Clara scoffed. 'Do you have any idea how thoroughly they scrutinise their employees? This man has served time in prison. The banks handle large sums of money on a daily basis so, by necessity, their employee checks are more stringent than most.'

'Yes,' Agnes whispered, only now realising her folly. 'He told me that when I interviewed him.'

Even Mercy, herself embarrassingly slow to appreciate how duplicitous and manipulating humans could be towards one another, recognised how clever Stephen had been. Banking was a solid profession – a position of absolute trust. It went without saying a bank clerk was of exemplary character.

'I should like to think that had you offered him the rooms, you would have at least followed up his references?' Clara said to her aunt. Agnes's flushed pink cheeks said it all.

'I always knew there was something off about you,' muttered Gilbert. Stephen's body language had gone from defensive to aggressive. It was as if now that he'd been exposed as a fraud, he had nothing left to lose. He spun to face the younger man.

'Says the man faking photographs for grieving families, creating the illusion the spirits of their relatives have returned, and charging them money to contact the dead. I had a word with your sometime assistant Charlie Taylor – his and my paths have crossed before – so you're in no position to judge me, you pasty-faced, sneaky excuse of a man.'

'Is this true?' asked Agnes, looking quite upset to find out that more than one person in the room was concealing things from her.

'Oh, what a dark, cadaverous horse you are, Gilbert,' Clara exclaimed, clearly enjoying all the revelations.

Mercy jumped to her feet. She wasn't having this. Stephen would not take Gilbert down with him. 'You know nothing about Gilbert's life or the reasons for the things he does. What he does he does from a place of kindness, misguided though it is, to ease the pain of people who have suffered like he has. Not for personal gain.'

'You don't have to defend me,' Gilbert mumbled.

'I do because I will always stand by those I love, and will not have a man like Stephen compare his crimes with your well-intentioned fabrications.' When her brain finally caught up with the dramatic admission her tongue had made without her knowing, her whole face flushed a deep red.

'Oh, darling, how marvellous. You do love him, after all,' Clara said. 'But as sweet as your proclamation is, I fear Mr Thompson is trying to deflect us from our mission.'

Mercy, unable to meet Gilbert's eye without fear of acknowledging that truth, looked at Stephen instead, and thought she caught a flash of amusement in his eyes. She wanted to walk up and slap him across the face for everything he had put poor Mr Gorski through. How cruel to offer such hope, only for it to be a lie. But she was astute enough to recognise the slap would be for Roland too, and the way he had manipulated her and taken away any chance she'd had of happiness. Naturally, she did nothing.

'Unfortunately, Aunt, this rather proves that you can go to church and still be a rotten egg,' Clara said, squashing her cigarette into an abandoned saucer.

'If you are all quite finished, I must take my leave,' Stephen said. 'I think you'll find I have committed no crime.'

He turned to Gilbert, who stood firm and pulled back his thin shoulders.

'Let him go,' Alexander said. 'He is not worth our time.'

'If poor Mr Blandford hadn't died so unexpectedly you would never have found your way to Burlington Square,' Agnes said, frowning and folding her arms across her wide chest.

'Indeed.' Stephen turned his head back to those in the room. 'How unfortunate that he contracted blood poisoning from the application of an unclean bandage proffered by a stranger on a most regrettable wound in a public house on a sticky June evening.'

Those last vicious words were the only victory he would get from this situation, and everyone in the room felt their blood run cold as he pushed Gilbert aside and stormed into the hallway, not one of them brave enough to articulate the implications of the words he had just spoken.

64

'We have to tell the police,' Agnes said.

'Tell them what?' Clara asked.

'He all but admitted to murdering Mr Blandford.'

'He knew Nathaniel,' Gilbert said. 'I saw them drinking together once at the Mad Hatter, at the start of the summer, but I've only just made the connection.'

'This is the man who had the rooms before Mercy?' Clara clarified and her aunt nodded. 'The one who was fond of his drink? Oh, it's all starting to make sense.' She stood from her chair and paced in front of everyone, preparing to deliver a denouement like an elegant female Holmes or the more recent Hercule Poirot. 'He bumps into Mr Blandford by chance, or perhaps even knew the man from frequenting the public house. After too much of the old giggle-water, Mr B, who, by all accounts could talk to anyone about anything at length, spills Mr Gorski's sorry tale of woe and Stephen's interest is piqued.'

'Yes.' Alexander leaned forward in his chair, animated by the possibilities. 'Nathaniel was my friend. I told him things I had not told anyone for many years, I think perhaps because I was painfully aware of my mortality.'

Clara continued her pacing in front of the rapt audience.

'He realised he was close enough in age to pass as the missing son – and with the details of the baby so scant, and such a minuscule chance of anyone ever tracking down the child, all he had to do was reinvent his birthday and drop a few hints to a melancholy, lonely old man, desperate to make amends for the betrayal of his first love and their illegitimate child. And poor Mr Gorski fell for it.'

'Clara,' Mercy whispered, 'he is in the room.' She was mortified that Alexander's weakness was so carelessly discussed.

'Not at all, dear lady. I was, as you English say, hornswoggled. *Mądry Polak po szkodzie* – a Pole is wise after the harm's been done. And I think when you want something so very much, you can convince yourself of anything. I am fortunate that Miss Humphries' niece appeared on the scene to save me from my foolishness.'

Clara shuddered. 'Just think what could have happened if you'd let the rooms to him...'

It would take a long time for the dust from the disturbing revelations to settle, Mercy realised, and for the unbearable stench of deception to leave the house.

'It doesn't seem right than he can walk out of here and face no consequences,' Agnes tutted.

'Worry not, oh dearest aunt of mine. Revenge is a dish best served cold. I have sufficient contacts back home and in London and will be certain to deliver the unpalatable meal. But now—' Clara launched herself dramatically across one of the armchairs '—after all that drama, I rather fear I am in desperate need of a stiff drink.'

'Absolutely. Madeira for everybody,' Alexander announced, slapping both hands down on the chair arms. 'There is still cause to celebrate, for I have realised, watching you all rally to support me today, that I have family here in this very room, had I but known it.'

Clara didn't need telling twice. She leapt back up and headed to the decanters on the sideboard, as Agnes looked over to Gilbert.

'We really must have words about your unsavoury contacting of the dead. I don't think your activities are very Godly, my dear.' She patted the chair beside her.

'Oh, Aunt Ag, we all know Gilbert is somewhat of an oddity, but darling, I was utterly convinced he was selling saucy photographs to dubious publications. It could be *so* much worse. Besides, I've often dabbled with the Ouija board myself. I really do think poor old Mitzy actually believes her great aunt Elspeth was murdered. I must get around to telling her that Neville has been having her on for months...'

Excusing herself from the assembled company, Mercy announced she would make sandwiches for them all, and slipped silently down to the kitchens before someone remembered her startling admission regarding her true feelings for Gilbert.

* * *

In the quiet of the kitchen, the repetitive nature of slicing bread, carefully buttering each slice and making up plates of sandwiches with a variety of fillings, soothed Mercy's troubled mind.

She would find the courage to return to Alexander's room with food for them all because the others would be present to dilute the embarrassment, but wondered how she could ever face Gilbert alone again. He knew the truth now. Perhaps they'd both always known. But there wasn't anything she could do to act on those most all-consuming of feelings.

It would be sensible, she supposed, to move out, but she was determined that there were no circumstances under which she would willingly head back to Suffolk. When she'd first run away, there had been an inevitability about her return. It was simply a matter of time until they tracked her down, and whilst that remained true, she'd been exposed to such kindness here at Burlington Square, that she could finally admit to what she had always known in her heart – what they had done to her at Home Farm was wrong and she did not have to endure it again. Let them come, she thought, and I *will* fight them.

Remembering that Agnes had a pretty green glass cake-stand in the front room, she wiped her hands on her pinny and covered the plates with clean tea towels – Inky was fond of fish paste and she wasn't certain of his whereabouts.

As she stepped into the hallway, the universe, which really had been having too much fun at everyone else's expense of late, presented her with the very person she had hoped to avoid.

'I, erm... I thought perhaps... Agnes sent me down to...'

I'll bet she did, Mercy thought, and waved her arm in the vague direction of the front room, her own words catching in her throat.

'Cake-stand,' she finally managed to utter.

'I'll, erm...'

Their bodies brushed together as they tried to pass each other in the narrow, cluttered hallway. At the point when they were completely parallel, they both paused. Mercy looked up into his hollow, searching eyes. Yet again, she wondered at the strange force that tugged her heart so violently towards his that it pounded fiercely inside her chest every time he was near.

'You defended me,' he said, as their heads were only inches apart, and he ran his hand nervously through his hair again.

She swallowed, not knowing how to respond. He blinked slowly and then stared briefly at her lips, before swaying towards her, and flicking his eyes back up to hers for permission, but she pulled back for the second time.

'Um, yes. I thought perhaps we could be friends again,' she said her wide eyes begging him to accept this compromise. 'I... I'd like to see where you develop your pictures. I want to learn... to try and understand.'

He bit at his lip and dropped his eyes to the floor.

'I can't be your friend, Mercy. I would always want more and it's obvious you can't or won't allow that to happen.'

'It's... complicated.' She closed her eyes but felt, with a jolt, his cold fingers brush her cheek. Opening them to see his confused gaze, her heart wrenched in his direction and her body betrayed her so completely that any further lies were pointless. Unable to fight it any more, she leaned in to his hand as her tears began to fall. He caressed her skin, wiping away her pain with his thumb, and she inhaled his glorious scent. Allowing her head to fall against his chest, she absorbed his warmth as his arm encircled her body, gripping her tightly. His lips dropped to the top of her head and she felt his breath across her scalp, heard his breathing accelerate.

'I don't understand,' he mumbled into her hair.

'It's all such a dreadful mess, and I'm so scared.'

'I'm here for you. Whatever it is, I'm here,' he reiterated.

Funny, really, how those simple, heartfelt words changed everything. All those years with no one on her side, and suddenly she was reminded there was a whole houseful of people who cared. Perhaps she could do this. Perhaps if he understood that it could never come to anything. Hadn't she promised herself to experience new things – to make memories?

She tipped her face up to his then and allowed his mouth to drift slowly down towards hers, as he gave her time to pull away again, if that was what she wanted. Instead, she pressed her body further into his, as one of his hands pushed into the small of her back, and the other slid up her body to angle her face just so – his fingers finally knotting in her hair. And as their lips met, Mercy Mayweather, at the grand old age of twenty-seven, finally came alive.

Every nerve-ending, every cell in her body, cried out for his. Like a tiny pebble skittering down the mountain, their emotions gathered momentum, sweeping up everything in their wake, and cascading towards the inevitable avalanche – powerful and totally unstoppable. Ashamed and strangely liberated at the same time, she scrabbled to tug his shirttails from his trousers, sliding her hand underneath the cotton fabric and up the smooth skin of his warm back, as his kisses intensified. There was no thought to the people gathered on the first floor or who might come tripping down the stairs. The moment was theirs and nothing existed outside it.

Yes.

This.

She lost herself in him – his touch, his breath, his eyes – knowing this was what she'd been searching for. It had always been out there somewhere and she deserved to finally claim it.

As their passion began to overtake all common sense, there was a sharp knock at the front door and they pulled apart. Perhaps it was for the best, she thought. Making love in Agnes's hallway in broad daylight was not sensible, even though she doubted they would have been able to prevent it had the interruption not jolted them both back to the reality of their present circumstances.

She patted her hair and smoothed down the front of her dress, glancing nervously at his pale face, as she walked to the door. Gilbert hovered behind.

And then her whole world crumbled. Could the universe not look kindly upon her just once?

'Found you at last, you ungrateful bitch.' There was the face she had so hoped to avoid.

'What the hell is going on?' Gilbert asked, stepping forward.

Mercy tried to find the words to explain what was about to unfold but nothing would come from her mouth.

'Roland Mayweather.' The man stretched out his hand in greeting but his eyes were far from friendly. 'Mercy's husband.'

65

Mercy faced Roland and felt herself start to shake, from fear or anger, she couldn't decide.

Three confused people stood together in the doorway. She had known her happiness was too good to last, but had hoped she might have a bit more time pretending that she could love Gilbert and that they could be together. It was a childish and unrealistic daydream, but it had comforted her for those brief moments.

'Pack your bags. I'm taking you home,' Roland demanded. 'Mother is waiting at the hotel.'

Mercy dropped her head, unable to meet her husband's eye. Everything felt heavy, from her heart to her toes. She shook her head slowly from side to side.

'You are my wife, and you will do as I say.' The coldness of his tone was unsettling.

Had he tracked her down a few weeks ago, she would have acquiesced without question but things had changed. In this house she had found friendship and, dare she admit it, love. Agnes had taught her that duty was commendable but love... *love was every-thing*. Alexander was proof that you never recovered from finding and losing your one true love. Gilbert was her destiny – she knew it from her bruised lips and thudding heart – and she was not prepared to let him go. If Clara had been brave enough to disentangle herself from a lie, she could do the same. Mercy Mayweather was not the same woman who'd walked through this door back in August.

She tipped up her chin and finally met Roland's eyes, as her heart thumped uncontrollably. Clara's confidence, Alexander's wisdom and Agnes's frankness all flooded through her at that moment.

'I'm not returning with you, Roland. You don't love me and I certainly don't love you.'

'I see how it is,' he said, his eyes turning to Gilbert. He stepped into the hallway and pushed the door violently to a close. 'You've taken a lover, you whore.'

Had her husband not arrived moments ago, Mercy knew that his words may have been accurate, but there was no time to correct his assumption as Gilbert rushed at him and shoved him up against the wall. The thud of their bodies echoed through the very fabric of the house and alerted everyone to the disturbance below, as a flurry of haphazard blows ensued.

'Oh, how delicious. A love triangle!' Clara appeared at the top of the stairs, hands on hips. 'Do I need to send for the police or might we play nicely?'

Her words were enough for both men to pause their frantic scrabbling. Roland looked up to the beautiful woman who was beginning to descend the stairs as though she were walking onto a film set, and Gilbert turned to look at Mercy.

'I need to talk to my husband.'

Gilbert narrowed his eyes but stepped away, and Clara raised a silent eyebrow at the news her friend was not the tragic widow she had led them all to believe.

Mercy directed Roland towards Agnes's front room, knowing her landlady wouldn't mind. He nodded, and straightened his crooked tie, before leading the way.

'Gilbert, be a total sweetheart and help me bring the sandwiches up,' she heard Clara say from the hall. 'I'm absolutely famished. Drama rather does that to one, don't you find? And we've certainly had our share of that today...'

66

Mercy had known Roland for most of her life because his family's farm bordered that of her parents. The Mayweathers' land, although far more substantial, did not have access to the river, like theirs – useful for watering the livestock, irrigating the land during dry spells, and a handy travel route to market. It made the combining of the properties an appealing prospect.

When they were younger, and with only two years between them, there were inevitable jokes about a future match. Initially, the suggestion was quite appealing to Mercy. Roland was a tall boy with a handsome face, and attracted many an admiring glance from the local girls. She was flattered when he started to pay her particular attention – singling her out to carry her school bag or turning up at their farm and offering to lend a hand. But as a quiet girl, Mercy was an observer of people, and often on the periphery of the world around her. She began to notice an edge to him that worried her. He was charm personified to those whose respect he valued, but he would sometimes kick out at his dog when he was cross, or pick on smaller boys in the schoolyard. She pushed these concerns to the side whenever they were alone, because he was never anything but kind and attentive to her, but his shine was already dulling by the time Germany declared war. The adolescent flame she had held for him had burned itself out.

Too young to enlist at the start of the conflict, and part of a reserved occupation, it wasn't until 1917 that Roland was finally allowed to serve his country. She worried for him then. His quick temper and eagerness for a fight would lead him into danger. Even though she had now fallen out of love with him, they had a tearful parting the evening before he left for London. She had, after all, known him her whole life.

'Marry me?' he'd begged.

'I'm barely seventeen, Roland, and my mother still needs me.'

'And I need a reason to return, Mercy. I need a reason to survive.'

It was an awkward situation. Everyone expected this union, especially her parents, who were anxious for her future since her father's first suspected heart attack. Yes, her body thrilled when Roland kissed her, but there was something about him that made her uncomfortable. She was, however, desperately aware of the huge numbers of young men falling in foreign fields, and that many of her generation would not have the opportunity to become wives and mothers. Before her was a handsome young man begging her to be his. Perhaps she should be grateful for his proposal.

'When you return, and I am older, ask me again.' It was the best she could offer.

'And you promise to give me an answer?'

'Of course,' she replied. It was something for him to cling to, a commitment of sorts, and it gave her an escape route.

But twenty-year-old Roland Mayweather was wounded in the summer of 1918; a shell exploded at his feet and they were told he was lucky to survive, albeit with considerable injuries. And in so many ways, she did lose Roland in the war, because from that moment on he was not the same man. Taken to a casualty clearing station from the front line, he underwent emergency surgery before being shipped back to England to convalesce when his condition became more stable. Mercy eventually took a train down to a requisitioned country house in Devon to see him, despite warnings from his mother that she would find him considerably altered. It was her duty to visit and comfort, and when her father finally passed away from a further heart attack, her future, and that of the farm, became paramount.

After Mrs Mayweather's warning, she was not sure what to expect, but apart from his pale pallor, tired eyes and short, clipped hair, he looked much the same. No missing limbs or visible disfigurement.

Roland's perplexed stare ate away at the silence between them.

'What are you doing here?' he said, looking almost angry. 'I told Mother you weren't to come.'

His coldness overwhelmed Mercy, as she stood in a high-ceilinged drawing room with oak panelled walls, lush velvet curtains and crystal chandeliers. The opulence of her surroundings contrasted with the utilitarian nature of the mundane objects before her – enamel bed pans, simple steel-framed beds and rows of broken men.

'I say,' said the fellow soldier in the next bed, leaning towards them both, 'please tell me she's your sister, Rolly, and let me have a crack at her. Smashing ankles.'

Mercy shuffled from foot to foot, feeling like a prize heifer at market, and Roland took a moment to realise what his neighbour was asking.

'She's my girl,' he'd answered, clearly ruffled by the thought of the brazen chap beside him muscling in on Mercy. He looked at her with serious eyes. 'You are my girl, aren't you? It was only the thought of you waiting for me that kept me going through the carnage. Knowing that you would be there for me when all the horror came to an end.'

She looked at the damaged man before her and tried to reconcile him with the Roland of her youth, even though they hadn't seen each other in many months. He was still handsome, but she suspected he would be much altered in his mind. She knew this from others. She swallowed.

'Of course.' After all, she'd made him a promise to at least consider the prospect of marriage. What these men had been through, she couldn't even imagine, and those they had left behind owed them so much.

The lad in the next bed shrugged, accepting defeat, and Roland stared at her.

'Ask Matron if you can wheel me outside. Let's get some goddamn air.'

She bristled at his language but, with the help of a nurse, he was transferred from his bed, wrapped up accordingly, and wheeled out into the crisp afternoon. She parked him near a bench and sat gingerly on the damp wood. He looked so angry, and she couldn't blame him. All these wounded men, whose lives would never be the same, paying a terrible price for a fight they hadn't started. Finally, he spoke.

'We shall marry soon,' he said, grabbing her hand and staring into her eyes. There had been no proposal, no chance to decline. 'Before Christmas. A winter wedding whilst the farm is quiet.'

Perhaps she'd hoped seeing him again would rekindle something, but she felt nothing for him but pity. Surely they couldn't build a life together based on that?

'Let's not rush things,' she said, her heart beating faster and her stomach agitated. She had not agreed to this, but he'd suffered so much and wore this weariness across his pale face. He was looking for peace and needed a future.

'You can't keep me waiting any longer. I nearly died for my homeland and was prepared to lay down my life for my fellow countrymen. Be the homeland I fought for and have returned to. Yes, I am altered, but I know that a sweet thing like you would not hold that against me.'

Perhaps he'd noticed the hesitancy in her eyes, her crossed arms and the tilt of her legs away from his. But ultimately, how could she refuse? There had been much in the newspapers reminding the women of this country to do justice by the returning heroes. These men deserved a full life; work, marriage, children.

'Of course, Roland. I will see to the arrangements.' But there was no joy in her heart, and all she clung to in those following moments was that her mother would be pleased.

The date was settled and he bent forward to kiss her. Whatever she expected, she was disappointed, because she felt nothing as their lips touched – not like back in the meadow when she had fooled herself into believing it was love. No racing heart, no breathlessness, no stirrings in her body. Only the cold lips of a man who had somehow always been her destiny, regardless of her wishes.

And she wondered then if she had made a dreadful mistake.

* * *

Her mother had made Mercy a nightgown especially for her wedding night – cream silk, with lace detail and tiny bows along the hemline. She slid underneath the covers, almost shaking with anticipation.

Roland entered the room and came over to her, bending down to kiss her forehead.

'Goodnight, little one,' he said and walked to his side of the bed.

She didn't turn, her back to him as her stomach began to spin wildly. What would it feel like to have his hands and lips dance across her body, to have him inside her, to experience the mystical uniting of two bodies that was hinted at in novels and whispered about by giggling young ladies? All these thoughts rushed around her head as he blew out the lamp and got into bed. Her mother had been so terribly vague about the details that she had no idea what to expect. She waited in the darkness for him to touch her but there was nothing, so she rolled over to face him and found he had his back to her. Still nothing. Gingerly, she put out her hand to his shoulder, thinking perhaps it was a little forward of her, but she couldn't work out what was going on. Weren't husbands supposed to take the lead? Shouldn't he be guiding her on this most auspicious of nights? She was pinning her hopes on this lovemaking, hoping it might bridge the yawning gap between them.

'Goodnight,' he said, in a more definite tone this time, and she let her hand drop, half frustrated and half relieved.

It was several weeks before she found out the truth – before she understood his anger and despair, before she realised she had been tricked.

She sat on the edge of the bed one evening, having finally pushed the issue. Tears of confusion rolled down her face as she begged him to explain what was going on. Did he not find her attractive? Had she done something wrong? So, he moved to stand in front of her and began to undress. He untucked his cotton shirt from his trousers and slowly unbuttoned it.

'I need you,' he said out of nowhere, as she was hypnotised by his fingers working their way up the cotton. Her heart jumped. Was this a prelude to their lovemaking at last? Was their long-anticipated union finally to take place? 'And you owe me. Everybody who stayed behind on these shores and let us face a relentless foe on their behalf, owes us. Part of my payment is a strip of land that takes me down to the river, and the other will be to have you as my

companion and housekeeper. When my parents pass away, I refuse
to see out my remaining days alone.'

Prickles of unease travelled around her body. *Had he married her
for access to the river?* There was no talk of love. These were practical
and calculating considerations.

'A land fit for heroes – ha!' he scoffed. 'What a joke.' He tugged
the shirt off and it fell to the carpet, as he began wrestling with his
belt.

Mercy gave a slow swallow as she studied the jagged scar on his
right side. She knew his legs had been badly damaged but the
surgeons had saved them, and he could walk. Did he think horrific
scarring would frighten her? She would never love him, but she'd
also hoped for the companionship he talked of, and she would love
their children, and take solace from that. She swallowed hard and
prepared herself as he unbuttoned his fly and let the trousers drop
to the floor.

It was only at that moment she realised why the truth of his
devastating injuries had been deliberately kept from her. The shell
that had exploded beneath Roland Mayweather had left him with
nothing he could make love to his wife with and she stared open-
mouthed at the most God-awful mess she'd ever seen. There was a
deep red mass of twisted flesh and scarring between his legs. She
might be an innocent but knew enough from growing up on a farm
to understand that there were certain things you needed in order to
procreate, as her father had often castrated animals to prevent
exactly that.

Roland had nothing.

Mercy couldn't pull her eyes away from his damaged body as
her brain scrabbled to make sense of what she was seeing, or more
accurately not seeing. She had no idea of the medical repercus-
sions, how he functioned or what the loss of his appendage might
mean to him, but her first reaction was an overwhelming wave of

compassion. Was it worse than losing a limb? Surely it was what defined him as a man, and the psychological impact of such a loss must be enormous. The inability to procreate, she knew, made both sexes feel inadequate – women labelled as barren, somehow downgraded to lesser women. All her immediate thoughts were for him, and him alone.

'... Knowing that all my sacrifices had been worth it – the months stuck in a mud-filled trench, surrounded by rats, watching my pals killed before my eyes, hearing their screams in my sleep, surviving out there and discharging my duties in the most horrific conditions to give everybody back home a better world, to give *you* a better world.' Her tears were falling now, and still each and every one was for him. 'You won't leave me, will you? You won't abandon me after all I have been through? I honestly don't think it would be worth living if you did.'

For the first time he acknowledged his wound by lifting his hand and resting it across his scars.

'Never,' she said, without thinking. She had been deceived and the implications of this deception would take time to sink in, but how could she deny him? Mercy stood up from the bed and he allowed her to encircle him in her arms.

He had covered her in kisses, held her close, and wept. They lay wrapped in each other's bodies for the whole night, as she stroked his hair and told him everything would be all right. How could she say otherwise after all the sacrifices he'd made? She owed him her loyalty, if not her love.

And had he been kinder to her in the intervening years, she might have been able to bear it.

67

Roland wiped the back of his hand across his face and checked for blood, but the tussle with Gilbert had merely been the pair of them locking horns, and no real damage had been done.

He stared at Mercy for several moments before he finally spoke.

'Who is he?'

'Mr Adams. He's another of the lodgers here and my friend.'

'I'll bet he bloody is.'

'If you think I've been unfaithful, you're wrong.' Had Roland arrived half an hour later, she was absolutely certain she could not have claimed such a thing. She dropped her gaze to the floor.

'What the hell did you hope to achieve by running away? You must have known I'd track you down? You're my wife and you swore to love, honour and obey.'

Mercy dug deep for the courage that she knew had been building in recent days.

'And yet our marriage was always about the farm. My feelings were never a consideration.'

He said nothing so she continued.

'I overheard your mother talking to you once. She'd been so worried I would find out about your injuries before agreeing to marry you, said I was a good little worker, costing you nothing, and even though there would be no heir to the farm, at least I'd never be distracted by children. And you laughed, Roland. I *actually* heard you laugh.'

Again, there was no attempt to deny her accusation. Instead, he asked her a question. 'Why should I be the only one to suffer?'

She thought then of the mill owner's son, who had embraced his injuries, and achieved fame and fortune because of them, not despite them. He had never once allowed his blindness to justify unkind behaviour. Quite the contrary; he was generally thought of as one of the nicest people in the village.

'I have served a nine-year sentence for a crime I did not commit,' she said. 'I have suffered enough. Keep the land, you have it with my blessing. I have no desire to return to Suffolk now that my parents have died. I'm not tied to geography – I never was. It is people who matter.'

It wasn't the not having children; after all, she had no way of knowing if she herself was fertile, and she did not blame Roland for his injuries. It was the calculated deception.

'Perhaps I could have borne it had you loved me,' she said. 'But I honestly believe had you not been injured, you wouldn't have remained faithful to me. Our marriage was convenient and planned for the advancement of the farm – love was never a factor.'

He snorted. 'You're wrong, actually. Despite always knowing my father had planned our union, I was surprised what an attractive woman you grew up to be. From a skinny child, all elbows and awkwardness, you blossomed, Mercy, and what made it all the more enchanting was that you couldn't see it. All the lads in the neighbourhood could, though. The guy in the bed next to me at the hospital saw it when you visited and didn't stop saying what a lucky bastard I was for days. The dreadful irony is that by the time I left for the front, I did love you, and wasn't lying when I said it was thoughts of you that kept me going in my darkest hours.'

But Roland's excuses were falling on deaf ears. She understood that the unfairness of his injuries made him bitter, but he wasn't the only person to ever suffer an injustice. Agnes had every right to be furious with the world after years nursing her father and letting the man she loved walk out of her life, but she was the kindest lady Mercy knew. And the traumatic loss of his brother had clearly affected Gilbert, but he would never lash out at others because of it. In fact, he was now devoting his life to easing the pain of the bereaved – however misguided his methods might be. Nor had Alexander taken Alina's loss out on those around him. And, as she stood in that cluttered room, she drew on their strength.

'Then your love is a twisted thing, because you shouldn't behave towards the people you love the way you've behaved towards me. I've been treated worse than a servant by you and your mother. You have every right to be angry about your injuries. You have absolutely no right to take that anger out on me. I want our marriage annulled.'

His eyes narrowed.

'Goodness, what a difference a few weeks out in the big, wide world has made to the timid little mouse. Please don't tell me you hope to remarry. No one would have you.'

'You'd be surprised.'

'The answer is a resounding no. I will not have my injuries exposed and held up to ridicule to extract you from your vows.'

'And I will not remain a moment longer in a marriage that has not been consummated.'

Roland, angry now, stepped forward and slapped her hard across the face.

And Mercy briefly put her hand to her raw, red cheek, before summoning every ounce of strength she could find and slapped him back.

68

THE HATBOX FULL OF LETTERS

It stood on top of the wardrobe, at the very back, behind two other hatboxes. They, naturally, contained hats; the one she had worn to Daphne's wedding – wide-brimmed and covered in lavender satin and pink flowers; and the one purchased for her father's funeral – a black toque hat with an ostentatious arrangement of ostrich feathers splaying several inches upwards. Daphne, who frequently tried to persuade her sister to part with some of her gathered clutter, had repeatedly impressed upon her that such feather arrangements were no longer fashionable, and when Mr Blandford had passed away, had instead loaned her a simple cloche hat with a wide black ribbon. But, like everything else at Burlington Square, Agnes kept the feathered monstrosity for sentimental, rather than practical, reasons.

But the caramel-coloured plywood hatbox at the very back did not contain a hat. It held thirty-seven letters from Mr James G. Hunt Esq., all with Cochin postmarks, and sent to a young Agnes Humphries between the years of 1889 and 1896. They were bundled up in date order, so that should she wish to read them from the beginning, she could do so. And there had been several occasions over the years when she'd carried the kitchen steps into her room and heaved that circular box from the top of the wardrobe, before sitting on the edge of her bed with her memories.

After his proposal, the young lovers had naturally been desperate to find a solution, Agnes almost as much as James. But there was no family close enough to step into her shoes, Daphne stamped her small, booted foot down at the thought of moving to a foreign country, and the doctor advised against such a move for her father – as Agnes knew he would.

As May approached and no solution could be found, she failed to understand James's need to take the position, as much as he failed to understand the situation with her father. And yet they loved each other with an ache that was tearing them both apart. With his passage booked and departure the following morning, he came to Burlington Square late one evening, determined to elicit some sort of promise from Agnes.

'At least accept my proposal and put this on your finger? I'm sure we can work things out given time.'

She clasped her soft hands over the proffered ring but shook her head. Her problems were her own, and she would not allow James to suffer or make sacrifices because her options in life were currently so limited.

'We have no way of knowing how long I will be required here. I can no more tie you to an engagement that could last for years, than I can abandon my father.'

'Then let me pay for a nurse? I have the funds.'

But this had all been discussed before and he didn't understand that the only person the old man wanted to nurse him was his oldest daughter. She shook her head.

'I will never love anyone like I love you, Agnes Humphries.'

'But you have my blessing to try.'

He leapt from his seat and paced the room, his hands behind

his back and his eyes downcast. And finally, in desperation, he faced her. 'Because if it comes down to a choice between me and your father, you choose him?'

She nodded. 'In the same way that when it came down to me or your career, you chose your profession.'

'That's not fair,' he said, halting his steps.

'Perhaps not, but the difference is I *do* understand.'

* * *

It was only as the front door closed and his hansom cab pulled away, that Agnes noticed his top hat sitting on the top of the hall stand. Instead of chasing him into the street or sending word to his apartments, she decided that if part of him was left behind, he might one day have a reason to return.

Despite the pain of their parting, he kept his promise to write. There followed heartfelt words of apology from both sides at how they had left things, and his first few letters were filled with details of his new life in India. Perhaps they were an attempt to entice her out there, to persuade her to change her mind, for they always ended with sincere affection. Sometimes, her tears fell on the page and spoilt the ink as she read his words, but her replies had never once belied her regret. She, in turn, talked of her darling father, and described his more lucid moments, those when he knew his daughter – perhaps to prove to James that she could not have left him behind.

As one year bled into the next, she lapped up every description James sent of the busy port, marvelled at how much of his life remained quintessentially English, with their games of cricket and afternoon teas, and was fascinated by his descriptions of the customs, clothing, food and heartbreaking poverty of the locals. He even included sepia photographs of his house, perhaps as a poignant reminder of what she could have been part of.

The last letter she received from James was read just the once. After that it was never to leave the envelope again. Because it was the full stop to any hopes she harboured of future happiness.

Cochin, 12th June 1896

Dear Agnes,

One of the things I have long since admired is your honesty, and so I write with equal frankness to you now and hope this letter does not bring you too much heartache. I have mentioned in previous letters the Forester family, and the Reverend Forester is doing invaluable work amongst the locals, as well as delivering our weekly dose of spiritual instruction. Perhaps I have also mentioned his daughter, Ruth? She is a quiet woman but has a kind heart. I wish to be the first to inform you that I have offered her my hand and she has accepted.

I have held a candle for you for so long, and always found all young women wanting in comparison. But time waits for no man, and whilst I harboured foolish hopes of your situation changing (and please do not think ill of me for wishing you would be relieved of your caring duties, but I am matching your candour with my own) I now accept that you will be with your father until the end, however many years that might be. And in so many ways, I love you all the more for it.

My position here necessitates a wife, and although I cannot have the woman I want, I do believe I have found a woman who will love, cherish and obey, and I will endeavour to do those things in return.

I have valued our friendship over recent years, and often think of the vibrant young woman in the Bayswater gallery who stole my heart on a warm July afternoon, and wonder what might have been. However, to continue our correspondence would be inappropriate when I am married and, truth be told, I have nothing of importance to say to you now. You know I will always love you, and I wish you every happiness for the future.

Think of me often but do not allow yourself to live with regret.
Yours, always
James Hunt.

She had written back that she understood perfectly and was delighted that he had found someone to share his life with.

Then Agnes Humphries took herself to bed and cried into her pillows for two days solid.

'Married?' Agnes kept repeating, as though someone had just announced a man had landed on the moon. 'Well, I never.'

Roland had stormed out the house after the slap, threatening all sorts, not least of which was that he would return the following day, but Mercy was strangely calm. She was surrounded by friends, and they would not let her face this alone, any more than they had let Alexander confront the conniving Mr Thompson by himself. She'd walked back up to Alexander's rooms to find Gilbert had retreated to his attics after the fight, but with her husband's arrival, she owed these people her honesty.

'I always told you I was married,' Mercy said. 'I've never lied to you about that; you heard what you wanted to hear. I did lose him in the war because the Roland I knew never came back to me, physically or mentally. The young lad who kissed me in the meadow became the man who would throw my meals across the room when they weren't hot enough...'

She told her friends brief details of his injuries and how she'd not been told until weeks after their marriage.

'Poor man,' Agnes muttered, looking as though she might burst into tears at any moment.

'Yes, poor man, but don't you dare make Mercy feel guilty,' Clara chipped in. 'It's one thing to honour an arrangement made to a man you love – to be told the situation and make the decision to marry regardless. But quite another to be emotionally blackmailed into being with someone.' She stood up to pour another drink, also topping Alexander's glass up, before sinking back into her chair.

'It certainly explains the virginal look you wore when you first arrived, darling. I thought it was an act.'

'No.'

'No,' Clara echoed solemnly, and reached for her friend's shoulder.

Agnes blushed and Alexander buried his face in his drink.

'I didn't tell a soul,' Mercy continued, 'Not even my own mother when she was alive. It was a combination of the shame I felt, and my compassion for Roland. I didn't want him to be subjected to pitying looks or whispered half-truths. Perhaps I could have borne it all if the Mayweathers had been kinder, but I was the scapegoat and, in the end, I realised that simply was not fair.'

'How did you find the courage to run away?' Agnes asked, so wrapped up in Mercy's sad tale that she'd shuffled to the edge of her seat.

'Do you remember that novelist woman, Agatha Christie, disappearing last December? Whatever the truth behind it, it made me think. She just upped and left her life, albeit only for eleven days, and I thought perhaps I could do the same. The schoolmaster's wife had long been worried about me, and helped me with money. She knew a lady who worked at Pemberton's and wrote me a reference and I slipped into a life that was liberating – not subjected to the constant demands of others.'

'And then dear old Aunt Ag found you,' Clara said, finishing off

Mercy's tale. 'Thank God at least one of us has found our happy ever after.'

'Oh, Clara, you will,' Agnes said with great conviction. 'I wonder if I can't clear some of the things in that spare room and offer you a bed for a while... just until we can think of something useful you could do with your empty life.'

'What a simply splendid idea. Daddy is furious about Jack, and Lily refuses to have me back. She claims I'm a terrible house guest. Can you imagine?'

No one spoke for a moment until Agnes cleared her throat. 'I do have house rules though, young lady.'

'Oh, tish, rules are there to be broken. Ask Mercy.' She winked at her friend.

'Perhaps you can start by giving young Jemima some of your time?' Agnes suggested. 'Help her out with the children?'

'Children?' Clara was horrified. 'Oh darling, I simply don't do those. Far too sticky.'

'I think the whole household should spend an afternoon in the park together before the weather turns,' Mercy said. 'Gilbert can push Alexander in his Bath chair and we could take the girls. Agnes and I can easily make up a picnic, and between us we can marshal the little ones to give Jemima a break.'

'I should like that very much,' said Agnes.

'So should I,' Alexander agreed.

'Then all that remains is for you to pop up to ask Gilbert if he'd like to be part of it...' Agnes placed her hands on her plump, but increasingly cooperative knees, and let out the happiest sigh.

'Now?' Mercy asked, a rolling feeling in her stomach.

'Yes, now,' her landlady said, quite firmly. 'And Clara and I can sort the dishes.' She heaved herself to her feet and began to walk across the room, winking at Mercy as she passed. 'We won't wait up...'

THE SCRAP ALBUMS

Agnes pulled three scrap albums from the right-hand drawer of the sideboard, and collapsed onto her much-cherished sofa with them balanced on her knees.

The top album was a glorious deep red leather, with an embossed border of ivy, which had been gifted to her on her eighth birthday. Her love of the sentimental was already apparent, and her father thought her growing collection of postcards and theatre programmes would be better kept in such a book, rather than the oblong Huntley and Palmers biscuit tin she'd appropriated from Cook. Her mother helped her decorate the pages, showing her how to paste the 'scraps' – delicate die cuts of pretty girls in summer bonnets, children in their winter mittens throwing snowballs, and playful kittens with balls of yarn.

The first album came to an abrupt end with the solitary and heartbreaking addition of her mother's memorial card. The cluttered pages, however, reminded her that her childhood was a happy one, and she still carried that little girl, so full of hope, deep inside her somewhere.

The following album was bottle green with a picture of a

Regency-era young lady on the front, and the contents centred almost entirely around Daphne. Endless photos taken of the ringleted, cherubic child, pictures drawn by her sister's childish hand and details added by Agnes noting Daphne's first words and achievements – worthy of any proud mama, which to all intents and purposes, she was.

The third album, also of red leather, was filled with magazine cut-outs of country cottages, images of brides taken from newspapers, and foreign postcards of places she wanted to visit. But as her dreams, and the album, progressed, her father's health had started to deteriorate.

A calling card from *Mr J. G. Hunt* was given its own page, so precious had it been to her. As was her first and only Valentine: a paper lace card covered with embossed flowers. Inside he had simply written *Yours forever*. The sad reality was their romance was over hardly before it had begun. But it had been a romance. He'd been the love of her life...

There were several blank pages at the back that she'd never bothered to fill after James had left, even though they had continued to correspond for several years afterwards. As always, she clutched the thick albums to her chest and hugged them tightly, before returning them to the cupboard for another day, when she wanted to remember the start of a life that had not turned out as she anticipated – as if looking through it again from the beginning one more time might make the ending change.

But it never did. And she wondered if she'd ever be able to bring herself to fill those remaining pages.

PART IV

AGNES HUMPHRIES

71

FRIDAY, 5TH AUGUST 1927

Agnes dipped the nib of her pen into the pewter inkwell and began to write to Mr Thompson, offering him the rooms at Burlington Square, feeling inordinately proud of herself for basing her decision on logic rather than sentiment.

She heard Gilbert coming down the stairs as she sealed the envelope and dabbed the stamp on the roller of the little cut-glass letter licker, but as he reached the bottom step, she heard him curse and return up the stairs. Doubtless, he had forgotten something.

She gazed through the lookey outeys at the trees in Burlington Square, sighed and rubbed at her knees. Agnes had been about to ask him to post the letter for her but it was a beautiful summer's day, and perhaps the walk would do her good. Shuffling to her feet, she went to the hallway and grabbed the green straw hat with the drooping brim that Daphne had bought for her recently. The top hat caught her eye, as it often did, and her heart shifted in her chest. Checking she had her key with her, she stepped out into the bright day, lifted her face to the sun and smiled.

She followed alongside the black railings until she reached the bottom of the road, and then turned right. Checking one of those pesky motor vehicles wasn't haring up the street, she crossed over and spotted the bright red postbox in the distance. Lost in a multitude of thoughts – worries about the quiet young widow, pondering the truth of the scandal her niece was embroiled in, and contemplating what she might cook Gilbert and Mr Gorski for tea – she heard a shout from behind.

'Agnes Humphries? As I live and breathe!'

Her heart stopped, as did her feet, and her mind swept her back to a moment in time, thirty-eight years previously, when she'd stood before an emotional young man, begging her to be his wife, telling her that she was his everything. She turned slowly and was confronted by the same sparkling eyes and ridiculous ears, even if time had softened his face and years of hot sun had weathered his skin.

'To think you are still in the area,' he continued. 'I am only passing through the city today on my way up north, and did not imagine for one moment that you might still be local. How fortuitous to have bumped into you.'

How fortuitous indeed. Had she sent Gilbert out to post the letter, James might have drifted three hundred yards from her life and she would never have known.

'I'm a few pounds heavier, and several decades older, but little else has changed since you left.' She smiled to show him that she wasn't angling for sympathy, merely stating facts.

'Nothing wrong with curves, my dear,' he replied.

They stood facing each other for a few moments, both searching for the familiar and the altered. Despite the passing of so much time, it was as though she had only seen him yesterday, and all those years of longing and disappointment threatened to overwhelm her.

'I assume your father is no longer with us?'

She nodded. 'He passed away the same year as the queen.'

'Goodness, your care must have been quite exceptional for him to be with you for so long.'

'I wouldn't have had it any other way.' She tried to swallow but her mouth felt dry and her heart was thudding. 'And how is your wife? Ruth? Is she with you in London? I had no idea that you had returned from India. I have, on occasion, asked my brother-in-law if he knew anything of you. Oh, I'm gabbling. I always talk too much...'

'You certainly never struggled for things to say, as I recall.' That familiar twinkle flashed across his eyes. 'I have returned to these shores to be nearer to my sons, David and Michael, but we lost Ruth unexpectedly two years ago.'

'I'm so sorry. Losing loved ones is never easy.' So many interpretations open to so few words.

'She was a good wife to me but it was never love. There was only one woman who ever truly captured my heart, even if the universe had other ideas.'

This time, neither could bring themselves to look at the other.

'I'm sorry. Can you ever forgive me?'

'We both made our choices. I was as guilty as you, putting my career above all else. Besides, "*you do not stay angry forever but delight to show mercy*,"' he replied. 'My father-in-law was forever quoting from the Good Book.'

There was a pause. He looked down at his shoes and Agnes tugged at her bottom lip.

'May I accompany you on your journey to the postbox?' He nodded at the letter in her hand.

Agnes felt something ripple through her that she couldn't explain. She clutched the letter and tipped her head to the side.

'No,' she replied.

'Sorry.' He looked momentarily crestfallen. 'I shouldn't have assumed... I'm intruding on your day.'

'Not at all,' Agnes blustered. 'That's not what I meant. I'm not going to the postbox—'

'But the letter, dear lady?'

'It's a sign – seeing you, you talking of mercy. This is wrong. I just know in my gut.'

Her explanation only served to confuse the poor fellow more.

'Ah, you're married. Me accompanying you would be unseemly,' he surmised.

'Forgive me, I'm talking in riddles. Posting the letter is wrong – not bumping into you. I need to dispose of this letter and write another one. I'm renting out rooms and believe I've made an error in offering them to a particular gentleman. Not that he is at fault in any way, but there was a young lady whose need, I believe, is greater. I don't know her story but I do know that I can help her. Mr Thompson and my feisty young niece will be just fine but I need to show mercy to Mercy.'

'Oh, Aggie,' he said, smiling. 'You were always one to be led by your heart rather than your head...' He paused. 'Even when it meant letting me go.'

'That decision was the hardest one I've ever had to take in my entire life. I cried myself to sleep for months.'

He couldn't take his eyes from her earnest face. 'And you are still living at number 23?'

'I could never leave that house, despite my longing to see the world. That was part of the problem.'

'Yes.' He nodded. 'A house packed with memories. It's not too late though, you know? Women older than you have undertaken foreign adventures. Perhaps we could arrange a trip together?' he offered, bravely.

'I think the time for such escapades has passed,' she said, thinking of her troublesome knees. 'Besides, I still find enormous pleasure in reading about the travels of others, whilst I remain safely at my beloved house, with not one jot of seasickness, surrounded by all my precious possessions.'

'Then let me at least see you to your door. May I?' He put out his arm and she allowed him to loop it through hers and they meandered back up the hill.

They climbed the stone steps together, and Agnes nodded at Jemima, who was embarking on an outing with her brood. That poor woman would have four little ones before the year was out. As much as Agnes adored children, her heart went out to the young mum – someone else she worried about in her quiet moments.

'Do you have time to stop for a cup of tea?' she asked. 'We have much to talk about. Although, before I pop that kettle on, I must write to Mrs Mayweather.'

He nodded, and followed her through the front door. As they entered her narrow hallway, he looked to the top of her hallstand.

'Oh, my hat. I often wondered what happened to it. You kept it all this time?'

Agnes smiled. 'You know what a sentimental old fool I am... I hoped that one day you might return for it.'

And there was a look that passed between the two friends that spoke of broken hearts, frustrated affections, regret, and hope. And as he lifted it from the shelf and spun it towards him one complete rotation, before landing it perfectly on the top of his head, the overwhelming emotion circling in that small space at the front of Burlington Square was hope.

EPILOGUE

LONDON, 1949

'Agnes really was quite the hoarder,' said Gilbert, surveying the mountains of clutter. 'It's not fair of Clara to ask you to sort everything out. She always was an entitled madam. Surely she can fly over? It only takes about an hour from Paris and she made it back for the funeral.'

'Her business interests can't be left for long. Besides, you know Clara – she's not in the least bit sentimental and would sell the lot,' said Mercy, heaving a large red scrap album from a drawer in the sideboard.

She looked across at her husband, thankful that their two boys had been too young to get caught up in the war. The Great War had destroyed her first husband, and Gil had been posted to the front for this one in his role as a civilian photographer. Since their marriage, his whole career had been built on recording truths, however unpalatable, and he was making the world a better place in his own way – one photograph at a time. It sometimes seemed, however, that it was his destiny to be in the presence of death. Please God there would never be a third world war...

Mercy rested the album on the desk and opened it up. I

contained an assortment of photographs and newspaper clippings, and she flicked through until she came across the wedding of Agnes and James. It had been a miserable day in December, barely months after he'd moved back to England, but Agnes had pooh-poohed the naysayers, insisting she'd wasted enough of her life waiting and neither of them knew how much time they had left. As it was, they had squeezed in nearly twenty happy years together, although poor old Agnes was back to her caring role for the last six months of his life when a stroke unkindly left him in need of her ministrations. Mr Gorski had lived out his remaining six years with them, having moved down to the ground floor, and formed a close friendship with James. Gil and Mercy had been regular visitors over the years, their boys treating Aggie and Jim as surrogate grand-parents.

Mercy turned the page to find a handful of photographs from her own wedding. The annulment had taken a while to sort, Roland difficult until the end, but by the summer of 1928 she was finally free to choose love over duty. Gil stood beside her, as she clutched a small posy of cream roses, wearing a simple off-white gown. (She could not bring herself, in all good conscience, to wear white.) The photographs of the wedding party on the steps outside the church made her smile, Clara outshining them all, and Agnes in the largest hat you ever did see, clutching at James like he might disappear for another forty years.

She ran her hand over a newspaper clipping from 1930 detailing the opening of yet another of Clara's nightclubs. Marlene Dietrich had performed there on the opening night and there was an image of Jemima and Clara standing together outside the premises. They were listed as business partners and stood apart from each other, but those that knew, knew. Little had Mercy known what wheels she'd set in motion when she'd formed her friendship with the pair of them. Swept up in her feelings for Gil, she hadn't noticed the other romance slowly smouldering before her very eyes. Life had never been straightforward for the women, but together they faced every adversity with fortitude. Fleeing from Berlin in 1933, they had relocated to Paris and opened *Dodies de Danse*, named in homage to Clara's grandfather, apparently, which had made Agnes laugh so hard, she cried. Would her dear friends find their place in a shattered post-war Europe? She hoped so.

Then Mercy came across something she hadn't seen before. A clipping from the London Evening Chronicle, 16 December 1934.

> Yesterday evening a homeless man was stabbed in Regent's Park after a violent altercation and died shortly afterwards. The victim was named as fifty-nine-year-old Stephen Thompson. He was known to the police after serving four years at Brixton Prison for robbery. Originally from Hexton, Hertfordshire, Stephen leaves behind a mother and four brothers...

Interesting, she thought, how close Agnes had come to offering the rooms to him all those years ago – after all, he'd been the most logical lodger. There had never been enough proof to link him to the death of Nathaniel Blandford but Mercy felt his unhappy life and untimely death were perhaps justice of a sort. She shuddered. How strange it was that one simple decision could have so many ripples.

She closed the album and sighed at the monumental task ahead of them. The thought of anyone other than Agnes living in the house was heartbreaking.

'We can put an offer in,' Gilbert said, as if reading her thoughts. 'I know you're fond of the place, and if we sell our house and approach the bank... My salary is healthy and with the small nest-egg Agnes left you...'

'Can we really afford it?' she asked.

'I'm sure we could negotiate. After all, we've remained good friends with Clara, and the pair of you have always exchanged regular letters. Perhaps we could offer to keep a room for her, in case she ever pops back to England.'

Mercy smiled. 'That woman was always trouble, and I have a feeling she always will be.'

Gilbert chuckled. 'But she's a good sort, is Clara, and she has a kind heart.'

'She does, indeed. And it's extremely generous of her to let us take what we want from the house. All she's asked for is the albums to be shipped out, and this threadbare old thing.' Mercy walked over to the pale blue sofa and rested her hand on one of the shabby arms.

'Perhaps she's more sentimental than she'd have us believe,' he said.

'Yes, the sofa I understand,' she said, remembering how it was one of Agnes's favourite places to dispense her wisdom. She slid onto the sagging seat and patted the fabric beside her, indicating for Gilbert to join her. 'You're right. Let's make Clara an offer. It's a very special house and she might surprise us. After all...' She smiled as her husband lumped down beside her, sinking further than he anticipated. 'Agnes always insisted that anything is possible.'

ACKNOWLEDGMENTS

Give a man a fish and you feed him for a day. Give a girl a laptop and you'll keep her amused for years...

I can hardly believe novel number five is out in the world. It's been an unreal journey since the publication of my debut novel in 2019, and yet here we are. It is still a miracle to me that other people get to read the words I merrily type into my keyboard, humming along to my music, as I let my brain take me to many a strange place. Thank you to all who came along with me on this particular journey to 23 Burlington Square. As always, there is a whole host of people to thank, from my incredibly enthusiastic editor, Isobel Akenhead, to my ever-supportive (award-winning) agent, Hannah Schofield. I am incredibly excited about the future with both of you by my side.

The Romantic Novelists' Association continues to be an important part of my writing life, and the Norfolk and Suffolk Chapter, in particular, have been a fabulous source of support and encouragement. Special hugs, as always, to my virtual office buddy Clare Marchant, and to the rest of the gang who keep my spirits up on a Friday – Heidi-Jo, Kate, Ian and Pam.

Congratulations to Frida Lindström, who won the international competition on the wonderful Heidi Swain and Friends Facebook Book Club to name the pub in this book. The Mad Hatter is entirely down to you.

To Sue Baker and Fiona Jenkins for their ongoing love and support, and Fiona for her 'pearls' of wisdom.

Also huge thanks to Catherine Lister who sensitivity read an early version of this novel, as well as recommending some fabulous resources for Clara's story. Your guidance was invaluable.

And lastly, to my family. When the headphones are on, and the empty coffee cups are stacking up, thank you for not interrupting.

Jenni x

ABOUT THE AUTHOR

Jenni Keer is the well-reviewed author of historical romances, often with a mystery at their heart. Most recently published by Headline and shortlisted for the 2023 RNA Historical Romantic Novel of the Year.

Sign up to Jenni Keer's mailing list for news, competitions and updates on future books.

Visit Jenni's website: www.jennikeer.co.uk

Follow Jenni on social media here:

 facebook.com/jennikeerwriter

twitter.com/JenniKeer

instagram.com/jennikeer

bookbub.com/authors/jenni-keer

Boldw☾☽d

Boldwood Books is an award-winning fiction publishing company seeking out the best stories from around the world.

Find out more at www.boldwoodbooks.com

Join our reader community for brilliant books, competitions and offers!

Follow us
@BoldwoodBooks
@TheBoldBookClub

Sign up to our weekly deals newsletter

https://bit.ly/BoldwoodBNewsletter

Made in the USA
Las Vegas, NV
29 March 2024

87981785R00233